Brumaire

Mark Logan

Brumaire

St. Martin's Press
New York

Library of Congress Cataloging in Publication Data

Nicole, Christopher.
  Brumaire.

  1. France—History—Revolution, 1789-1799—Fiction.   I. Title.
PZ4.N6425Br   [PR9320.9.N5]   813   77-15864

ISBN 0-312-10677-7

By the same author

Tricolour
Guillotine

CAST
IN ORDER OF
APPEARANCE

Italics are fictional characters.

Characters marked with an * appeared in the two previous novels of this series.

* George Bryan Brummell	Nicknamed Beau, English dandy and friend of the Prince of Wales
* *Paul de Lancey*	Husband of Lucy Minnett
* *Priscilla Minnett*	Mother of Nick and Lucy Minnett
* *Lucy de Lancey* (nee Minnett)	Nick's sister
* *Anne Yealm*	Nick Minnett's mistress
* *Harry Yealm*	Anne's father
* *Percy Minnett*	Nick's father
* *Nicholas Minnett*	Proprietor of the House of Minnett, England's leading private bank
* *Elena Reyes*	Spanish girl befriended by Nick Minnett
Richard Parker	English seaman; leader of the mutiny at the Nore in 1797; cousin of Anne Yealm
Lorna Grant	Irish spy in French pay
* Robert Stewart, Viscount Castlereagh	English Tory politician

* Alexander Minnett	Caroline Minnett's son
Alice Mawlton	Farmer's wife
* Belair	Nick Minnett's horse
* Jack Morley	Butler at the Minnett country home
* William Pitt	Prime Minister of England, Nick Minnett's closest friend
* Marie Josephine Rose Bonaparte	Napoleon's wife
* Francois Athanase (Jean-Louis) Charette de la Contrie	French royalist leader
* Lazare Hoche	French general
* Eric	Nick Minnett's valet
* Maureen Morley	Wife to Jack Morley; housekeeper at the Minnett country home
Admiral Colpoys	British naval officer
* Etienne de Benoît	French royalist leader; friend of Nick's
* Honorine Damas	French royalist agent
* Richard, Earl Howe	British admiral
* Lord George Moncey	Caroline Minnett's brother, Nick's brother-in-law
Edward Pellew, Viscount Exmouth	British naval officer
Lord Edward Fitzgerald	Irish republican leader
* Judith Yealm	Anne Yealm's daughter by Nick Minnett
Harry Yealm Junior	Anne Yealm's son by Nick Minnett
* Henry	Butler at the Minnett town house
* Lady Caroline Minnett	Nick's wife
* John Turnbull	Chief clerk at the House of Minnett
* Lord John Ratsey	Owner of Ratsey's Bank, rivals to the House of Minnett
* Prince George Augustus Frederick, Prince of Wales	Heir to the British throne, son of George III
* Princess Caroline	Wife of the Prince of Wales
Mrs Prout	English landlady

*Aurora de Benoît	Sister of Etienne de Benoît
*Vicomte Paul Francois	
Jean Nicolas de Barras	French politician
Lieutenant Calham	British naval officer
John Evans	British mutineer
Charles Smith	British mutineer
Captain Listowel	British naval officer
*Horatio Nelson	British admiral
Sir William Hamilton (Willy)	British ambassador to Naples: Emma's husband
Lady Emma Hamilton	Wife of the British ambassador in Naples
Maria Carolina	Queen of Naples
Ferdinand I	King of Naples
Sir John Acton	Englishman who is Prime Minister of Naples
Johannes Szen	French/Hungarian agent
Seraphine Condorcet	Nick's erstwhile accomplice in Paris
Joachim Castets	French agent
*Andoche Junot	French officer
*Napoleon Bonaparte	French general
Louis Berthier	French general; chief of staff to Napoleon
Francois Brueys	French admiral
Louis de Casabianca	French naval officer
Louis Condorcet	French revolutionary
*Joachim Murat	French general
Louis Desaix	French general
Edward Berry	British naval officer
Garthwaite	Detective employed by Nick Minnett
*Henry Addison	British politician
Robert Canning	British politician
Count and Countess of Seend	Parents of George Moncey and Caroline Minnett
Clayton	English detective
Lucas	Anne Yealm's neighbour
Pat	Irish smuggler
*Charles Maurice de Talleyrand-Perigord	French statesman
Lucien Bonaparte	French politician

Brumaire

1

"A fox," shouted George Brummell, sweeping his plate from the sideboard and holding it high with only two fingers and his thumb as he threaded his way through the throng to the table. "Today I shall have me a fox."

"Why, Beau," remarked Paul de Lancey. "He will likely die of fright at the sight of you."

"Or jealousy, my dear Paul. Or jealousy."

Both men wore red jackets, as indeed did every other man in the room. But Brummell had replaced his cravat with a thin black string, and his entire lapels were crimson velvet, making the padded shoulders behind them seem even larger, which was the intended effect. He was a thin young man, with narrow, almost pinched features and darting dark eyes.

Now he secured himself a seat close by the head of the table. "Will you not ride with us, Mistress Minnett?"

Priscilla Minnett smiled at him. She smiled at everyone in the high-ceilinged breakfast room—at the men, eager, bubbling with excitement; at the women, mainly in blue or brown riding habits, beavers already perched precariously on top of their upswept hair, cheeks sparkling with anticipation. Only their hostess remained calm. Though her greying brown hair betrayed her fifty years, the superb bone structure of her smooth oval face remained almost girlish.

"I am too old to go cavorting across the countryside, Mr. Brummell. I shall be represented by Lucy."

Lucy de Lancey—merely a younger edition of her mother—was seated opposite; but she reserved her smile for her husband. "And we shall gain the beast first, Paul."

"Not today, my dear. Not today," Brummell insisted. "Today I feel a rush of energy coming over me. Why. . . ." He paused as the whole company turned to gaze when the double doors which led from the breakfast room into the hall suddenly opened. Unruffled, Brummell drowned out the chorus of greetings. "Mistress Yealm. Kedgeree. Eggs?" He winked. "What would the little fellow like today?"

Anne Yealm inclined her head with a graciousness which was entirely natural. "I think a cup of coffee, Mr. Brummell."

She came up the room, moving slowly, while the other guests hastily stepped aside to make way for her. Though eight months pregnant, she seemed to carry her swollen belly with all the self-possessed confidence in the world. Her plain blue gown, worn with a low ruff in white gauze, only augmented her beauty, which eclipsed the glittering crowd to either side of her.

She was tall, only a few inches under six feet. Her auburn hair was undressed, fluttering gently beside her cheeks, then falling straight on her shoulders and beyond. She was strongly built, with good shoulders and wide thighs, long legs, and a consciously athletic movement despite her pregnancy. But beside the greater beauty of her face, none of these beauties mattered. Every feature—high forehead, widest blue eyes, long, straight nose, flat, wide mouth, pointed chin—was perfectly formed, perfectly fitted to every other. Save for the colour in her cheeks, the quiver of her lips as she smiled, she might have been an animated statue, carved by a master.

Paul de Lancey was holding a chair for her, next to his mother-in-law's, and she sat down. "You would think they were about to fight a battle," she murmured.

"Oh, indeed they are," Priscilla Minnett agreed, resting her

2

chin on one finger to gaze at her. Suddenly she flushed. She had almost thought, "daughter-in-law." What an incredible idea, and a ridiculous one. Down to a week ago, in fact, she had been in a state of some alarm that Nick's determination to introduce his mistress into society might prove the disaster of the century. Oh, she was truly beautiful, and she possessed a remarkable presence. But she *was* the daughter of a lighthouse keeper, and the widow of a common fisherman. That Harry Yealm had been Nick's best friend was neither here nor there; Nick had always been notorious for his peculiar friends. Priscilla could understand that Nick might feel responsible for Harry's death, and thus even more responsible for the young widow. That mutual respect and affection between the two should have developed into love was perhaps natural. Yet the fact remained that socially they were as far separated as the earth and the sun. And to bring the girl to Windshot for the Christmas festivities, as pregnant as she was . . . Priscilla just could not imagine what Percy would have said.

But Percy was dead. Nick was now the head of the House of Minnett, and a law unto himself. And more even than that; since Percy's death four years ago, the entire world had been turned upside down. Why, at Christmas 1792 there had still been a king in France, however uneasy his throne. Since then not only Louis, but also his wife and most of his friends and relations, had all lost their heads, and war had come to Europe. Nick had been married and estranged, all the while becoming more and more involved with Mr. Pitt's schemes, both financial and political . . . and Anne Yealm had entered Nick's public world.

She smiled at the girl. Because, incredibly, her visit had been a success. The men could not resist her, swollen as she was. The women no doubt tore her to pieces behind her back, and yet were themselves conquered by her remarkable good humour, her calm confidence, her ready deference, so ready, indeed, it might almost be mistaken for arrogance—they had the titles and the family background. Anne Yealm had Nick Minnett, a prize for which any woman present (saving his mother and his sister) would give five precious years of her life.

Anne returned the smile, and then looked towards the doorway, as did everyone else. For Nicholas Minnett was at this moment entering the room.

Like all the men, Nick wore hunting pink. Unlike them he carried his hat and his crop, and was pulling gloves over his fingers.

"Ladies," he said. "Gentlemen. Shall we make a start?"

When he smiled, he was handsome. In repose, Priscilla Minnett thought, his face was too hard. His features were regular, the oval face an ideal setting for the superb Minnett bones, at once delicate and refined; but his mouth had settled into a steel trap, and his grey eyes were like flints. Similarly his body suggested a taut spring, hard muscled and alert; no doubt his pleasure sailing had much to do with this, as it had so much to do with Anne's carriage and bubbling health—she was his only crew. But his movements carried more than a hint of suspicion, a readiness to surge into violent action at the first hint of opposition. She sighed. He was no more than thirty, at once the wealthiest and the most haunted man in the kingdom.

Having started the throng moving to the doors, he joined them at the head of the table, kissed each on the cheek, gave Anne a quick squeeze of the hand. Their mutual adoration always dissipated the very last of Priscilla's doubts.

"But Nick," she said. "Where have you been? Won't you eat something?"

"Later," he said. "I've been looking at my mail."

"Bad news?" Anne asked. Her voice was as quiet as the rest of her, and as soothing.

"I doubt there is such a thing as good news. Elena Reyes fears now that with Spain at war with us, she will never see us again."

"And is she not right?" Priscilla Minnett asked.

"I doubt it will be a very long war, Mama. The wonder is that she got her letter out at all. She also complains. Don Pietro is thirty-seven, and she considers him old enough to be her grandfather. Then there are some accounts."

"From Caroline?" Priscilla Minnett asked, and watched Anne's face. But not a shadow crossed that serenity. She did not fear Nick's wife. Priscilla wondered if she feared anything.

"Why do you not just pay them?" she asked.

Nick shook his head. "Should I do that, she will merely laugh at me all over again. Should I push her into a debtor's prison, I might just get the name of her lover."

Priscilla Minnett sighed. "It seems so unfair. You have a lover who is also the mother of your child. Caroline is merely wild. Was merely wild, perhaps." She rested her hand on top of Anne's. "I do not seek to criticise you, child. Or harm you, in any way. But . . . I'm afraid it can only end in another duel."

"There is no chance of that, Mama," Nick said, patiently. "Carrie can sleep with whomever she chooses. As I am sure she does. But if I am to divorce her I must have a name. That is all I wish."

"To divorce her. But she too is the mother of your child."

"You know that's not true. And besides, that family . . . did they not try to have me killed? I will divorce her, Mama, if it takes me the next year to obtain the proof." His face broke into that irresistible smile. "And there is a sombre subject for the Windshot Hunt. Anne will keep you company. And you must have a word with Mr. Parker."

"Ah, yes. Mr. Parker," Priscilla Minnett said. "You must bring him to my parlour, Anne. After the hunt has left."

"I will do that, ma'am." Anne rose, accompanied Nick into the hall. Outside the mounts were already waiting, the first of the riders already being assisted into their saddles. The dogs howled, anxious to be released from their pens; the chatter of conversation filled the air; the maids were already circulating with their cups.

"You'll take care, Nick," Anne murmured.

" 'Tis the fox who is in danger this morning, sweetheart. And so will you take care. Those stairs are steep."

She made a moue, and then frowned. "I do not think your mother approves of Richard."

"I do not think anyone approves, Anne. But he is your cousin, and he is welcome. Why, Mr. Parker. A very good morning to you."

Richard Parker was a tall young man, with a ruddy complexion and a powerful physique; he was a seaman in the Royal Navy, and looked the part—save for the uncommonly serious expression on his face. It was, in fact, a fine face, intelligent and interested. But in the two days he had been at Windshot Nick had discovered he held a most unsailorlike view of the world, at once sombre and anxious.

"And to you, Mr. Minnett. Anne."

"Richard. Mistress Minnett would talk with you."

"Mistress Minnett? What an honour." He glanced at Nick. "Am I then allowed above stairs, sir?"

Sarcasm? Oh, certainly. But was the man not right?

Nick smiled at him. "Custom, Mr. Parker. Convention. It makes us all less than we are. I apologise for my guests. Yet must I humour them, as they are also my customers. You are welcome at Windshot, now and always."

"Aye," Parker agreed. "As Anne's cousin. May I attend your hunt, sir?"

Nick frowned. "Ride to hounds, you mean? You've no pink."

"I would not so intrude. I would like to follow at a suitable distance. Mr. Morley has offered me the use of his mare. I have never seen the gentry enjoying themselves."

"Why, you shall be welcome, Richard. Mind you are not ridden over."

"I shall, sir. Anne, I shall attend Mistress Minnett in an hour. That is as long as I can sit a saddle, to be sure. Fortune with your fox, Mr. Minnett."

"He'll not fall to me," Nick said. "I am happier on the deck of a ship than the back of a horse, and shall no doubt lag far behind. You'll excuse me." He kissed Anne on the forehead, ran down the stairs. And cursed his own embarrassment. The fellow was just intelligent enough not to know his place. But the fault was his own. Anne had merely begged him to allow her to return to Lyme Regis for a day to see her cousin. Richard could come visiting seldom enough, with a war on and His Majesty's ships more often at sea than in port. But it had taken him four years to persuade Anne to leave Lyme in the first place, and bring their daughter Judith to live at Windshot—she still would not consider a London House, as he wished—and he was not going to let her go again, especially within a month of her confinement. So he had invited Parker to visit them here. The fellow could hardly expect to be asked to sit at table as well.

A maidservant presented her laden tray. Nick took the cup and smiled at her. She was indeed worth smiling at; a tall young woman, in black gown and white apron. Though her dark brown hair was confined in a tight bun behind her white cap, her long thin face was filled with a delightful suggestion of humour, almost wickedness. Her brown eyes sparkled, her lips constantly suggested a smile.

"Good fortune to you, sir," she said. Her Irish brogue was a match to her expression.

"I thank you, Lorna," he said, and blew her a kiss.

A thought for the future? One to be rejected, certainly at Windshot. But there was something about her which troubled him, or perhaps "intrigued" would be the more accurate word. He almost felt he had met her before. She certainly reminded him of someone, although he could not for the moment think who.

"Nick," shouted Paul de Lancey. "Come on, man. The beast will have left the county."

"A wager, Nick," Lucy screamed, cheeks pink in the December breeze. "The brush will be mine."

"A fact I accept." Nick swung himself into the saddle, then raised his cup. "Tallyho." He drained it, handed it to the maid, and spurred his horse.

iii

The hounds were loosed, and cascaded out of the gate like a river of howling sound. The horses thundered behind, red coats and blue bobbing in the bright winter sunlight, breaths clouding, voices shouting. The earth shook, the aged grey stones of Windshot Castle seemed to tremble—the keep dated back to Norman times, erected by some grim visaged seigneur to keep the turbulent west country Saxons in check. Paul and Lucy de Lancey led the rout, George Brummell and Viscount Castlereagh were close behind. The Christmas house party at Windshot was a memory from several years in the past, revived this year for the first time by the latest Minnett. Who

7

cared that all the world seemed to be at war, that French armies were plodding across Holland and Germany, surging across Italy, that the Royal Navy patiently and wearily patrolled the Channel and Biscay? England was inviolate and would remain inviolate just as long as the Navy *was* there. Thus protected, the gentry vowed to enjoy themselves, and their bankers vowed to allow them the means.

And how glorious it was to be out in the open air, on a sunlit winter's morning. It almost equalled being at sea, and Nick had not been to sea for too long. The affairs of the House had kept him in London since his last return from France—nearly a year ago, after that remarkable visit in the summer of 1795. And then, when he had once again found leisure, Anne had been pregnant, and he'd not risk either her health or the babe's. He loved Judith as much as he loved her mother, and he looked forward to loving another child within the month. Perhaps a son.

A sobering thought. He possessed a son. Or did he? Alexander was Caroline's son, not his. Of that he was sure. How she remained, always, her glowing blonde beauty ready to fill his mind, her presence ready to make his anger rise. But supposing, just supposing, Garthwaite did manage to produce the evidence of adultery necessary for a divorce? Or indeed, supposing that Caroline herself ceased defying him, and agreed to supply a name, what then? He could envisage no happier state than to be married to Anne, to be able to give Judith a name and a position. But Nicholas Minnett, head of the greatest bank in the world, married to the daughter of a lighthouse keeper? His friends accepted Anne at table at Windshot, because she was Anne, and because Nick's little social eccentricities were known and accepted. But would they accept her in *their* houses, as Mistress Minnett?

And should he care whether they did or not?

The hounds found a fence, wriggled beneath it, charged a farmyard. The horses roared behind, rising together, thudding hooves into the beaten earth, scattering dust into the still air. Chickens and cattle were locked away this day, when Mr. Minnett would ride to the hunt. Faces peered at them from the windows, cheers were raised and scarves were waved. So the fence would suffer, and so would the yard. Flower beds would be trampled into mud. And

Master Bowen would present his account at the Castle on Monday morning, sure it would be met in full. And no doubt he would tack on to it every little repair he had hoped to make and been unable to afford. It was a game, based on the Minnett millions.

The hunt burst into open country again, with a copse of trees fringing the road, and a wagon came into view, rumbling along slowly.

The huntmaster blew his horn, rising in his stirrups to do so, and then waved. The hounds charged up the bank, baying and howling. The driver dragged on the reins, and the wagon creaked to a halt.

"Out of the way, man. Out of the way," yelled Paul de Lancey, driving in his spurs to set his horse at the embankment.

The huntmaster gave another blast on his horn. The hounds swarmed around the wagon for a moment before setting off down the farther side, streaming through the copse, the fox now in sight as it left its lair to make for the open country.

The lead horse of the wagon gave a rear and a whinny, and his companion joined. Desperately the driver dragged on the rein, but the horses were out of control, surrounded for a moment by their fellows, and now sought to escape, as the hunt flowed away from them and down the farther embankment, streaming behind the hounds.

"Whoa," screamed the driver. "Whoa." He was standing now, leaning back, face crimson as he strained on the reins. A woman had appeared behind him, also reaching for the brake.

Nick drew rein on the road itself, allowing his companions to gallop away from him, and watched the wagon careering down the uneven slope, bouncing and swaying on the ruts.

"Crazy fool," someone shouted as he galloped by. "He must have heard the horn."

Then the last of the riders was gone. When the hunt was out, it paid to stay at home. Nick turned his horse to follow, gave a last glance over his shoulder, and checked in dismay as he watched the wagon wheel hit an obstruction, the whole equipage rise into the air, and then come down on its side, pitching the man one way, the woman the other, leaving the horses struggling in the traces and neighing, while pots, pans, and loaves of bread scattered across the trampled grass.

Nick swung his horse, trotted down the embankment, gave rein, and galloped towards the overturned wagon.

"Help," screamed the woman. "Help me."

She was in fact hardly more than a girl, and now he saw what had brought down the horses; they had stumbled into boggy ground. He drew rein, dismounted, knelt beside the apparently unconscious man, who had fallen on his face. There was only a trace of blood, but the woman was screaming again, her voice soaring even above the terrified shrieks of the horses.

She had been thrown the other way, where the earth was covered by a film of water, deeper than it looked, for she already floundered up to her thighs, while mud clung to her arms and obscured the flushed pink of her cheeks.

"My apologies, Alice," Nick said, recognising her as he waded in, sinking to his ankles as he seized her shoulders.

"Oh, God," she gasped. "Oh, God," and made a convulsive effort to drag herself into his outstretched arms, with such force that she pulled him off balance, so that he fell beside her with a tremendous splash, sending mud and water cascading in every direction.

"Easy, Alice," he gasped. "We'll have you out."

He turned on his knee, still holding the girl, and discovered that he could not move. He had already sunk to his thighs, as the girl had disappeared to her waist.

"Oh, God," she screamed. "Oh, God."

Quicksand. He sucked air into his lungs, expelled it again as he seemed to sink farther with the effort. His face was smothered in mud and his hat had come off. He could inhale nothing but the noxious smell of the mud, could feel nothing but the tug at his legs and the woman squirming in his arms.

"For God's sake," he shouted in her ear. "Lie still."

She obeyed, panting, her cheek pressed against his, both arms round his neck. Her cap was gone and her pale yellow hair scattered across the mud. She was very young, and very frightened. And was not he very frightened?

He gazed at the equipage, twenty feet away. It was not sinking, and neither were the horses, for all their frantic endeavours. Neither was the girl's husband, still lying unconscious on the ground beyond. And neither was Belair, his own stallion, now peering at him in turn, and cautiously pawing the turf with a forefoot.

There was nothing else to be seen, save the distant trees, the embankment marking the road. The hunt could be heard receding into the distance.

And the mud was now gripping his thighs, seeping through his breeches to dampen his groin.

"Oh, my God, sir," whispered the girl. "We're sinking."

"We've a way to go yet," Nick promised her. "But keep still. Belair. Belair, old chap."

If he could just reach the drooping rein, the stallion could pull them out.

Belair pricked his ears, came slowly forward, sank to his hock, extricated his foot with a great jerk, and retreated. He gazed at his master, brown eyes a mute statement of uncertainty. But there was no point involving the horse as well.

"You'll not make it," Nick said. "Stay. Stay, Belair."

"You're Mr. Minnett," the girl said, peering at him from a distance of six inches. "Oh, Lord, Mr. Minnett. What will happen to us?"

"We must wait on your husband to wake up," Nick decided. He could just see the man's boots, on the far side of the upturned wagon. They did not move. The horses had regained their feet and stood gazing at Belair with silent concern. Silence. Even the hunt had faded. How quiet it was.

"He's dead," wailed the girl. "I know he's dead, Mr. Minnett. And we'll drown."

"Shhh," Nick said. And listened. Because there was sound, drifting across the morning. Or was it his imagination? But it had to be sound. He was Nick Minnett. He had survived too many dangers—in France at the hands of the sans culottes, in the Channel from hurricane force winds and mountainous seas, in London from the bullets of an assassin, the vengeance of George Moncey, his brother-in-law—to drown in a bog. He found himself smiling at the irony of his situation. No one would ever be sure where he had actually gone down—he would just have disappeared. There were sufficient people who claimed he was in any event a spawn of the devil. So, the devil would merely have reclaimed his own.

But not this time. Because there were hooves. The girl had heard them too, and recommenced her squirming. "Mr Minnett . . ."

"Aye," he said. "But keep still, child. Or we'll not be here when he reaches us."

The water was round his waist.

And there was Richard Parker, sitting on the steward's old grey mare, gazing down at them.

"Mr. Minnett," he said. "There's no place for a man of distinction."

iv

"We must have Mr. Parker in," Priscilla Minnett decided. "Mr. Morley, you'll require Mr. Parker to attend us."

"Immediately, ma'am," Morley agreed, and withdrew through the double doors of the great withdrawing room. In here the fire blazed in the grate, and the chandeliers gleamed with candlelight. The hunt had returned in triumph. The riders had bathed, and were now dressed in their best—the men either in uniform, for most were at least colonels of volunteer regiments, or in black; the ladies in their very brightest colours, their most daring gowns. Fashion was beginning to incline towards sheer materials and less and less petticoats, though any man who glimpsed a female curve on a December evening could be sure it was shrouded in woollen stocking or shift.

They drank mulled wine, and toasted Nick.

"It really is too bad," Brummell complained. "To gain the fox, as I said I would, Bob, you'll remember that, and have Nick steal the glory at the end."

12

"Glory?" Nick demanded. "There was no glory. I had no idea the girl was fast."

"But you stopped and went to her assistance," Castlereagh pointed out. "Some farmer's wife?"

"I've known Alice Mawlton all her life," Nick said. "And Harry. They've farmed here for fifteen years."

"Then they should know by now to keep out of the way of the hunt," Paul de Lancey said.

"Mr. Mawlton is all right?" Priscilla Minnett whispered.

"Oh, aye. Just a severe bang on the head. And I'll make good the damage to the wagon," Nick said, also speaking in a low voice. "What a sorry lot they are, to be sure." He was referring to his guests. Because he was, indeed, more than a little angry. Presumably his life had been in danger. But to suppose that one should ride on and let a young woman drown, merely because she happened to be a farmer's wife. . . .

"Here he is." Anne stood in the doorway, holding her cousin by the hand. Her face glowed with pleasure, Parker's with embarrassment.

"The hero," someone shouted.

"You'll take a glass, Mr. Parker," Lucy said, herself carrying it towards him.

"Why, Mistress de Lancey . . ." Parker took the glass, gazed at the gentry. "It was nothing, I do assure you."

"Nothing?" Priscilla Minnett cried. "Why, sir, the House of Minnett is forever in your debt. You'll not forget that. Nick?"

"Aye." Nick seized Parker's hand. "You'll not forget that, Richard. Anne, where would I be without you and your family?"

"I'm so happy," she said, squeezing each of their arms. "So proud. Nick. . . ."

Morley was standing behind her, clearing his throat.

"What is the matter?"

"Why, nothing, Mr. Nicholas." He spoke in a low voice. "Mr. Pitt has arrived."

"Billy? He could not have chosen a better moment."

"Yes, sir. But he has gone straight to his room, for a bath and a change of clothing. He has been on the road these two days. He asked me to inform you, sir."

Nick squeezed their hands again, smiled at them. "You'll excuse me, Anne, Richard?"

"Of course, sir," Parker agreed. "For where is a common hero when the Prime Minister himself pays a call."

Nick gave him a quick frown; it was difficult to say whether his impertinent remarks were meant as a jest or not. Then he ran up the stairs, banged on the door, and entered the bedchamber. He discovered Pitt seated in an armchair with a glass of port in one hand, while Eric, Nick's valet, tugged at his boots.

"Billy." Nick closed the door. "We had given you up for lost."

" 'Tis a fact I cannot stay long," Pitt agreed. "And you? What are all these tales? You very nearly *were* lost."

"A hunting accident. It can happen to anyone."

Pitt sat up, wriggled his toes. "Thank you, Eric. Give us half an hour, will you?"

"Yes, sir." Eric left the room, carefully closing the door behind him.

"I do not know what to do with you, Nick," the Prime Minister grumbled, finishing his drink. "There must come a time when you will learn some discretion."

"Discretion? A woman was drowning."

"A farmer's wife?"

"You sound like everyone else. A woman."

"Forgive me. I know the value of human life as well as you. But some human beings are more valuable than others. It is a fact, and sooner or later you will understand it, if you do not already. Will you fill my glass?"

Nick poured, took one for himself. "What kept you?"

"News. Of one sort or another. Bonaparte has gone into winter quarters. So they say. No doubt he will pop up again, somewhere, unexpectedly. But then again, perhaps not. They say his wife has gone to join him in Italy. You knew her as well, I believe?"

"I met Rose before I met Bonaparte."

"Ah. I wonder how the Republic manages to turn up these men

of such frightful energy, and not a little talent, while we must stumble along with our incompetent asses."

Nick smiled at him. "For a start, you must execute everyone over the rank of colonel."

"My God, you do say the most terrifying things. However, it was not the successes of Bonaparte, or his marital bliss, that kept me in London. I have a report from my agent in Brittany."

Nick put down his glass, the smile leaving his face. "Charette?"

"Is taken and hanged."

Nick sat down, slowly. "My God." How memory came back to him, of that huge, jovial, black bearded figure. Charette had survived constant destruction for four years, only to find a rope at the end of it.

Pitt sighed. "So there is the very end of any hopes we may ever have had of the Vendée. Any hopes. Of course, I never had any great hopes there. You were the one."

"They're my people. Perhaps I should say, *were* my people."

"Now, for sure. Anyone who would sport a white cockade has long been executed. But that is not the least of my problems. My agent does not only bring word of the past. He talks of the future, too. There is a fleet assembling in Brest."

"There was always a fleet in Brest."

"This one is bigger than the last. They are fitting out every available ship, every transport as well as every man of war. And there is an army of forty thousand men encamped around. Hoche is there."

Nick frowned at him. "To descend on us?"

Pitt shrugged. "It would hardly be to invade the Americas."

"But . . . would they risk the Channel fleet?"

"Even the Channel fleet cannot be everywhere. They need but two days of offshore wind, and they'd be away. Where do you think, Nick? Precisely."

"Who knows?" Nick said. "Brest. Up Channel for Wight, or this very coast. Or Scotland . . . I'd wager you'd give a year of your life to find out, Billy."

"Ten years." Pitt sat bolt upright. "But not from you." He wagged his finger. "I have given orders that if the 'Golden Rose' is seen at sea again during this war, it is to be arrested. Your place is here, raising money. At this moment there is no duty greater than that."

Nick grinned at him. "As you say. Anyway, what—me take the 'Rose' to sea? With Anne about to deliver, I have no crew. Which reminds me. I had best rejoin my guests. I'll expect you down to dinner, Billy."

"Just give me time to have a bath. But not a word of this to anyone, Nick. There'd be a panic."

"Not a word," Nick promised, and opened the door, to step back in surprise as a young woman tumbled into the room.

♦

2

It was the Irish maidservant, Lorna Grant. She landed on her hands and knees, gazed at the two men with an expression of embarrassment and dismay, colour flaming in her cheeks.

"By God," Pitt was on his feet.

"Lorna?" Nick demanded. "What were you doing?"

"About to knock, sir, truly." She scrambled to her feet, straightened her gown, attempted to do the same for her cap and only succeeded in dislodging it.

"To knock? She was listening," Pitt declared. He pointed. "Irish."

"Why, sir, so I am." She had regained most of her composure. "Now what would I be doing, listening to two fine gentlemen like yourselves? I was reaching for the door, sir, to tell Mr. Pitt his bath was ready, and why, bang, it swung open on me. 'Tis the truth, sir."

Nick had already dragged on the bell pull, and Eric and Morley were hurrying along the corridor.

"Lorna?" Morley demanded. "What is the meaning of this?"

"Well, I. . . ."

"She was listening at the keyhole," Nick said.

"Oh, no, sir," Lorna protested. "I'd not do a thing like that." But as she looked around the circle of faces, her own expression settled into firmness, her mouth hardening. She recognised her danger.

"How long has she been in your employ, Nick?" Pitt asked. "Morley?"

"Why, sir, Mr. Nicholas, only a week. She is one of the temporary staff my wife employs to cope with the Christmas holidays."

"Temporary?" Pitt asked.

"Maureen," Nick called, as Mistress Morley climbed the stairs. "Do you know this girl?"

Maureen Morley peered at the maid. "She had very good references, Mr. Nicholas."

"We'll have a look at those. Thank you, Eric. Morley."

"Can I go, sir?" Lorna inquired.

"You'll step inside," Nick said.

She hesitated, then walked farther into the room. Nick closed the door, and Pitt sat down again.

"A spy, eh?" he mused. "For whom, girl?"

She stood before him, her hands clasped behind her back. "I'm no spy, sir. I was about to knock . . ."

"As you said." Nick seized her wrists, pulled them round in front, and turned over her hands. The soft white flesh was only recently reddened with physical labour. "You'll raise your skirts."

"I will not, sir. 'Tis indecent."

Holding both her wrists in his left hand, Nick seized her skirts and pulled them above her knees. There was a knock at the door. "Come."

"Indecent," Lorna declared, although she made no effort to free herself. "I'd not realised you were that kind of man, Mr. Minnett."

"Why, Mr. Nicholas," Mistress Morley said. "Whatever are you at?"

"Come round here, Maureen," Nick suggested. "Would you say those knees had ever knelt on a wooden floor?"

For the flesh was smooth and indeed remarkably clean.

"Bless my soul," Maureen Morley said.

"Hold the skirt a moment," Nick said, and stroked the flesh, pushing the material higher.

18

"Why, sir," Lorna said, giving a little shudder, possibly because his fingers tickled.

"Nick?" Pitt asked.

"Calloused," Nick said. "Above and behind the right knee. You must spend a lot of time in the saddle, Lorna."

"Why, sir . . ."

"In the saddle?" Pitt demanded. "A housemaid?"

"Makes you think, doesn't it? All right, Maureen."

Mistress Morley allowed the skirts to fall back into place.

"Well, sir," Lorna said. "I am from Ireland . . ."

"Where the housemaids ride side saddle," Nick said. "One learns something new every day."

"Side saddle, sir?"

"That callous is on the outside of the knee, Lorna. The right knee. It has been created over several years—of riding to hounds, I'd say." He took the sheaf of papers from Maureen Morley's hands and sat at the table.

"A very odd business," Pitt said.

"A disgraceful business, sir," Maureen agreed. "Let me take her downstairs, Mr. Nicholas. A few strokes of a cane will have her telling the truth."

"You touch me with that cane and I'll have your eyes," Lorna said, quietly enough, but there could be no arguing with her tone.

"Why, you little. . . ."

"Easy, Maureen." Nick turned over the second letter. "George Grenville. You've worked for some famous people, Lorna."

"Thank you, sir."

"Saving that this is not George Grenville's signature."

"Sir?"

"He banks with me," Nick pointed out. "He is also Mr. Pitt's first cousin. Billy?"

Pitt took the letter. "By God."

"Forgery," Nick said, "is a hanging offence, Lorna. So is treason."

The girl gazed at him. Her tongue showed for a moment, and then disappeared again.

"You'd best send for the magistrate from Exeter," Pitt declared. "Hadn't you best tell us, Lorna?"

"You're having sport with a poor defenceless girl," she said. "All I wanted was the job. Starving, I am."

"You'll have me looking at your belly, next," Nick said.

She backed away.

"Have her to the magistrate," Pitt said. "I want her disposed of, and quickly. Those were most secret matters she must have overheard."

"D . . . disposed of?" Lorna whispered.

"You'll be hanged," Mistress Morley said severely. "And it'll be no more than you deserve."

The girl looked at Nick again. "You'll not hang me, Mr. Minnett. I only wanted the money."

She was willing him, with her eyes, with her mouth, perhaps with the memory of her legs, of the softness of her flesh. Supposing Nicholas Minnett could any longer be tempted by a woman's flesh. But *she* thought so, and that was important.

"Supposing she would tell us who sent her here, and with what in mind, Billy," he said, "we might be able to exercise clemency."

"Supposing," Pitt agreed.

"She'll tell you nothing, Mr. Nicholas," Maureen said. "I've already marked her as a right stubborn hussy."

"None the less," Nick said, "it's worth a try. Give me an hour or so." He opened the door for her. "After you, Lorna."

ii

The girl hesitated, then stepped on to the gallery, walking in front of him towards his bedchamber. She knew where they were going.

"Sir?" Eric inquired.

"I'll have a bottle of port, Eric. No, make it two. And two glasses."

"Yes, sir, Mr. Nicholas." But Eric's blunt features were a picture of mixed disapproval and bewilderment. He of all people knew that Nick's reputation as a rake was largely undeserved, though he also knew that his master was the most pragmatic of men, and would use any means that came to hand to obtain his desired end.

Lorna Grant was hesitating again, at the door to the bedchamber. Nick reached past her to open it, and she stepped inside.

"A servant would have opened the door for me," he said.

She remained with her back to him, gazing at the bed. Eric was already returning with a laden tray.

"Thank you, Eric." Nick took the tray, closed the door, and turned the key in the lock. He placed the tray on the table by the bed, poured two glasses. "Drink."

At last she moved, sufficiently to lift the glass. But she did not drink.

"You'll not pretend you've never tasted port," Nick said. "Even a housemaid would have sneaked a glass from time to time, while the butler stroked her bottom."

She sipped. "And do you, sir, intend to stroke my bottom?"

Nick sat down in the chair on the far side of the room. "You may undress."

"Yes, sir." She put down her glass, reached up, took off her cap.

"You do know that I can have you hanged?"

"Yes, sir. But would it not be a waste?" She laid the cap on the bed to free her hair. Thick and long and brown, it tumbled onto her shoulders. He realised that she was a quite lovely woman.

"Finish your port." He got up.

"Sir?"

"Drink it. You are too tight. I like my women easy."

She hesitated, then drained the glass. Nick filled it again.

"You like your women drunk, sir," she said.

"Oh, aye, I'm a man of strange tastes." He leaned forward, brushed her lips with his.

She gave a little gasp, reached for the back of her apron, released it, allowed it to fall to the ground. Nick held out her glass.

"I'd sooner . . ."

" Drink it," he said.

She gazed at the expression in his eyes, then tossed her head, seized the glass, and drank it. Nick refilled it.

Now she was definitely panting. She fumbled as she unfastened her gown, her hands seeming to lose themselves on her shoulders. " 'Tis naught but a scheme," she protested.

"All life is naught but a scheme." He held out her glass. She shook her head. "No. My head spins as it is."

"Drink."

She hesitated, shrugged, drained the glass, and sat down heavily onto the bed. Her gown flopped forward to expose her shoulders and the straps of her petticoat. "You'll have to help me," she yawned, and fell back. The glass left her fingers and rolled slowly across the coverlet, the dregs staining the pale blue material as it did so.

Nick sat beside her, looking down on her splendid face. Her eyes were shut, and he held her chin between thumb and forefinger, moving it gently to and fro. "Lorna."

"Leave me be," she muttered. "Leave me be."

He lowered his head and kissed her on the mouth. Her eyes opened, and her tongue sought his. Her arms went round his shoulders. Even drunk, she was a strong young woman.

"Lorna," he whispered into her ear, working his body on hers. "You'll not hang, Lorna. I'll not let you hang. I'd help you, Lorna. These people, they are not my friends. Tell me of your friends, Lorna."

She held his face again, brought him down for another kiss. She seized his right hand, placed it on her belly, gave a faint frown of bewilderment; no doubt she had forgotten she was still fully dressed. He gave her groin a gentle squeeze.

"Time for another drink," he said, and pushed himself up to pour.

Her head flopped to and fro. "Another drink," she said, and gave a little giggle.

He got his hand under her shoulder blades, lifted her up, kissed her eyes, her ears, her nose, her mouth. "You are a delightful creature," he whispered. For once he was not telling a lie.

She laughed, and he drained some port into her mouth. She

coughed, shook her head again, and rolled on her stomach. "You are a devil, Nick Minnett," she said. "Oh, a devil. You're all devils. Moncey's a devil."

He lay beside her, put his right leg across hers, his mouth next to her ear, his heart pounding, while his belly filled with lead. "Who? Who did you say?"

She pushed him away, rolled on her back, arms and legs flung wide. And gave a shriek of laughter. "I'd forgot. You're wed to his sister."

He held the bodice of her gown, fingers pressing against the softness under the fabric, then pulled her upright. "Moncey? You've dealings with George Moncey?"

She gave another peal of laughter. "Oh, aye. He'll bring you down, Nick Minnett. And all the Tory rascals with you. Oh, he'll laugh at *your* hanging."

Nick shook her, gently. "Where is he now?"

"Is he? Is he?" Her head flopped from side to side.

"Have another drink." Nick held her face, poured some liquid down her throat.

She gagged, and retched. "Wi' the frogs," she muttered, her eyes closing. "Wi' the frogs."

"Where? Where with the frogs?"

Her head drooped on his chest. "Where'd you expect. They gather at Brest."

"And Moncey is there? But why? Where does he hope to guide them?"

Her eyes opened again, and she belched. He was enveloped in port fumes, and in her smile. "They're for Ireland," she said. "We'll all be free, come the spring." Her eyes flopped shut, and she was asleep.

iii

"Ireland," Pitt said for the fiftieth time. "My God. I should have suspected it immediately. They are all Papists over there. The French have ever designed on it."

"Yet these French are no longer Papists," Castlereagh said. "They'll be looking to find their own sort—professional brigands."

"Aye, well, it takes an Irishman to know his kind," Pitt remarked. "None the less, the matter is serious enough."

"George Moncey," Nick said. "George Moncey, by God. The fellow must be mad."

He gazed down the sweep of the withdrawing room. Everyone at dinner had sensed that something of import was afoot. Now that the meal was over, the politicians and their host had been allowed to withdraw to the far end of the room. The other guests gathered around the fire, as usual, drinking port and exchanging gossip regarding the hunt, all the while casting glances at the trio in the corner.

"Oh, he is," Castlereagh agreed. "Mad with hatred of you, Nick, for giving him that public beating last year, and for wishing to divorce his sister into the bargain. How you ever got involved with such a crew is a mystery to me."

"It was to me too, at the time," Nick confessed. "But there is a personal matter. . . ."

"Not to him," Pitt said. "He confounds you with the entire administration, as we are your friends as well as your customers. Nick, I must be away."

"You've only just arrived," Nick pointed out.

"Aye. I'll sleep in the coach. Bob, you'll accompany me."

"Eh?" Castlereagh looked down at the glass in his hand, glanced at the company, and the fire. And sighed. "I suppose, if duty calls. What do you intend?"

"Why, to alert our people."

"Where? There are several hundred miles of undefended coastline, every fifty miles a bay which is a perfect natural harbour, every village filled with men and women who hate the very name of England."

"We must do what we can," Pitt said, and got up. "I am sorry, Nick. You understand."

"Aye," Nick said, thoughtfully. "I understand." He also rose, watched the two men invade the throng at the far end, and bring their chatter to a stop with their farewells. He went into the hall. "Morley, you'll prepare Mr. Pitt's carriage. Fresh horses. And fetch his and Lord Castlereagh's boxes. Well, Richard? No peace for the wicked, eh?"

Parker stood in the hallway leading to the pantry. "Trouble, Mr. Minnett?"

"Affairs of state."

"But personal matters too, Nick." Anne Yealm had left the withdrawing room to join them. "I heard the name of Moncey."

He nodded. "Quite a responsibility, to think that a personal feud encourages him to make war on the entire country. If only . . ." he paused as Pitt and Castlereagh and the de Lanceys hurried out.

"Nick," Lucy cried. "They'll not say a word, save that they must be away in haste."

"You'd think the French were landing," Paul complained.

"Aye," Pitt agreed. "Consider that, if you wish." He squeezed Nick's hand. "I'll have my week at Windshot next year. And remember what I said. Your place is here. Mistress Yealm." He kissed her cheek. "Hail and farewell." He released her, gazed at Parker in mystification for a moment, then hurried out of the door, Castlereagh at his heels.

"Who'd have thought it," Parker remarked. "Me and the Prime Minister in the same house, if only for a couple of hours."

"What did he mean, Nick?" Lucy asked. "About his words to you?"

"The whole thing smacks of mystery," Paul said.

"Affairs of state always appear so. You'd best rejoin our guests."

They hesitated, then returned to the drawing room. Nick felt Anne's fingers on his arm.

"What *did* he mean, love?"

Nick sighed. "The French are massing a fleet and an army around Brest—for an invasion, to be sure. Mr. Pitt would give a lot to know where and when."

"Admiral Colpoys is on station off Brest," Parker said. "They'll not get through."

"In December, with a gale a week? There is always the chance."

"And you'd be there to find out what you can," Anne said softly.

He smiled, kissed her on the forehead. "As would you, sweetheart. Don't deny it. But I told Mr. Pitt it was impossible, with my crew unable."

"I sometimes curse the frailty in us women that enables this to happen," she said, releasing him.

"And I adore it. Now then, Parker, you'll excuse us, I'm sure. What with one thing and another I have sufficiently neglected my guests for one day."

"I'd crew you, Mr. Minnett."

Nick frowned at him. "You?"

"I hold the rank of Able Seaman. I'll wager I know more of the sea than do you, sir."

"I'd not deny that. But you are holidaying from the sea, surely."

"None the less, if you really wish to go, I'm your man."

"In December," Anne said softly. "With a gale a week."

"If you would . . ." Nick chewed his lip, glanced at her, threw his arm round her shoulders to hug her against him. Brittany called him like a magnet. His family had come from there, much of his boyhood had been spent with the Benoîts at St. Suliac. He had financed Etienne de Benoît's futile invasion, had fought with Charette de la Contrie against the Republicans. He had shared some of the most traumatic moments of his life with Honorine Damas.

But Anne knew all of these things. "If Hoche, and an army, were to get ashore, in Ireland . . ."

"Oh, aye," Anne said. "I'll not beg you, Nick. You seem determined to leave my children fatherless at the first possible moment." She sighed. "The cause is not the French. It is merely that you have not sailed the 'Rose' these six months. I sometimes think you have salt water in your veins, and not blood."

He turned up her chin to kiss her mouth. "Do you?"

Her smile was shy. "I said, sometimes."

"I'll get my gear," Parker said. "Believe me, sir, it will be an honour to crew Nick Minnett."

"Aye. But it must be done privily. I'd not excite the others."

26

"What, disappear for a week, and not excite the others?" Anne inquired.

"Three days. No more. Tell them I have decided to follow Mr. Pitt and Lord Castlereagh to town, but I shall be back for Christmas. Aye . . ." He frowned at Maureen Morley, hurrying down the main staircase, panting, and with her cap gone from her head. "Maureen? You've seen the ghost?"

"I've lost one, sir. You'll need a stick to my back. That girl, the Irish one. She's not in her room."

3

"Did you not lock her in?" Parker demanded.

"I did, Mr. Parker. She left by the window."

"That is three storeys up," Anne cried.

"Aye, but there's a vine. She must have opened her casement and climbed down—or jumped."

"My God." Nick ran out of the front door, down the steps, and round the side of the keep. His father had purchased Windshot some twenty years before, as a country retreat, but had only troubled to maintain the keep itself. The curtain walls and the other buildings, save for the stables and the dog pen, were in a state of tumbled, ivy grown ruin; and ivy certainly swarmed up the walls of the keep as well. But strong enough to support a woman?

He stood beneath the overhanging roof, gazing up at the windows. His imagination clouded with a picture of Lorna Grant, skirts and hair flying in the December breeze, climbing down the wall. But climb down she had; the ground at the bottom was imprinted with her feet—deep where she had landed, then trailing off into the night.

Parker stood beside him, a torch flaring in the wind. "How long ago, do you reckon?"

"It can't be more than an hour. Horses. Morley, saddle them up.

And prepare some food. Cold stuff and some bottles of wine. Do you ride, Richard? Of course you do. You were up this morning."

"I can stay in the saddle," Parker agreed.

"Two horses. We'll catch her." He hurried round to the front of the castle; Anne waited at the top of the steps, hugging herself against the wind. "We'll fetch her, sweetheart," he said.

"Why?"

"Eh?" He pulled on his cloak. "Well, she's a spy."

"Who you'd hang?"

"Who I'd use for further information." He held her shoulders, looked more closely into her eyes. "Not jealous of an Irish maidservant?"

"Jealous of your safety, Nick," she said. "As you well know. Do you still mean to put to sea?"

"Aye. There and back in three days, Anne. The weather is settled."

"The weather is never settled in December. Take care, Nick, please take care."

"I'll be here for your confinement, you have my word. Richard?"

Parker was already mounted, holding the second horse by the bridle, the saddle bag of victuals in front of him. "Where do you think, sir?"

"She'll make for the coast road," Nick said. "And thence Exeter. She'll know she cannot survive on the moors in winter."

He waved to Anne, cantered out of the yard, then remembered that he had forgotten to say goodbye to his mother and sister. But that was best. They would certainly protest, and their objections might well alarm the rest of the party. This way he would be back before anyone could decide what to do.

The breeze was like a breath from the arctic. If the girl did not possess a cloak she would be frozen by the time they caught up with her. They topped the rise, looked behind them at the twinkling lights of Windshot, and down the far side at the empty darkened moor. Though the moon was bright, she could easily stumble straight into a bog.

"There." Parker pointed. Nick, straining his eyes, caught a distant glimpse of movement.

"You've considerable eyesight, Richard."

"I'm a sailor, Mr. Minnett. May I ask what you intend?"

"Not to hang her, if that is what bothers you."

"It does, sir."

"I mean to take her with us."

"Sir?"

"Brittany stretches a long way, Richard. That girl will know where we must go. Come on."

He cantered down the slope, increasing his pace to a gallop at the bottom, and leaving Parker behind. The wind sang in his ears, and now the distant figure had disappeared. Gone to ground at the sound of his horse? Yet she had been there.

As Belair bounded over the uneven ground, the figure rose from behind a hummock and ran again, fleeing blindly now, aware that she could not escape.

"Whoa," Nick called. "Whoa. That goes for you as well, Lorna."

Still she ran, panting, feet stumbling, slipping to her knees and regaining her stride. Nick rode Belair alongside, reached down to seize her hair, and she turned to strike at him. But his gloved fingers were lodged in the rich brown locks—she had lost or discarded her cap—and he brought her to a halt, panting against the heaving flanks of the animal.

"Kill me now," she gasped. "Shoot me down, Mr. Minnett, as you are a man. I'll not have my gut drop away at the end of a rope."

Nick dismounted, still holding her hair. "Hang you, Lorna? Did we not agree that would be a waste?"

When he had brought her close, he noticed that her eyes were glazed. She exhaled port and staggered a bit. That she had got this far was evidence of her determination.

"Unless I have to, of course."

Parker rode up to them. "What now, Mr. Minnett?"

"Lyme," Nick declared.

"With the girl?"

"Oh, aye. She'll be our pilot, if she wants to live."

ii

Lorna settled herself on the saddle, leaned back against him. Her hair clouded his face.

"Pilot you?" she asked. "Where, do you suppose?"

"I wish to have a word with Lord Moncey," Nick said, letting the horse pick its own way; Belair knew the road to Lyme well enough—it was only ten miles distant.

"He's in France."

"You are a bright and intelligent girl, Lorna. We are going to France."

She turned her head. "We have no ship."

"I have a ship."

"But 'tis December."

He squeezed his arm round her waist. "I'll keep you warm, Lorna. But you are right in supposing we should make haste. So you'll tell me where to go."

"I will not."

He sighed. "Well, then, it's the rope. Jeering men, your legs flopping about, your gut . . ."

"I've seen women hanged," she said. "The thought makes me blood crawl."

"Then you'll not wish to experience it."

"You're asking me to betray my people, Mr. Minnett."

"I'm asking you to direct me to the biggest scoundrel on the face of this earth, in exchange for your own life."

"You'll set me free? No prison? No transportation?"

"Free," he agreed. "Think about it."

She relapsed into silence, only occasionally changing her position to make herself more comfortable. Lorna Grant. A housemaid. The devil she was. An Irish spy, and no doubt as well born as himself. But wars and revolutions always made for strange bedfellows. He smiled, at his inadvertent choice of simile.

31

Lights glowed at the foot of a rise, and the breeze had freshened. They rode down the cobbled streets of Lyme and stabled their horses at the inn.

"Mr. Minnett?" John Humphrey peered at them. "You'll not be putting out tonight?"

" 'Tis a fresh breeze, John. Nothing more."

"Aye, sir, and a high glass. But it'll be near freezing on the water."

Nick chewed his lip, but there really was nothing for it. "Aye, well, we'll not be long." He held Lorna's arm and escorted her down to the jetty. Parker had already located the tender, and was unshipping the oars.

"What did he mean?" she asked. "Talking about a glass?"

"He means his barometer. It is high and steady. That means fine weather, but an east wind. It comes all the way from Russia. Cold."

"So where's your ship?"

He pointed. The tide was half up, and the ketch was just leaving the sand, still bumping on the wooden legs bolted to each side to hold her upright when she dried. She was eighty feet long, her principal mast being forward, with the mizzen to supply additional canvas by the helm. She was built of oak on oak frames, according to Harry Yealm's own design.

"That?" Lorna glanced at him. "Why," she said. "You look like a boy, Mr. Minnett. You love that thing."

"So I do," he agreed. "More than anything in the world. Saving Mistress Yealm."

He sat Lorna in the stern of the dinghy with himself, while Parker handled the oars with all the expertise of a seaman.

"The 'Golden Rose'," the sailor said. "Anne has told me so much about this boat, Mr. Minnett. You'd not believe how much I wanted to sail in her."

"She'll not let you down, Richard. Up you go."

The dinghy came into the varnished topsides of the ketch, and Parker scrambled aboard with the painter, made it fast, then turned to help Lorna.

"Below with you," Nick said, and gave her the saddle bag. "You can make us some coffee. And put in a dollop of rum; you'll find a bottle in the locker."

She hesitated, then slid back the hatch and went down the companion ladder to the cabin. The keel gave a last bump on the sand.

"Well, sir?" Parker asked.

"Let's get to it." Between them they unshipped the legs, secured them on deck; hoisted the dinghy on its falls, and stowed it amidships; removed the sail cover from the main, left it loosely secured on the boom; pulled the foresail from its bag, clewed it on to the forestay. The easterly wind was beam on to the harbour entrance. But there was now enough water for manoeuvre within the breakwater. "We'll have it up," Nick decided, and they hoisted the mainsail, sheeted it hard. Now 'Golden Rose' curtsied to her mooring, running up into the wind and falling away again as the chain held her fast.

"Let go," Nick said, hurrying aft to take the wheel.

Parker threw the buoy over the side, and the ship immediately came alive. Nick put down the helm and she swung away from the wind and gathered way.

"Foresail," he bawled.

Parker was already heaving at the halliard, and the canvas slipped up the stay, ballooning, resisting the efforts of the man. Nick brought the ship back into the wind again, and Parker seized his opportunity to swig the sail tight, before securing the halliard. The next time she fell away Nick let the sails fill properly. 'Golden Rose' gave a bound, then sped through the entrance into the sudden whitecaps beyond, picking up a bowfull of spray to toss over her shoulder.

"Well, Richard?"

Parker came aft to set the mizzen. "She's a good ship, Mr. Minnett. With a good skipper. You handle her like if you were born to it."

"I was, just about. Take the helm."

"Where, sir?"

"South will do for the moment. I'll get a course from our passenger." He slid down the ladder, paused in dismay. The lantern had been lit, and swung gently to and fro immediately in front of him. A bag of coffee lay on the deck, split and rolling in company with a bottle of rum. And Lorna Grant lay on the port berth, vomiting into a bowl.

"Oh, Christ," she wailed. "Oh, God in Heaven. Put back, Mr. Minnett. Put me ashore."

"In France," he promised her. "Tell me where."

"Oh, Christ," she said. "Oh, God, I'm not intended for the sea, Mr. Minnett."

"You'll get used to it. Where, Lorna? Where? You'll not want to prolong the voyage."

"Oh, Christ," she said again. "Palue, Mr. Minnett. That's all I know. The château at Palue."

"Palue," he said. "L'Aberwrach. Oh, 'tis unlucky you are, Lorna. That's a hundred and fifty miles. We'll not make it before tomorrow afternoon."

iii

"Noon, Mr. Minnett." Parker pushed the hatch shut behind him. "I've left you some grub."

Nick slowly unclamped his fingers from the spokes of the wheel. The sun was out, and it was somewhat warmer than last night, when he had supposed he'd freeze. But the end was in sight. He pointed, and Parker followed the direction of his finger. "France?"

"Aye. Ushant, down there to the west. Keep her as she goes, just west of south. We've a tide carrying us over."

"L'Aberwrach," Parker remarked. "An iron coast, they say. And no entrance, to speak of."

"There are reefs," Nick said. "But not for another three hours, at least. And that's ideal. We'll enter at dusk."

"And you know the way, Mr. Minnett?"

Nick grinned at him, clapped him on the shoulder. "I know the way, Richard. There's a reef called Libenter, and the tide is nearly half down now. It'll show. Call me when you see the rocks." He went down the ladder, pulling the hatch shut behind him, then rubbing and slapping his hands together. He could be sitting down to luncheon at Windshot, his back to a roaring fire, his fingers closing on a crystal goblet filled with best claret. Instead every bone in his body seemed frozen to the marrow, and his fingers were closing on a hunk of bread and cheese and a mug of buttered rum. But how good it tasted.

He chewed, leaned against the starboard bunk, and looked at the girl. Her back was to him, and she seemed to be asleep. But she must feel like merry hell. She had not eaten since leaving Windshot, and at the end had vomited green bile. Lorna Grant. On board 'Golden Rose'. This was the first time since Harry's death that he had taken the ketch to sea without Anne at his side. And in her place there was this one. In her own eyes she was a patriot. But to Billy Pitt she was a spy, and thus an enemy to any of Billy's supporters.

He leaned over the bunk. "We'll be to land by sunset," he said.

She made no reply, although her eyes were opened. She sucked air into her lungs, her nostrils expanding.

"At least take a drink," Nick said.

She shook her head feebly, not rising from the pillow.

"You'll feel better once we're into the river," he promised.

He finished his meal, returned on deck with his mug. Now land could clearly be seen through the flurries of spray where the Atlantic swell was pounding the rocks. Truly an iron bound coast. He remembered the last time he had been here. Then he had been on board the 'Queen Charlotte', flying Admiral Howe's flag, and the voyage had ended in the battle now known as the Glorious First of June, England's greatest victory since the Battle of the Saintes. Two and a half years ago, and there had been no victories since.

"That girl, sir," Parker remarked. "She'll guide us to the château?"

"Aye."

"You're sure of that, sir? When she gets her stomach back, will she not betray us? She'll be sure of a welcome in France."

Nick nodded, finishing his drink. How good it felt to trace the liquor's heat down his chest and into his belly. "I have that in mind, Richard. So we'll keep her close."

"We could leave her on the ship, and find our own way."

"Not a good idea. Were she to work herself free, we'd be trapped without a ship, most like. I like my enemies where I can see them."

" 'Tis a thought. Rocks."

Nick took out his telescope, inspected the land. Isle Vierge stood out clearly enough, and the high ground behind. The Pendant rock rose from the sea like the diamond it was named after. Then the Libenter reef, ugly black heads peeping through the surf. The main entrance was west of the reef. But there was a passage between La Pendante and Libenter. And there was a battery on the headland to the west. To be sure, he was flying the tricolour just to be safe, but they might yet bring him up.

"Give me the helm. And stand by your mainsail. When I call, I'll want it down, and quickly."

"Aye, aye, sir." Parker went forward.

Nick settled his hands on the spokes, looked aloft at the pennant which fluttered away from the mainpeak, showing him the direction of the wind. He altered course a point to larboard and the wind came in abeam, throwing 'Golden Rose' on to her side, sending her scorching along at ten knots, straight for the flurry of foam.

Parker looked forward and aft, his mouth opening and then shutting again. He'd not question his helmsman. And now the moment was upon them. 'Golden Rose' thrust her bow into the terribly narrow stretch of relatively calm water, La Pendante close enough to port to touch with a boathook, the seething waters of the reef equally close to starboard.

"Mainsail," Nick bellowed. "Bring her down, Richard. Bring her down."

The halliard was let fly—a knot at the end would make sure it could not free itself from its block—and the sail ballooned outwards as it came down. Parker's face was crimson with exertion as he gathered in the stiff canvas. But already the yacht was losing speed, and under foresail alone Nick could turn her up into the narrow passage. With rocks all around them now, the passage itself seemed suddenly calm.

Parker secured the mainsail, and came aft. "You're in the wrong profession, Mr. Minnett. Surely anyone can count money. It takes a sailor to handle a ship like that."

Nick grinned at him. A successful voyage always left him bubbling with exhilaration. "That was the easy part, Richard. Now we have to get ourselves ashore."

iv

"Land." The dinghy had no more than crunched on the sand when Lorna Grant was over the side, wading through the last of the water to fall to her knees.

Parker helped Nick pull the dinghy above the high water mark, then stared into the darkness; it was not late, but the December evening had already closed in. The yacht was anchored in the first bend of the river, sheltered from the sea by the reefs through which they had just come, and protected from curious eyes by the trees which fringed the shore, hiding the upper reaches. "Where is this château, Mr. Minnett?"

"Le Palue is a little village, around the bend of the river," Nick explained. "We shall be well secured here, and should we be away again by sun up tomorrow, no one will know we have been here at all."

"Saving Lord Moncey, eh? What do you intend?"

Nick held Lorna's arm and pulled her to her feet. "To take him back with us. Come on, now, me darling. And Lorna, I have here a knife and a pistol." He showed her the pair. "The knife is for you if you make a sound more than you ought."

She looked at the weapons with contempt; as he had prophesied, her spirits were returning minute by minute, now she was off the ship. "What are you doing?" she demanded.

"Just making doubly sure." He tied a thin length of line around her waist, securing it tight so that she could not slide it past her thighs. He made the other end fast around his own left wrist.

"You'd think I was a dog," she grumbled.

"Let's go," he suggested.

She shrugged, led them up the beach, and over a grassy bank, just visible in the gloom. They came upon a fishing boat drawn up, and then a rough roadway leading towards the trees. "Now remember," Nick said. "Leave the talking to me." He spoke French with a Breton accent, and as he and his companions were all decked out in woollen caps and sailing smocks, they made a fairly presentable picture of fishermen and their woman home from a day at their pots.

They were in the trees, and they could see the houses beyond. Candles gleamed at windows, and there was some activity in the pension. It was just on supper time. And then the château itself came into sight, not very large, but with at least one tower reaching above the steeple of the church.

A dog barked, and Lorna hesitated.

"Is there a way round?" Parker whispered.

"Then would the animal start in earnest," Nick said. "We shall only come through this by boldness." He moved closer to Lorna, held her elbow, guided her up the street itself. They passed a man, leaning on the gate of his garden, and smoking a pipe, and exchanged a 'bon soir'. Nick wondered what were these people's true feelings. He had campaigned with them, or with their brothers, twice in the past four years, both times unsuccessfully. Now they were cowed and beaten, by the might of the Republican army, the genius of Lazare Hoche. But who did they support, in their hearts? Or who *would* they support, when the choice was presented?

As they passed the church, the dog came up to them, sniffed Lorna's gown, then turned and walked away.

"Good girl," Nick said.

"Animals like me," she said simply. "There is your gate."

"And a guard," Parker muttered.

Nick glanced over his shoulder. The village had faded into the darkness, and the bulk of the church lay between them and the pension.

"Good evening, citizen," he called in French.

"Who is it?" inquired the sentry. "Hold there."

"Jacques," Nick said. "You remember Jacques, citizen."

"Jacques?" The sentry left his gate, peered at them "I know no Jacques. I . . ."

He was close enough. Nick sucked air into his lungs and drove his right fist, with every ounce of strength and power at his command, into the man's belly. The sentry gasped and doubled up, and Nick closed both fists together, using them as a club on the nape of the man's neck. His knees hit the ground and then his chin, and he lay still.

"My God," Lorna said. "Is that how you normally treat people?"

"I must remember to stay on your right side, Mr. Minnett." Parker picked up the musket. "What of this fellow?"

"Take off his belts," Nick said. "Bind and gag him."

Parker obeyed, and then rolled him into the shadows. Nick studied the distant lights. "Where is the dining chamber?"

"To the right," Lorna said.

"Show us."

She glanced at him, then led them off the gravel drive and across the grass beneath the trees, along a path walled by topiaried hedges. They emerged before the huge mullioned windows, blazing with light.

"Hold her," Nick said, and handed the end of rope to Parker. "And if she utters a sound, use this."

He gave the sailor his knife, and both Parker and Lorna gazed at the gleaming steel.

"Don't forget," Nick said, and stole across the path to look through the window. The table in front of him was laden with food, and surrounded by four men. Three he did not know, but the fourth was unmistakable. Lord George Moncey was a big man, taller and broader than Nick, with the fresh bold features of all of his family; excessive weight had given him a coarseness where his sister had managed to retain her looks, at least, up to the last time Nick had seen her. And he used both hands with equal freedom now—the terrible wound Nick had given him when first they had fought, seven years ago, had quite healed.

Nick stole back to the shadows. "He is there."

39

"Can it be so easy?" Parker inquired.

Nick smiled at him. "It is not so easy. Now we must get in, and out again. How many people are within, Lorna?"

"How should I know?" she asked.

"How many were here when last you visited the place?"

She shrugged. "Perhaps a dozen."

"How many women?"

Another shrug. "Perhaps half."

"And one man is accounted for. Four more are eating, and two are serving. That leaves mostly women. I think boldness is our best course, Richard."

"And the girl?"

"We shall tie her up and leave her here. She should be safe for half an hour, and we should not need longer than that. Indeed, should we take longer than that we are done in any event." He released the rope from round Lorna's waist, used it to secure her wrists. "Sit," he said.

Her eyes gloomed at him, and then she sat on the grass; he pulled her ankles together and tied them, using the same length of rope.

"Now open your mouth," he said, taking the woollen cap from her head.

Once again she gave him a long stare, then she opened her mouth and, as he made to thrust the cap in, unleashed the most piercing scream.

4

Nick was so taken aback that Lorna had time to give yet another fearful howl. He had completely underestimated the girl. While his instincts had been telling him that she was a good deal better than she pretended, he had yet supposed her to possess the docility of the servant she appeared. He had never expected that she would risk her life for her friends, and that she would wait—with patience and despite great discomfort—until she could work the maximum damage to her captors.

But now she was drawing breath for yet a third yell. He grasped her throat, throwing himself on top of her and rolling with her into the bushes.

Parker knelt beside him, the knife thrust forward. "Let me get this into her ribs, Mr. Minnett."

Nick hesitated, still squeezing her throat, listening to the tumult from within the house. "No," he snapped. "Run for it. Make away from the shore, give them the slip, then double back. Quickly now."

Parker hesitated. Then he dropped the knife and ran down the drive. By now the front door was opening, men were clustering in the entrance, and women, too, judging by the high-pitched voices.

And Lorna was panting against his chest, reaching for the last of her breath. He relaxed his fingers, just enough to allow her to breathe.

She licked her lips. Her momentary spurt of courage was past; she knew that now he probably *would* kill her. "I'll wait with a basket, for your head, Nick Minnett," she whispered.

He left his fingers on the soft flesh of her throat, kept her still with his weight. Gravel crunched as men came down the steps. "He runs, over there," said someone. "The guard. Where is the guard? Wandered off, by God. You. Get down to the village."

"Thieves, you think?" Moncey was speaking, his voice harsh.

"Screaming?" asked one of the Frenchmen.

"Perhaps they assaulted a servant," said another.

"The servants are all here."

"Well, then, lovers, perhaps."

"Quarrelling? It could be. In which case no harm is done. But we must assume the worst."

"Spies?" Moncey demanded.

"It is possible. These Bretons are not really Republicans at heart. Half of them even dream of independence. They are a mutinous crew and would betray us to the English without a thought."

"Then they must be caught," Moncey said. "And executed. Should Pitt learn we are bound for Bantry . . ."

"Ah, bah," said the first Frenchman. "No one could warn England in time. And if they could, Pitt could not get word to Ireland. The fleet is embarked. The wind is east. Colpoys is off station. We sail tomorrow. Only an act of God could stop us now."

They went back inside, banging the door behind them. Lorna's breath rushed against his fingers. "Well, then," she whispered. "You have found out everything you came for, Mr. Minnett. What a pity it is of no value to you."

Nick looked down at her. Because she was right. It would take him until tomorrow night to return to Lyme, then at least two days to London. Then another week to get a message across to Ireland. By which time the French would already be moored in Bantry Bay, their artillery no doubt disembarked.

So then, what was left? Presumably he could break in and

murder Moncey. But where was the point in that? The man was an enemy, and a traitor into the bargain. But the fleet would sail whether he was alive or dead.

"Why do you not surrender?" Lorna asked. "Release me, and I will present you as my prisoner. I will save your life, Minnett. I will ask for you, as my servant. You will enjoy being my servant. I will only whip you every other day."

He still held the woollen cap in his right hand. Now he slipped his fingers up her throat to hold the base of her jaw, forced her mouth wide. She realised what he was doing a moment too late. Before she could protest, the wool was balled into her mouth, leaving her silent.

Nick rose to his knees, thrust the knife into his belt, listened. There was a good deal of noise from the village, but it was already dying as the fishermen returned to their bottles of wine. The château had subsided back into quiet; the candles still glowed in the dining room.

He got up, lifted Lorna to her feet and threw her over his left shoulder, legs dangling across his chest, thigh bumping his ear, face bumping his back. She made a resentful gurgling noise deep in her chest.

The guard still lay in the shadows, bound and gagged, eyes rolling. They had not seriously tried to find him. But why should they not be confident? They were protected by their reefs from any sizeable landing force, and they were confident that the odd spy was no longer a problem.

Leaving the road, he made his way through the bushes. He crouched whenever he heard noise, which was often enough. Lorna lay in the crook of his arm, trying not to swallow strands of wool and staring at him with pure venom in her eyes.

It took him an hour to make the two miles back to the beach, all the while wondering what he would find there. But 'Golden Rose' still rode to her anchor, although the dinghy was gone. And by now the night was again empty; the biting cold had driven the villagers back to their firesides.

He laid Lorna on the sand, rubbed his hands and his lips and uttered one shrill whistle, then another. A moment later he saw

Parker climb into the dinghy and stroke it towards the beach.

"Mr. Minnett? I had given you up."

"I'm not that easy to lose, Richard. All well with you?"

"Oh, aye. They were not that enthusiastic. Did you learn anything, Mr. Minnett?"

Nick placed Lorna in the bottom of the boat. "The fleet will sail within the next couple of days, bound for Bantry Bay."

"Bantry. There's a sheltered harbour. But . . . within a couple of days? What's to be done, Mr. Minnett? We'll not return in time."

"That's why they were not bothered. But we've a trump they've forgotten, Richard. Admiral Colpoys is out there. With the Channel fleet. They claim he's off station. But that can be no more than a snare. We'll find him."

ii

Dawn found them rolling in the big Atlantic swell north west of Ushant itself, a blue haze on the horizon. By now Lorna had once again retired to her bunk, although the wind had dropped, and there was much less movement than the previous day.

Nick and Parker peered through their telescopes at the empty sea.

"They are there, sir," Parker insisted. "This is their station, and this is where they will be."

"I have no doubt of it at all," Nick agreed. "But even if they are temporarily south of station, a frigate should have been left in sight of land."

"There," Parker cried. "There, sir."

And now Nick could also make out the topsails, slowly rising above the horizon.

"Harden in those starboard sheets," he shouted. "We'll run down."

They ran as best they could, for the breeze had indeed dropped away, although it remained easterly. But the glass was also showing signs of falling; the high pressure area which had kept the weather fine over the previous week was beginning to slip away into Europe. And what then, he wondered?

He handed over the helm and went below. The Irish girl lay on her back, staring at the swaying lantern as if attempting to hypnotise herself. She was no longer secured; at sea there was no need.

"An English frigate," he said. "We'll soon have completed our mission. As best we may."

Her head did not turn. "And I'll be hanged," she said, half to herself.

"There would be a waste," he smiled. "I'm growing quite fond of you, Lorna. And it was a bold thing you did, outside the château. Now, if you'd start telling the truth, and behaving like a lady instead of a pirate, we might even find it possible to be friends."

At last her head turned. "Friends, Nick Minnett? With you? You're Pitt's creature."

"And whose creature are you? Not George Moncey's, I hope."

She rolled on her side, her back to him. Nick sighed, and went on deck. The ship was now full in sight, and there was no doubt that she could also see them. She had altered course towards them.

Nick levelled his glass. "That's no ordinary frigate. The 'Indefatigable' forty four," he said. "Edward Pellew. There's fortune."

"A friend of yours, Mr. Minnett?"

"Oh, indeed. A very old one."

"I should be obliged, Mr. Minnett, if you'd not tell him I am Navy."

"I see what you mean. There'll be no questions from Edward Pellew, I promise you that. Not if you sail with me."

"I am sure of that, sir. None the less, I would be obliged."

"As you wish. Which ship is yours, Richard?"

" 'Queen Charlotte', sir."

"Howe's flagship. My God, I sailed on her two years ago."

"At the battle just off this island, sir. Oh, indeed. I remember it well."

"You were on board?"

"She is my ship, Mr. Minnett."

"And I never knew."

"There were better than a thousand of us, sir. And why should the head of the House of Minnett know the name of a common sailor? Sir Andrew Douglas died in your arms, as I remember." He gave a crooked smile. "I'd not have been so willing to sail with you had I not known you'd been under fire."

"Aye," Nick said. "It was a great occasion, if a sobering one. How long have you served, Richard?"

"Eleven years, sir." Another twist of his lips. "I volunteered, Mr. Minnett. Can you imagine? Oh, I was a patriotic fellow."

Nick frowned at him. "And you are no longer? I'll not believe that."

"I had no idea what I was entering, and that is the truth, Mr. Minnett. Or I'd have cut off my right hand."

"Have you ever known the lash?"

"No, sir. If you do not count a rope's end used by an enthusiastic midshipman. But I have friends who have."

"Surely, discipline must be maintained."

"Oh, aye, discipline. I do not quarrel with the principle, Mr. Minnett. But it is not human to place every single power of life and death in the hands of one man, for several months, sometimes several years, on end together. They may be friends of yours, Mr. Minnett. At sea they are raging devils."

"I'll not believe that of Ned Pellew. Or Dickie Howe."

"There are exceptions, sir. I have never sailed with your Mr. Pellew. The Admiral, why, he is an honest man and a good one. But then, he no longer seeks either fame or promotion. He has sufficient of both. 'Tis the young man making his way we of the lower deck must fear."

"Hm," Nick said. "I suppose that must be true."

"And when you consider, sir, into the bargain, that a seaman receives the same pay now as he did when Blake commanded, that this is the first furlough I have received in three years, and I am not a married man, sir . . ."

"I had not realised things were so bad. Yet will they surely be remedied, soon enough."

"Why, sir? When they have existed for a hundred years?"

46

Nick glanced at him. A puff of white smoke appeared on the bow of the approaching frigate; water splashed a hundred yards away where the ball plunged into the sea. "We'd best heave to, as that is what she wants. And you had best keep your thoughts to yourself, Richard. At least while we are in her company."

iii

"Nicholas Minnett?" Edward Pellew was a short, stocky man with a thrusting chin, which seemed elongated as he peered at his visitor. "What in the name of God are you doing in mid Channel in December?"

"Looking for you, Ned. Or for someone. Where is Colpoys?"

"Biscay. He'll return." Pellew peered over the side of his frigate. "That yacht is yours?"

"It is. With two on board."

"Invite them up. She can remain fast there."

"Aye, well, one is seasick, and the other would rather stay with the ship. Ned, the matter is urgent."

Pellew frowned at him. "Come below. Make that ketch secure, Mr. Robinson, and send them down a bottle of wine. You'll accept that, Nick?"

"I'm sure Richard would be grateful. Why is Colpoys not on station?"

Pellew led the way into the great cabin, snapped his fingers, and the marine sergeant saluted and withdrew.

"I am a serving officer, Nick, unlike you. I do not criticise my superiors."

Nick sat down with a sigh; the frigate, herself only a small ship, seemed stable after the constant motion on board 'Golden Rose'. "You may do so to me, Ned. The Admiral's duty is to watch the fleet in Brest."

"Aye. But he grows bored with beating about here. It is not the most comfortable place in the world, especially in winter. Today is the first calm we've had for a month. And it will not last; the glass is dropping as if it had lead weights tied to it."

The sergeant returned with a bottle and two glasses on a tray.

Pellew sat opposite his friend and filled both glasses. "Muscadet. The Bretons bring it out to us after dark. They play a two sided game, those fellows."

"For which I at the least must be grateful." Nick drank. "You'll not be telling me Colpoys has gone round the corner looking for better weather?"

Pellew peered into his own glass. "He has formed the opinion that the Brest fleet is there until the spring, and that we do no more than wear ourselves out. We can fetch him back in three days. Tom Blackman is just over the horizon, by the Isle de Sein, and Jack Halliwell beyond him."

"The wind is easterly, Ned."

"For the time. It is going to veer, believe me."

"Not soon enough, perhaps. There are thirty men-of-war in Camaret Bay."

"Thirty-one," Pellew corrected him.

"And forty transports."

"They have nowhere to go," Pellew pointed out.

"They are at this moment loading with troops," Nick said. "Hoche commands. They know your admiral is away and they plan to sail today or tomorrow."

"Eh?" Pellew raised his head. "Where bound? The West Indies?"

"Ireland, Ned. Bantry Bay."

"The devil!" Pellew leapt to his feet, ran to the door. "Steward. summon Mr. Robinson. Haste, man." He turned back. "You are sure?"

"I left L'Aberwrach but six hours ago, having learned their plans."

"The devil," Pellew said again. "Robinson. Make all sail. We will contact 'Audacious'."

"Aye aye, sir." The lieutenant hesitated. "And the ketch?"

"You'll cast me off," Nick said. "I must know what you intend, Ned."

"To summon Colpoys."

"You said three days. Will you leave Ushant unguarded for that time?"

Pellew hesitated. "I can reach Blackman, and be back, by dusk."

"One ship?"

"Christ, what a foul up," Pellew suddenly shouted. "Aye. One ship. Listen. Make haste back to England."

"I cannot get there before tomorrow."

"I may hold them until then. They may well assume, seeing my topsails, that I represent the fleet. Since that beating Dickie Howe put on them two years ago . . . you were there."

"I was. And as you say, so was Dickie Howe. Not Tom Colpoys."

"Aye. But they remain nervous. I will do what I can." He squeezed his friend's hands. "You'll not charge my overdraft to Susan."

"It is written off, as of this moment," Nick promised, and returned the pressure. "God speed you, Ned."

"And you, Nick. Make haste. Remember that glass. In December, if it comes on to blow, it will blow." He smiled. "That may be our salvation. But not yours in that cockleshell. Make haste."

iv

"He's a brave man." Nick watched the frigate, already hull down to the south.

"Or a foolhardy one," Parker commented. "Oh, I'd not deny his courage, Mr. Minnett. Any of their courage. Not even my own."

Nick grinned at him. "Neither would I, Richard. Neither would I. Bring her up a point. We'll be there by dawn."

"Saving that." Parker pointed, at the wisps of cloud which spread across the sky from the west. "You need no barometer to judge that."

Nick went below to check the glass anyway. It had dropped an inch since dawn, so there was certainly weather coming. He checked his course on the chart, heard movement from the bunk.

"I had supposed you asleep."

"I was. What has happened to the warship?" she asked.

"Gone about her business. And we're about ours. England."

"Aye." She sighed. "As usual with you, Mr. Minnett. Everything turns out fine. They say you're born under a lucky star."

"Who says?"

She pushed hair from her eyes, sat up, just avoiding bumping her head on the low deck beams. "You've a mirror?"

"Not on the 'Rose'." He winked. "But you'll do. You look a perfect sight. But there's colour in your cheeks."

"I'm that hungry."

He gave her some bread and cheese and a glass of wine, and watched her tear at the food. She had not, indeed, eaten for some forty-eight hours.

"So you're going to live."

"Until they hang me." Her eyes gloomed at him.

"Aye, well, we'll have to think about that."

"Wind's freshening," Parker called down the hatch.

Nick scrambled on deck, watched the whitecaps. It was just west of south, now, and thus with them as they made north. But it was veering all the time, and increasing all the time, as the glass dropped. As Pellew had said, a south westerly blow might just stop the French. But it left 'Golden Rose' with a long haul, and on to a lee shore into the bargain. "We'll take a tuck in the main," he decided.

Parker nodded with relief, and lashed the helm as he came forward to assist Nick to lower the mainsail by some feet, wrapping the loose canvas around the boom and securing it with the reefing points. Her speed reduced, the ketch rode more easily.

"It'll be a dirty night," Parker said.

"Aye. Take a spell." Nick held the wheel, straining now to keep 'Golden Rose' on course. He remembered that terrible night—how many eternities ago?—when he had last conned this ship through the Race of Alderney. A full gale had howled about his ears, steep sided seas threatened to tear out his masts every moment. All the while, a revenue cutter was close behind him, well aware that his holds were full of claret. And Harry Yealm was dying in the same bunk where

Lorna Grant now lay—although mercifully Nick had not known then how badly hurt his friend had been.

This evening, however hard the wind might blow, the seas were unlikely to be as dangerous, at least until they neared the English coast; seven years ago he had known he was moving into shelter; this time he was going to be more and more exposed.

The wind commenced to whine, and the time was three o'clock. 'Golden Rose' began to surge off the waves, crashing into those behind. Parker came back on deck.

"Another couple of rolls, Richard," Nick called. "And hand that jib. Run up the storm canvas."

His words were whipped away by the wind, but Parker knew what was required. He might continuously utter mutiny in his comments on the Navy, but he was a seaman, through and through. Yet even under storm canvas 'Golden Rose' was travelling much too fast, smashing through the waves with stomach-rending force, making him wonder for the safety of her timbers, the security of her masts. Now the entire sea was a mass of nothing but whitecaps, and spray was flying even over the stern when the occasional foaming crest caught up with them.

Parker came aft, holding on to the shrouds for security. "Banging a bit," he shouted.

Nick chewed his lip. To reach England, to get word to Billy Pitt, was his first duty. But not to get there at all would be a sight worse than arriving a few hours late. "You're right, Richard. We'll heave her to." He looked over his shoulder, chose a relatively long run between crests, and brought up the helm. 'Golden Rose' turned in almost her own length, heeling as the wind caught her amidships, and then rearing to the next wave as she pointed up wind. Nick lashed the wheel, joined Parker on the foredeck, green water foaming about their knees and threatening to tear them from the deck. They dragged on the sheets, backing the foresail so that the wind blew on the inside, pushing the bows round again. The mainsail was then sheeted tight. As the bows fell away, the mainsail filled, and the bows came up again. Then the jib filled, and they fell away to repeat the entire

51

manoeuvre over again. She'd do that forever. Spray broke on the bows, and occasionally a whole wave flooded aft, threatening the hatch covers. But with the ship stationary, there was no more pounding.

It was time to take stock. So far nothing had carried away, and they could do no more—save think of themselves. The afternoon sun had disappeared, and dusk was already upon them, adding to the blackness which was spreading out of the west. And their hands were as numb as their cheeks.

"Below," Nick bawled in Parker's ear. "We can do nothing up here."

They dropped into the cabin, securing the hatch behind them. Parker caught the swinging lantern and set it alight. The noise below was quite tremendous. To the whining of the wind and the crashing of the seas was added the creaking of the timbers and the slurp of the water in the bilges. Parker stripped off his wet clothing, and Nick did the same. Lorna was being sick again; she gazed at them in horror.

"We're lost," she muttered.

" 'Tis just a gale. This time tomorrow it will have blown itself out. Maybe sooner. Move over."

"Aye?" He was down to his drawers, but now he pulled on a dry woollen smock to keep himself warm.

"I'm coming in beside you," he said.

"Who'll sail the ship?"

"She'll sail herself, better than I could do it." He lifted the blanket and crawled in next to her. Parker, who had already taken refuge in the other bunk, was rubbing hands and legs together beneath the blanket in an effort to get warm. Nick took the girl in his arms, extracting warmth from her burning body.

"Christ," she said. "I'm not in the mood, Mr. Minnett."

He held her close, and slowly stopped shivering. She raised herself on her elbow to vomit again, and then lay back with a sigh. "What a way to die. Why'd you not just hang me, Mr. Minnett?"

"You'll not hang," he promised. "You'll not even drown, Lorna." He squeezed her against him, kissing her on the ear. The storm shut out the entire world, shut out even Parker in the next bunk. It was just the woman and the man, cocooned beneath their blanket, seeking warmth and comfort from each other while the world exploded about their ears.

"Oh, God," she whispered into his throat. "Oh, God. Oh, Ned. Oh, Ned."

"Eh?" he asked. "The name's Nick."

Her head went back; her face was only a pale glimmer in the gloom as he was between her and the lantern. "Aye," she said. "Nick."

"But you said Ned."

She blew a kiss at him and shut her eyes. He shook her awake.

"Tell me about Ned."

"He's me brother," she said. "Me half brother, anyway."

He stared at her, and suddenly knew her face. It had troubled him from the beginning. Close enough, anyway. "Fitzgerald," he said. "I knew it. Ned Fitzgerald. Lord Edward, by God. I'm to apologize, my lady."

"Ah, begone with you," she said. "I was born outside the blanket, Mr. Minnett."

"But Leinster is your father?"

"Oh, aye," she said. "Or so he says." Her eyes were closing again.

He shook her again. "There's a warrant for Lord Fitzgerald's arrest. Did you know that?"

"Oh, aye," she said. "We fight in the same cause. No doubt there's one out for me, as well." With that she fell asleep.

5

Nick awoke with a start, amazed to discover that he had actually been sleeping. The howling of the wind and the slapping of the waves had been restful. And now, though the wind had dropped and the motion was definitely easier, big seas still crashed against the hull.

He raised himself on his elbow and looked down at the girl. She also slept, but hers was the sleep of exhaustion; there were shadows under her eyes, and her breathing was stertorous. The Duke of Leinster's daughter, even if an illegitimate one. With whom he had shared a blanket for some six hours, though their bodies were separated by several layers of woollen clothing. A remarkable thought.

And one fraught with problems. Lorna Fitzgerald. Her brother Edward was sufficiently notorious as the leader of the United Irishmen, as they were known, who sought to expel the British from their lovely island. It was not a business he had ever considered very deeply, except in so far as he advanced money to English landlords of Irish property, money which was ostensibly for the improvement of their estates, but which was invariably squandered on wine, women and cards in London. But that was no concern of his. Surely. The security was good. A banker should have no politics. He supported Billy Pitt's

54

administration because he believed that was best for business; their personal friendship was something else again.

And bankers should have no hearts, either? The girl sighed, and blew hair from her face. Her people had a long history of mistreatment and violence. Cromwell was but an episode, terrible as it might be, in a chain of catastrophe reaching all the way back to Strongbow. Thus now they fought with an equal violence, an equal desperation. Given the chance this girl would drive a knife into his ribs without hesitation.

Or would she?

Her eyes opened, and she frowned at him, clearly uncertain as to her whereabouts. Then her tongue came out, white coated and dry, to lick her lips.

He raised the blanket, rolled out, made his way to the pump and filled her a mug of water. He held her head up while she drank and looked curiously around herself.

"We're still afloat," he said. He smiled and kissed her on the nose. It was a nose made for kissing. And Anne would not be jealous of a kiss.

"Where are we?" she whispered, reaching up to push more hair away and rub sleep from her eyes.

"Afloat, I said. As to exactly where, we shall have to wait a few hours to tell. I will get out my chart and estimate our drift from our last known position, which was just before we hove to. Then come noon, I will take a sight . . ."

"A sight?"

"I will use an instrument I possess, called a sextant, to measure the height of the sun above the horizon."

"And that will tell you our position?"

"It will give us our latitude, for certain."

"How?"

"I have an almanac, which gives the sun's height, in these waters, and in most other waters as well, at noon on every day in the year. So all I need is an accurate clock, which I possess, and a glimpse of the sky. That done, I will lay course for Lyme Regis."

"You make it seem so easy," she said. "Are all seamen as confident, and as competent, as you?"

"All who stay alive," he said.

"Aye," she said. "And I thought you no more than lucky. Seeing you here, on your boat in a storm, explains much about you." She smiled. "My people think nothing of you. You are a clerk, they say, and of no account. That is because you have never been to war, never commanded men. I shall have to tell them they are wrong. That to command a ship at sea, even a small one, is equal to commanding a regiment." The smile faded into a frown. "Or will I have the chance to say so, to anyone?"

His turn to smile, and to kiss her nose again. "We'll talk about that when we come safe to Lyme."

ii

"Mr. Minnett." Tom Price, old and bent, supporting himself with a stick, stood on the jetty in Lyme to watch the 'Rose' moor. So did most of the townspeople. "No damage?"

"No damage, Tom," Nick shouted. "When is the stage due?"

For it had taken them two days to beat up against the north westerly wind, and Parker was at the end of his furlough.

"Why, sir, in half an hour."

"You'd best be away, Richard," Nick said. "Tom can bring back the dinghy."

Parker finished stowing the mainsail and stepped down. "Aye. Well . . ." He hesitated. "It's been a memorable voyage, Mr. Minnett. At least for me. I'll not forget it."

"Neither will I, Richard. Nor your help. Nor your saving of my life, in fact. The door of my house, at Windshot or in London, is always open. You'll not forget that?"

Parker smiled, a rare sight. "I'll not, Mr. Minnett." He hesitated, then thrust out his hand. "If every skipper was like you, sailing would be the pleasure God intended it to be." He frowned. "What of the lady?"

"You'd best leave her to me."

Parker nodded, turned to the hoists to get the dinghy over the side. "You'll give my love to Anne, Mr. Minnett. Tell her she can forward the rest of my gear to the Nore. That's where we're stationed for the summer."

Nick stood with hands on hips, watching him scull for the shore. A last barb? A warning? Or a reminder? He was a strange fellow, and there was the truth. With that sharp a tongue he would be lucky to survive service in the Navy.

While Nick was silently musing, he noticed Lorna Fitzgerald combing her hair with her fingers. She was as unwashed and dirty as either of the men, more so in fact, as she had been vomiting during a large part of the voyage. Yet she remained an entrancing picture, enhanced now that he knew who she really was, of what she might really be capable. As a woman? Or a lover? Certainly as a delightful companion. She had recovered from her sea sickness after the storm, and though he had found no further reason to share her bunk—he and Parker had stood watch and watch all the way home—she had from time to time sat with him on deck.

She glanced up at him, resumed her work. "Is the fellow gone?"

"Hardly a fellow." He descended the ladder. "I owe him my life. And he proved himself a fine crew."

"I wish I had a mirror." She sat at the table. "God, how good it is not to be heaving about the place. What happens now, Nick?"

He sat opposite her. "No one in Lyme knows your identity. I've a couple of guineas in my pocket. If you've somewhere to go."

"Oh, I've somewhere to go." She frowned at him. "You'd set me free?"

"Don't you suppose you've been punished enough? There can hardly be a harsher sentence than to be kept at sea for two days in a gale, if you're not a sailor."

Her tongue showed for just a moment, and was then withdrawn again. "I'll not change my politics."

"I'd not expect you to. I'd just beg you to be careful. The punishment for spying, or for inciting rebellion, is death. I'd not see that body dangling."

Again the tongue. "You've never seen this body, Nick. You'll not know what you've missed."

"Would you pay for your keep?"

"I'd pay for my life. It would be a pleasure."

He got up. "Next time we meet, Lorna, I'll sleep with you before I give you to the hangman. There's a promise."

She caught his hand, pulled on it, and he leaned over the table. She kissed his mouth, her tongue sliding across his. "Next time we meet, Nick. I promise, too."

iii

He rode across the moor, mounted on Belair, leading Parker's horse by the rein. It was a crisp, cold morning; there was a trace of snow clinging to bushes on the hillocks. And it was Christmas Day.

It had been a quite remarkable week, though something of a failure. Not his, perhaps. Had Colpoys been on station . . . he could only hope that Pellew had survived his gallant delaying action, and that the French had taken a battering in the storm. But they must be near Bantry by now. Messengers would already be making for London with the news. He could no longer affect the situation.

He frowned. Then why was he exhilarated? He was not used to failure, neither his own nor other people's, if they were connected with his schemes, his adventures, his plans. But this morning his heart bubbled. Of course, they would be sitting down to Christmas luncheon at Windshot, and he was arrogant enough to suppose his appearance would make the occasion. He would be reunited with Anne, sufficient cause for joy at any time.

But his face was distorted this morning. It was not a problem within his experience. He had entered a man's world like anyone else, eager for love—and had fallen in love with great promptitude. But Aurora de Benoît had rejected him, and while he had still been in a mood of uncertainty, he had been neatly entrapped by Caroline Moncey. Poor, poor Aurora. Poor Caroline. The one had sought only power and position, and had been so shattered by her experiences that she now occupied a single room, paid for by the House of Minnett, and ventured forth only with the aid of her maid. Only Nick could make her smile, and he resolved to visit her when he returned to London.

Caroline, on the other hand, had sought only the wealth which had accompanied the name and position of Mrs. Minnett. But she had overplayed her hand to such an extent she was now a perpetual debtor, and her brother's head was now threatened by the noose as well.

But between them they had all but ended his quest for love. He used women, now, as he used men—discovering their weaknesses, turning their strengths to his own best advantage. As he was Nicholas Minnett and, as he was young and handsome as well as wealthy, women succumbed the more easily to his charm when he chose to exert it, and thus suffered the more heavily. Seraphine Condorcet, Honorine Damas, both lay heavy on his conscience. But he had not loved them.

His love for Anne was something quite distinct. It had, indeed, been there, for Anne Yealm the person, before he had really discovered Anne Yealm the woman. Now it embraced so many facets; Anne Yealm the calm, quiet personality; Anne Yealm, the ideal crew; Anne Yealm, the perfect companion; Anne Yealm, the most beautiful woman he had ever known; Anne Yealm, the most passionate woman he had ever known—at least when in his arms. And now, Anne Yealm the mother of his children as well.

So then, why, as he rode towards Anne on a Christmas morning, did he still think of Lorna Fitzgerald?

As if it mattered. Even Lorna would have the sense to disappear until the Irish troubles were solved, one way or the other. And that meant just about forever.

The sun gleamed on the walls of Windshot. He walked the horses into the yard, and the boys came forward to take his bridle.

"Well, Jack?" he called. "No ghost."

"Mr. Nicholas." Morley came down the steps. "We were that worried, sir. There was a lot of wind, two days ago. But you were safe to port?"

"I was hove to in the Channel approaches, Jack. Safer than in most ports, I reckon." He slapped the steward on the shoulder and followed his nose to the dining room. Standing in the doorway, he gazed at the crowded table, felt the warmth from the huge fire seeping into his bones, and inhaled the magnificent scent of hot red wine and brandy, roasted turkey and boiled ham.

"Nick." Lucy de Lancey gave a scream and leapt to her feet.

"Nick," her husband shouted, and came running up the room, followed by the rest of the guests.

"My God," Brummell shouted. "You look a positive scarecrow."

"And I feel one, my dear Beau." Nick reached the top of the table, his back and shoulders already sore from the slaps and hugs he had received. "Mama?"

She held his hand. "You are the most wretched son any woman could suffer," she said, her eyes bright, and then hugged him. "But to have you back."

"Now, Mama," he said. "I only went with Billy Pitt and Castlereagh."

"You went to sea," she said.

He frowned at her, and she smiled.

"Anne confessed the truth of it. But even had she not, why, there is dried salt encrusted on your hair." She stroked his chin. "And on your beard."

"Anne," he said. "Where is she?"

"In her bed," Priscilla Minnett said. "If you hurry, you may be in time to see your son fed."

He ran from the room, while the assembly burst into a chorus of cheers. Heart pounding, he took the main staircase three at a time, gave Maureen Morley no more than a smile at the top, wrenched open the door to his bedchanber, and paused to scoop Judith from the floor—she was almost two, a bundle of auburn-haired delight, already beginning to look like her mother. He stood at the foot of the bed and gazed at Anne, and at the little scrap of humanity which was gnawing at her left teat.

"Sweetheart."

"Nick, love." She smiled at him through her tears.

He gave Judith a last squeeze, replaced her on the floor with her blocks, and sat on the bed. Anne put up her mouth to be kissed.

"Mama said a son."

"I'd not fail you twice."

"You have never failed me even once, Anne."

"They say he has your eyes. But then, they will say that. Harry, will you not greet your father?"

The babe continued to suck.

"He has my appetite, and there's a fact. Harry?"

Her cheeks were pink. "If you've no objections."

"I think it is a splendid name, Anne. And you?"

"This one was easy. Not like Judith. But what of you, and the 'Rose'?"

"We rode the storm hove to."

She nodded. "I thought as much. I think that of everyone here, I was least frightened. And the French?"

"Are away. Colpoys was not on station."

"Mr. Pitt will not be pleased about that," she said. "What will you do now?"

"I should get up to London."

"Can you not stay a while?"

"I'll stay tonight, Anne. There's a promise. We have much to discuss."

Her eyes were watchful.

"You'll remember I spoke of opening a branch office in Naples? I have been in correspondence with Sir William Hamilton, the ambassador, and the court there are all in favour of it. So is Pitt. Naples is one of the few neutral countries left, and with the French owning the rest of Italy it gives us a window into their world."

"You've not discussed banking business with me before."

He got up, paced the room, carefully avoiding Judith's growing house of blocks.

"I would like to go there personally, to see the situation, to inaugurate our business. I would like to take the 'Rose'. And you."

"Me? Naples? Why . . . what of the children?"

"We'd not go before next summer. Harry will be weaned by

61

then, or could be. And Mama would be happy to care for them until our return."

"Which would be?"

"The following year, I should think."

"A whole year?"

"Eight months, more likely."

"But. . . ."

He sat down again, held her hand. "Naples, Anne. The most beautiful city in the world. The Mediterranean is the most beautiful sea in the world. You'll love it. And I would holiday with you, alone for a while. It is something I have long wanted to do."

"Did you catch the Irish maidservant?"

He frowned. "As a matter of fact, we did. Is that important to you?"

"It just crossed my mind. Is she hanged?"

"I set her free. She gave us the information we required."

Anne smiled. "I'm glad you did that, Nick. Naples. Forgive me. Since knowing you, my whole life has turned topsy turvey. Paris was only a name to me, before I found myself there, with you. Naples is even more remote. Scarce a name, even. More a dream."

"But you'll come, Anne."

"You have but to beckon, Mr. Minnett," she said. "Convince me my children will be cared for, and I'd follow you to the end of the earth."

iv

"Mr. Pitt will see you now, Mr. Minnett," said the secretary.

Nick nodded, rose, and the secretary opened the door of the Prime Minister's room. From here one looked out at the Thames, at the hustle and bustle of the main thoroughfare of the great city which dominated the country over which this man ruled. Mr. Pitt looked, as usual, exhausted, if pleased to see his banker.

"Nick. I have the most tremendous news."

"I'm glad to hear that." Nick sat down. "Mine is of a sombre variety. You've heard from Ireland?"

"Not a word."

"Ah, well, will you have mine first?"

"No. You have mine. You'll be aware there was a gale in the Channel last week?"

"Oh, indeed." Nick smiled. "We get the wind at Windshot. Hence its name."

"Aye. Well, two days ago a Frenchman came ashore on Deal Beach. Swept he was, all the way from Ushant, out of control."

"A man-of-war?"

"A transport. Three hundred soldiers on board, with horses. All sick and dying, and lucky to be ashore. The fleet sailed, Nick, only three days before Christmas. Would you believe it. Into a gale."

"The wind was easterly," Nick said, his heart pounding.

"Oh, indeed, when they left. Although the glass was falling. But they decided to risk it, because Colpoys had gone off station. Their scouts told them there was not a British ship to be seen."

"Not one?"

"Not Colpoys, and that's certain. I mean to have his command, indeed I do. I may not be able to chop off these incompetents' heads, but by God I can have them cashiered. It was left to 'Indefatigable'. Only a forty-four, but she sailed amongst them and scattered them like a fox in a hen coop. The wind did the rest."

"And Pellew?"

"I have no idea. This fellow got set downwind of the others, and at the time was happy to be in that position. But I mean to find out. Pellew. He'll go far. Your news?"

"Why , I have none at all. Save that I am mighty relieved to hear yours."

"What of your spy?"

"I let her go."

"Let her go?"

"I discovered that she is actually Lorna Fitzgerald. Edward's half sister. An outside child of the duke's."

"My God. One scarce knows where to turn, nowadays. There will have to be a warrant."

"Oh, aye. But she cannot harm us now."

"I suppose not." Pitt pulled his nose. "And to say truth, I'd rather not put a Fitzgerald on trial unless I have to. It will only exacerbate matters. I have a scheme, Nick, to settle this Irish question once and for all. Supposing I can persuade my colleagues. Why should a man be barred from political office, or any other kind of office, for that matter, merely because he is a Roman Catholic?"

"No reason at all," Nick agreed. "It is a matter of history."

"Quite. And where would a Catholic conspiracy get anyone today? Spain is a ruin. The French are totally atheistic. The Pope himself is their prisoner. And if we could get rid of the Irish question, a running sore in our side, Nick, why, then, our strength, our ability to prosecute this war to a successful conclusion would be doubled. Oh, it shall be done. One nation. I see Irish representatives at Westminster."

"And I will say amen to that," Nick agreed. Then would Lorna be able to return to England openly. There was an interesting thought. If a dangerous one, for Nick Minnett. " Well, then, as we have solved the entire problem of the nation in a matter of minutes, I will get on home. There are one or two problems remaining in the banking business." He got up, then remembered. "Billy, do you have anything to do with the Navy?"

"The Navy? God forbid. I am no sailor. Melville looks after that." He frowned. "Why?"

"You'll admit it is our right arm," Nick said. "Without the Navy, we would indeed be helpless."

"I'll not deny that."

"Then dc you know that a seaman in this right arm of ours has received no increase in pay since the days of Cromwell?"

"Rubbish."

"It bears investigating," Nick said. "Think about it. I'm for a bath and bed. 'Tis a long ride from Windshot."

But only a short one from Westminster to Park Lane. He walked his horse, alone; his valet, Eric, had already gone to the Minnett town house to alert the servants that their master was back. On a January afternoon the streets were empty, as the wind whistled between the houses and chilled cheeks and hands of the lone rider. One kept warm with one's thoughts. Billy Pitt was a great man. He sought an end to the French rebellion. Well, there was an ideal, because if unchecked, it might spread, heaven knew where. So no doubt part of it was England's historical fear of a too powerful France. And this France, mismanaged and anarchic as it was, was certainly becoming powerful, thanks to men like Bonaparte and Hoche. Had Hoche survived the storm? He must find out about that.

But in the midst of this war, which spread every day, Billy could still think about the rights of people. There was greatness. Thus he could also think about the rights of men like Richard Parker, and thousands of others. It was surely not enough for England to dominate the oceans of the world. Were she to do so in an inhuman fashion she would be remembered as nothing more than a seafaring version of Genghis Khan.

But he himself had only become interested because the man was Anne's cousin. Just as he had only become interested in the Irish question, because of Lorna Fitzgerald's smile, the feel of her body against his, the memory of her twisting in his arms.

There was a sobering thought.

He dismounted in the yard of the Minnett house, went up the stairs. Henry, the butler, looking older than ever, but as straight as ever, waited to take his hat and stick.

"Mr. Minnett, sir. Welcome home. Was Christmas a happy event?"

"Oh, aye, Henry. A happy event."

"Madame is well? Mistress de Lancey is well? The young lady is well?"

"All are well, Henry. They'll be up within a week. And the young lady is again a mother. You may congratulate me."

"I do indeed, sir." Henry cleared his throat. "There is a guest, sir, to see you."

"Eh? I really am not in the mood, Henry. All I desire is a hot bath."

Henry cleared his throat again. "I know, sir. But this lady, sir. It is your wife. Lady Caroline."

6

Nick pulled open the door to the parlour, strode in, checked. Caroline Minnett wore a pink velvet gown, cut low in the bodice, and white gloves. Her hair was concealed beneath a lavender silk bonnet. She had been seated before the fire, but rose as he entered, inflating her lungs and throwing back her head to appear to best advantage. Not that she needed a great deal of effort. It was two years, almost to the day, since she had left this house for what he had supposed was the last time. And yet now, as so often in the past, he was confounded by the voluptuous boldness of her beauty, the aggressive sexuality which she exuded like a perfume.

And as yet she had not spoken. There was an un-Carrie like suggestion.

He closed the doors behind him. "Dumb?"

"With the sight of you, Nick? Should I not be?" She spoke quietly, and thus again unnaturally. "You always look so splendidly healthy. So . . . so virile."

"You also look well, Carrie. Will you take something to drink?"

Slowly she sank into her chair. "I would adore a cup of tea." Her eyelids fluttered. "Unless there is cold champagne."

"There is always cold champagne, Carrie," Nick said, and pulled the bell rope.

"I had not expected you to be so hospitable," she said. "When last we spoke . . ."

"I ordered you to leave this house upon pain of a whipping."

She smiled at him. "And have you changed your mind?"

He sat opposite her, on the far side of the fire. "After you have had your drink, perhaps. Henry. A bottle of the Bollinger. And two glasses."

"Yes, sir, Mr. Nicholas." Henry withdrew.

"You have just returned from Windshot, I understand," Caroline said. "Did you have an enjoyable Christmas?"

"Very."

She took off her gloves, slowly, finger by finger, concentrating on what she was doing. "Rumour has it that your guest list was a remarkable one."

"Anne Yealm was there, if that is what you mean. She lives there, now."

"Anne Yealm," Caroline said, putting as much contempt into her voice as could be managed. "You are besotted with her, Nick. I am doing you a favour by refusing a divorce. Were you free, you'd marry the girl. Nick Minnet, married to a fisherwoman."

Henry returned with the opened bottle and the glasses. Nick poured.

"You have a very limited scale of conversation, Carrie."

"And you . . . you sit there, treating me like a stranger. You do not even ask after Alexander. Your very own son."

"Alexander is not my son," Nick said, quietly and patiently. "I have a son."

Her head came up.

He smiled at her. "Anne has just become a mother for the second time. You may congratulate me."

"Oh, you—" She rose, paced the room. "You enjoy nothing so much as to humiliate me. Alexander . . ."

"I have no desire to discuss him, unless you have come to give me the name of his father."

She paused, turned, stared at him. Then she drained the glass, set it on the tray.

"I am sorry, Nick. I did not come here to quarrel. I am so very upset. This terrible news about George . . ."

"Ah," Nick said, and poured some more champagne. "Conspiring with the United Irishmen. A treasonable matter."

"Nick." Caroline sank to her knees beside his chair. "He means no harm, Nick. He has doubtless been led astray. Edward Fitzgerald, oh, the man's a villain."

"Some would accuse him of being a patriot."

Her brows came together. "You, Nick?"

"Oh, the man is the enemy of me and my friends. Do not doubt that. But he is open about it, and I can respect him. Why, General Bonaparte is my friend, at the same time as he is my enemy. But Moncey, crawling about in his gutter . . ."

"Nick. He does not deserve to die."

"I entirely disagree with you."

"Nick." She scrambled to her feet again. "Your own brother-in-law?"

"Carrie, your effrontery amazes me. Truly it does. Anyway, I have nothing to do with the warrant out for George. He is a traitor, and there is an end to it."

"You are a friend of Pitt's. Were you to intercede . . ."

"And why should I do that?"

"Nick?"

Nick sipped his wine. "On the other hand, Carrie, I might do that, were you to behave towards me like a civilised woman, give me the name of Alexander's father, and allow us to obtain a mutually civilised divorce. I might do more. I might repeat my offer of two years ago, all your debts settled, and an income for life. For you and the boy."

Her fingers were tight on the stem of the champagne glass. "So that you could marry that . . . that harlot?"

"The next time you use that word about Anne I shall most certainly have you thrown into the street. So that I might be free of you and your family. Well, Carrie? I consider I am being more than generous."

"You—" Her face hardened, losing its beauty and in the process becoming almost brutal. Then she hurled the still full glass into the fire, setting up an enormous sizzle. "I'll see you damned, first," she said, and stalked from the room.

ii

The huge doors of the marble fronted building swung open, and the liveried doormen stood to attention. Threadneedle Street disappeared behind Nick as his boot heels clicked on the marble floor of the main building. The clerks and tellers, accountants and submanagers, lined up to say, "Good morning, Mr. Minnett," and Eric was at his shoulder to take his hat and cloak and stick.

He smiled and nodded to them all, mounted the marble staircase beyond the hall to the mezzanine floor, where his secretaries also waited, every one in a black coat with a white cravat, again chorusing, "Good morning, Mr. Minnett."

The doors to his office stood wide. The room was twenty feet deep, ending in the tall windows which even on a wintry day allowed what light there was to enter, although the crystal chandelier necessarily glowed all the time, and a fire roared in the grate. Nick sat behind the huge mahogany desk, padded with leather, leaned back in his chair and felt the warmth creeping through his boots into his toes, his fingers slowly beginning to unstiffen. He watched Turnbull, short and stout and perspiring, bustle into the room, a secretary at his side, while another closed the doors.

"Good morning, Mr. Minnett."

"Good morning, John."

"Great news, sir."

"Oh, aye, John. Jervis is to be raised to the peerage. Although they do say the victory was the work of that fellow Nelson. How odd, that so unlikeable a man should possess so much talent. What have we today?"

The secretary placed the pile of folders in front of Nick, stood to attention. As did Turnbull. It had been Nick's custom, since becoming owner of the House, to have his chief clerk sit with him, but Turnbull always waited to be invited.

"Sit down, John. Sit down. What's this?"

"Mr. Brummell, sir. Seventeen thousand and rising."

Nick lifted the sheet of parchment on which the account was contained, glanced through the attached documents.

"There is not much security, sir," Turnbull remarked.

"There never was. He is a friend of the Prince, John. We shall humour him a while longer." Nick opened the next folder. "Let me know when it touches twenty. Henry Arbuthnot?"

"You set his limit at five thousand, Mr. Minnett. He is only just over."

"Too far. You'll write Mr. Arbuthnot, John. Tell him we must have a reduction, and immediately." Another folder. And a deep frown. "Paul de Lancey? Did I authorise this?"

Turnbull mopped his brow. "Well, no, sir. It happened in December, sir. You were already gone down to Windshot. Mr. de Lancey was going to join you the next day, sir, you may remember, when he dashed in here, said he dared not leave London, in fact, he would not be allowed to leave London, did he not settle that debt."

"*That* debt? Six thousand, four hundred and three pounds? To one person?"

"Lost at cards, I believe, sir."

"And you authorised it."

"Well, Mr. Nicholas . . ." Turnbull's handkerchief was busy.

"Where is your security?"

"Well, sir, Mr. Nicholas, there is Miss Lucy . . ."

"What, do you have a lien on my sister?"

"Oh, Good Lord, no, sir, but as the bank . . . well, sir . . ."

Nick leaned forward. "The bank belongs to me, John. To be sure, Lucy has a lifetime's interest, but as Lucy Minnett, not Mrs. Paul de Lancey." His finger prodded the paper. "I gave him five thousand a year. And he promised to live within that. Close this account to bad debts. And the next time he dashes in here with a tale of woe, refer him to me."

"Yes, sir." Turnbull sighed. Even after four years he was never sure what would happen next in his dealings with this young man.

"And as we are discussing bad debts," Nick said, "where is the Prince's?"

"Well, sir . . ."

"How much?"

"Seventy-three thousand."

"Great God in Heaven." Nick leaned back in his chair.

"You could talk with Mr. Pitt, sir," Turnbull suggested.

"I did that, three years ago," Nick reminded him. "And the solution was an increased grant from the Commons, on condition he married. So he married. What is the gossip there?"

Turnbull cleared his throat. "Well, sir, the Princess Caroline and her babe are not in residence . . ."

"They never were in residence. He hates her and she loathes him. How they ever stayed in the same bed long enough to produce that unhappy child I'll never know." And yet, did he not know? Were not his circumstances, as regarding his own Caroline, exactly the same? "I will have a word with Mr. Pitt," he said. "Although what proposition he will put forward now is a mystery to me." He sat up again, leaned forward. "John. Naples."

"Mr. Nicholas?"

"Thought I'd forgotten, had you? I want you to assemble all the correspondence I have had with Sir William Hamilton on the subject of opening a branch of the House there. Have it on my desk tomorrow. I'll write personally, and to Lady Hamilton." He smiled. He remembered the tizzy which had been created when old Willy had married the young woman who could most euphemistically be described as an actress. He wondered what ten years of being wife to an ambassador would have done to that ebullient personality.

"Yes, sir. The French . . ."

"Have the entire peninsula, from Rome north. But they are at peace now, and brooding only on us. Naples is a foot in Europe, at a time when our other footholds may be becoming precarious. Besides, Ratseys is there already."

"Yes, sir." Turnbull remained doubtful.

"How much of that stock do we hold?"

"Thirty-one percent, sir. You'll know Lord Ratsey has been trying to buy into Minnett?"

"He'll not succeed. We are a family concern. His mistake was in scattering his stock around like manna, looking for over capitalisation. I'll have his Naples business, for a start." Nick got up, smiled at his clerk. "Besides, we must recoup. Since Mr. Pitt saw fit to give away my Alexandrian holdings, we have a great hole in the Mediterranean. I shall go in May, as soon as the weather settles. Mistress Yealm will accompany me. She is coming up to London, John. Is that not splendid news?"

"Oh, aye, sir. Splendid." Turnbull continued to look unhappy. "You'll be away a long time, sir."

"Several months, to be sure. So no increases in borrowing limits while I am gone, eh?" He slapped his friend on the shoulder. " 'Tis an adventure, old friend. Not a catastrophe. With profit at the end of it."

iii

An adventure. With Anne. But then, all life was suddenly an adventure, to her. As he walked the phaeton through the park, she looked from side to side, smiling at the passersby and being smiled at in turn. She wore a dark blue redingote over a pink gown, with a high pink felt hat decorated with dark blue ribbons; she was a foretaste of summer which put the spring flowers to shame.

To ride, with Anne, in the Park. How long had he wanted to do that. "Happy?"

"I had not supposed it was this possible."

"And how does London compare with Paris?"

"Not so exciting." A quick glance and a flush. "Or should I not say that?"

"You may say what you like. In any event, I agree with you." The phaeton rolled out from beneath the trees and on to the road. "Will you wait?"

She shook her head. "I'd come up."

"You do not have to."

"I would like to. Unless you think she would prefer not to see me?"

"I'm sure she would love to see you." He reined the horse, locked the brake, placed his whip in its holder. Anne was already dismounting from the far side; she could never remember always to act the lady, and it would no more occur to her to wait for his hand than it would to Mama, for instance, to think of descending from a carriage without assistance.

He escorted her into the downstairs lobby of the tall building, and Mrs. Prout hurried forward. "Mr. Minnett." She smiled at Anne.

"Mistress Yealm. Another friend of Madame Condorcet's."

"Oh, aye." The smile tightened for just a moment, and then returned. No doubt she knew the name. Nick Minnett was London's principal source of gossip. "Madame will be pleased to see you, I am sure."

They climbed the stairs. "It must be nice for her, here," Anne said. "Looking out over the trees and the park. So quiet. After Paris."

"And the Conciergerie." He knocked, waited for the door to open. Seven years ago his heart would have pounded fit to burst. He had loved Aurora de Benoît almost from birth. They had played together as children, and he had assumed no other future than with her at his side, before she had been swept up into the false glitter that had been the court of Versailles, to be dragged into the intrigue and immorality which had accompanied the collapse of the Bourbon edifice—married to a man she despised, and nothing more than a pawn in the great events which had accompanied the Revolution. Her strength had not been able to sustain so much; the loss of a husband and a brother, her own degradation. At the end of it all, only Nick Minnett had remained constant, and now it was too late for either of them.

The door swung in. Aurora peered at them, her face tight and frightened, her yellow hair, once her greatest glory, already streaked with grey although she was a year younger than Nick, and undressed and scattered.

Slowly her features relaxed. "Nick. Mistress Yealm. How good of you to call. Come in. Come in, please. Mistress Yealm, I did not know you ever came to town."

She spoke English as if it were her mother tongue; she had spent much of her childhood with the Minnett family, both in London and at Windshot.

"My first visit, Madame." Anne entered the little parlour, waited for Nick. The room smelt sour, the windows were shut tight.

"And you are living every moment of it. Tea. You will take tea. I prepare it myself, you know." She fussed with the kettle suspended over the fire. "But it is good of you to call, Nick. So good. I am so very lonely." Tears dribbled down her cheeks, splashed on to the flames.

"It is, alas, to say goodbye, Aurora."

"Goodbye?" She turned, on her knees, the tea forgotten, her face collapsing once again.

"Only for a season," he hastily reassured her. "We shall be back in the new year."

"In the new year . . ." She gazed at Anne, her jaw slowly dropping. "You are going?"

Anne looked at Nick, uncertain what to say.

"You are," Aurora cried. "Oh, you fortunate creature."

"How do you know she is fortunate?" Nick asked, gently taking her elbow to guide her to a chair. Anne made the tea. "You have not asked where we are going. It might be the North Pole."

"Just to go. Nick, I shall be all alone."

"You will not be all alone, Aurora. Lucy will come every week. You have everything you wish?"

"Oh, I am comfortable, Nick. There are accounts . . ."

"Send them to Turnbull. And do not *worry*, Aurora. There is nothing can trouble you, in London. No Barras, no Tallien, no red capped revolutionary to torment you here."

She shuddered. "I see them behind every shadow. Oh, Nick . . ."

He disengaged himself, drank his tea. "We must be away. We sail in a week, and there is so much to be done." He held her shoulder, kissed her on the forehead. "You have a good rest."

"Madame," Anne said, and also kissed her cheek, then fled through the door behind Nick. "My God," she said. "To have collapsed so utterly. Will you have to care for her the rest of her life?"

"Aye."

"Has she nothing of her own?"

"Not a penny. What the family did salvage from the collapse in eighty-nine, her brother squandered on that futile expedition to Brittany. Which also cost him his life."

"And nearly cost you yours," she said. "But you will care for her, and pay her bills, for all eternity, because you once loved her. Will you do the same for me, Nick, when you cease to love me?"

He helped her into the phaeton. "When I cease to love you, Anne, they will be piling earth on the lid of my coffin. Now let us think about Naples."

iv

"Only the two of you." Priscilla Minnett shook her head. "There should be some men. Why is Eric not accompanying you?"

She stood on the wooden dock, just below Tower Bridge, peered down at the deck of 'Golden Rose', secured alongside, freshly painted and varnished, every shroud a blaze of bunting, fluttering in the breeze.

"Eric is taking passage on a frigate, Mama," Nick assured her. "No doubt he will be there to meet us." He looked utterly incongruous in the midst of the gaily dressed throng, for he was already wearing a faded blue sailing smock, as indeed was Anne, her hair caught up in a red bandanna.

"Oh, aye," Paul de Lancey said. "You'll be honeymooning, there and back."

"Biscay," said Lucy. "All those storms."

"Just take care, Nick," Pitt said. "I do not know why *you* cannot take a frigate, like any self-respecting gentleman. There is one at your disposal."

Nick embraced his friend. "I'd not realised you'd one to spare. What is this rumour I hear about a mutiny at Spithead?"

"Oh, some hot heads, pursuing the very point you raised with me a couple of months ago. Pay and conditions. They are right, there is the problem."

"And something should have been done a long time ago."

"Something will be done, I promise you. 'Tis the French I would have you consider, not our own people."

"The 'Rose' can outsail any froggy afloat," Nick said. "And will. Besides, will they venture forth with our latest hero on the prowl?"

"You'll not meet Nelson until Sardinia," Pitt said. "We have just dispatched him back to the Mediterranean."

"Not to look out for me, I hope."

Pitt closed one eye. "And to watch the French fleet in Toulon. It is building again. But certainly he will be using Naples as a base."

"Then I will be able to congratulate him in person. Alice, you'll take care of these two rascals?"

The nurse held Judith by the hand, wheeled the pram holding Harry Yealm.

"I shall, Mr. Nicholas. You'll not know them when you get back."

"And they'll not know me, there's the problem," Anne said, kissing each child in turn. "Mistress Minnett . . ."

"Mother, Anne," Priscilla Minnett whispered. "I would have it so. Take care of my son."

"As I am able," Anne promised.

"And I shall take care of both of us." Nick held his mother close. "And you take care of yourself, Mama. Paul."

"I shall keep them all, safe and well, Nick." Paul shook his hand. "I cannot tell you how sorry I am about that business, Nick. I am so very grateful to you. And I shall mend my ways, I promise."

As he had promised before. Nick smiled at him.

"I'm sure you shall, Paul. At least stay clear until I return. Lucy." He kissed his sister. "Billy. I'll bring you up-to-date news of the Mediterranean."

"Which I could do with, to be sure. This is a mad scheme, Nick. Were it any man but you I would absolutely forbid your departure."

" 'Tis you I worry about, old friend," Nick said. "You need someone like Anne, to take away some of those furrows."

Pitt smiled. "You'll have to find me one, then. You've no sister, Mistress Yealm?"

"Alas, sir, no," she said. She gave him her hand to kiss. He ignored it and embraced her instead, kissing each cheek in turn.

"So bring my banker back again," he said.

They were on board at last, free from the embraces and the waving hands, the farewells and the tears. The wind was westerly and light, the tide was ebbing; the ketch faced upriver. Anne untied the mainsail while Nick heaved on the windlass, and the canvas soared aloft. The crowd cheered. Anne was already releasing the mooring warps, and Nick had gone aft to the wheel. As 'Golden Rose' drifted away from the dock, carried astern on the falling tide, he put the helm hard over, while Anne sheeted the boom across and made it fast on the port side. Another cheer from the crowd, and 'Golden Rose' was heading down river at speed, pushed at once by wind and tide.

Anne was forward, running up the jib. Now she came aft to give a last wave as they rounded the first bend.

"At last," Nick said. "When did I first suggest Naples, sweetheart?"

"Three years ago," she thought. "I never supposed it would ever happen."

"All things happen," he said. "We'll round the Foreland by dusk, if this wind holds, and then it's heigh for Lisbon. You'll like Lisbon."

"I'll like just being at sea, with you, again," she said. "How many days, to Lisbon?"

"I reckon about ten."

"Ten days," she said. "With no one here, except us." She linked her arm through his. "Nick, I am so happy. I do not want anything in the world ever to change."

He kissed her temple. "Would you not settle for peace with the French?"

"I would love to have peace with the French. But not even that, if it alters you, and me. Am I very selfish?"

"Very," he assured her. "But it is a selfishness I like. Will you harden in those sheets?"

The river was bending. Now London and Westminster were both lost behind them, and they were racing past the docks where the great Indiamen lay alongside to discharge their precious cargoes, with the first reach stretching in front of them, and Greenwich with its palace and its observatory on the port bow. And there, in the distance, were the ships of the Nore fleet. The Nore fleet? Nick frowned, and reached for his telescope. No sail was set, and yet the great line of battle ships seemed to cluster in the very centre of the channel, as if all had been cast adrift. But their bows were facing upstream. They were anchored. Every one. Blocking the entire river.

Anne came aft. "I have never seen so many vessels at one time."

"Aye," he agreed. " 'Tis mighty strange. Take the helm."

She obeyed, and he went forward to drop the mainsail. He'd not get through that lot with all sail set. He doubted he'd get through them at all.

Under foresail alone, 'Golden Rose' lost more than half her speed, and now ghosted along, carried mainly by the current, with just enough wind filling the sail to give her steerage way.

"Whatever are they at?" Anne demanded. "Is it some kind of manoeuvre?"

"I can think of no other answer," he agreed. "What in the name of God . . ."

For the nearest man-of-war had suddenly exploded into white smoke from her forward port, and now the report of the blank cartridge drifted to him.

"She summons us to heave to," Anne said.

Nick seized the helm and put it up. There could be no arguing with any two decker, much less a fleet of them. 'Golden Rose' came about with her usual alertness, and lost way, although she continued to drift with the tide. And now a longboat left the side of the warship and came towards them.

"Ahoy there," Nick shouted. "What is the meaning of this? This ship is the 'Golden Rose', master Nicholas Minnett, proceeding about her lawful business."

The longboat came alongside. "Your ship has been identified, Mr. Minnett. I am to offer my apologies, but no vessels are being allowed either out of the river, or into it."

Nick frowned at the man. Incredibly, although the boat was fully manned, the coxswain appeared to be an ordinary seaman, if a well spoken one.

"Nothing of this is known in town," he said. "Is there a French fleet about?"

"No, sir," said the seaman. "It is by order of the commander, sir."

"The commander? You mean of the fleet? Admiral Howe?"

"Admiral Howe is not with the fleet, sir. Our commander is Richard Parker, Esquire. . . ."

"Who?" Anne cried, clinging to the shrouds.

"And it is he who commands your presence, Mr. Minnett, on board 'Queen Charlotte'."

Nick stared at him. "Are you gone mad?"

"On the contrary, Mr. Minnett. This fleet has come to its senses, and will neither fight nor permit trade until our grievances have been redressed. Come, sir, make haste. Mr. Parker is not a man to be kept waiting."

7

They offered Anne a basket, but she preferred to climb the ladder up the steep sides of the 'Queen Charlotte'. The gunwales were lined with seamen, eager to give her a helping hand.

"Three cheers for the lady, lads," Parker called. "She is my cousin. And for Mr. Minnett. He is my friend."

The rigging rang, and the applause was repeated on the other ships of the fleet.

"Richard?" Anne held his hand as she dropped to the deck. "Is it really you?"

Nick jumped down beside her, looked around him. The decks were gleaming white, the sails were neatly furled, the cannon were polished and secured. 'Queen Charlotte' looked as cared for as ever in the past. But there were no officers to be seen. And a red flag fluttered from her masthead.

"Welcome, Mr. Minnett," Parker said. "I can now repay your hospitality."

Nick frowned at him. "I suppose I am dreaming, Richard."

"Why, no, sir, unless justice is a dream. You'll come below. Oh, do not worry about the 'Rose'. My men will care for her as if she were their own. I have given the orders."

A marine sentry stood to attention at the companion hatch.

Parker ushered Anne and Nick inside, followed them down the varnished stairway to the wardroom. The doors to the sleeping cabins on either side were locked, and in the passageway there was another sentry, armed with musket and bayonet.

"I'll wager this brings back memories, Mr. Minnett," Parker remarked.

"Indeed it does," Nick agreed. "Although they are strangely distorted."

"You'll take a glass of port?" Parker poured from the bottles assembled on the sideboard. Through the stern windows the other ships of the fleet could be seen, swinging to their anchors.

"My brain is spinning." Anne sat down, accepted a glass. "We are bound for Lisbon, and thence the Mediterranean."

"And a splendid voyage you will have." Parker raised his glass. "The 'Rose'."

"I'll drink to that," Nick agreed. "Whenever we can continue."

"Oh, that will be soon, sir. Their lordships cannot resist us, as well as the Spithead fleet. And we have learned that Admiral Duncan's men are also with us. That will release the Dutchmen from the Texel, should this business not soon be settled."

"But this business," Nick said. "You are in a state of mutiny."

"Some would say that, sir, certainly," Parker agreed. "But we will defend the country, should the French make a move against it. We merely seek an adjustment of our grievances, sir."

"Which are as you outlined them to me, last winter?"

"Indeed, sir. We wish to receive a fair wage. We wish to receive reasonable periods of shore leave; no more of this being forced to remain cooped up on board ship while we are in port. And we wish those officers who scarce deserve the name of human beings to be dismissed from the service, or given posts ashore."

"Those are fair, Nick," Anne said.

"Oh, indeed, they are fair," Nick said. "I have never denied that. Were they presented in time of peace, rather than war . . ."

"In time of peace, Mr. Minnett, we could be laughed at, and ignored," Parker said.

81

"I suppose," Nick said. "These officers you accuse of being tyrannical. Who decides their names?"

"Why, sir, their lordships already know them, I have no doubt. In any event, we are prepared to give evidence. We have already sent ashore those we feel might have been in danger to remain."

"You mean you have not sent them all ashore?"

"No, sir." A slight shadow crossed Parker's face. "We have retained those of a reasonable disposition. They are confined in their cabins, but you will meet them, Mr. Minnett."

"They are hostages?"

Parker shrugged. "Call them what you will, sir. As I said, this will not be a long business. Our demands are known. They have but to be agreed."

"And if they are not?"

"They are just and reasonable, sir."

"They are made under a threat of blackmail."

"None the less, sir, they will be agreed." Parker rose. "A cabin is being prepared for you. Now I must return on deck. Anne. Mr. Minnett."

"And we are also hostages, Richard?" Nick asked.

Parker stared at him for several seconds, then turned and left the room.

ii

"Simpson, was his name," said Lieutenant Calham, as he walked along the poop deck. "Oh, he was not the sort of man to admire, no doubt, Mr. Minnett. Hard and brutal. Most disliked by the men. But you'd not deny his courage." He paused and peered over the gunwale at the other ships, then at the distant shore, and sighed.

Anne's fingers were tight on Nick's arm; they were allowed on deck as they chose, but the officers were only permitted to take air one at a time. "And was he killed, Mr. Calham?"

"Aye, well, you see, he was officer of the watch. In port, you'll understand, it is no more than an anchor watch, with but a single

officer. Even the midshipmen are allowed to take a watch by themselves. 'Tis good training, at least at keeping awake. And when the
mutineers presented their muskets and told him to surrender, he
whipped out a pistol and shot one dead on the spot. Not Parker,
more's the pity."

"Sir?" Anne cried.

"Oh, my apologies, madam. But that man is the encourager and
upholder of the entire business."

"And this Simpson was cut down?"

"Ah, no, Mr. Minnett. Nothing so civilised. He was seized and
subjected to a drumhead courtmartial, and hanged from that yardarm
over there."

"My God," Nick said.

"Did he not deserve to die?" Anne demanded. "As he had just
killed a man?"

"My dear Miss Yealm," Calham protested. "He was an officer . . ."

"And the man he shot was a common seaman," Anne said.
"Show me the passage in the Bible which divides people into officers
and men, one with the power of life and death and the other
without."

Calham stared at her for a moment, mouth opening and shutting, then turned and walked for the companionway.

Anne bit her lip. "I am sorry, Nick. It is pure fright. They hold
Richard responsible for his death."

Nick nodded. "He has taken on the responsibility of leading
these people. He will be judged for everything they have done, or will
do. Should it come to judging."

She seized his arm. "And will it?"

He hesitated. "No nation at war can be dictated to by part of its
armed services, Anne. And no navy can be run without discipline,
without the discipline of life and death over anyone who would
disobey orders. No army either, for that matter."

Slowly her fingers released him. "You are against Richard?"

Nick sighed. "I believe in the justice of what he seeks. If he had
only been patient . . . I put the matter to Pitt, and he agreed to

investigate conditions on board His Majesty's ships. If Richard had but waited. . . ."

"For how long, Nick? For how long has the entire navy just waited?"

Nick watched Parker walking towards him. "We have been hearing about Lieutenant Simpson."

"A murdering dog," Parker said.

"The officers call his execution murder," Anne said.

"Aye. Well . . . we have demanded a free pardon for every man on board every ship, regardless of what may have happened in the mutiny itself."

"And will you get it, Richard?"

"We must. Or we take the fleet to sea."

"And go where?" Nick inquired. "You'd turn to piracy?"

"There is a prospect, certainly. Or we could take our ships into Brest." He grinned at them. "The very idea of that would bring their lordships to heel."

Nick frowned at him. "You are joking, of course. But is that how you see the matter, one of bringing their lordships to heel?"

"Well—" Parker flushed. "It is certainly how they are referring to us, you may be sure of that, Mr. Minnett. And are we not men as good as they?"

"No one is denying that, Richard, but . . ."

"But they are gentlemen and we are not? I do not hold with that world, Mr. Minnett."

Nick's frown deepened. "You were happy enough to sail with me."

"So I was. And I am obliging enough to call you sir, although why I should do so I cannot for the life of me understand. You are no better than I. We stand the same height, we possess the same organs, the same muscles. I would wager my brain is as active and as shrewd as your own. Our difference, Mr. Minnett, lies in an event that happened over a hundred years ago, which resulted in you ultimately inheriting half the wealth of the kingdom, and me inheriting nothing but my body."

"And you would level all of that?" Nick said. "Why, sir, you preach revolution after the French style. Not justice. You would have to be opposed by every right thinking man and woman in these islands."

"You think so, Mr. Minnett? It pleases *you* to think so. I wonder, should you put that question to one of your own servants? Put it to Anne, here and now?"

They both looked at the woman. She flushed. "I have no cause to complain of the world in which I live," she said, softly.

"Because of Mr. Minnett," Parker said. "But do you believe in it? Can you believe it is as God meant it?"

Anne raised her head to gaze at Nick. "I do not know if any of us understands God's intention, Richard."

"Oh, bah," Parker shouted. "You are temporising, for fear of offending your lover. I will tell you this, Minnett. Our demands will be met, or by God, I will sail this fleet across to the French. Liberty. Equality. Fraternity. There are the watchwords for men. And we are men. Not slaves."

iii

Bells, ringing across the water. The sound of feet, marching to and fro on deck. The cry of 'all's well', drifting through the morning.

A fleet at anchor, guarding the Thames. But blockading it as well. To all intents and purposes an enemy fleet. Why, that had not happened since de Ruyter, in 1666.

"Awake, love?" Anne's head lay in the crook of his arm.

"Aye."

"What will happen, Nick? 'Tis all but a week."

"Aye," he said.

She raised herself on her elbow, brushing auburn hair away from her eyes. "Pitt will know that we have been taken. That you have been taken."

"I imagine he was informed of that within an hour of us coming on board. Your cousin regards me as his principal hostage."

She threw back the sheet and rose to kneel against his side. "And are you not, Nick?"

He smiled at her. It was five years since that spring day in 1792 when she had first come into his arms; she had been just twenty, and almost a virgin, for her marriage to Harry Yealm had lasted no more than six months, and most of that Harry had spent at sea. Nick had been on his way to fight a battle; she had been about to wait, to wait for him to conquer or die. So there had been no more time for friendship, for convention, for master and servant. And for the first time in his life, he had known love. As he had remained, actively in love with her, ever since. So perhaps he sometimes yearned for the poise of a Princess de Lamballe, the tempestuous energy of a Caroline Minnett, the bubbling vitality of an Elena Reyes, and, more recently, the surging humour of a Lorna Fitzgerald; here was bedrock, calm and strong, eager to be loved, but only by him. And worthy of love, in every way, for the strength of her mind, for the loyalty of her heart, for the beauty of her body. Motherhood had given her no more than a developing attraction. It had increased the pout of that flat belly, but left the muscles as hard and as strong as ever. It had given her always large breasts a greater fullness, and the slightest of sags. Which made them the more irresistible. He reached for them now, cupping them to draw her down on to his chest.

"No doubt I am, sweetheart. As are you."

She allowed him to kiss her, and then pushed herself up again. "So Pitt will give in to his demands. To save you."

"I have no idea."

"Would you, to save him?"

"I very probably would. But then, I am not a Prime Minister. I can afford to be more selfish. So forget about Pitt, and about Richard, Anne. We were hoping to honeymoon, remember, all the way to Naples. Our journey has been prolonged by a week or so. That is not relevant. It but gives us more time to enjoy each other."

Once again he pulled her down, and once again she resisted him.

"But you do not approve of what Richard has done. What he is doing."

"Dearest love, how can I approve? The man is in mutiny, in time of war. It is a matter of understanding what is most important in life.

86

The nation must come before all. The security, the prosperity of the nation."

Her elbows were on his chest. "The nation will always survive, and always be prosperous, Nick. The French nation survived their revolution, and is again reaching for prosperity. You are not concerned with the nation. You are concerned with a small governing class. That is what you are concerned may be overthrown."

He stared at her in surprise. Never had Anne spoken to him like that. Never, indeed, could he recall her speaking to anyone like that.

And she knew it. She flushed, and allowed her body to rest on his. "I'm sorry, Nick. But I have been thinking deeply this last week."

"So it seems. And if I am concerned that the nation continues in the way it has done, and prospered, these last hundred years, it is because I believe it is best for all. Best for you, as well as for me, Anne."

Her head rested on his chest. "I'll not deny it, Nick. But I do not know how proud I should be of that. You raised me from nothing, to stand at your side. How many tens of thousands are there like me, who will never know the embracing arms of a Nick Minnett?" Her head raised again. "What is that noise?"

He sat up, still holding her close. "It sounds like cheering." He got out of bed, pulled on his breeches.

"Oh, can it be, Nick? Can it be?"

"You'd best dress." He buttoned his shirt, dragged on his boots, ran for the doorway. The marine sentry was gone from the corridor, and the officers were opening their doors, to peer cautiously out.

"What do you think is happening?" asked Lieutenant Calham.

"Something good, by the sound of it." Nick climbed the companion ladder, emerged into the waist. Here was crowded with seamen, swarming into the rigging, waving their hats and cheering. They made room for him, and indeed for their officers, readily enough, touching their hats with suitable deference. They watched the sloop beating up river with the tide, her shrouds a mass of flags.

Calham levelled his telescope. "Terms agreed," he said. "By God. I would never have thought it."

"But you are content," Nick said.

"I am relieved, if that is what you mean," Calham confessed. "Had they been refused, I would not have given tuppence for our lives. Any of our lives."

The sloop was handing sail as it came into the side of 'Queen Charlotte', and a man was already climbing the accommodation ladder. "Who commands here?"

"I do," said Parker, standing at the break of the quarterdeck.

"Aye, well, you're to return to your duty, and immediately."

"Our terms have been met?"

"A full investigation of all our grievances has been promised, and promised publicly, by their lordships of the Admiralty."

"And you'd surrender on that promise?" Parker demanded.

" 'Tis the best we'll get," the sailor said.

"Ah, bah," Parker said. "Once let a few regiments of soldiers board these ships, and their lordships will sing a different tune."

"The promise is from Admiral Howe," said the sailor. "Black Dick himself. He'll not lie to us."

"Aye," said one of the men from 'Queen Charlotte'. "I'd take Black Dick's word, for anything."

Parker glanced around him, realising he was in danger of losing support. "Well," he said. "If the lads are prepared to trust him. You say all our grievances will be investigated, and remedied?"

"Where they are found to be true."

"No reprisals?"

"A full amnesty for all acts undertaken up to today," the man said. "There are exceptions, to be sure . . ."

"Exceptions?" Parker shouted.

"Aye, well, certain acts were committed which their lordships cannot condone. But the list is brief. No more than three names."

"Whose names?"

"Why . . ." The man thought for a moment. "Only three, I think. Men guilty of murder. John Evans, Charles Smith, and Richard Parker."

There was a moment of horrified silence. Then a ship went by, sails set, prow heading down river. There were officers on the poop, and men swarming to carry out their orders. The red flag had disappeared, and in its place the white ensign fluttered in the breeze.

"Scum," Parker muttered. "Lapdogs, hastening back to do their masters' bidding."

" 'Tis all we asked for, Dick," said someone.

"Aye? And what of me? What of Charlie Smith, here? What of Johnnie Evans? You'd see us hang?"

The men shifted their feet, looked at each other.

"Men—" Calham began, and was interrupted by Parker, who leapt to his side, and struck him to the deck with a swing of his arm.

"One more word out of you, *Mister* Calham, and it's over the side," he bawled. "Watch him." He advanced to the rail, looked down into the waist. " 'Tis all a trick," he shouted. "Maybe they'll keep their promise of amnesty to you lads. Indeed they must. They've no one else to fight their war for them." He paused, as if awaiting a cheer of support, but received only murmurs of agreement. "But you can bet next year's pay, if it comes, that once you're properly returned to duty, you'll be forgotten all over again. Oh, an inquiry will sit. It will be an excuse for a dozen half pay admirals to enjoy a glass of port at the nation's expense. Then they'll decide that we are exorbitant in our demands. That things aren't bad at sea, anyway. They won't be for *those* gentlemen. That we're no more than a pack of scum infected by the breeze from across the Channel. That's what they'll say, lads, mark my words."

"Aye," shouted Smith in support. "He's right, lads."

"Where's the alternative?" someone shouted.

"Not a hundred miles away," Parker shouted. "A hundred? Not fifty. Boulogne harbour, lads. Liberty, Equality, Fraternity. The French will welcome us, lads. They'll make us their flagship, I shouldn't wonder. And they're free men over there, lads, not slaves."

The seamen were exchanging glances. They had enjoyed their

few days of freedom. And despite Earl Howe's promises, they remained apprehensive of the future.

Parker smiled. He could see his victory.

Nick glanced to his left, at the companionway, where Anne waited, stark horror in her face. But there was no one could end this, save himself; these men would not listen to their officers at such a moment.

He seized the balustrade of the quarterdeck rail and vaulted over it before anyone understood what he was doing. His feet struck the deck and he spun Evans round, plucking the pistol from his belt as he did so, throwing the man back and seizing Parker round the neck before he could defend himself, the pistol presented at his throat.

"By God," Smith shouted, starting forward.

"A step more and I'll blow his head off," Nick promised.

"Mr. Minnett?" Parker gasped. "I'm your friend, Mr. Minnett. You said so. I saved you from drowning in that bog."

"And I am endeavoring to save you from an even deeper bog, Richard." He faced the men on the deck, still bemused by what had happened. "Listen to me," he shouted. "You think you can just sail away, turn your backs on old England, find new homes in France? You think you will be free men once you cross the Channel? Listen to me. I am Nicholas Minnett."

Parker gave a convulsive wriggle, and Nick clamped his neck tighter.

"I have visited France, several times, these last few years. And let me tell you, my friends, there are no free men over there. Times were bad, under the Bourbons. But they wanted only money. This new French government, this 'Directory', wants its people's souls as well. They will tell you what to think, what to say, what to dream. And they will make you fight, lads, against your own comrades here in England. They will put you in the van of their battle fleet, where you must kill your friends or be yourselves killed. And what of your moments ashore? Where will your wives and sweethearts be? Your children and your mothers, eh? Be sure that not one of you will ever be allowed back into England."

The men were muttering, and shifting their feet, to and fro.

"Of you all," Nick said. "Only these three have been excepted from the general pardon. Their case remains to be fought, in law. I give you my word that I shall assist them, that the House of Minnett will see to their defence. But they must stand trial. And you must return to your duty. That is the only hope for any of you."

He took a long breath and stepped away from Parker.

"Marines, do your duty."

The redcoats were already moving forward, two to each prisoner.

Lieutenant Calham seized Nick's hand. "By God, Mr. Minnett, I think we owe you our lives."

"Then take command," Nick said. "And quickly."

Calham hesitated, then hurried to the rail. "Three cheers for Mr. Minnett," he shouted to the seamen.

They gave them, readily enough, the rigging ringing to the sound.

"And now," Calham shouted, "let us get this ship back to her mooring, lads. And see her ready to fight the frogs."

Another cheer. Nick left the quarterdeck and descended the ladder. Anne had remained in the companion hatch. But when she saw him coming, she turned and went inside.

8

Nick dismounted, slowly, handed the reins to the yardboy, climbed the stairs, slowly. It was a splendid early autumn afternoon; the trees were still in bloom, a faint breeze rustled the leaves and wisped across his face. There was hardly a cloud in the sky. It was a day to be at sea. As he should have been at sea these last two months.

But now, perhaps, it was again possible, to think of the sea. He had not allowed himself to think of anything, this summer. Save what he had to do.

Henry waited to take his hat and stick. "Sir?"

Nick shook his head, went into the house, hesitated for a moment in the hall, then entered the parlour. Even in September Priscilla Minnett liked a fire in the grate. She spent most of her time in this room, partly because the glass doors looked out at the rose garden, partly because it contained the porcelain collection on which Percy Minnett had lavished so much time and money.

Lucy had been sitting with her. Now she jumped to her feet, ran to her brother. "Nick? Oh, Nick. Your face."

"Does that mean the appeal is rejected?" Priscilla Minnett asked.

"It is." Nick stooped to kiss his mother on the forehead. "Their lordships would not be moved from the facts in the case. There was a mutiny. Lieutenant Simpson was within his rights to use force, even to kill, any mutineer. His action was justified, and would have been condemned by no court in the land. Therefore the seamen's action in trying and convicting him was doubly illegal, doubly murder."

"But what of Billy?" Lucy asked.

"He says he cannot interfere with justice. And he forbids me to consider it either. I have no idea what he fears I might do. Where is Anne?"

"Upstairs with the children. You'll tell her?"

"She will have to know." He went to the door, paused, looked over his shoulder. "And where is Paul?"

Lucy sighed. "He went out. He said the waiting made him nervous. He said he found the atmosphere in this house oppressive."

Nick nodded, closed the door behind him, and slowly mounted the great staircase. He did not know what to expect. Because she, like him, had been waiting, all this summer, holding herself in check, certain that at the end of it all would be well. Was he not Nick Minnett? Did he not always make things come right, in the end?

He opened the nursery door. Anne knelt, assisting Judith in the dressing of a doll. Harry squirmed over the carpet on his stomach.

Nick knelt beside them, kissed Judith, swept Harry from the floor for a squeeze.

"They hang tomorrow."

Anne laid down the doll, got to her feet.

Nick remained kneeling. "I tried every argument I knew. I even reminded them that it was I brought an end to the mutiny. But their lordships insisted that justice be done."

"Justice?" She stood at the window, looked down on the garden. "Or vengeance? Would they be condemned if Richard was some misguided peer?"

Nick sighed, set Harry back to his journey, got up. "Vengeance, certainly, sweetheart. It had to be, I suppose."

"And you agree with them?"

"How can you say that?" He stood at her shoulder. "I have done all I can, Anne. I have neglected my own affairs, to secure for them the best defence possible, to give evidence myself in their favour. But now there is nothing left."

"I know that." She turned against him. "I know, too, how hard you have tried." She kissed him on the chin. "I honour you for it, and I am grateful. Believe me."

"So, now," he said. "Perhaps we can resume living our own lives. October is late, but not too late. We have but to get past Biscay before the autumnal gales."

"Did you see Richard?"

"I asked to, but he refused. I cannot blame him for that." He held her shoulders. "Anne. You need to get away. So do I. 'Golden Rose' is ready. We can be on board tomorrow, away the day after."

She shrugged herself free, went across the room. "I would prefer to go back to Lyme."

"Anne . . ."

"You are right that I must get away, Nick. But not with you, alone, on the 'Rose' for six months."

"Not with me?"

"I love you, Nick. Believe me."

"I have never doubted that, sweetheart."

"But perhaps loving you is a more serious business than I ever supposed. You are Nick Minnett. Oh, it is magnificent, it has always been magnificent, to know that you are there, that I can count on your power, your strength, that in all the world I need fear nothing and nobody, because I am your woman. It has never occurred to me that to be your woman, I must also see the world with your eyes."

"Anne . . ." He crossed the room.

"Please, Nick. Stop there." She turned to face him. "I want to see the world with your eyes, Nick. They are secure eyes. They see only happiness, only splendour. They see the objectives necessary to you, to England, with a clarity the rest of us can only envy. But here, in London, in your house, in your company, it is difficult not to sit back and allow you to do my seeing for me, to tell me what is there. But just this while I want to see, myself. I must see—for myself, Nick. Please."

94

He stood in the middle of the room, utterly confounded. Then sighed again. "Ah, well, Naples is not important, after all."

"No," she said. "It is important, Nick. I would have you go."

"Me? By myself?"

"You'll find a crew. Or you could take passage on a frigate. Mr. Pitt would provide that for you."

"Indeed, he has offered. But . . . it will be a matter of several months."

"We have been separated for several months before, Nick. And I have loved you the more at the end of it."

"We have never separated over a matter like this. And you say you would go back to Lyme? If you leave here, you must at the least go to Windshot."

"Lyme," she said. And smiled. "If you do not take the 'Rose', perhaps you will send her back to her mooring. I would like that. Then I can work on her, of an afternoon, and remember."

"And the children?"

"Will come with me," she said, firmly. "I was miserable at the thought of leaving them for so long, in any event. Please, Nick. Grant me this."

"And when I return?"

"We shall pray for your return, Nick. Do not make it long, I beg of you."

ii

"There it is, Mr. Minnett." Captain Listowel offered the use of his telescope. "See Naples and die, eh?"

Nick levelled the glass. They had been in sight of the towering, threatening cone of Vesuvius since dawn. Now the sweep of the bay was opening before them; the green mound of Capri and the heights of Sorrento to the south, all the way round to Cape Miseno and the volcanic splendour of Ischia to the north, behind which the grim walls of Castle Nuova reached for the sky. Two days ago the frigate had rounded the southern tip of Sardinia, to leave Ustica on the starboard bow. Then he had known the end of the voyage was in sight. Because how much memory had been brought back, to sail these waters once again. And with Listowel. This same ship, this same captain, had taken him, and Elena Reyes, away from Toulon, in the winter of 1793. They had spent Christmas in Gibraltar, on their way home to England.

This time he had again spent Christmas in Gibraltar. But in the four years which had passed, Elena Reyes had joined the ranks of his enemies. Gibraltar had been in a state of siege, at least on its landward side.

"You do not look particularly pleased," Listowel remarked.

Nick closed the telescope. "I have seen Naples before, Captain. This is a business trip, not a pleasure one."

Listowel took the glass, nodded, and resumed his slow pacing, up and down the quarterdeck. He had had very little conversation out of his distinguished guest since leaving England. But he had been warned that the ebullient young man he had known four years ago no longer existed, and indeed that his passenger was in a black mood. So he left him to himself. As now. Nick continued to lean on the rail, watching the dancing whitecaps, careless of the fresh, and cold May breeze which whipped out of the Appenines to flick the tops of the waves aft as spray, while the land rose every moment, and it was even possible to make out the masts of the English ships anchored in the bay. Nelson's ships. It was getting on for three years since he had last met that over-enthusiastic fellow. And in that time he had made himself quite a reputation.

To accomplish what, at the end of it? To hang a man, who would improve his lot? But then, what did any of them accomplish?

He was Nicholas Minnett. From birth he had known what he would inherit, where his destiny would lie. He had supposed. He had not supposed the byways down which he would wander. He had become caught up in the fury and excitement of the French Revolution entirely by accident, seeking to save the Benoîts from the axe. His involvement with the tragedy of people like the Princess de Lamballe and Madame Roland, had left him aware that adventure was not necessarily pure enjoyment, that death and disaster could lurk at even the most wealthy, the most apparently powerful elbow. But out of it, too, had come a belief in the individual's part, obeying the dictates of his ideals, his concept of duty. This belief had carried him along for four years, had enabled him to make friends of men like Bonaparte, who followed the same principle, if with a different end in view, as much as of Pitt, who stood for his own vision of the future.

Who *had* stood for it. There was the point. Could he still believe that? From the moment the first ship at Spithead had hoisted the red flag, someone had been certain to be condemned and hanged. That Parker and his two companions had actually executed an officer had made it easy for their lordships. The end would have been the same had they merely thrown Simpson over the side and allowed him to swim ashore. The mutiny, however justified, had been a challenge to the establishment. And the establishment, however willing to see that it was time for generosity, on the largest possible scale, would still have its victim.

And of them all, who was more a pillar of that establishment than the House of Minnett, and its head? The men on board this ship understood, or pretended to understand, his motives. They pretended to honour him, as the man who had returned them to the proper path, that of duty. But in their hearts, did they loathe him?

And in his heart, did he not loathe himself?

And what of Anne? He had hoped that a long slow voyage together, with all the rest of the world lost beyond the horizon, would serve to shut out this first unhappy memory they had ever shared, make them once again understand that their lives together were something special, something separated from the uncertainties of the world.

And she had feared that the memory of Richard Parker would have lain ever between them, that even more, the realisation that when it came to a conflict between truth and duty, Nick Minnett, the man to whom she had dedicated her life, would always choose duty.

Always? He did not know, himself. He did not know if Anne was right. He did not know, for sure, if he still believed in Pitt's Toryism. Anne had said she must be left alone, to find herself again. Had she not also known, in her infinite wisdom, that he needed to be alone, to find himself? For what use was a man, however wealthy, however powerful, who did not understand which force in life was dominant, for him?

Listowel stood at his side. "We shall be anchoring in a little while, Mr. Minnett. I have a boat standing by to take you ashore." He lifted his arm, almost as if he would have thrown it around his passenger's shoulders, then thought better of it. "A good place, Naples," he said. "For forgetting that there are cares in the world."

iii

A good place for forgetting. Oh, indeed. He had not been in Naples for ten years. He had last come here as part of his Tour, on his way back to France, to meet Father in Paris, to discuss a loan to Monsieur Necker. That had been a different world, a world it was difficult to believe had ever existed.

Except, perhaps, in Naples. Several years of war had flowed around this timeless kingdom, but had affected it not in the least. There were English tars and red-coated marines to be seen in the streets, thronging the taverns; but there had been English tars here in 1787 as well. The city itself was the same bustling, dirty, narrow-streeted place he remembered, the washing strung between windows to block out the sun might have been the same linen. The faces displayed the same fascinating mixture of laughter and suspicion.

But there *had* been several years of war, and if the Neapolitans had survived with a shrug, others had been less fortunate. Nick had to stop and stare, and hastily remember to use his left hand, as he gazed at the gaunt figure who would greet him on the dock. He had met this man only once, at Prince George's betrothal ball, an occasion entirely overshadowed in his memory by that disastrous fight with George Moncey. Nelson had but passed across his consciousness, somewhat irritatingly, as a man who spoke in superlatives.

But who perhaps lived in them as well. The black patch over his left eye, the empty right sleeve pinned to his breast, indicated the fighting sailor. Nor had they in any way diminished the almost feverish brilliance which remained in the other eye. His hair was loosely secured, and his dress remained as careless as ever in the past.

"Mr. Minnett." He squeezed Nick's fingers. "Welcome. You have news from home, I pray. Mr. Pitt would have us do something more positive then watch the French skulking along the shore?"

"There are despatches, Admiral," Nick agreed. "But have you not fame enough? All England drinks a toast to St. Vincent, nightly, and couples your name with it."

Nelson made a wry face. "A skirmish, Mr. Minnett. A skirmish. We are at war, sir, with France. Therefore the task facing His Majesty's fleet is to destroy the French fleet. Utterly. Until that is done, sir, why, we are but despicable failures." His expression lightened. "But you'll not want to discuss politics with me. I asked to meet you privily in the hope you would have a privy message." He turned, led the way towards the carriage. "Here he is, Sir William, safe and sound. As I said he would be."

The door to the berline was open, and Nick was being ushered up, to be seized as he got inside. Eric would look after his gear.

"Nicholas Minnett. My God, but you never change."

He smiled at Lady Hamilton. "Neither do you, Emma. Neither do you."

He knew that she was approximately his own age, just past thirty; but he would never have guessed it otherwise. In many ways she reminded him of his wife, saving that she had a reddish tint to her hair, which gave her an even more dramatic colouring. The features possessed the same bold handsomeness; her eyes the same predatory glitter. She half hid them beneath an enormous hat, silk and lace mainly in pale blue. Her gown was of lawn, in a darker blue, the neckline ending not very far above her naval, although she wore shoulders and sleeves. Her flesh was a glowing pinkish white.

"And yet," she said, pursing her lips, and extending her hand to trace her finger along his lip, "this used to turn up. Life has got at you, Nicky."

"It has that habit." He turned to Sir William and smiled, squeezing his hands. "You are well, sir?"

"As well as can be expected," the Ambassador grumbled. "You had a good passage?"

"Oh, indeed. Very restful."

"That is all to the good. Their Majesties are expecting you."

"Today?"

"There is a levee, and your arrival is expected. Get in, Horatio. Get in."

Nelson entered the carriage and sat beside Lady Hamilton. To Nick's surprise, Emma kissed his cheek, as tenderly as if he had been her son.

"There, now," she said. "You can stop fretting, Horatio. You have no idea, Nick, the torments this man goes through, the torments I have to go through with him. The sight of a French sail drives him into a frenzy. When you did not arrive yesterday, he all but developed a fever."

"Emma, please," Nelson murmured.

Nick recalled the slight, dark creole he had met on this man's arm, three years before. He wondered if Fanny Nelson would recognize her husband now.

But Hamilton was muttering into his ear. "All is arranged, Nick, as you wish. We have a site for you, and their Majesties are eager, oh, indeed, eager . . . mind you, it has not been easy and will not be easy, even now. The place is full of frogs."

"Eh?"

"Well, what would you? Naples is neutral. The fleet must put to sea every week, to preserve appearances. Horatio spends most of his time over in Sardinia, sheltering in the Maddalena Archipelago."

"What do you at all, Admiral?" Nick asked.

"Watch the French, sir. The Toulon Fleet. For when that sails, sir, we must destroy it. The West Indies—there will be its destination. Perhaps to link with the Dons on the way. Oh, indeed, sir, we must watch them, constantly, and wait, and pray for them to emerge. Then, sir, we will destroy them."

Presumably the man's confidence was his most precious asset.

"Diplomats," Hamilton grumbled. "Savants. Spies, for the most part. Oh, it pays to watch out for *them*."

"I am here on no military matter," Nick said. "Now, were you to tell me that Ratsey was here, slandering me to their Majesties, I might be alarmed."

"Take care, Nick. That is all I can say, take care. Do not go abroad after dark without a servant. Frogs. A despicable lot. Scarce a gentleman in the entire crew. Take care."

iv

The gates to the palace stood wide, and they drove by the enormous facade, row after row of Grecian pillars. Yet this magnificent edifice was a symbol of the grimmest oppression, a reminder that never in a thousand years had Naples possessed a native monarch. Here Guiscard had carved himself the greatest of the Norman empires; here the two Joannas had in turn scandalised and savaged their unhappy subjects; here Spanish and Austrian princelets had successively bought themselves a throne, until now, in the personages of a Spanish king and an Austrian queen, the two royal families were united. This was a period, Nick realised, which might well see the end of all European monarchies. Supposing the French had their way.

The courtyard was a mass of equipages and grooms, hastily clearing a passage for the ambassadorial coach. Dismounted cavalrymen stood guard at the doorways, sky blue uniforms faced with red, with red epaulettes and stripes on their breeches, and white crossbelts, elite troops, with red trimmed fur caps instead of ordinary shakos. They came to attention as Emma swept by them with a smile, holding Nick by the arm, now, leaving her husband and Admiral Nelson to trail behind.

"I swear you will be the handsomest man there, Nick," she said. "Ah, if you were only a soldier. How splendid you would look. You would put these fellows to shame."

Nick doubted that. Beyond the archway they entered a long, deep hallway, thronged with diplomats and their ladies, gossiping and giggling, muttering behind their fans, discussing matters of apparent urgency. And here the guards were grenadiers, big fellows in white uniforms with gold facings, and high white bearskins decorated with red pompoms, while their boots were topped with gold.

But here the crowd was slithering to either side to allow the English party through, Emma granting various people a gracious smile, almost as if she had herself been royalty, whilst a host of whispers clouded the air behind them, mainly in French, only distantly reaching their ears.

"The Queen's best friend."

"Her *only* friend, my dear."

"More than that. They say *she* really governs this country."

"And Acton. Oh, and Acton."

"Where would they be, without the British?"

"And now we are going to get an English bank. That is Nicholas Minnett."

"Who?"

"You must have heard of Nicholas Minnett, my dear. They say he is the wealthiest man in Europe."

"Perhaps the world."

The doors at the end were open, and they stepped on to crimson carpet. This inner room was almost empty, save for the guards, and a cluster of figures at the far end, two of them seated, but now rising to their feet as the party entered.

"Emma," screamed Maria Carolina, in English, running down the three steps from the dais. "You have brought him. Emma, you are a treasure. Nicholas Minnett. Oh, let me look at you."

Emma's curtsey was perfunctory. Nick bowed more deeply. Although here again it was difficult to decide who was the Queen. Emma was certainly the more beautiful, and had the more assurance, while there was little to choose between the vulgarity of their dress. But Maria Carolina, as befitted a daughter of Maria Theresa, had the presence, the certainty that however lacking in dignity she might be, however overweight, she was yet a queen, and the daughter of an empress, and the descendant of a line of emperors reaching back a thousand years.

"Your Majesty," he said, and bowed over her hand.

"Oh, I would like to *kiss* you," she said. "I shall. Later. When I think of what you did for poor, poor Antoinette. . . ."

"Tried to do, ma'am. I was of little value at the end."

"Because she would not let you have your way, silly girl. Oh, I know all about it. Campan sent me her diary to read. And she regretted it at the end, bitterly. Had she been married to a man, instead of that oaf . . . it is the misfortune of us Hapsburg women, to marry oafs. You've never met my husband."

King Ferdinand was shifting from foot to foot and looking extremely uncomfortable.

"Sire," Nick said, bowing again.

"A pleasure, Mr. Minnett. A pleasure. As my dear Carolina says, the man who risked so much for our sister will always be welcome in my kingdom. John. This is Nicholas Minnett. Sir John Acton. My Prime Minister."

The Englishman was tall, and distinguished enough; he wore his sixty years well. And were all the tales of *him* also true? Nick glanced at the Queen as he shook hands. But if the Prime Minister was her lover she seemed to have other things on her mind. She was seizing his arm again.

"Now, Minnett," she said. "You wish to open a branch of your bank."

"Indeed, ma'am . . ." Nick looked towards the king.

"Oh, do not discuss it with me, Mr. Minnett," he said. "I am allowed to know nothing of these things. Horatio, my dear fellow, how good to see you." He began to mutter at Nelson.

Acton cleared his throat. "Ahem. His Majesty really does not concern himself with such mundane matters, Mr. Minnett. But I regard the entire project as one of enormous importance to Naples. I look forward to receiving you in my office, tomorrow, and then taking you on a tour of the city to select a suitable site."

"But we have already chosen a site," Maria Carolina cried. "Have we not, Emma?"

"Of course we have," Emma cried, squeezing Nick's other hand. "You worry about your politics, Sir John. Willie says there are far too many frogs in Naples."

Acton shrugged. "There are far too many frogs everywhere, my dear Emma. What can one do? There are certainly too many to fight."

"*We* shall show you your site, Minnett," the Queen said, her fingers running up and down his sleeve. "My carriage will call for you in the morning. Early. I like to be abroad early, while it is cool. The afternoons are best spent in bed. Do you not agree?"

Her eyebrows arched at him.

"Oh, indeed, ma'am, in this climate." Nick had not supposed it would ever be likely that he should turn to Emma Hamilton for help, but he was very happy to see her frowning.

"I shall come as well," she announced.

"You, Emma? You *never* rise before eleven."

"I shall make an exception for Nicky," she announced. "It will be sport. And then you will lunch with me, Carolina, and we will entertain him together, at siesta."

Maria Carolina sighed. "As you will. She is a dreadful spoilsport, Minnett. And I had so many things to show you." Once again her eyebrows arched, and she leaned forward to allow him a glimpse down her décolletage.

"Your Majesty," Acton said. "There is a considerable crowd without, waiting for audience. And if you have finished with Mr. Minnett, for the time being." He gazed at Nick, remarkably benignly.

"Duty, Minnett. There it is. Duty. Ferdy, are you coming?"

She gave the King her arm and they swept to the doors, already being opened for them. And looked over her shoulder. "Come along. Come along, Minnett."

Emma seized his arm.

"I am not sure I have landed in the right place," he confessed. "This is a royal court?"

"Naples is Naples, my dearest Nicky," she said. "There is nowhere like it in the world."

"I can well believe that."

Her fingers squeezed his arm. "And only in Naples will you ever have the chance to sleep with a queen, supposing you are so minded. Supposing you are not satisfied with the mere wife of an ambassador."

Her invitation was so direct, so sudden, and so unexpected he could only turn his head to gape at her. They had passed the doors and were in the antechamber, where the throng was just straightening after bowing or curtseying to the Queen. And now he lost the ability to speak altogether. Nick found himself looking at Lorna Fitzgerald.

9

Nick had stopped before he really intended to. And Lorna's face was dissolving into that unforgettable smile.

"Nick Minnett, as I live and breathe," she said in French.

"Do you know this person?" Emma had also been brought to a halt.

"We have an acquaintance. You'll excuse me, Emma." He disengaged himself, took Lorna's hands. She was exquisitely dressed in an Empire style gown of white silk with pale blue Grecian designs on her hem, and a pale blue sash around her high waist, apparently the only security for the fold over bodice, cut into a décolletage as low as the Queen's. Her shawl was of crimson cashmere, to complete the tricolour design, and her reticule was also of crimson silk. Her deep brown hair was secured with pale blue bands in a Grecian style, gathered in an extended bun on the back of her head. And the pendant hanging around her neck was a diamond solitaire. "If you had not greeted me I'd have supposed myself dreaming."

"Because I have changed my clothes, Nick? May I present my husband, Johannes Szen."

Nick faced a slight young man, somewhat shorter than Lorna, and wearing a monocle, with which he inspected Nick.

"Charmed, I'm sure."

"My pleasure," Nick agreed. "I did not know you possessed a husband, Lorna."

"I did not, when last we met," she said. "I have only been married these six months."

"You are wearing French colours, madame," Emma announced.

"I am French, by adoption, my lady."

"Szen?"

"Johannes is Hungarian. But he also is French, by adoption. We believe in the future. France is the future."

"My God," Emma said.

"And you are here on official business?" Nick asked.

"Johannes is here to investigate the diggings at Herculanaeum. But what a happy chance, to find you in Naples. You will attend a soirée at my hotel, Nick. I insist. We have so much to talk about." Her mouth twisted in a deliciously wicked fashion. "And some unfinished business."

She withdrew her hand, still smiling at him.

ii

"The girl is Irish," Emma declared. "You can tell it by her accent. Therefore she is a renegade. Really, Carolina, you should be more careful about whom you allow into your country."

"Me?" the Queen inquired. "It has nothing to do with me. You must ask John. And he will say she travels under the aegis of the French. No one opposes the French. Or who knows, that dreadful Bonaparte person might return to Italy."

"And then at last poor dear Horatio would have something to do," Emma said. "He'd soon put a stop to any nonsense."

Nick was seated between the two women as the carriage made its way slowly down the street. The berline was closed, and officially the Queen was travelling incognito, but none the less there was the royal crest, and an escort of jingling pale blue clad horsemen, and another equipage behind with the maids; crowds gathered on every corner to stop and stare, and receive an occasional wave from both of the women.

"And what did she mean about unfinished business?"

"Ah . . . I have no idea," Nick said. "She is a Fitzgerald, you know. Edward's sister. Well, half sister."

"Oh, yes?" Emma remarked.

"A pretty child," Maria Carolina said. "I think it might be a good idea to see more of her." She smiled at Emma.

"Ha. There, Nick. What do you think of that?"

The carriage was stopping, and he gazed across the Riviera di Chiaga. It was a good site, certainly, on a corner, and looking down the street towards the harbour.

"Very good," he said. "Very good indeed. But I do not much care for the building."

A private house, he estimated, sadly in need of paint, and no doubt a rabbit warren of small rooms within.

"Building?" Emma inquired. "But that is no problem, Nicky. We shall tear it down."

"And build a suitable edifice for Europe's leading bank," the Queen agreed. "My own architect will design it for you, Minnett."

"I don't know what to say. Where does Lord Ratsey have his office?"

"It *is* no more than an office," Emma said. "He is concerned only with bills. But you will operate an entire banking service, will you not? So you said in your letters."

"Oh, indeed I shall. With permission."

"You have it, Minnett. You have it. Now that is enough business for one day." And indeed the berline was moving again, rumbling down the street and towards the Reale gardens, while the cavalry trotted behind. "We shall picnic," the Queen decided, "and you will tell us, Minnett. About Antoinette." She seized his arm. "Did you see her die?"

Nick stared at her in horror. "No ma'am. I did not."

"Oh. I am told that you used to pop in and out of Paris like a jack-in-the-box."

"Not entirely," Nick said. "Although it so happened that I was in Paris in the autumn of ninety-three. But I was recovering from a wound."

"Oh, what a tale you must have to tell, Nick," Emma cried, squeezing his arm.

"Imagine," Maria Carolina said. "Being exposed, to all those horrible people. Being undressed, in public. Being forced to kneel. My God, I go quite giddy at the thought of it." Her eyes rolled.

The carriage rumbled into the park, came to a halt. The doors were opened, the steps let down, the grooms stood to attention. The Queen descended heavily, sighing. Her maids had also disembarked and were setting up a table and some folding chairs, as well as an enormous umbrella, and laying out food and iced drinks. It was, Nick supposed, a delightful spot, close to the sparkling waters of the Mediterranean, overlooking the ships anchored in the bay, surrounded by gently waving palm trees. Amazing to think that in England the flowers would just be coming into bud.

But he did not wish to think about England at all, this morning. And it had nothing to do with his present company.

Lorna. What a strange chance, that they should be once again thrust into each other's company. A happy chance? That was surely up to him.

Maria Carolina picked at her cold chicken. The maids and the grooms had withdrawn out of earshot, and were devouring their own luncheon. The cavalry were farther off yet, restraining curious passersby.

"Where will it end, Minnett? Where, do you think?"

"It will end when the French land in England," Emma declared. "One way or the other."

"Land in England?" Nick inquired.

"Have you not heard? Bonaparte prepares an invasion. He has established an enormous camp around Boulogne, and waits only for a favourable wind. Boulogne, why it is scarce thirty miles from Folkestone."

"You expect the French to conquer?" Carolina asked.

"They have conquered everywhere else," Emma said.

"My God, what a dismal dilly you are to be sure. And what of your Lord Nelson?"

"Ah," Emma said dreamily. "They will not conquer Nelson. He will sail away, to some far off land, the West Indies—"

"And you will go with him," the Queen said. "Poor Willy. Poor, poor Willy."

"Willy is far too old to stand the rigours of a long sea voyage," Emma declared. "I do not know how we will ever get him home from here. We shall have to wait for the war to end, and travel overland."

"Then no doubt you will be here for the rest of your life," Carolina said. "Emma I think I would like to spend the afternoon in this pleasant place. It is far too hot to return to the palace. Perhaps you would like to take the berline back. Leave the smaller coach."

"And desert Your Majesty?" Emma cried. "I shall do no such thing."

"I shall not be alone, silly. I will have Minnett to keep me company."

"I am sure Nicky would like to see some more of Naples," Emma said. "Wouldn't you, Nicky?"

"Well, I . . ."

"He is not leaving tomorrow," the Queen pointed out. "He will spend this afternoon with me, and we will . . ." She smiled at Nick. "Talk. He will tell me about Antoinette. And about England. I should love to visit England."

"It would be a pleasure, ma'am," Nick said. "But . . ."

"It would not be proper," Emma said. "And in any event, there is an audience this afternoon. Have you forgotten? And Nick is dining with Willy and me."

"Am I?"

"Yes," she said severely. "Had *you* forgotten?"

"Well, I . . ."

"I will not have it," Maria Carolina announced. "Nick is a guest in my country, and I will . . ." Again she paused to smile at him, and for a terrible moment he thought she might be about to say 'have him first'. ". . . be responsible for entertaining him. After all, Emma, you spend so much time looking after dear Admiral Nelson that I really do not see how you can spare any for Minnett."

"Well," Emma said. "Really. You must be more careful of your words and your actions, Carolina. There is too much gossip as it is."

"Bah," the Queen said. "If people do not have gossip, then they turn to intrigue. Minnett—"

"Your Majesty," he said firmly, and rose. "This has been a magnificent morning, a magnificent lunch. And you may believe that I would like nothing better than to spend the afternoon, the evening, the night in your company. Both your companies," he hastily added, bowing in Emma's direction. "But I am here to work. Oh, yes, indeed. And this afternoon I already have an engagement, with Sir John, to discuss government investments. A bank must be profitable, Your Majesty. So I really must ask you to excuse me."

"You cannot walk," the Queen said.

"I will borrow a horse from one of your guards."

"And you will come to dinner," Emma said.

"Alas, I have a previous engagement. Ladies. My most humble apologies, my most heartfelt thanks." He hastened towards the waiting guardsmen, before the two women could catch their breaths.

iii

And soon caught his own, when he had finally got out of sight of the royal party. The impression he had formed the previous day, that he had abandoned the real world for some unending carnival, seemed stronger than ever. Perhaps it had to do with the warmth and the sea, perhaps it was the presence of Vesuvius, towering above the town and the bay, reminding puny mortals how irrelevant their lives and their wars and their problems were when compared with the immensity of a volcano. Certainly it was affecting his senses as well as everyone else's. Never before had he experienced two women fighting over him, at least in his presence. That one was a Queen and another an ambassador's wife seemed hardly more incongruous than the event itself, here in Naples.

His own sense of discretion was fled. They had awakened a great deal in him. He had used the voyage for thinking, and reached no conclusion. Memories of Anne had been no more than painful, because he had no idea whether or not *she* had reached a conclusion. One of the reasons he had fallen in love with her had been his realisation that beneath her quiet, almost deferential, exterior there lay a great deal of strength, of character as much as will. He had never supposed that power would ever be exerted in opposition to himself. But she would always follow the dictates of her heart, no matter what the risks or penalties involved.

And once again her memory was now distorted, by a smile, and a promise. He could remember their last words to each other as if they had been spoken yesterday. An idle promise, because it could never be fulfilled. Except that there was no such word as "never."

He drew rein, inquired of a gentleman seated at a roadside café. His Italian was limited, but the man spoke enough French to communicate, and to give directions. The hotel was on the Toledo, and he had ridden by it only a few minutes before. He turned his horse, walked it back up the slope, and through the opened gates into the courtyard.

"Monsieur has business here?"

The fellow actually wore a red cap. Nick dismounted. "I wish to call upon Madame Szen."

"Citizeness Szen is taking her siesta."

"Give her my card," Nick said. "I will wait."

He crossed the yard into the portico, the servant hurrying at his heels. "Nobody disturbs the siesta, citizen." He checked, as a butler emerged from the interior of the house. "This gentleman insists upon seeing Citizeness Szen."

"Madame is resting," the butler said, with dignity.

"I told him that," said the yardboy.

"And I have told him that I will wait," Nick said. "In there." It was a cool hall, with a fishpond in the centre, secluded from the sun and almost gloomy, and thus the more pleasant.

The butler peered at the card. "Ah," he said. "I will give this to madame's maid."

"Do that," Nick said. "And bring me a bottle of wine. Chilled."

He brooded at the red and yellow goldfish, darting to and fro between their weeds. He was being deliberately objectionable. Because he knew why he was here, and already hated himself for it? Or because he did not know what to expect?

He left the pond, strolled across the marble floor to another archway, found himself in a comfortably furnished parlour, again with a marble floor, although in here there were some scatter rugs, and divans along the walls. The effect was almost oriental. And how quiet the building was. Naples, in siesta.

"Your wine, sir."

He turned. Lorna wore a pink negligee; the bows were released and her white silk nightdress drifted through as she walked. Her feet were bare, her hair was loose. And she smiled, and carried a silver tray on which there was a bottle and two glasses. But what a contrast to the black gowned, slightly defiant maidservant.

"I hope it is chilled to sir's requirements," she said, and bent to place the tray on one of the occasional tables near the divans.

He caught her shoulders, his fingers sliding on the silk, and she turned into his arms. Her tongue just showed, to touch his, and then she moved her head back. "I wish you had told me you were coming."

"I had almost determined not to."

"And then you remembered that Johannes spends his afternoons digging," she smiled, and kissed him properly, passionately, working her body against his as she did so, before sliding away from his embrace to pour the wine.

"Something like that. And I am glad I surprised you. I would not have had you acting, for me."

"Acting?" She returned close to him, a glass in each hand. She drank from one, and then gave it to him, drank from the other. "Not for you, Nick. Never for you. Who knows you are here?"

"Why, no one. Not even Eric. It was an impulse."

"Oh, happy, happy impulse. My God, what an awakening. To find Nick Minnett waiting on me. My heart is running wild. Would you not quieten it?"

She took his free hand, rested it on her left breast, and gave that little shudder he remembered when he had touched her knee at

Windshot. Then she was back against him, crushing his hand between them, while her own slid down the front of his shirt to caress his breeches.

"Or perhaps I have not awakened," she said. "Perhaps I am enjoying the dream of all dreams."

"And would you awaken, Lorna?"

"No," she cried. "Never. Never, never, never. Come." She put down her glass, held his hand, led him to an inner hallway, where there was a small staircase. "This house is riddled with secret ways. All Naples is riddled with secret ways."

She was climbing in front of him, and he could wait no longer. He reached for her thighs, brought her to her knees, raised her hair to kiss the nape of her neck, inhale the sweetness of her perfume. She half turned, so that she fell back into his arms.

"So then," she whispered. "Carry me, Nick. Carry me to bed. My feet. Kiss my feet, Nick. Kiss me from head to toe." She laughed, a deep gurgle in her throat. "I meant, from toe to head."

Nick obliged. She communicated a quality of animal eroticism he had not known since Seraphine Condorcet, and possibly not even then, because Lorna also had a sophistication, and an experience, which Seraphine had lacked. It occurred to him that here was the perfect mistress, just as Anne would be the perfect wife. Something to be considered.

But not at this moment. She had splendid toes, perfectly shaped, cool and faintly dusty from where she had walked on the marble floor. And then he could trace with his mouth the gently muscular curve of her calf, the firmer ridges of her thighs, the impish undulation of the buttocks as she rolled on her face, legs spread wide, body squirming deeper in the sheet. When he kissed between her shoulder blades she rippled like a snake, all the way down to her toes, and was then on her back again, presenting the deep forested groin, the gentle pouting belly, the uncannily small breasts, magnificent little mounds from where the nipples darted to scrape his cheek and fill his mouth.

All this, and the smiling mouth, the laughing eyes, remained to come. As did the penetration, which was accompanied by a surge of

114

feverish energy, as she wrapped her legs around his, locked her belly against his, beat on his shoulders with her clenched fist.

A time to reflect, lying on the softness of the woman, breathing her hair. On the impulse which had driven him here? Oh, no impulse. He had supposed he had been escaping the cloying attentions of Emma and the Queen. But in truth he had been coming here from the moment he had seen her, yesterday morning. Or perhaps he had been coming here, somewhere, before even that, all of last year, without even knowing where he was going.

Then thought was lost again, as she rolled him on his back, to wash him with warmed water and gentle hands, before pirouetting about the room, long brown hair flailing behind her, long, strong legs flexing and straightening, small breasts bobbing.

"Oh, happiness," she shouted. "I knew, from the first time I saw you, Nick, that you would bed me. Some day. And I knew that I would adore it. Adore you." She descended on him like a tornado, straddled him, shook her hair into his face. "I adore you."

He kissed her nose. He had done that before, on board 'Golden Rose', and wanted then, to do so much more.

"And when did you first see me. At Windshot?"

"Oh, no." Again she shook her head, trailing the hair across his face. "I saw you, oh, it must have been five years ago. At a ball. Just before war was declared it was, in the winter of ninety-two-ninety-three. You were pointed out to me, Nicholas Minnett. You had been imprisoned by the French, they said, and had escaped the September massacres. You had sailed your yacht down the Seine in a storm, they said, with the French shooting at you from the banks."

"Not quite true," he smiled at her.

"But very romantic. You were romantic. When I looked at you then, I knew . . . that's why, when they wanted a spy, I volunteered. They were horrified. But I persuaded them. Let me go to work for Nick Minnett, I said. All the Tory ministers gather at his house, for cards, and to drink port, and to talk politics. There I'd be, at the centre of England's affairs. Windshot was to be only a start. I was planning on getting up to your London home."

"And instead got caught out."

She made a moue, shook some more hair into his face. "I think I wanted to be caught, by you."

"And hanged?"

"You'd never have hanged me, Nick. I thought you might beat me. Why did you not beat me? Whip me until the blood ran?"

"It never occurred to me. Would you have enjoyed that?"

"Oh, yes," she said.

"You have some very odd tastes."

"I like to feel. To know that I am alive. Is that odd? I know, Nick. You can beat me now. Tie me to this bed and whip me and whip me and whip me."

"Next time," he said. "I doubt I have the energy."

She gave a little shriek of laughter. "Oh, you have the energy. If not for that . . ." She squirmed on him, and indeed, he did possess the energy, for Lorna Fitzgerald, for feeling so much womanhood, so much aware womanhood, in his arms, for losing himself in the softness and the passion, the loose smiling mouth, the sharp little white teeth, the silky hair which enmeshed him.

And at last she seemed as exhausted as he, lay half across him, cheek to cheek, her lips against his ear, her shoulders rising and falling as she breathed. He thought she slept, and indeed dozed himself. Vaguely he wondered what time it was. The room seemed to become more gloomy, the heat began to leave the air. Johannes Szen would hardly continue digging after dark.

Johannes Szen. He had not given that young man a thought.

Because Lorna had not apparently given him a thought. Was not apparently giving him a thought, now. She was a bride of only six months, she had said. And her husband was already no more than an inconvenience.

But he had not come to Naples to fight a duel.

"Lorna," he whispered into her hair. "I must be leaving. What time does your husband return from the excavations?"

She raised her head to look at him, her eyes only inches from his face. She wore an expression he had not seen before, at once wistful and determined.

"You would not like to have to kill him, Nick?"

116

"I would not like to have to kill him, Lorna."

She shook hair into his face, but slowly this time, allowing the strands to tickle rather than stroke. "And will you always love me, Nick?"

"I will always want you, Lorna."

She smiled. "That is good enough. For the moment. I am aware of the rival I possess." She rolled off him, got up, picked up her negligee and slipped it round her shoulders.

He also sat up, and she shook her head. "Lie there, and rest, Nick. I will make sure it is safe for you to leave. If it is not, you are best in here. And I will fetch that bottle of wine, for a drink." She stepped outside, closed the door behind her. Nick allowed his eyes to droop shut once again. Lorna Fitzgerald. He had spoken no more than the truth. She was perhaps the most desirable woman he had ever known. So there was a world of difference between desire and love. So he could recognise that there were none of the qualities which made Anne what she was in that quivering bundle of lascivity. But if desire was all she wanted, then was he a fool not to accommodate her.

Because it was all he wanted, as well.

The door opened. Opening his eyes to smile at her, he instead gazed at four men.

10

For a moment Nick was too surprised to move. He had recognised the first of the men, short and stocky, with a neat moustache and a bland expression.

"Castets?" he demanded. "What in the name of God are you doing here?"

Joachim Castets smiled. "I am here for you, Mr. Minnett." He presented a pistol and walked into the room, the other three spread out to either side of him. "Will you get dressed?"

Nick considered the matter. But he knew Castets to be a dangerous man, and a totally unprincipled one. They had first met when Castets had been playing a double game, working for both Manon Roland and Count Mirabeau. After that he had identified himself with the Jacobins, then deserted even them to take service with Talleyrand. In the line of his considered duty he had twice saved Nick's life. But he would carry out his present employer's commands without question, unless he could be persuaded to change sides.

Yet the anger bubbling in his belly called on him to resist, even at the cost of his own life. Lorna Szen. An irrational desire, which had brought him to this. He dared not attempt to analyse his feelings towards her. Because desire remained uppermost. So then, he would kiss those smiling devilish lips even as he strangled her.

"Haste, Mr. Minnett," Castets said.

His men waited; they also were armed.

Nick got dressed. "One day, Joachim," he said. "One day soon, I am going to throttle you."

"I mean you no harm, Mr. Minnett. You must know that. Me? I am your friend."

"Oh, yes?" Nick pulled on his boots. "And supposing I refuse to come with you?"

"Ah, well, then, it would be necessary to hit you on the head."

"But not to harm me?"

"I would endeavor not to, sir."

"And where are we going?"

"On a journey, sir. There is someone wishes to speak with you."

"I am being kidnapped."

"You are going on a journey, sir," Castets repeated. "Now then, we shall leave this house, and enter a coach. I must repeat, sir, that should you try to escape us, we shall be forced to bring you down. I am an excellent shot."

"I thought you might be." Nick sighed, walked in front of them, down the staircase up which he had carried Lorna Szen, only two hours earlier. Now he understood why she had been so interested in whether or not he had told anyone he was coming here. How her brain must have been clicking, as she had hastily sent for Castets and his men, and then set herself to entertaining her guest until he could be taken.

And how efficiently she had done that.

But why? There was the question. How had she known he was going to be in Naples at all? How had she had Castets and his men available? He had arrived but the previous day.

And even that was insignificant beside the question of what happened now. What could he do now? Nothing, except wait. He had been in this position before. He had been taken prisoner in circumstances far worse than this, before, and had made himself wait, for the opportunity to escape, the opportunity for someone to come to his aid.

It was only the woman's part which rankled.

And there she was, waiting in the parlour, fully dressed and wearing a cloak and a low, flat hat.

"You did not resist them," she said. "Thank God for that. I had hoped and prayed, and expected, that you would be sensible."

"I seem to suffer my lapses," he said. "But on the whole, I suppose I am a sensible man. Or I would not merely stand here and look at you."

Her face was unusually serious. She gazed at him for some seconds, then turned and walked in front of him, into the courtyard. It was quite dark, now, and cool. Around them Naples was coming to life, for its usual gay evening. And in the centre of the courtyard there waited a berline, curtains drawn, coachman and postilion already in place.

To his surprise Lorna got in first, held the door for him. He sat beside her, Castets sat opposite, still holding his pistol. One of his men sat beside him. Their precaution was presumably a compliment, Nick thought. The carriage sagged as two other men climbed up behind. The whip cracked and the equipage moved through the gate.

Lorna took off her hat, nodded at the hamper beside Castets. "Will you take a glass of wine?"

"Will it be poisoned? Or drugged?"

She poured, three glasses, drank from the first, and then gave it to him. "Does that satisfy you?" She sipped from the other glass. "I would like you to know, Nick, that I volunteered for this mission, as well."

ii

She was smiling at him, over the rim of her glass.

"Volunteered?" he echoed. "But I only arrived yesterday."

"And I have been here a month," she said. "Waiting for you. I could hardly believe my eyes when you just walked into my house this afternoon. I had supposed a long and arduous task lay ahead of me." She rested her hand on his arm. "It *was* a labour of love, Nick."

"Aye," he said, "As you'd destroy a horse with a broken leg. How did you know I was visiting Naples?"

She shrugged, moved to the end of the seat, leaning against the swaying carriage wall. "I was merely told you would be there."

"By whom?"

"You will discover soon enough." Her teeth flashed in the gloom as she smiled. "It is not George Moncey, if that is what you mean."

"There are others who might wish my death."

"No." She leaned forward again. "Your life is not in danger, Nick. This I swear. I can even say that you will be pleased to discover where you are going. Believe me. Trust me."

"I have always enjoyed your sense of humour, Lorna. It is the most attractive thing about you."

She gazed at him for a moment, then gave another little shrug and retired into the darkness.

The carriage pulled to a halt as they were challenged by the guard. Presumably they were at the border; they had been on the road several hours. Nick gazed into the muzzle of Castets' pistol, pointed at his chest. Lorna remained a silent shadow in the far corner.

"Should I shout, Joachim, and you fired," Nick said, "you would hang. So, no doubt, would you, Lorna. You seem to have a weakness for courting that unpleasant end."

"It is an occupational hazard, hanging," Castets said. "And I *will* fire, Mr. Minnett."

"I believe you, Joachim. So you believe me when I say that one day I *will* throttle you."

Castets sighed. "I have long suspected that would be my fate, sir."

The carriage was moving again, and gathering speed. Nick leaned back. He did not bother to question his courage. He had given up doing that. He trusted his instincts. To die, in a closed carriage, even with the certainty of immediate revenge upon his captors, was pointless. Especially when they were captors of the breed of Joachim Castets and Lorna Szen. Time enough in the future to consider them. But more than that, he was now too interested in the cause of his predicament. In how news had leaked of his passage to Naples. In why anyone should be interested in kidnapping him. And in the identity of the kidnapper. He had never supposed this was a merely Irish plot. It would not have involved Castets, and certainly would not have been so smoothly conducted an operation. Undoubtedly he was now, for the fourth time in his life, a prisoner of the French.

Of Barras? Barras considered he had been betrayed, in October 1795. He had held in his hand Nick Minnett, an invaluable hostage, at once Pitt's best friend and the wealthiest man in England. The ransom, for Nick as much as for Aurora de Benoît, had been the House of Minnett's Egyptian funds. And the funds had been assigned to Barras. Before word had come that the government of Mehemet Ali had sequestrated the Minnett holdings in Alexandria, undoubtedly at Pitt's bidding. By then events were crowding too fast upon the French government. In the confusion surrounding the day of the barricades and Bonaparte's whiff of grapeshot, in the death of the arch-Jacobin Louis Condorcet, Barras had temporarily lost control of the situation, and, egged on by Talleyrand, and Bonaparte himself, had agreed to let Nick, and Aurora, and Anne, and the 'Golden Rose' go, on the understanding that the House of Minnett would make every effort to implement the original agreement. Well, Nick thought, he had made representations. But Mehemet Ali had not been co-operative. He had almost contemplated a voyage to Egypt, and decided against it. The money lost there could be recouped in Naples.

Supposing he ever got back to Naples.

He dozed, eventually, and then slept. He awoke as the equipage came to a halt, to discover that it was again daylight, a bright crisp morning.

The door swung open. Lorna had already left the carriage, as had Castets, but he had taken his pistol with him. Nick climbed down, found the postilions spreading breakfast, cold meats and bread and wine, on a cloth laid on the ground beside the road. He stood, hands on hips, gazing at the mountains looming on either side of him, and guessed they were somewhere beyond Rome. He walked round the coach, and found Lorna standing in a stream that bubbled down from the distant peaks to course beside the road. She was wading, skirts held high, bare legs streaming water.

"Oh, it is magnificent," she shouted. "It reminds me of County Down."

She possessed no conscience. Clearly she had already forgotten that he might be angry with her. That he might hate her, indeed, for betraying him. Or was the fault entirely his? He had known she was an enemy. That she had smiled at him, had beckoned him into her arms, had not necessarily meant that she had changed.

He sat beside the food, began to eat. He had discovered a very healthy appetite. Now his mood was clearer, his resentment more accurately directed. He could blame no one but himself. Last night he had been inclined to seek for scapegoats, to blame the Queen and Emma for titillating and disgusting him at the same time, even Anne, for not accompanying him in the first place, for exposing him to that long and tedious and sexless voyage. Today there could no longer be a doubt. He was Nick Minnett. He believed in himself, in his power to charm, to bribe, to accomplish whatever he sought, to conquer, by the sheer force of his personality. Thus he had assumed, without proper consideration, that Lorna had been conquered, on that night of the storm in the Channel. And had given her beliefs and her patriotism, her own concept of honour and of duty, not another thought.

And he must now pay most bitterly for that over confidence.

She sat beside him, stretching her legs out to dry in the morning sunlight, skirts folded neatly across her knees.

"You are not still angry, Nick?" she asked. "Do they not say that all is fair, in love and in war? Do you remember what I said to you, lying in the grounds of the château at Palue? If you surrender, I will ask for you as my servant? Now I have caught you. You could at least appreciate my determination."

Castets was pouring wine. "I do not think Mr. Minnett feels like talking," he said. "But you will take a glass of wine, Mr. Minnett."

Nick took the glass. "I will even talk, Joachim," he said.

"But not to me," Lorna remarked.

123

"To anyone, who will tell me where we are going."

They exchanged glances, then Lorna smiled. "It can do no harm, now, as we are beyond the reach of pursuers. We are bound for Toulon."

iii

Soon after breakfast they stopped to change horses, and then continued on their way. Now the signs of French occupation were everywhere, tricolour flags flying from the *hotels de ville* in every town they passed, French soldiers in garrison. They travelled, day and night, stopping only for their meals—invariably a picnic by the roadside—and to change their horses. And always fresh mounts were waiting for them. This was a highly organised journey, Nick realised.

And organised around his reputation. There were never less than three people in the coach with him. Lorna, always, and two men, each armed with a pistol, one watching him while the other slept.

And they were going to Toulon. He could gain no additional information. As Lorna pointed out, accurately enough, that at the speed they were travelling, they would be there in a few days. But what memories Toulon would bring back. What memories, indeed, did the very name bring back. He had arrived there in the company of Colonel Napoleon Bonaparte, a fugitive from the Committee of Public Safety, his life privileged because he had managed to save Bonaparte's. He had left there in the midst of the greatest explosion he could recall, when the magazine had been blown apart by Sydney Smith, and he had found himself in the water with Elena Reyes in his arms. He still had nightmares about that December evening.

They were across the frontiers of Savoy, now, and the end was in sight. And in the morning, after breakfast, as Nick climbed into the coach to sit beside Lorna, he was amazed to discover they were alone and the door was being closed behind him. He sat opposite her in his surprise.

"Do you know," she said. "You have hardly addressed a word to me, these three days."

"There has not been very much to say."

124

"Three days," she said. "Confined in a coach with a beautiful woman, and nothing to say? That is not the Nicholas Minnett of legend. It is not even the Nick Minnett I remember from the 'Golden Rose'."

"Then our positions were reversed," he said.

"Oh, indeed." She sat beside him. "And I learned to come to terms with my situation. Can you not do the same? We are alone, now. You could strangle me, if you chose."

He looked out of the window. A horseman rode to either side.

Lorna smiled, and reached across him to draw the blinds and to plunge the coach into a quiet gloom.

"Now," she said, and kissed him on the mouth, and then withdrew as he would not respond. "Do you hate me that much?"

"Perhaps I hate myself."

"For being taken so easily? But think of this. Had you not been taken, so easily and so unexpectedly, perhaps you had not been taken at all. You are Nick Minnett. Without total surprise would you have surrendered?"

"I also dislike women who prostitute themselves."

"Prostitute themselves? Can you believe that, Nick? Can you remember a single moment of those hours we spent together, and even consider that I did not want them? That I do not want you, now? Why do you think I commanded us to be left alone? By this afternoon we shall be in Toulon."

"And what will happen to me then?"

"I do not know. But you will be well taken care of. This I have been promised, or I would not have taken part."

"A promise, Lorna, is generally as valid as the person who makes it. No more. So until I know your employer, I can hardly feel as reassured as you."

She sighed, rested her head on his chest. "And I am sworn to reveal his name to no one. But I trust in him, Nick, and I am sure you will do the same."

"Then what does he want with me, if he means me no harm?"

"That too must remain a secret, for just a few hours more. Nick

. . ." She raised her head. "Can you not find it in your heart to forgive me, to love me, one more time?"

"I really am not in the mood, Lorna. I find women more complicated, not less so, as they and I grow older. Either they are totally mindless, and thus delights in bed but bores out of it, or they are a bundle of ideas and prejudices and ambitions, and quite impossible to trust or believe or sometimes even to like."

She threw herself away from him, sat in the far corner of the seat. "What is complicated about me, may I ask? Listen." She leaned forward again. "You gave me two guineas and told me to remove myself. I understood there should soon be a warrant out for my arrest. Two guineas. How far do you think that got me? Well, I can tell you, it got me to France. But what then? I am a bastard aristocrat, neither fish or fowl. I am pretty. I have brains."

"And a total lack of scruples."

"Scruples are for those who can afford them. I offered myself to the French government."

"All of them?"

"Oh, your wit is immortal," she said. "They accepted me, in their employ. Their first command was that I marry. I had a choice of three. I chose Szen. He is pleasant enough, and he is more interested in holes in the ground than in any I might possess. Also, as a savant he is acceptable in most European capitals, unless their governments actually happen to be at war with France. So I play the spy, the agent provocateur. It is my profession. And one day, perhaps, Nick, I will be able to play it as I would like best, with Ireland's freedom at the end of it. I will not deny that. For Ireland, I would kill. Even you. Not for France. But for France, I was happy enough to be told that my mission this spring was to be Nick Minnett. I was overjoyed. And now we have wasted all this precious hour in talking when we could have been doing." She pulled back the blinds, leaned out of the window. "Toulon."

Nick leaned out of his window in turn. The coach was at the top of a rise, but they were already close to the sea, the road having descended from the mountains, still towering on their right. And

126

there again was the Mediterranean, less placid than in the Bay of Naples, but even more blue. And the superbly sheltered harbour of Toulon, nestled behind the bluffs of Cap Sicié. The first time he had seen this port it had been a mass of ships. Ships of the Royal Navy, and ships of the Spanish Navy, then their allies.

And now . . . he frowned. The harbour was again filled with ships. Even a brief inspection informed him that this was a fleet of war. And more than that. There were too many ships for a French fleet. At least half had to be transports.

"My God," he said. "But what does that intend?"

"You will have to ask the commanding general," she said, joining him at his window to rest her chin on his shoulder.

"Oh, yes? And who might that be?"

"Why, the employer about whom you were just asking questions. An old friend of yours, Nick. Napoleon Bonaparte."

iv

Nick's head turned in incredulity. "Bonaparte? But he is at Boulogne, preparing for the invasion of England."

Lorna smiled at him. "Not correct. Bonaparte is here in Toulon, preparing this army, and this fleet for . . . only he knows where."

Nick's head turned back to peer through the windows of the coach as it entered the town. Certainly Toulon was filled with soldiers and sailors. On the harbour front cannon were being embarked, as well as munitions and stores. This fleet was on the point of sailing, he would estimate. And under the command of Bonaparte, the Republic's most brilliant general. Bound where, from Toulon? Naples? Would it not have been easier to march through Italy, already half conquered? A descent upon the coast of Spain. Certainly possible. Or Nelson's perpetual fear, the West Indies?

There was the most likely of all.

And where precisely did Nick Minnett fit into this scheme of things? But he would not now have long to wait. The berline was drawing to a halt before the largest hotel on the front, where the tricolour floated in the breeze, and bearskinned guardsmen stood to attention at the door. And there, bare-headed but wearing the blue coat, white breeches and high knee boots of a French general officer, was Andoche Junot, large features looking as happy as ever, curly fair hair rippling in the breeze.

The door was opened, and Lorna was being assisted to the ground.

"Andoche," she said. "I have fulfilled my task."

Junot peered into the interior. "Mr. Minnett," he said. "Welcome back to France."

Nick got down. "Am I welcome, General?"

"Indeed, you are, sir. The commanding general is awaiting you. Citizeness Szen, General Bonaparte is pleased with you. Well pleased. Your husband is with you?"

"He takes a different route," she explained. "To confuse pursuit. He will be here this evening."

Junot nodded. "Good. General Bonaparte is anxious to put to sea. There is warning of a mistral on its way, and Admiral Brueys informs us that Nelson cannot maintain station north of Corsica when the north wind blows. Mr. Minnett, will you accompany me?"

"Do I have a choice?" Nick asked.

"You are a guest, sir, really. Excuse us, citizeness."

Lorna held out her hand. "Good fortune, Nick. I shall see you again, I hope. And soon."

Nick hesitated, then took the strong brown fingers. "It will be my pleasure, Lorna. As a pendulum swings, who knows what our respective roles will be by then?"

She gave her delicious laugh. "I can hardly wait. Au revoir." She drew her cloak around her shoulders, got back into the coach where Castets waited for her, patiently.

"This way, Mr. Minnett," Junot said.

Nick followed him into the house, up a flight of stairs. The door at the end of the gallery stood ajar; he could see a desk and another uniformed officer, but this was a man he did not know. He was somewhat older than the normal run of revolutionary generals.

Junot went first into the room. "Mr. Minnett."

"Nick." Bonaparte came round the desk, both arms outstretched. "My dear fellow."

Nick allowed himself to be embraced. It gave him time to collect his thoughts. For Bonaparte had changed. The pinched-faced, somewhat nervous young man with whom Nick had shared a carriage from Paris to Toulon five years before—and the equally tense young brigadier who had commanded the guns to fire on the Paris mob three years ago—both had disappeared into the confident aura of a successful general. The little mannerisms which Nick had noted in the past were now becoming characteristics; the throwing back of the head, the thrusting of the left arm under the tails of his coat, as he was doing now, as he stood back to look at his friend. And the face itself had filled out, the cheeks rounding to a suggestion of plumpness, an idea immediately dissipated by a glimpse of the short hard-muscled body.

Only the eyes had not changed at all. They glowed, reflecting the multi-faceted fires which burned constantly in that over active brain.

"Well? Have you nothing to say?"

"I am still somewhat bemused," Nick confessed, and glanced at the other officer.

"My chief of staff. Louis Berthier. Nicholas Minnett."

Berthier held out his hand. "I have heard a great deal about you, Mr. Minnett. It is a pleasure."

"And Andoche you know, of course. Gentlemen."

The two officers left the room, closing the door behind them. Bonaparte continued to stare at Nick.

"I will apologise for the manner in which you were brought here. You are not hurt?"

"Only my pride," Nick said.

"Ah. It will recover." He gave that flashing, irresistible smile. "And had I merely invited you, would you have come?"

"No."

"Exactly. Sit." Bonaparte sat behind his desk. "A great deal has happened, since Paris."

"Oh, indeed." Nick sat down. "You have become a famous general."

"Bah," Bonaparte said. "To defeat a few irresolute Austrians, a few frightened Italians, makes a man great? I would test my skill on better mettle."

"So I understood. It was even said you planned to take on the English."

Bonaparte wagged his finger. "I do not rate the English any higher than the Austrians, as soldiers, Nick. But as sailors, now, there is a different matter. To invade your country I must have a fleet, capable of putting to sea and staying at sea, for at least a week. Not one likely to be scattered in the first storm that comes along."

"That was a considerable storm," Nick said. "I was out in it."

Bonaparte's brows drew together. "In December '96? You will not say you had something to do with Hoche's failure?"

"A little."

"My God." He leaned back in his chair. "I might have known. You are, indeed, my lucky star, Nick."

"Because I suggested you for the command against the Paris mob?"

Bonaparte leaned forward again. "Because in some way, I cannot say how, you are connected with every fortune I have ever enjoyed. Consider. We met, the day before I was due to leave for Toulon. My first command, Nick, and one which earned me a reputation."

"I should have thought that was skill, not fortune," Nick objected.

"Everyone needs fortune. How was my reputation made? I spotted—you were with me, remember—that the La Grasse promontory was not properly defended by the British, and I realised that if I could mount a battery there we would make the harbour untenable. Now suppose your Admiral Hood had had the foresight to fortify that point? There was nowhere else. With the best skill in the world, I could have done nothing."

"I told him so," confessed Nick. "But he thought he knew best."

"And that is not fortune? And then, as we have just recalled, it was your presence in Paris, entirely by chance, that earned me the command of the Army of the Interior on that day which established the Directory. And that, my friend, earned me the command in Italy. I needed small fortune in Italy. Some of my victories there *were* close affairs. But I gained them, because the Austrians had no stomach for hard fighting. The Directory was not altogether pleased with the haste with which I made peace. It did me no good to tell them that I was short of almost every wherewithal to wage war, that I had conquered half of Italy with a band of starving sans culottes. So what happens? They seek to remove me far from Paris. But where can I go? Then word comes, Hoche, the darling of the Republic, has failed in his attempt to invade Ireland. His fleet is scattered, his reputation shaken. So they send me, the man with the reputation, to take over his command. And now I learn that you had a hand in that, as well."

"And that is fortune?" Nick demanded. "Anyone appointed to the command of an army to invade England sacrifices his reputation on the instant."

"Oh, indeed. Supposing he is a fool. I am not a fool, Nick. I could see, after one morning's ride along Gris Nez, that an invasion of your island was impossible, unless in some mysterious fashion I could blow away the Royal Navy. But I have been given an army, and the use of a fleet, to harm Great Britain. That was the fortune. I went to Paris. I told them that if those were my orders, then I knew how to harm you English in a far more serious way than by crawling up the white cliffs of Dover. And they agreed."

"Well, I am totally mystified," Nick said. "Just what do you propose?"

Bonaparte stared at him for some seconds, then got up and went to the window to look out at his fleet. Both hands were locked behind his back.

"That too is a result of you, Nick. Of our talks, on that first journey we made together, down here to Toulon. England is the wealthiest country in the world. But she does not obtain her wealth from her own soil, her own husbandry. She obtains it from her Empire. From the Indies, east and west."

"You aim for the West Indies?"

Bonaparte turned, smiling. "Then would I again be a fool. What, a mass of small islands, every one of which must be conquered by a fleet, and may be defended by a fleet? No, no, Nick. I am prepared to risk one sea crossing, no more. Then my army marches. We are bound for Alexandria, and thence, thence, Nick, I will carry the tricolour into India."

11

"Egypt?" Nick cried in sheer horror. "India?"

"Why not? Did I not once tell you that there was the center of the world? All the riches of the world, certainly, despite the looting of you English. We shall walk behind Alexander, only with greater success. Now, come. Let us embark. I was waiting only for you. We must be ready to take advantage of the mistral, the moment it arrives." He rang a bell on his desk, and immediately the doors to the office opened, Junot and Berthier returned, this time accompanied by half a dozen valets, bearing cloaks and hats.

"But wait a moment," Nick shouted. "Why do you need me, to go to Egypt? I know nothing of that country."

Bonaparte smiled at him. "I need you, Nick, for three reasons. Firstly, you are my fortune. I am sure of that, now. Indeed, I will confess to you, dear friend, that my decision, although moulding in my mind, was still but an idea, until I heard that you were going to visit Naples, and therefore would be within my grasp, so to speak. Then it became, a decision."

"Heard I was going to visit Naples. But . . ."

Bonaparte was already out of the room, hurrying down the corridor, while guards presented arms. On every side doors were opened and officers and clerks were putting papers together.

"The second reason, Nick, is that you have unfinished business with Mehemet Ali, eh? That small matter of the House of Minnett's Egyptian investments, which by right now belong to France? You will get them back. I will get them back for you."

"Yes," Nick panted at his heels. "But . . ."

Bonaparte emerged into the daylight, paused briefly to salute the flag, and hurried down the steps. The street outside had been cleared, and a barge was already alongside the steps, waiting for the general.

"And the third reason," he said, "and possibly the most important of all, is that I go, not merely to conquer, to plunder, to destroy the British eastern empire. I go to *found* an empire, Nick. Empires must be managed. Financially more than any other way. You will be my minister of finance, Nick. I have never understood why Pitt never made you Chancellor of the Exchequer."

"Mainly because I have always refused the post."

"Ah." Bonaparte held his shoulders, peered into his eyes. "You will not refuse me, Nick."

"Why not, do you suppose?"

Bonaparte gave a short laugh, turned away, and climbed into the barge. Junot patted Nick on the shoulder. He looked around at the rows of armed guards, sighed, and also went on board. Junot and Berthier followed, with several of the clerks, and the barge cast off, the oars propelling it across the dancing water. The wind was already freshening, and from the north west.

"You will not refuse me, Nick," Bonaparte said again, "firstly because you are my friend, and secondly, because you are my prisoner." The smile died for just a moment. "Who can be shot if he tries to escape."

"Ah," Nick said. "Yet I had supposed you *my* friend, Napoleon. You must know that I have a bank to manage, that I have a family to care for, and to descend to very mundane matters, that I have no change of clothing. In fact, as I have been wearing these rags for the past four days, I would rather have a change of clothing than anything else in the world, right this minute."

"A change of clothing? Why, there is one waiting for you, on board 'L'Orion'."

"Eh?"

"I had clothes made up, especially for you, Nick."

"But . . ."

"As for your bank, you well know it has managed without you for months on end in the past. This may take a year or two, to be sure, but I am equally sure the House of Minnett will continue to prosper."

"Perhaps," Nick said. "But how did you know my measurements?"

"As for your family . . ." Bonaparte wagged his finger. "I know who you are really thinking of. That splendid mistress of yours. Oh, yes, indeed. But you are a married man, Nick. Married men should not spend their time thinking about their mistresses. No, no. I have given up all of mine, since my marriage to Josephine. It is best. Your measurements, why they were given to me by your own sweet wife."

Nick gaped at him. "Caroline?"

Bonaparte pointed at the side of the line of battleship they were just coming under. "She waits for you. Why, who else do you think told me you were visiting Naples?"

ii

Nick could only stare at the ship, for there was certainly Caroline Minnett, looking down at him from the gunwale, and now waving her hat.

Bonaparte climbed the ladder, Nick at his heels, while the boatswain's whistle coooeed and the sailors and marines stood to attention. Waiting in the waist was the admiral, François Brueys, accompanied by several of his officers.

"Welcome on board, General. The wind will be fair by nightfall, I promise. All is ready."

"Then let us begone." Bonaparte frowned at him. "You are sure the English will not be there?"

"As the wind freshens, citizen, they will have to seek shelter."

135

"How will it be too fresh for the English, and not for us?"

"Because we will be travelling with it, General. Whereas they must either beat into it, or attempt to maintain station, both of which are extremely difficult in such conditions."

"Hm. I hope you are right. I would have you meet Nicholas Minnett, my new minister of finance."

"My pleasure, Mr. Minnett," Brueys said. "And may I present to Your Excellency, my flag captain, Louis de Casabianca."

The captain, a swarthy fellow with an enormous nose, saluted. "It is my privilege, General. Would you greet my son? He is a great admirer of yours."

The boy, wearing the uniform of a midshipman, was hardly more than sixteen, Nick estimated.

Bonaparte shook his hand. "Sailing with your father, eh? Capital. One day, one day, Captain, I shall have a son to ride into battle beside me. Oh, indeed, it is my dearest wish. Now, Nick, come along."

He led the way aft, where Caroline waited; at a discreet distance there was a further group of people, mostly women.

"Napoleon," Nick protested. "This is madness. Women, on an eastern campaign?"

"I told you, I go to found an empire. Women are necessary."

"But you do not risk your own wife."

Bonaparte glanced at him. "Josephine is the most Parisian of all Parisiennes, although she was born in the West Indies. Besides, I have hopes . . ." He laid a finger on his nose. "That son I spoke of. She will join us for Christmas. I promise you that. Lady Minnett, you will see that I have not failed you."

Caroline gave a slight curtsey. "I never supposed that you would, General. Nick. Will you not kiss me?"

"No," Nick said. "What are you doing here?"

"Why, you have made England quite untenable, for me and my family. What else could I do? But as I was going to be an exile in any event, I came to the conclusion that you should share it with me. Is not a husband's place at the side of his wife?"

"I ought to throw you over the side."

She smiled at him. "But General Bonaparte would not like that, Nick. And think of it, Egypt. I have always wanted to go to Egypt. I am told it is the most beautiful country in the world."

"The most dramatic, the most historic," Bonaparte agreed. "Now come, let us discover our cabins. But first, Nick, you must meet our travelling companions. These are the most brilliant minds to be found in France, you know. We are going to do more than conquer. We are going to explore—the pyramids, the tombs, the country. We are going to add to mankind's store of knowledge. Now let me see." He paused in front of the group, while Nick's jaw once again dropped in total consternation. "You know the Szens, of course, Johannes. Lorna?"

Lorna Szen made a deep curtsey. "Mr. Minnett and I are old friends, General."

iii

Even south of Corsica, the mistral howled, although at last the seas were starting to go down. For over twenty-four hours the fleet had careered along, driven by gusts of up to forty miles an hour, making ten knots even under shortened canvas, while the waves had built into twenty and thirty feet, up which the ships soared before surfing down the far side in a welter of foam. The storm had been a blessing in one way; the ladies had all kept their bunks, and even Caroline, with whom he shared a cabin on the General's orders, had been prostrate with sea sickness since leaving the shelter of Cap Sicié. He would almost have been amused, that she should so rapidly be forced to regret her decision to take part in this madcap enterprise. And to involve him in it.

Had he been in the mood to be amused. For the mistral had also, as Brueys had prophesied, driven the Royal Navy off station. Nick clung to the port gunwale now, and peered eastward. Visibility was very good, and he could even make out the distant shadow of the Appenines, if not Vesuvius. Naples was over there. But no Nelson.

There would have been another cause for amusement, had he been in the mood, that he should actually pray for a sight of Nelson's topsails. Then he would be involved in a battle, from the wrong side. Something to think about, as he, in common with everyone else, did not doubt that should Nelson appear this fleet would be destroyed.

It was a gamble. One of the worst Nick had ever considered. More so, he would have supposed, than to risk the Channel, which after all would only have involved six hours instead of sixteen days. The truth of the matter was, he thought, wiping spray from his eyes and holding his cloak tighter about his shoulders, that for all his confidence when it came to fighting on land, Bonaparte knew he would have too tough a nut to crack in England, where he might expect the people as well as the army to repel their traditional foes. In Egypt he might expect less resistance, in a nation already resenting their long centuries of Turkish misrule.

"Not there." Bonaparte stood beside him, cloak also tight. "You do not still expect to see them, Nick?"

"I'm an optimist." He considered the general, who had certainly suffered these last two days. "How do you feel?"

"Envious of you sailors. But I am told the storm is all but over."

Nick nodded. "The wind drops every moment."

"So long as it carries us south of Sicily, all will be well."

He clapped Nick on the shoulder. "Now, come, no more resentment, Nick. This is an adventure."

"A gamble, I was just thinking, in which the odds are not very good."

"This is not a hand of cards, Nick. But let me get ashore, at Alexandria. Let my men get ashore. You are thinking of that untrained rabble who marched behind Hoche and Condorcet. These are veterans who have confidence in me. For I am also a veteran. Do you not agree?"

"Oh, I do. But still, you are but what, forty thousand men? You have little hope of replacements, at least with any regularity. Every man you lose is worth a regiment to the enemy."

Bonaparte nodded, his face serious. "Of course you are right. I must conserve my people. But yet, think of Cortes, who conquered Mexico with hardly five hundred. Or Alexander himself, taking on the Persian Empire at even greater odds."

"Indeed," Nick said. "If you succeed, you will be immortal."

Bonaparte gave him a sidelong glance. "And you think I only seek immortality? I suppose you are right. But not militarily, Nick. Oh, I wish to be remembered as a great general. I think I am a great general, although we must await the end of my life to decide that finally, eh? But to *rule*, Nick. To know what is best to be done, and to be able to do it."

Nick frowned at him. Here was an unsuspected ambition.

Bonaparte flushed. "Because I believe I know best what should be done, Nick. Laws. I have ideas about that. Mankind labours under laws that are unnecessarily complicated, where they are not just unnecessary. And not enough people know them. You English are the worst offenders in that respect, with your unwritten customs, your common law. But Europe is as bad, where every district has its own laws, its own customs. Think how much simpler life would be, for everyone, were the law to be codified, to exist for all men." He brooded at the dancing whitecaps. "And then, communication. Do you know, not one decent road has been built in Europe since the Romans? There is a confession of failure. And the organisation of wealth. Oh, I am proud to have you as a friend, Nick. But yet, were I Pitt, the Minnett millions should belong to England, not a single family. You would control it, but in the end, money on that scale should belong to the nation." He peered at his friend. "Now I have offended you, all over again."

Nick smiled. "No. I think you have been suffering from inactivity, these last months. And surely, if you think on a scale that grand, your attention should first of all be given to France?"

"Oh, no doubt. Would the French give me the opportunity. But that is not possible, for a common soldier who is a Corsican to boot. I will tell you this, Nick, in confidence; France is probably being worse governed now than even under the Bourbons. Yet those politicians will not let go of what they have. No, no. My only hope is to demonstrate for the world my gifts as a governor, that I may perhaps be invited to undertake that task for my own people. And where, do you think, could you find places more needing good government than

India, and Egypt? There is a perfectly Augean stable of custom and tradition and mismanagement, would you not say?"

"I would," Nick said. "You do amaze me, Napoleon, really you do. A professional soldier, as you say, worrying about administration?"

"Should I not? Do you know what is the trouble with mankind, Nick? They have a brain. Tens of thousands of little grey cells, we are told. And they use but a hundred or so of them, all of their lives. What a waste. I shall not waste anything. Any part of me."

A cough behind them announced the presence of Admiral Brueys.

"You'll excuse me, gentlemen. The mountains of Sicily are in sight. With this wind holding, we shall be through the Strait of Messina by nightfall. And not an Englishman in sight."

"And then Malta," Bonaparte shouted. "Capital. My gamble, Nick. It has succeeded." He slapped him on the shoulder. "Now come, say you forgive me for kidnapping you."

Nick could not help smiling. "As you say, it will be an adventure. Had you provided me with more suitable company . . ."

"Nick," Bonaparte said. "Nick. Your wife is beautiful, she is loving, she wishes only to be at your side."

"You do not know her very well," Nick said.

"Perhaps she has changed. And she is the mother of your son."

"She is not, Napoleon. There is the main cause of our difference."

Bonaparte frowned at him. "You have proof of this?"

"Alas, no."

"Hm. It is a point worth considering. But just to have a son. I should not consider it very far. You know, I have now been married two years, and nothing? Is it in me? It must be in me, Nick. Josephine has two children already, by that fellow Beauharnais. It must be me." He turned from the rail, all his animation gone. "A son, Nick. If you have that precious commodity, do not look too far."

Bonaparte levelled his telescope at the distant, brown stone walls. Then closed it with a snap. "The white flag. The Knights of St. John are not the men they were. Fortunately for us. That castle looks as if it would take some storming. We shall go ashore." He rested his arm on Nick's arm. "Not you, Nick. I am sorry, but I do not feel sure that you have become reconciled to your position. You will go ashore in Egypt. You have my word."

He turned away, went down the ladder to the waist, where the officers were already gathered, as the boats, filled with blue-coated French guardsmen, were already lowering into the calm water.

Nick sighed, gazing at Malta. He had never been here before. The eastern Mediterranean was beyond the reach of his experience. Not that he minded whether he went ashore or not. He thought he would, indeed, be glad of a few hours peace to consider himself and his situation. And besides, the island looked brown and arid, the houses a gleam of too brilliant white in the midday sun. It was also uncommonly small, even when considered along with its neighbour, Gozo. But he could see its importance; it lay directly on the route through the central Mediterranean, and it contained a magnificent natural harbour, off which the French fleet now lay, hove to, but awaiting the occupation of the fortress by the soldiers before entering the security beyond.

And the Knights of St. John had surrendered without firing a shot, although they must be aware an English fleet was in the Mediterranean, and that therefore to withstand even a short siege would be to put the entire expedition in jeopardy. Yet Bonaparte had not apparently doubted that they would surrender. Presumably French agents had been at work.

But this was no more than another manifestation of the care, the planning, the foresight which went into all this man's preparations. Nick thought of his very rapid understanding that an invasion of England, however brief the command necessary of the Channel, would be a far more hazardous undertaking. No wonder the Directory, those untalented men Barras and Tallien and their cronies, were happy to have so formidable a brain, especially when in command of an army, removed to the farthest possible distance from France.

And they must very well suppose that he *would* conquer the Middle East countries for them. Certainly Nick could no longer doubt that possibility, excepting only a certain amount of reasonable fortune in matters like personal health. So where did he fit into the picture? If he believed in Bonaparte's ability, and he did, then was he taking part in one of the great adventures of all time, with a great deal of profit at the end of it, and untold opportunities for the House of Minnett to expand, into India, through Egypt and Persia, perhaps even farther afield, into China and the forbidden empire of Japan. It was a prospect to dazzle even the sober mind of a banker.

And where did his anger arise? Only in his kidnapping. Only in the way his desire for a woman had led him into a trap. Only in Bonaparte's quite juvenile insistence upon the joys of marriage. As if his own marital future, wed to that West Indian friend of Madame Tallien's, could in the long run be any happier than his own. What a contrast between Rose de Beauharnais and his only other West Indian acquaintance, Fanny Nelson. And how odd that both Napoleon Bonaparte and Horatio Nelson, the one bidding fair to be France's greatest general and the other equally likely to become England's greatest admiral, should both have chosen to marry West Indian ladies. Which but proved his point, he thought with grim satisfaction: Nelson's marriage was already all but over.

But the thought of Nelson ended his daydream with the effect of a slap in the face. Here he was, considering being partner to an empire, without considering that the empire would be French. So his ancestors were French, and there remained more French in his blood than English. And so indeed, the religious persecution which had driven those early Minnetts to flee La Rochelle and Nantes and seek refuge in Protestant England no longer existed in this new France. The fact was that the Minnetts had chosen Great Britain as their country, and out of that choice had come his own friendship with Billy Pitt. However grand his schemes, however splendid his visions and his abilities, Bonaparte was an enemy and must remain so, and his downfall must be as much a concern of Nick Minnett's as it was of Horatio Nelson's.

"My God, to think that this deck has stopped heaving."

He turned, found Caroline at his elbow. They had hardly exchanged a word on the voyage, as she, like Lorna, had been incapable of speaking. Lorna had still not appeared on deck.

"For the moment," he said.

"Even a moment is long enough for me," she said. "I swear I have lost pounds of weight. Nick. Was that you, beside me at night?"

"It was somewhere to sleep."

"Nicky," she said, and held his arm. "You are the cruelest of men."

"On the contrary," he said. "I am the most generous. Yes, Carrie, I slept beside you while you were unable to do more than groan, and I never once strangled you. Is that not generosity?"

"Nick."

"Consider," he said, ticking them off on his fingers. "You made me drunk, inveigled me into your bed, and then screamed rape, so that marriage became a necessity. Two. You outraged my servants. Three. You inflicted upon me, and have endeavoured to inflict upon me, ever since, the most astronomical debts. Four. You nearly had me killed by your brother, and were then a party to my attempted assassination. Five. You became pregnant by some unnamed man, and had the effrontery to pretend the babe was mine, flying to my bed when already impregnated just in order to create a possibility. Six. You betrayed me to the enemies of England. Every one of those is a reason for me to hate you, and I have only stopped because I am running short of fingers."

She gazed at him, tears forming in her eyes. "I deny none of them. Oh, I am the most wretched of women. If I trapped you into marriage, Nick, it was only because I love you so. If I acted to your detriment afterwards it was only an excess of temperament. I have ever suffered from it. I know it, and hate it in myself. If I have had to snare you again, it was because I could think of no other way to be near you. And if I am not near you, Nick, I will surely die."

Her tone was so genuinely contrite he almost believed her.

"If this is some trick to get me into your bed again, now that you are feeling better, Carrie, let me inform you that I really doubt whether I shall ever again feel like taking a woman, any woman, in my arms, after my last experience."

She sniffed. "Oh, Lorna. She really is a detestable child. Too confident by far." She sidled closer, leaned against him and looked over the gunwale beside him. "But of course I wish you back in my bed, Nick. If you do not feel like it at the moment, you must allow me to persuade you."

"Oh, yes?"

"Nick," she whispered. "I swear it. I wished only to be near you again. To prove to you that I am as valuable to you, if you would but permit me, as any woman. Even Anne Yealm."

"Indeed?"

"Yes," she said fiercely. "But give me the chance."

He considered. Could she possibly be of use? Could she possibly be trusted? But if Bonaparte was determined to continue treating him as a prisoner in any event, what did he have to lose? However tenuous a hope Carrie was, she was his only one.

"You would have to help me to escape from this captivity," he said. "And regain Naples, to warn Nelson of Bonaparte's destination."

She hesitated, then nodded. "If that is what you wish. He trusts me, as my brother is proscribed in England."

"And you would help me?"

"Yes," she said fiercely. "I shall. But call upon me, at the first available opportunity, Nick, and be sure I will either see you free or die in the attempt."

12

Was escape possible? Certainly not without the aid of the woman. He had observed that there was someone watching him, surreptitiously, all the time. Except when he was considered to be alone with his wife. As now. She lay half across his chest, her golden hair scattered on his shoulder. She clung to him with a total desperation. Which was reassuring. Whatever her ultimate motives, she knew this was her last chance to make him love her again.

Then what *of* her ultimate motives? To regain the position of his wife, the wealth and the power which went with such a position? To gain for her son the certainty of inheriting the House of Minnett? To use her husband's influence to secure a pardon for her brother? All of those things, undoubtedly. And to accomplish them she had had her husband kidnapped, and assaulted him nightly like a prostitute.

Then need he have any scruples about using her? About enjoying her undoubted charm? About utilising her relations with the French to enable his own escape to become a possibility? About letting the future take care of itself? Undoubtedly she would become pregnant, or claim pregnancy. That too was a weapon. Undoubtedly, the fact that they had spent several days together, after his discovery of her infidelity, would be used by her defence, when it came to that, as an implicit condonation of that infidelity by her husband. But the truth of the matter was, there could be no future at all for Nicholas Minnett unless he escaped from the French. That was the essential, and to do that he must use whatever means came to hand. Analysis of a situation was his business, both from his training in the House and from his training at sea. Where essentials were concerned, all else became irrelevant details.

He realised what had awakened him, so early in the morning. 'L'Orion' had hove to. And now he was aware of a great rustle throughout the fleet, accompanied by a sudden beating of a drum. General quarters. Nelson. It had to be, Nelson, caught up with them, after all.

He sat up; they needed no coverlet, in the south eastern Mediterranean, in summer. Carrie rolled on her back, protesting in grunts. He climbed out of the bunk, pulled on his clothes. They fitted well, as Bonaparte had promised, and yet were untidy; he had no Eric to care for them. Poor Eric, waiting patiently in Naples for his master to return.

Carrie sat up, her face and breast and belly alike pink. She was a splendid figure of a woman, a true Moncey, tall and bell shouldered and utterly voluptuous. Her breasts sagged and then ballooned again as she breathed, the inflation reaching all the way down to her navel.

"Nick? What is that noise?"

"The call to arms. I must see what it is about. Get yourself dressed."

He opened the door, ran into the corridor, climbed the stairs to the quarterdeck, paused to watch the regulars falling in on the deck below him, while one of the boats, already crowded with blue-coated soldiers, was swinging out.

"Nick." Bonaparte stood above him, at the break of the poop, wearing a somewhat shabby green topcoat, despite the heat which already filled the morning air. "Come up here."

Nick climbed the ladder, followed the direction of the pointing finger, gazed at the low line of shore, and to the right, the gleaming walls and towers and minarets of the city. "Alexandria?"

"Indeed it is. We are here." Bonaparte looked over his shoulder at the empty Mediterranean. "If Fate will give me but one hour more, Egypt is mine. Well, Admiral?"

"Oh, indeed, Your Excellency," Brueys agreed. "I doubt there is so much need for haste. The chart shows me a sheltered harbour, over there in Aboukir Bay, where we may lie to our anchors without fear of attack by anyone, and from whence you may land your men at leisure. Assaulting an open beach will be costly."

Bonaparte wagged his finger. "There is no such thing, as time, in war, Admiral Brueys. The landing will be costly in any event. Have you seen those fellows?"

Nick inspected the beach through his telescope, watched the brightly cloaked horsemen riding up and down the sand, waving swords and no doubt uttering their war cries. Those he could not hear, but he could see the puffs of black powder as they fired their muskets at the approaching boats, the first soldiers splashing through the shallows.

"They are ashore," Junot said, having also been watching through a glass.

"What did I tell you? My brave Lannes will soon disperse a few Mamelukes. We will force the surrender of Alexandria this morning, Admiral, and then, then your ships may truly anchor in safety. Have my barge made ready. Andoche, you and Berthier will accompany me, and you Nick. Tell the ladies and the savants to make ready to go ashore. And make a signal to Murat; as soon as the beach is ours I will have the cavalry disembarked. Alexandria is but an outpost. Our destination is Cairo. We will commence our march tomorrow."

ii

The cavalry went first, hussars out to either side as skirmishers, pale blue capes gleaming in the sunlight, thrown back because of the heat and to show the gold braid on their crimson jackets—riding briskly, or standing motionless on distant sand dunes, peering at possible lairs where the Mamelukes had fled, driven from the beaches and from Alexandria itself by the fury of General Lannes' assault. As Bonaparte had predicted.

Then the smaller group of curassiers, a compact mass of steel and blue. Then the camel corps, hastily recruited, their riders wearing long skirted red jackets and high dark red shakoes with even higher red plumes, and to complete the gaudiness of their uniforms, red boots; it was part of Bonaparte's strategy to entice the Copts into his ranks where possible, as he calculated they liked the rule of Mehemet Ali no more than that of his nominal master, the Sultan. The rear was composed of foot soldiers. The light infantry wore green jackets instead of blue, loose white trousers instead of breeches, and low black kepis, or caps. Each man carried a blanket roll and a knapsack, and, being light infantry, they marched in extended order, and were allowed to chat and gossip amongst themselves. The line infantry, originally intended also to wear green but owing to shortage of the proper material decked out in a variety of colours, including red and grey and black, marched more formally and less enthusiastically. And last of all came the blue clad artillerymen, caissons whipping up vast clouds of sand which drifted slowly away down wind. Apart from the splash of colour against the brown of the sand, Nick realised that this army must be visible for miles.

The staff rode in the centre, accompanied by the baggage wagons, and the savants and the women. Most of the ladies rode in the wagons; some few were mounted, amongst them, naturally enough, both Caroline and Lorna Szen. Lorna's husband stayed in a wagon. He, like most of his fellow professors, was deeply disappointed at having been unable to explore Alexandria to his heart's content, and even Bonaparte's assurance that the city would still be there for them when the campaign was completed, had not sufficed to allay their chagrin. But the city, having refused the summons to surrender, had had to be carried by assault, and was not at this moment a particularly salubrious place. And time was pressing. Bonaparte sought the main Egyptian force.

The army followed the river. The river was everything, at once protecting their flank (they were accompanied by a flotilla of hastily armed boats), showing them the way to Cairo, and providing them with water. No one had ever been guilty of hyperbole, Nick thought, when describing the Nile as the mother of all rivers. The army had left a garrison in Alexandria and moved east, along the coast, past the securely anchored ships of the fleet resting in Aboukir Bay, their part in the campaign over for this season, and reached Rosetta, where the main flood of the great stream debouched into the Mediterranean. Here they had camped, to form their ranks before commencing the hundred mile march to Cairo. Perhaps here Bonaparte had hoped the Mamelukes would again assault them. But the fierce cavalry had found the musketry and the bayonets of the French infantry too daunting, and had preferred to join their general. Because Mehemet Ali was there, claimed their prisoners, with a mighty army, waiting to swallow the invaders—if the desert did not do so first.

At least the visit to Rosetta had been rewarding to the savants. They had discovered ruins, and unearthed some stone tablet which they considered of great value. Apparently the inscription was at once in the ancient, indecipherable hieroglyphics of the Pharoahs, and underneath, in Greek, which could be understood. Their delight had known no bounds. Was this the answer mankind had been seeking for over four thousand years?

But the general had decreed the march, and the Rosetta Stone would have to be deciphered at a later date. Another cause for resentment and disappointment, accentuated by the heat. What had the prisoners said? "If the desert does not swallow you up first?" The sun rose out of an empty sky at dawn, and hung close above the army until dusk, scorching every last drop of moisture from every body, bringing men crashing to their knees, to be hauled to their feet once again by their comrades. They had early learned the fate of stragglers, stripped and spreadeagled, lips, noses, ears and genitals sliced away, in most cases while the men had still lived, and screamed.

Which, Nick reflected as he dropped over his horse's neck, effectively disposed of any ideas he may have had for escaping while on this march. It had seemed an easy prospect. But he spoke no Coptic, and he would be a fugitive from a French army. Not even Caroline could intentionally be exposed to such a horrible death.

Relief came at dusk, when the temperature dropped, so rapidly indeed that it was necessary to draw a cloak tight about the shoulders, for then too a breeze sprang up out of the desert, to come soughing through the encampment.

Camp was generally pitched about four in the afternoon, so that every tent could be erected, every picket line laid out, well before dark; the Mamelukes hung on their desert flank like an ever present rain storm. Now fires were lit and hot food prepared, and weary limbs could stretch upon the sand. The savants would produce their notebooks and make lengthy entries, jabbering amongst themselves at some unusual rock formation passed during the day, the soldiers would take out their flasks and their pipes and their cards, and forget that tomorrow need ever come.

And Bonaparte, seated on a camp stool, his table in front of him, would examine maps and reports and interrogate flankers and the occasional prisoner, continuing far into the night while his aides held flaming candles above him. His energy was quite remarkable. He issued a constant stream of directives, orders, comments, his secretary taking constant notes, even while he was dealing with some other problem. He seemed to need no more than four hours sleep a night, and regardless of the heat during the day would wear his green topcoat, daily growing more shabby, buttoned to the neck.

His generals: Junot, broad and perspiring; Murat, uniformed as a hussar in a blaze of crimson and gold and sky blue cape, constantly pulling and caressing his moustache, restless as a thoroughbred horse because he was unable to close with the enemy; Berthier, placing paper after paper in front of his commander; Lannes, dark and quiet, a man who reminded Nick of a steel spring, merely waiting to be pointed and released; Kleber, blond and hearty; Menou, dark and pessimistic—Nick watched them all, and wondered. Junot he had known as long as Bonaparte himself; Menou and Murat he had met in Paris in 'ninety-five. Lannes was new to him, but the way he had forced a landing at Aboukir and then stormed Alexandria was a fitting complement to the reputation he had earned in Italy . . . not one of these men had been ranked higher than lieutenant when the revolution had begun, nine years before. Now they sought to emulate Parmenio and Perdiccas, Eumenes and Ptolemy, Lysimachus and Seleucus, as they marched behind this self-proclaimed reincarnation of Alexander. And who could doubt, watching and listening to them, that they would succeed.

"Seventy miles," Bonaparte declared. "And the total is a hundred. We should be upon them tomorrow, Murat. Another company on the right flank, spread them wide. What is this? Thirty-three men in a company, down with sunstroke. I will not have it. Less water, there is the ticket. They are being permitted too much. No, Citizen Decazes may not have an escort of cavalry to explore the oasis. He would be cut off and chopped up. Tell him, tell them all, there will be time enough to explore oases when the Mamelukes are crushed. Tell them I will personally explore their oases with them. Wounded? Wounded? We have not yet fought a battle. Half of those men are malingerers. Tell them I will consider the return of the wounded to the coast after we take Cairo. A caisson lost? Soft sand? This is absolute nonsense. Did we lose any caissons when crossing the Alps. I will not have it. That captain will be reduced to the ranks. Well . . ." He peered at the officer who had just arrived, and his features lightened. "Desaix? Good news?"

The young man smiled. He had a singularly winning smile and was always enthusiastic and eager. He was Bonaparte's favourite officer, there could be no doubt about that.

"I have something for you to see, General."

"Eh? I am not in the mood for games, Desaix. What is it?"

"Will you not come, sir? I promise you it will be worth your while."

Bonaparte glanced at his aides, then sighed, and got up. "Nick?"

Nick stretched his legs. "I am content."

Bonaparte shrugged, mounted his horse. Murat and Junot went with him. Berthier came across to the fire. "You should smoke a pipe, Mr. Minnett. You would find it very soothing, after a long day." He filled his own. "How is your wife?"

151

"As well as can be expected," Nick said.

"An army engaged upon a campaign is no place for ladies," Berthier agreed. "But what can we do? We could not just abandon them to be murdered, or to entertain the sailors. The commanding general sees us as a nation on the march, and a nation must be composed of both the sexes." His head jerked. "What in the name of God is that?"

The noise was a chorus of screams from the river bank, now accompanied by several musket shots.

"We are attacked, by God," Nick shouted, scrambling to his feet and running towards the sound. Berthier was at his side, while in front of them green-coated infantrymen hastily snatched their weapons and formed a line, which parted to allow Caroline and Lorna through. Each woman wore only a loose robe and dripped water.

"For God's sake," Nick demanded. "Whatever have you been at?"

"We wished a bath," Lorna said. "Is that so terrible?"

"I stank enough to frighten a goat," Caroline declared. "And to be beside all that water . . ."

"Until the dragon," Lorna said. "You should have seen it, Nick. Thirty feet long, and scaled like something out of antiquity."

Nick frowned at them. "You'd best try to become decent again, or it will cause a riot." He joined the men on the river bank, staring at the darkening water.

"The ladies spoke the truth," a sergeant said. "There was something there. Made a snatch at them, it did. Huge mouth, big as a cannon."

"And those teeth," remarked a private.

"It is called a crocodile," Nick said, "and is a reptile which inhabits this river. And it will indeed snap you up, or anyone else who ventures into its domains. Or even come ashore after you, so you had best look out." He walked back, Berthier at his side.

"They are delightful creatures," the general remarked.

"Crocodiles?"

"Women. Not another crisis?"

An aide was galloping his horse into the officers' enclosure.

152

"General Berthier," he called. "Mr. Minnett. General Bonaparte commands your presence at the southern perimeter."

"No rest for the wicked," Nick said. But the guardsman appointed his batman was already leading his horse forward.

"Nicky," Caroline shouted, leaning out of the back of her wagon, exposing a vast area of breast to the gaze of the interested guards. "Will you not inspect me? I swear the beast all but removed my leg."

"And mine," Lorna said, leaning out beside her. The two women were, remarkably, friends, despite their mutual interest in himself and the ten years or more difference in their ages.

"In a little while," Nick said. He cantered his horse beside Berthier's, through the various regimental camps, until they reached the southern edge of the whole encampment. Here Bonaparte and his aides were gathered, staring at the desert.

"Nick," Bonaparte shouted. "Here. Look at that."

Nick drew rein, took the offered telescope, waited for his breathing to settle while he focussed. Frowning, he saw the strange looking triangles which popped above the horizon. They looked like tents, but were too far off, unless they were very large tents indeed.

"The enemy?"

"Oh, they are there. But those, Nick, those are the Pyramids."

vi

The sound of the bugle brought Nick instantly awake, and Carrie with him. She sat up and said, "Oh, Nick, is there really to be a battle?"

"Indeed there is. We had best learn what is to be our position." He dragged on his breeches, went outside, discovered the servants already making ready to dismantle the tents.

"Mr. Minnett." Junot, fully dressed and mounted. "We have made a reconnaissance. The army opposed to us is some sixty thousand men."

"But that is double our number," Nick cried. Apart from their losses, a considerable force had had to be left to garrison Alexandria.

"Indeed it is, but some forty thousand of those are mere peasants, infantry so untrustworthy Mehemet has placed them in a fortified camp, supported by guns. No, no, it is the Mamelukes we must destroy. They are mounted, and will prove worthy of our metal, have no fear. The general commands you and the other non-combatants to remain within this brigade, which will march in square, and take up that position to receive the cavalry. Good fortune."

He trotted off, and Nick was surrounded by the savants, normally jealous of his privileged position regarding the general as the rest of the army was of *their* privileged position regarding everyone else, but this day anxious only for news. "Why, get dressed," he said. "And be prepared to march."

Carrie was already dressed and mounted on her wagon, and now she was joined by Lorna Szen. "Nick," they shouted. "Nick, you will stay close." Lorna was in a state of high excitement.

"Aye," he said, and climbed up beside them; from there he could obtain a better view. "I will stay close."

And was he not also excited? He had been in several battles, but always opposite these men, this revolutionary army, this tremendous body of concentrated enthusiasm. He had read often enough, how they had conquered Austrians and Germans and Italians at odds of ten and twenty to one. Here again they were about to face odds, as well as the most feared horsemen in the world.

The infantry advanced in four vast columns, almost as wide as they were long; the cavalry hung back, and the artillery had been divided up to march with the infantry. The flotilla, like the cavalry, remained back. They would await the outcome of the decisive encounter.

He stood up, the better to see the enemy. As Junot had said, somewhat to the right, in front of the pyramids themselves, immense structures rising out of the sand, there was a palisaded camp, from which muzzles protruded, and behind which there came the cries of the mob within. No discipline there, but a great deal of enthusiasm. They would become dangerous only should the French have to retreat. The real enemy were to the left, close to the river, milling about, a constant cloud of dust through which the brightly coloured cloaks and the burnished helmets with the glittering spikes of the Mameluke cavalry could be discerned as they awaited the command to charge.

The command to halt came down the column. Instantly all was ordered confusion. The horses were led into the centre of the brigade, and released from their traces; the wagons were arranged not in a Bohemian laager, as Nick would have expected, but in a row. The infantry formed square around them, each side several ranks deep, each with bayonets fixed. The men were mostly young, but in their march they had been allowed to grow their moustaches and their beards, and looked like a set of perfect veterans. As indeed they were, regardless of their age in years.

"Oh, my God." Lorna's fingers bit into Nick's arms. "I am so excited I could wet myself. I believe I have already done so. I was wrong, Nick. A storm at sea is nothing like this. It is too isolated, too lonely. Here you can feel the beating of all these hearts, ours and theirs, waiting."

"A storm at sea?" Caroline demanded. "When were you in a storm at sea, with Nick?"

"Hush," he said. "Napoleon."

Bonaparte walked his stallion past the ranks of his soldiers. Murat and Lannes and Junot and Berthier trotted at his heels. Now he raised his hand, and the little cavalcade pulled to a halt.

"Soldiers," Bonaparte shouted, his voice clear in the sudden silence. He pointed at the great tombs looming above them. "From yonder Pyramids, twenty centuries this day behold your actions." His gloved hand swung around, to pick out Nick. "We fight together once again, Minnett," he shouted. "And this time, once again, shall we conquer."

The soldiers uttered a cheer, and Nick felt like joining in. These people were his enemies, and no matter what the pretence, he was their prisoner. But yet their magnificent élan and the daring confidence of their little leader communicated itself to him, sent his blood pulsing through his veins. Suddenly across the desert there came the thunder of hooves and the immense roar of twenty thousand throats uttering their battle cry. Napoleon had disappeared, riding to his post with his staff, and now they could see the flashing sabres, the bared teeth of the horses as the Mamelukes surged at them.

"Oh, God," Caroline screamed. "Oh, God. Hold me, Nick."

He found one of the women under each arm. But the square was commanded by Desaix himself, walking up and down, mounted and therefore clearly visible, talking the while. "Hold!" he said. "Hold and wait. Hold and wait." The cavalry surged at the first square. Muskets rippled in the morning, black smoke rose into the still air, accompanied by the screams of men and horses.

"Hold," Desaix shouted. "Hold and wait. They will soon be here. And there will be enough for all."

The cavalry was flowing away from the first square, repulsed by deadly musketry and bristling bayonets. Now they came hurtling on.

"Fire," Desaix shouted. "First rank will retire. Second rank advance. Reload. Fire."

The morning burst into unforgettable sound. The crackle of the musketry seethed around the wagons like waves on a stormy sea, black smoke obliterated the sky, made breathing difficult.

"Fire," Desaix screamed. "First rank will retire, second rank will advance. Reload."

Again the volleys crashed through the morning. A puff of breeze momentarily cleared the air. Nick stared at a mob of dying men and horses, their blood streaming into the yellow sand, screaming their last farewells into the powder clouded air. But he saw too a company of the Egyptians, their horses rearing desperately from the French bayonets, turning their mounts round and forcing them to walk backwards. Men of such desperate courage, he realised, scarce deserved to lose.

Supposing they would lose. Egyptian horses shrieked in agony as French bayonets sought their rumps. But the line was momentarily broken, and Desaix was on the far side, bellowing his orders; the colonel left to command this side was dead. Nick wrenched himself free from the women, jumped to the ground.

"Nick," Carrie screamed.

"Nick," Lorna shouted.

He scarce heard them, already running across the sand, stooping to pick up the dead officer's sword.

"Reform," he bawled. "Reform. To me. Bayonets."

Men clustered around him, forming a second line some thirty yards inside the first, but the Mamelukes were through, great sabres carving the air as they hurtled at this last French stand, as they supposed. "First rank, fire, second rank bayonets," Nick screamed. "First rank retire, second rank present. Load. Load."

A horse reared above him, scarce visible through the churning dust. Desperately he threw up his arms, and the hooves landed beside him. He glimpsed a bearded face, threw up his sword and heard the clash of steel, and was then overtaken by a searing pain. The horse galloped away, leaving its dead rider behind on the sand.

Nick sank to his knees beside him, and the morning faded into nothing as he too hit the sand.

13

Surprisingly, the pain had gone. Even more surprisingly, the noise had also dwindled to nothing more than a murmur. And the sun had disappeared. Nick lay in a tent, covered by a blanket, aware of a throbbing in the head, of some discomfort in his thigh, of a great weariness.

And of Caroline. "Nick," she whispered, kneeling beside him. "Oh, Nicky. You," she said to someone standing behind his head. "Fetch the general, quickly."

Nick licked his lips, and she raised his head to hold a cup of water to his mouth. The process was painful. But the liquid tasted delicious.

"What happened?" he asked.

"You were ridden down by a Mameluke. I think you must have killed him before he actually reached you, but his sword still caught you a blow on the hip, and your head seemed to be hit by his horse as it went by."

"I remember. But what of the battle?"

"It is finished," she said. "Ours was the only square broken, and thanks to your efforts the line was restored. The cavalry finally retired, and then the Egyptian infantry fled. Oh, it was tremendous. General Bonaparte sent General Murat to chase them. You should have seen *our* cavalry charging, Nick. Oh, it was splendid. They say thousands of the Egyptians were killed, or threw themselves into the river to drown."

Her eyes glowed, with passion and excitement. Her hair was loose, and seemed to tremble. Her lips drew back over her teeth.

"And Nick," she said, lowering her voice. "I have a plan. For you and me. As you are hurt . . ." She glanced up as the tent flap opened.

"Awake, Nick?" Bonaparte stepped inside. He gave no indication of having been in a battle at all. "That is good. My doctors tell me your wound is slight. And it was a gallant action, to take upon yourself the restoring of the square. We will make a soldier of you yet." He knelt beside his friend. "Are you in pain?"

"Not a great deal," Nick said.

Bonaparte shook his head. "You were impetuous, and you are untrained in the proper use of a sword. But it was gallant. Now, come, you must get well. Cairo has surrendered. We must explore the city, eh? And we must explore the pyramids themselves. This is a strange country. A mystic country. It makes the blood run hot in a man's veins."

"It gives fever," Caroline said. "And Nick is not that slightly wounded, Napoleon. I do not think he should stay here. The heat is too great."

"And where would you have him go to get cool?"

"You are sending your wounded back to Aboukir," Caroline pointed out.

"The seriously wounded."

"And who can say that Nick's wound will not become serious?" she demanded. "Fever could set in. I beg of you, Napoleon. Let him go to the coast. I will go with him, and nurse him back to health, and we can rejoin you here."

Bonaparte frowned at Nick. "You wish to do this?"

By now Nick had caught Carrie's drift. "I doubt that I will be much use to you, lying about in a tent."

"Hm. I suppose . . . very well. You will accompany the convoy to the coast." He wagged his finger. "But mind you come back. And soon. He is in your charge, Caroline. See to it."

ii

Once again the river. Always the river. He sometimes supposed that the river would be imprinted on his brain forever.

But that was the fever. He had not supposed he would actually succumb. His wound was nothing more than a scratch; his bang on the head no more than an inconvenience. And yet he sweated, and trembled, and felt cold despite the heat.

"I knew it." Carrie held wet compresses of eau de cologne to his forehead. "Oh, dear God, you are not going to die?"

"No. I am not going to die." He settled himself more comfortably as the vehicle lurched, gazed out of the back. The wagons formed an endless trail, kicking dust slowly into the air, leaving it hanging on the breeze behind the convoy. The escort added their share; they were hussars, their pale blues and crimsons forming multicoloured balls bobbing to either side. He doubted they were really necessary. The Mamelukes had withdrawn, some said south into Nubia, others suggested across the Sinai desert to Palestine. To escape now would be a simple affair. There was the irony of the situation. Carrie had kept her word, placed him in a position to get away, and he was left weak and trembling in a wagon, rumbling onwards towards the sea.

She stroked his temples, caressed his neck. She slept beside him, awoke at his slightest movement, was immediately there with drying towel or cooling drink. No man could ask for a better nurse. But she was Caroline Moncey, first, Caroline Minnett second. He could not get that out of his mind.

"You are better," she said, perhaps to convince herself. "I swear you are less hot, less wet. Oh, Nick, you are going to be all right."

"I have no doubt of it," he agreed. "But what then?"

She propped herself on her elbow beside him, golden hair stranding across her face; she sweated almost as profusely as he did. "We shall steal two horses, at night, and make our escape."

160

"And go where?"

"We shall ride east," she said.

"Into the desert?"

"The Egyptians are there, Nick. Watching us from the other side of the river."

"And there is another problem you have not considered," he pointed out. "How do we cross the Nile?"

"Oh, we shall," she said. "Will the horses not swim?"

"They will. But so will the crocodiles."

"Well, then," she said, patiently. "We must ride west."

"Into Algeria? That is a thousand miles. And supposing we get there. They make Christians slaves, in Algeria. They would take you into the harem of the bey."

"Would they?" She sat up.

"You find that an exciting thought?"

"Well . . . it would be different. Oh, Nicky, I am so desperate for love. For your love, mainly. But . . ."

"As I am incapable you'd settle for an Arab sheikh."

"Oh, all you do is insult me. Nicky . . ." She lay beside him, her body shuddering with the uneven movements of the wagon. "Nicky, am I not being a good wife to you?"

He considered. But she was being a good wife to him. "At the moment."

"I will be, always, from now on. Nicky, I'll go down on my knees, and apologise to Mistress Morley. Really I will. And I won't say a word to Mistress Yealm. Truly I won't. I don't mind if you have a mistress, Nicky. I just want to be your wife."

He thrust his fingers into the thick golden hair. He supposed he must really have a fever and be in a state of delirium. Carrie, the most arrogant of women, suggesting that she would apologise to a servant.

"Don't you believe me, Nicky?"

He massaged her scalp with the tips of his fingers. "Let's say I'm finding it difficult."

"But it's true. Oh, Nicky, you do that so beautifully. And then, Nicky, when you get to know Alex, you'll love him, you cannot help

161

but love him. And you'll recognise that he really is a Minnett, really is your son. He has all of your characteristics, even if in looks he is really a Moncey."

"I'm sure of it," Nick said, releasing her. "And at last you are making sense. I believe that to have me recognise Alex as mine, to have me make him heir to the House of Minnett, you'd cut off your arm. Well, perhaps your finger."

"Oh, Nicky." She reared on to her knees. "You are so bitter."

"I'm not at all bitter, Carrie. Not any more. I'm just attempting to present you with the truth. The fact is, I know, and you know, that Alex is not my son. Therefore I shall never make him my heir. I am still prepared to educate him, and care for him, providing you let me divorce you. Because that is another piece of the truth you have just got to face. I do not love you, Carrie. I have never loved you. I married you out of duty."

"Nicky. When I think of us in bed together . . ."

"You're a beautiful woman, Carrie. And I'm a healthy man. That still doesn't make love. But I am in love . . ."

"With Anne Yealm."

"With Anne Yealm. And I would like to marry her, as you know. Just as I am sure that you, with an allowance from the House of Minnett, could make a very successful second marriage yourself. Can't you just be sensible, for once in your life?"

"You . . . you are a horror," she shouted. "Suppose I tell you that I do not believe in divorce? That I believe a marriage is a marriage in the sight of God, and must endure forever?"

"I would reply that you are lying."

"Oh, you . . . you . . ." She reared above him like a snake about to strike, and he realised that he scarce had the strength to resist her.

They were interrupted by a cough. The guard had come back from his seat beside the driver. "Begging your pardon, Citizen, Citizeness, but Aboukir Harbour is in sight. The fleet is waiting for us."

162

"Citizen. Citizeness." Admiral Brueys smiled at Caroline. "Your health. I give you General Bonaparte." Once again the quick smile. "He gains all the glory, while we but sit and wait."

The officers applauded. Like the new colonels and generals of the army, they were mostly young and enthusiastic, glorying in their blue uniforms with red facings. Unlike Lannes and Murat and Junot, they as yet had no list of victories to set to their names. And so they sat beneath awnings stretched across the quarterdeck of 'L'Orion', the remnants of their lunch before them, drank their wine, and dreamed of glorious events.

But Aboukir was a place to dream. The harbour was shallow, protected at either end by redoubts, and at the western end by a castle, all their fortifications repaired and improved by the French. Across it, in a long line, were the twelve French battle ships, positioned so that they occupied the entire area, with just room at either end to swing to their anchors; the smaller vessels were moored closer to the shore. This evening, as the wind was north west, the great ships faced west. 'L'Orion' was exactly in the middle of the line. She carried a hundred and twenty guns, presently secured beneath her red ports, and compared with any warship afloat. To either side of her were two eighty gunners, 'Franklin' forward, 'Torrent' aft. The other nine ships of the fleet were seventy-fours, 'Le Guerrier' forming the western extremity of the line, 'Genereux' bringing up the rear. It was a sobering thought, Nick decided, that the best British ship in the Mediterranean, Nelson's 'Vanguard', herself only mounted seventy-four guns. Not that the French, in this position, with their flank firmly protected by the sand dunes, through which only a trickle of water led to Lake Elco, were thinking of fighting anyone. They had merely sought to make sure that they themselves could not be forced to fight. They were the base from which Bonaparte could conduct his operations, safe in the knowledge that he had Aboukir to fall back upon.

"You are pensive, Mr. Minnett." Brueys cut his cheese into little cubes. "Your wound disturbs you?"

"No, Admiral. This week, sitting here in the seabreeze, has done wonders. I shall soon be able to ride again."

"You are anxious to regain the army," Brueys said sadly. "But I have heard you are a sailing man, for sport. Or perhaps you wonder why Nelson has not found us."

"It seems strange," Nick said. "You have been anchored here a month."

"Ah, but he has found us. I think."

"Eh?"

"There was a sail, sighted this morning, before we sat down. And then another."

Nick frowned at him. "You do not seem disturbed about it."

Brueys smiled at him. "I am not disturbed about it, Mr. Minnett. I knew he would come, eventually. But we are here for the rest of this year, I suspect, and your Admiral Nelson is perfectly welcome to stay off there—for the rest of this year, if he chooses. When I leave Aboukir, I shall do it with a southerly wind, dash through his fleet, and return to France before he can regroup. This is not the Channel, Mr. Minnett. There the storm weather blows from the west, giving the English the advantage. Here the sirocco, when it comes, will be to our advantage." He pushed back his chair. "Come, let us see if it is indeed your fleet."

They climbed the ladder to the poop, and Brueys stared through his telescope. "Four, six, eight, ten, twelve ships. And I would say one or two frigates as well."

He offered the glass, and Nick peered at the white canvas which filled the northern horizon. He felt his heartbeat quicken. The last time he had seen a sight like that he had been standing on the poop of 'Queen Charlotte', and it had been Dickie Howe offering him the glass. Howe had never questioned the certainty of his victory, could he but catch up with the French. Just as Brueys had no doubt that he would only fight a battle to his own advantage. He closed the telescope. "It is certainly Nelson."

"Oh, indeed. He will come and make sure that we are all here, then he will retire across the horizon again. You mark my words. The frigates will be left to watch us. Ah, well, I shall have my siesta. Mr. Minnett?"

"I will stay here," Nick said.

Brueys hesitated, then smiled, and slapped him on the shoulder. "And dream, Mr. Minnett? I prefer to dream in my bed."

He went below. Nick placed his elbows on the rail, looked out to sea. He could now make out the ships, propelled onwards by the sea breeze. Nelson was apparently going to take a close look at his prospective adversaries. Nelson. Oh, to be over there, on board 'Vanguard'. Because although his wound was all but mended, he was more and more coming to realise that escape was a quite impossible idea. No doubt he could drop over the side one dark night and make the shore, but what then? Only the desert, and the Arabs. And with Carrie in tow? She certainly would not allow herself to be left behind.

He felt her beside him. "Aren't they splendid?" she said.

"I thought you were off the British?"

"I still think they make a splendid sight. Nicky, it is nearly four. Let us have a short siesta, at any rate." She remained as desperate for sex as on their wedding night, a perpetual lust. Perhaps she had not been joking when she had claimed she would not mind being captured by the Arabs.

"Just let's watch them back out of sight." He frowned. Because the ships were still growing, and now taking on a formation of line ahead.

As the officer of the watch had noticed. He levelled his telescope, then snapped at his midshipman, the boy Casabianca. "Fetch the admiral. Quickly, boy."

Brueys was up in a moment, coatless, fair hair flapping in the breeze. "What is it, man?"

The lieutenant pointed. The leading English man-of-war was very close, apparently making straight for the spit of land which formed the western side of the harbour.

"The man is mad," Brueys said. "It is too shallow there for a warship."

The lieutenant was still looking through his glass. "His ports are open, Admiral."

Nick's heart pounded. For he had suddenly realised a truth which had escaped Brueys, and which would probably have escaped any admiral afloat. Save only Nelson. But then, perhaps only Nelson would have the courage to act upon it. "And when you say too shallow, Admiral, there is room for your lead ship to swing, is there not?"

Brueys stared at him. "Room? For one ship to swing? Your admiral would attack through a gap that narrow? I tell you he must have lost his senses."

The afternoon was punctuated by noise as the British warship opened fire.

iv

"Mad," Brueys shouted. "Mad. To arms. Sound the drums. Run out those guns."

Nick stared in fascination as the English ships held their course, as the afternoon swelled into a crescendo of beating drums and scurrying feet. 'Le Guerrier' was completely surrounded by flailing water where the shot was plunging around her, and she had apparently already been struck, although from his position he could not see clearly. Now the three lead English ships were all engaged, and the rest sailed silently on, while the remainder of the French fleet could only watch in helpless agony.

"We could cut our cables, Admiral, and engage them at sea," the lieutenant suggested.

"Bah. That is what Nelson wishes. They would destroy us as we tried to form line. Supposing we could make sail at all, with the wind blowing us on to the beach."

"But they will pound us in turn, Admiral."

"Bah," he said again. "We must engage them as we can. Perpaps they will run aground. There. One of them has done it. The rest will follow."

Nick levelled his telescope. One of the English men-of-war had certainly struck bottom; her sails were hastily brought down to prevent her driving farther on, and the whole vessel was commencing to heel. But her plight made no difference to the line of battle; those behind merely avoided her, using her, indeed as a marker to show the shallow water.

"Ashore," Brueys said. "You must be put ashore, Mr. Minnett. The general would not have you killed."

"Oh, allow me to stay, Brueys, I beg of you. I have been in a battle at sea before, and if your theory is right, Nelson will not even reach your position."

Brueys chewed his lip.

"But I would be obliged if you would send my wife ashore," Nick said.

"No," Caroline said. "I will stay with you. We will die together, Nick. I have always wanted to die in your arms."

"Oh, really, Carrie. No one is going to die on board 'L'Orion'. Ask the admiral."

Brueys merely snorted and walked away. The noise was now quite deafening, and the entire head of the anchored French line was a swirl of smoke. The relative peace of the rear seemed quite uncanny. But it must be equally uncanny on board the English rearguard, Nick realised, holding silently on.

"Look," shouted the watch lieutenant. "Admiral." They ran to the port gunwale, watched a ship ghosting towards them, still wreathed in smoke. She was so close they could read her name, 'Goliath', and she was between them and the beach, in water so green it seemed that she must strike at any moment.

"Open those ports." Brueys ran to the rail, bellowing his orders. "Fire as you bear. Haste. Haste!"

His words were lost in the explosion from 'Goliath's' broadside as she came abeam. It was a sensation Nick had never known before, because the British ship's guns had been double shotted, and they were aimed into the hull of the Frenchman, not at the decks or the spars. The entire enormous hull trembled as if seized and shaken by a gigantic hand. The deck shuddered as if every timber had been torn loose. He found himself lying on the wood, his ears reverberating with screaming men and shattering timber, and with the explosion of

Brueys' reply. And with Caroline, screeching into his ears as she clung to his arm, her hat gone and her hair scattered.

"Below," Brueys bawled at him. "Get below."

He shook his head. They were probably safer here. He rose to his knees, peered into the smoke which whirled around him. 'Goliath' had gone, but now in her place there came another, 'Zealous', and another nostril strangling, belly tearing explosion to send him once again tumbling to the deck.

He lost track of time. He remembered that it had been five o'clock when the first English ship had opened fire. And it had been dusk when she had reached 'L'Orion'. Now it was dark, and still ship after ship of the English ranged by, hurling steel into Frenchman after Frenchman. And still the French replied, whenever their gunners saw a target. And still the smoke swirled and the ship trembled and the senses reeled. Carrie huddled on the deck beneath the gunwale, unable to move, knees drawn up. But for her wide, staring eyes he thought she must be dead. There was no question of walking up and down this quarterdeck, as he had done with Andrew Douglas at the Battle of the First of June. This was a duel with cannon at point blank range, a seething hell from which there was no escape and no respite.

"Admiral. Admiral." An officer, hat gone, uniform torn, crawling across the deck. "This is a slaughter. Admiral—we must strike. Admiral."

His voice choked. Nick regained his feet for the seventeenth time, joined him, felt another gust of hot air, realised that miraculously he was unhurt, but that Brueys was no more. His body had been almost cut in two by flying shot, and he lay in a pool of already stagnant blood; his captain lay beside him. How long had they lain there, not twelve feet away, separated from their men by the smoke and the noise and, now, the pall of death?

"My God," said the officer. "What to do? What to do?" His head jerked. "My God."

"Fire," someone screamed from below them. A seaman staggered up the shattered steps, holding on to the balustrade. "The ship burns, Admiral. Admiral?"

He stared at Brueys' body.

Another officer pounded up the steps. "The ship is on fire. We must abandon."

Another set of sails drifted alongside; the wind had by now fallen almost entirely. The first officer slowly straightened and said, half to himself, "I am in command."

"Then give the order, Jean," shouted his junior. "We must abandon."

"The flagship? No, no."

"But . . ."

"There is your enemy," shouted Jean, hand outflung. "There is your task. Serve your guns. Sink me that Englishman." He nearly drove them from the deck. "Boy?"

Casabianca knelt beside his father's body. The boy too had lost his hat, and there was blood on his jacket.

"Oh, God," Caroline moaned. "Oh, God." She knelt. "Oh, God," her voice rose to a shriek as she saw the flames licking upwards out of the shattered hatch in the waist of the ship, surrounding the mainmast with glowing light.

'L'Orion' trembled as her broadside once again exploded. Nick watched Casabianca who was weeping as he gazed at the shattered remains of his father. Nick stood above the boy, touched him on the shoulder. "He will be remembered," he shouted, his voice hoarse. "Now we must leave."

The boy raised his head. "Leave? He would not have me leave, Mr. Minnett."

"He would not have you die, unnecessarily," Nick protested. And then further speech was cut short as 'L'Orion' herself exploded.

14

The whole evening seemed to split into kaleidoscopic light, the deck opened up, throwing those on it backwards. Nick found himself in the water, arms and legs moving instinctively, brain swimming. Despite the light wind, the water was seething as if a gale were blowing. He could see nothing, save glowing fragments of wood splashing into the water around him with enormous hisses; one dropped on his head and he sank beneath the surface, before struggling back to gain his breath.

'L'Orion' had disappeared. And so, for the moment, had the sound of battle. It had not been mere deafness. So overwhelming had the explosion been that even combatants well removed from the centre had been stunned into silence. But now noise began to seep back into the darkness. Cries, first of all, screams for help, shouts of men who clung to burning pieces of wreckage. Then a cannon shot startled the night, and this was followed by a broadside, as the battle recommenced.

Nick began swimming away from the still-anchored French line, towards the ghosting shape of an English man-of-war he could see not a hundred yards away. And then realised that one of the screams was very close at hand, at the same moment as he remembered that Carrie had been holding his arm when the explosion had commenced. He turned on his back, kicking off his shoes to take some of the weight from his feet.

"Carrie," he shouted. "Carrie."

"Nick. Oh, Nicky." She was not twenty feet away, golden hair plastered to her face, breath coming in great gasps, but to some extent better supported than he was, by air trapped under her skirt. "What happened?"

"The fire reached the magazine."

"God, my ears are singing. Nick, help me."

He reached for her, insensibly ducked both their faces into the water as the ship for which he had been making loosed a broadside, filling the air above their heads with flying steel.

Carrie began to scream, and he slapped her face. "That won't help. Come on. We'll make the shore, if we don't make that ship."

"Oh, God," she gasped. "Oh, God." Her mouth filled with water, and she spluttered.

"Hush," he begged. For now he could hear sound. Rowlocks grating. Someone had lowered a boat.

"Over here," he shouted. "Over here."

"Who calls?" The voice spoke English. He wanted to scream himself, with relief.

"Nicholas Minnett," he shouted. "Over here."

Oars splashed, and the boat approached. Nick waved his arm, while supporting Carrie with the other. She was by now apparently incapable of movement. Around them the night continued to reverberate with explosions accompanied by searing light.

"Mr. Minnett?" Hands reached down to drag them on board and deposit them, dripping and shaking, into the bottom of the boat, while the lieutenant peered at them. "The word is that you were kidnapped, from Naples."

"Quite true," Nick agreed. "To accompany this expedition. It has taken you some time to catch up with us."

"Give way," the officer called. "Give way. Indeed, sir, we had despaired of regaining you at all. But the admiral will be pleased, sir. Pleased indeed, should he survive."

"Eh?" Nick sat up, allowing Caroline's head to bump on the

boat's timbers; water drained from her hair into the bilges. "Nelson is hurt?"

"Grievously wounded, sir."

"How do you know?"

"Why, sir, we are from 'Vanguard'." The boat was at this moment pulling into the side of the flagship, and men were swarming down the accommodation ladder to assist them on board. "We have Nicholas Minnett," the lieutenant called.

Another officer peered at Nick as he climbed into the gangway; Caroline was being hoisted up in a basket; swinging from side to side as 'Vanguard' once again exploded in a broadside.

"Mr. Minnett? Edward Berry. The admiral's flag captain. My compliments, sir."

"Glad to be aboard, Mr. Berry. But I have heard ill news of the admiral."

"Wounded, sir. But not seriously."

"Thank God for that. This is a great victory."

Berry laughed, and slapped him on the shoulder. He had lost his hat, and his fair hair was tousled and streaked with powder, as was his face. "A victory, sir? It is an annihilation. Bonaparte is done, lost in Egypt."

ii

An incredible thought. But nonetheless it was true. Of the French fleet only one seventy-four escaped the slaughter in Aboukir Bay, and a few days later that fell a victim to a cruising British man-of-war. The fleet had been destroyed exactly as Nelson had claimed it would be.

"It is a start, Mr. Minnett." They walked the poop deck together. "There remains the Channel fleet." He spoke seriously, seeming to suffer no ill effects from his wound. It had indeed not been as dangerous as had first been supposed; a flying piece of steel had ripped across his forehead, leaving a flap of skin that had fallen over his remaining eye, which, combined with the pain and the flooding blood, had made him suppose he had been totally blinded. Now the

172

wound was dressed, and in the voyage from Egypt he had regained his strength and his composure.

He had also regained his confidence. And his ambition. "For you'll admit, Mr. Minnett," he said, "there has been no victory like that in British naval history. You were at the Glorious First of June, sir. Seven ships struck or were sunk. Howe got a peerage. Rodney did no better at the Saintes, and he also received a peerage. Now, sir, what do you think?"

"You shall have your peerage, Admiral," Nick promised. "There can be no doubt about that."

"There is no money, there is the trouble," the admiral said. "No patronage behind me. Oh, Prince William was kind enough to witness my wedding, but we were scarce more than lads, then."

"Patronage will not be necessary," Nick said. "After a victory such as this. Believe me."

"Emma would be so pleased," he said, turning once again, and stopping, for the fleet was entering the Bay of Naples. "Viscount Nelson. Will that be it, do you think?"

"I should think so," Nick said, biting back the question which automatically came to his lips, as to whether Fanny would not also be so happy.

"You'll have a word with Mr. Pitt? I know he is a friend of yours. We shall go over the plan again, Mr. Minnett. It was risky, no doubt. But it worked. A man must take risks, sir, if he is to win, well. They say, sir, that the fleet must remain in being and that it is unseamanlike to hazard a command. And that is true, Mr. Minnett, where the enemy remains to be fought. But surely sir, were there ever a climactic battle, the side which retained but a single ship, providing every one of the enemy was sunk, would rule the seas to at least the same extent as the side with a superiority of say, twenty to ten in capital ships."

"More so," Nick agreed. "Believe me, Admiral, I am quite lost in admiration. The nation will be lost in admiration. Why, the world."

"The world." Nelson moved to the rail, gazed at the swarm of small boats already putting out to greet them; he had sent one of his frigates ahead to relay the news of his triumph. "There is fame. And at the end of it all, what has a man got, but the fame of his name?"

Nick left him standing there, went down the companion ladder to the cabin given Caroline and himself for the voyage. "We are coming into the harbour." He closed the door behind him.

"Nicky." She had remained in her bed for most of the journey; in the beginning she had been suffering from shock, as had he, and then the seas had been high. But there was nothing the matter with her now, as she sat up to hold his face and kiss his lips. "And then home. Say we'll be going home."

"Aye, well . . . you'd best get dressed."

"In these rags?" she complained. "I shall be the laughing stock of all Italy."

"Once we are ashore we shall find you some proper clothing, I promise." He sat on the bed, watched her brush her hair. A time to think, very deeply. About her. But all he wanted to do was think about Bonaparte and his army of veterans, about Junot and Murat and Berthier and Lannes. They were like a right arm, strong and valiant, suddenly severed from the trunk, left to twitch spasmodically until it finally drained of blood. As an Englishman, as an enemy of all things French, he should be throwing his hat in the air and shouting for joy. But in all her armies, did Great Britain possess so much talent as had been contained in that one small force? And could any country, anywhere, lay claim to a general with so much ambition for mankind, so many ideas on how the quality of life could be improved, as Bonaparte. He could not help but compare him with Nelson. He thought that as a fighting seaman Nelson possessed perhaps even more talent, even more genius, than did Napoleon as a fighting soldier. But there it ended. Nelson sought only fame. Napoleon sought that, obviously, as he was a human being. But he sought it on a scale which made Nelson's dreams of a peerage puerile.

And there was not the end of his brooding. Lost in that endless desert with that dwindling army was Lorna Szen. Another enemy. A woman who had said quite openly that were it in the cause of Ireland she would slip a knife into his ribs without hesitation. And yet a woman whose laughing face and utterly uninhibited body filled his

174

mind, a woman who he knew had but to beckon, and he would again follow her down whichever dark alleyway she led.

"Nicky." Caroline sat beside him, brush still in hand. "You can look more serious than any man I know."

"Aye, well, I have a great deal to be serious about. I hear the cheers. I'd best get back up. You'll dress and join me."

"Nicky." She held his arm, bit her lip. She did not dare ask for the blanket reassurance she sought. But she was the greatest of all his problems. He could not have expected even Anne to have stayed so close, so loyal, as had his wife over these past few weeks. But then, she had placed him in Bonaparte's power in the first place. Where did that crime cease, and her apparent loyalty begin?

"Let us get ashore, Carrie, and then we can think, and talk. About the future."

He freed himself, climbed the ladder, watched the royal barge come alongside; the entire waterfront was decked in flags, and the cheers of the populace as well as the salute from the guns on the castle came booming across the water.

Emma Hamilton was first through the gangway, skirts held in her left hand, to be released as she stared at Nelson, her mouth slowly opening. "Horatio?" she whispered. "Horatio? My God." Her voice rose to a scream. "Horatio, what have they done to you?" Her knees gave way, and she fell to the deck in a dead faint.

iii

"Good evening, Mr. Minnett." Eric hovered, looking suspiciously down the sloping street behind his master. He clearly felt that whenever Nick went abroad in Naples he was in some risk of not returning. "A very good evening, Eric." Nick took off his hat; he wore no coat in this overheated climate. "They have found us a passage. We shall leave next week."

"For England, sir? Oh, thank God."

"And I will say amen to that." Nick's heels clicked on the wooden boards as he climbed the stairs. "Lady Minnett at home?"

"Oh, yes, sir." Eric cleared his throat, and Nick paused to look back at him. The blunt features were red with embarrassment.

"What is the trouble?"

"If I could have a word, sir."

Nick frowned at him, then nodded, came back down the stairs, and turned into the library. Or the best thing the house had to a library—it was nearer to a study. But the hotel had been selected by the Queen herself, and chosen for its nearness to the royal palace rather than its elegance or its appointments. On the other hand, poor Maria Carolina, if her principal rival was effectively disposed of—for Emma had dropped even the slightest pretext, now, and spent her entire time with Nelson—had no chance against the constant, and constantly loving, presence of Caroline. He was indeed no nearer to solving his problem, and had welcomed the delay, irritating though it was, in finding a passage home. There had been no letter from Anne. He could not reasonably have expected any. He had intended to write to her the moment he settled in here, and been kidnapped before he could do anything. News of his disappearance had certainly been returned to England, but what was she to do then? He had despatched a letter, to her as well as to his mother and Turnbull, informing them of his safe return, but of course there had not been time for a reply; indeed he had suggested that they need not bother to reply, as he would be on his way home in a week or so anyway.

Yet the fact remained that it was September 1798, and he had last seen Anne in December 1797. Ten months of separation. The longest ever. He could still dream of her, could still awake sweating with the suggestion of her in his arms. But after their parting, he did not know whether she would ever be in his arms again.

And Carrie was now on the way to becoming irrevocable. She had played a part in his kidnapping. Perhaps that had been cancelled by the part she had wished to play in his escape, not that she had actually done anything at all. But she had been his wife in every possible way during the month they had lived in Naples; it was not possible to share a house with Carrie and not a bed, and it was not possible to share a bed with Carrie and not share her body as well. She remained occasionally petulant, perpetually extravagant. Her treatment of inferiors angered him as much as ever in the past. Yet was she a faithful and passionate wife. All of which counted for nothing when compared with the original cause of their separation. But to return to England with her *as* his wife would completely change the situation.

On the other hand, could he be so churlish as to drive her away again, now?

"Well?" He turned, his back to the rows of leatherbound books.

Eric closed the door behind him. He seemed, if anything, more embarrassed than ever; his face was crimson. "I do not know if I dare, sir."

"For God's sake, man. How long have you been in my service?"

"Why, sir, ten years."

"And you dare not speak your mind? Anyway, having started, you had best continue."

"Yes, sir." Eric's face became frozen. "Lady Caroline, sir."

Nick's frown gathered once more. "Yes?"

"Well, sir . . ." Eric shifted his feet. "It began three weeks ago, sir. Five days after your return from Egypt."

"Eh? What began?"

"Well, sir . . ." Eric shifted his feet some more. "It was the night of the great ball, you may remember, sir, given by the Queen to celebrate your safe return."

"Yes. I remember."

Eric cleared his throat. "You had enjoyed yourself, sir."

"I was drunk, if that is what you are trying to say, Eric."

"Yes, sir. And so you went to bed, and thus to sleep. Lady Caroline, sir . . . well, sir, she did not."

Nick sat down. "You are confusing me, Eric. So my wife did not sleep. I do not see what concern it is of yours. Or even how you know of it."

"Well, sir . . ." Eric's feet did another scatter across the floor. "She saw that you were sound asleep, sir, then she left the house."

"Eh?"

"This was reported to me by one of the servants, sir. It seems she was gone for two hours, returning shortly before dawn."

"My God. And you have waited this long to tell me of it?"

"Well, sir, it is so good to see you together again, sir, to see how much she loves you, sir . . ."

"Loves me? And she is keeping midnight trysts?"

"Ah, well, sir, who was to know with whom she met? Thus I said nothing, sir, but decided to wait and see."

"Eric, you must have been taking lessons from Castets. So, what did you discover?"

"Three nights ago, sir, Lady Caroline left the house again."

Nick scratched his chin. "Last Wednesday . . . why, we were early to bed."

"And you slept very heavily, sir."

"Indeed I did. I put it down to the heat. Or that toddy you made for my nightcap."

Eric cleared his throat. "Lady Caroline made the toddy that night, sir."

"My God." What a fool he had once again been, where she was concerned.

"Yes, sir. Observing this, sir, I remained awake, and sir, once again she left the house, after being abed some two hours. This time I followed her, sir."

"And?"

"She met three men, sir."

"*Three* men?" Nick shouted.

Eric's complexion again glowed. "This was no lovers' tryst, sir. Of that I am sure. They remained on the street, and talked, nothing more. But for some time. It was impossible for me to approach closely without being seen, and so I could not hear what was discussed. But it was an animated, at times vehement conversation. Then, sir, when she turned to leave them, she spoke more loudly than before, sir."

"And you heard what was said?"

"Yes, sir. She said, 'Until Saturday, then'. Tonight, sir."

iv

"Your drink." Caroline wore a pale blue negligee, which clouded at breast and shoulder to reveal the thrusting white beneath. "I made it myself."

178

Nick had already undressed; in Naples he wore no nightshirt, and had even folded back the covers on the bed. "Why, that's very kind of you, Carrie. You should not have gone to the trouble. Eric would have looked after it."

She placed the cup between his hands, sat beside him on the bed, leaned forward to kiss him on the mouth, slowly. "I want to do it. I want to be a good wife to you, Nicky. I am trying so hard. Will you not let bygones be bygones?"

He put down the cup, squeezed her against him. She was a magnificent woman. Even her evil was on a magnificent scale. He wondered what she would do if he closed his fingers on her throat and threatened to kill her. He wondered what she would look like, as he squeezed the life from her body. She would look magnificent even then. "You have not taken your drink," she whispered, scraping her silk clad nipples over his chest.

"I'd rather make love to you first, Carrie." He dragged his fingers up her back, taking the material with it; she half rose to release it from beneath her, so that soon enough he found himself on bare flesh.

"Oh, Nicky. You do love me. After all."

"You are a woman difficult not to love," he admitted.

"And you will let me come home with you, Nicky. I should like that so much. I promise I won't waste money, Nick. I promise I won't ever say a rude word to Mistress Yealm. I'll never interfere, Nick."

He rolled her on her back, smoothed golden hair from her forehead. Her nightdress was rolled round her waist, and her legs enveloped him, her groin working against his, pubic hair mingling with his.

"Oh, Nicky," she whispered. "Oh, Nicky. I do love you so."

And strangely, he did not doubt that for a moment. But love, to Carrie, was a weapon, to be used as well or as badly as everything else.

"As I love you, Carrie," he whispered, and thrust. And again, and again. To lie across her breast, and inhale her hair. And then to sigh, and close his eyes. "As I love you."

She lay beneath him for some seconds. "Nicky," she said at last. "You haven't taken your drink. Nicky."

For reply he gave a snore.

"Nicky," she said again, more loudly.

He sighed, and shifted his position, slightly, so that his weight no longer trapped her.

Another brief hesitation, then she pushed him aside, rolling him on his back. He gave a snuffle, and a snore, kept his eyes shut, his face relaxed. And heard the bed creak as she left.

He could just hear; she was quiet about her movements. But the privy door opened and closed, and opened again. There came a splash of water from the basin in the bedroom. An occasional rustle as she dressed. And then her scent close to him; she was standing above the bed, looking down. Then the very soft thud of the bedroom door, closing.

Here was the moment of risk. Were she a conspirator born she would now reopen the door, and catch him as he sat up. He had to continue to lie still for several minutes. And then to act with haste. His clothes had been discarded in such a fashion as to make them simple to pull on. Only his boots wasted a moment. He had already primed two pistols, to thrust into the pockets of his greatcoat. He hurried down the stairs. The front door was shut, the hallway quiet. But the bolts were open.

Gently he pulled back the door, stepped into the warm night air, stopped to watch the empty street, to listen for the faint sound of feet.

A shadow materialised out of the darkness, and Eric stood beside him. "That way, Mr. Minnett," he said. "May I come with you, sir?"

"No. You have but to sound the alarm should I not be back by dawn. And thanks, old fellow."

"Then at least take this, Mr. Minnett." He thrust a heavy cudgel into his master's hand. "That will turn a sword thrust, and you have no sword."

"I have no knowledge of them, and that is a fact. My thanks, Eric. I'll be back."

He ran down the steps, hastened into the street Eric had indicated, stopped to gaze along the length. There was a moon, being chased by high cloud, which meant that the street alternated in

180

shadow and brilliant light, left the very stones seeming to move. But there was someone moving, perhaps four hundred yards away. Her cloak swung as she made her way along, deliberately rather than in haste.

And the uncertain light now became a help. He could hurry, and close the gap between them, with little risk of her being aware of it.

He followed her down a succession of side streets, close now, concentrating on the chase. And nothing else? Surprisingly not, he realised. He possessed that rare ability to concentrate utterly on what he was doing. He would neither condemn nor forgive, until this matter was brought to a conclusion. But in his heart he knew that forgiveness, yet another forgiveness, was a remote possibility.

Caroline stopped at a door set in a wall. The wall itself was only seven feet high, and therefore clearly enclosed a garden rather than forming part of a house. Nick waited on the far side of the street, while she knocked, three light and two hard blows. Almost immediately the gate swung in, and she stepped through. He could not tell who had admitted her. Was this, then, her lover? Or was it something more sinister? There could be no going back until he found out. And the wall was within his scope.

He waited for two minutes, counting the seconds, then crossed the street, took a deep breath, ran at the wall and jumped. He got his hands over the top, and after a brief kick pulled his body up behind, swinging his right leg over to sit astride, to gaze down into a darkened garden, some fifty feet from the house itself, and at a group of people, gazing up at him.

"There is the scoundrel," said the unmistakable voice of Lord George Moncey.

15

"The man himself," Moncey said. "Carrie, my congratulations."

"Nick," Caroline screamed. "Oh, Nicky."

She was only one of half a dozen people beneath him, but it never occurred to him to drop back on to the street; he was too angry. With a roar of rage he dropped into a flower bed, just as a pistol was presented and fired. The flash of light half blinded him, but the ball merely struck the wall behind him, crunching into the stone.

He regained his balance, at the same time freeing the cudgel from his belt, and faced them.

And another pistol, presented by one of the men.

"No," Caroline screamed, running forward.

"She's right," snapped one of the men. "You'll alert the watch."

"Aye," Moncey said. "We'll settle this with swords."

"Nick," Carrie said, standing immediately in front of him. "I thought you were asleep."

"So I understand," he said.

"Get aside, woman." One of the men seized her shoulder and bundled her to one side: she lost her balance, tripped, and fell.

Nick faced Moncey, who had drawn his sword, and now advanced across the path separating the flower beds. Once before he had drawn on Nick, but then Pierre de Benoît had been standing near, to

182

supply him with a weapon. As Moncey remembered. He smiled. "This time, dear brother-in-law, this time."

Nick brought up the cudgel, swung it from side to side in desperate blows, driving Moncey back. But the sword point, flickering to and fro, prevented his advance, and a cry from Caroline, still sitting in a rose bush, warned to him only just in time to avoid a knife thrust from behind him. Stumbling back against the garden wall, he realised that his life might indeed be in danger.

And then he remembered his pistols. He stuffed the cudgel into his belt, thrust his hands into the pockets of his coat, and brought out the two guns. The five attackers hesitated.

"Two of you," he said. "At the least."

A thud came on the door leading to the street. "Mr. Minnett? Mr. Minnett?" Eric. Oh, faithful Eric, even to the point of disobeying an order. "I have the guard, Mr. Minnett."

Nick smiled at them. "All of you, gentlemen. We shall have a silken halter for you, George."

"You'll not see it. Timothy, shoot him down," Moncey commanded, and the Irishman raised his pistol.

Nick levelled his own; he would match any man in the world with a pistol. At the same time he sidestepped to reach the bolted gate.

The pistols exploded together; flashing in the darkness. Timothy gave a shriek and fell backwards; where his bullet went Nick had no idea. He dropped the used pistol, transferred the other to his right hand, and seized the bolt with his left.

"Cut him down," Moncey shrieked. " 'Tis only one man."

They surged forward again, and Nick fired again. There was another scream of pain, and a man dropped to his knees. Then the bolt was pulled, and the swinging door caught Nick in the back. He fell forward, and Eric, with the guard, rushed past him.

"Run," someone shouted.

"Come on." Moncey stopped to grasp Carrie's arm and drag her to her feet. "Hurry."

"No," she shouted. "No."

He stared at her for a moment, in total consternation. "You'd stay?"

"Seize that man," Nick commanded. "Take him alive."

The three men of the guard moved forward, and Carrie seized her moment to pull herself free. She stumbled across the garden and into their arms.

"Nick," she screamed. "Do not let him take me, Nick."

Moncey drew a pistol. "Faithless wretch," he shouted, and fired. Caroline gave a moan and fell to the ground.

ii

For a moment even Moncey seemed stunned by what he had done. The echoing report of the pistol shot followed its predecessors into the night. Then he turned and ran into the darkness of the garden, followed by those of his companions who could still move.

The guards stood irresolute; Eric remained close to Nick. But Nick was already thrusting them aside, to reach Caroline.

She lay on her back, half in and half out of a flower bed, golden hair sinking into the recently watered soil. Her body was twisted at an unnatural angle, and she gasped rather than breathed. "Nick," she whispered. "Oh, Nicky."

"Carrie." He tore open her cloak, dug his fingers into the bodice of her gown—the material was only lawn, and tore readily enough—and checked in horror at the blood which came welling out of that perfect valley to smother his fingers.

"Eric," he snapped. "Fetch a surgeon. Haste, Man."

"Oh, Nicky." Her fingers closed on his arm. "It hurts so."

"Aye, well, there is help coming." He folded the torn material back into place; he could not bear to look at that tortured flesh. It had lain against his, uncovered, only an hour before. But now the white material was itself pink.

"Nick," she whispered. "Listen to me, Nick, he is mad—utterly demented, with his hatred of you."

"Aye. But to shoot his own sister . . ."

"Nick, I swear, I meant you no harm. He was here, seeking me, seeking means of harming England, of harming you. And when he sent his messengers, Nick, I had to attend his meeting, for fear of something desperate befalling you. He wanted me to bring you to a secret place, Nick, where he could murder you. And I refused, Nick. I swear. I refused the first time, and I was going to refuse again tonight."

"Only I came anyway," he said. "Now hush, sweetheart. You have not the strength to talk."

"Strength," she muttered. Blood rolled down her chin. "I have no strength at all, Nick. Nicky, say you forgive me."

"I forgive you, Carrie."

She smiled at him. "You are too good to me, Nick. But we had a good time, in Egypt. And in Naples. Say we had a good time, together, Nick."

"We had a good time, together, Carrie."

"Nick." Suddenly her fingers ate into his arm. "Nick, say you love me, Nick."

He was holding her so close her head was against his cheek. "I love you, Carrie," he said.

"Oh, Nicky," she whispered.

He held her close, her cheek against his, wondering at the coldness of the Naples night. But he had spoken no more than the truth. In a strange way he had loved this woman, even while she had been tormenting him, screaming at him, throwing things at him. She possessed a vitality which was rare, and perhaps she had spoken no more than the truth when she had claimed it was her vitality which had made her sometimes wish to harm him.

The garden door banged again, and he was aware of feet around him. A man knelt beside him, gently lifted one of Caroline's arms.

"But signor," he said. "This woman is dead."

iii

Slowly Nick lowered Caroline to the ground. Equally slowly he then stood up. He was aware of no emotion, save anger. His brain seemed to be consumed by a white hot heat, which eliminated pity,

185

sorrow, grief. These things lurked, at the back of his consciousness. They had nothing to do with the present, but were a promise for the future.

"Where is Moncey?" He did not recognise his own voice.

"They fled, signor," said the sergeant of the guard. "But we have two of them. One is dead, the other sore wounded. We must get him to a surgeon."

"Horses," Nick said. "I must have horses."

"It will take time, signor. They had horses. We have heard their hooves."

"They can be tracked," Nick said. "Get horses. Eric . . ."

"It is but a short ride to the frontier, signor," the sergeant protested. "We will not catch them now."

"But we will catch them," Nick said. "Beyond the frontier. Horses."

"We cannot cross the frontier, signor," the sergeant said. "There is nothing we can do, about them, now."

"Nothing?" Nick shouted. "Those men have just murdered my wife."

"And one is dead, signor. The other will surely hang. There is vengeance enough."

"Vengeance," Nick said. "What do you know of vengeance, signor? If you will not accompany me, I shall go by myself. Eric. Get back to the hotel and saddle two horses."

"Signor," the sergeant said. "You will be killed."

"That is no concern of yours."

"It is my concern, signor," the sergeant said. "Your safety is my charge, given me by Her Majesty herself. If necessary, I will place you under arrest."

Nick hesitated, looking down at the silent body of his wife. But already the insensate anger was passing. He knew they were right. Even supposing it was possible to track Moncey and his companions now, for him to enter French territory would be to risk at the least a new imprisonment. And this time all those who would be his friends were lost in Egypt. The directors would be pleased about that. They would have no compunction about dealing with Nick Minnett. And that would accomplish nothing. Whereas the world was not so large that he would not again find George Moncey, somewhere, sometime.

"Signor?" The guard sergeant was anxious.

"You are a man of sense, sergeant. I shall commend you to your mistress." He stooped, lifted Caroline into his arms, straightened. "When I have buried my wife."

16

"Deal me one." Nick Minnett did not even look at his hole card, left the seven of spades lying carelessly on top of it, snapped his fingers. "And bring me a drink, for God's sake."

George Brummel licked his lips, slid the card across the table, hesitated, and then turned his attention to the player on Nick's left. Some of the tension left the air in the crowded room; it would return as the play came round. Even those, like Paul de Lancey or Lord Melville, who had known Nick, and played cards with him over a great many years, had never seen anything like this.

The waiter stood at his elbow, with a tray. Nick took the glass of port, drained it, took another and set it beside him. Brummell faced him, licking his lips. There were seventy pounds in notes lying on the table, in front of Nick alone.

"Well?"

Nick looked at his hole card for the first time, tossed the six of hearts on top of the seven, then turned over the card he had been dealt, added the three of clubs.

Brummell allowed a long sigh of relief. "Sixteen. Now you have given away your hand, Nick."

Nick's smile was cold. "But I have not yet ceased to play, Beau."

He placed ten pounds beside the already enormous pile of coin and currency. "Deal."

A gasp went round the onlookers. They had all abandoned the game now, just to watch this particular hand, to watch Nick drink, as he was again doing.

Brummell licked his lips, glanced at the anxious faces to either side, slid the card across the table. Nick turned it over, placed the four of hearts with the others.

Once again Brummell sighed. "Twenty. You have the fortune of the devil, Nick. A strong hand. We must see what we can do." He studied his own two cards. "We shall see."

"I beg your pardon, Beau," Nick said. "I am entitled to try for five."

"With twenty already there?" Castlereagh shouted. "You are demented, Nick."

"Or drunk," someone said.

"Of course I am drunk," Nick acknowledged. "Why should a gentleman not be drunk?" He thrust ten pounds into the pot. "Deal."

"Nick," Paul de Lancey whispered. "You cannot."

"I have," Nick pointed out. "Well, Beau?"

Brummell mopped his forehead with a silk handkerchief.

Nick smiled at him. "And I am not so drunk, Beau. No ace has yet appeared this round. I would say the odds were at worst even."

Brummell slid the card forward, slowly. Nick turned over the nine of spades.

"Ha ha," Brummell shouted. "Ha ha ha ha. You risked too much, Nick. Oh, it was a crazy thing."

"I still think the odds were as good as any," Nick said. He pushed back his chair, stood up, lost his balance, and sat down again.

"Home, Nick," Paul said. "It is late."

"I'll help you." Castlereagh took Nick's other arm, got him to his feet. "Nick, Nick," he said, as between them they moved towards the door, attracting curious glances from the other tables, bringing the hubbub of conversation to a temporary halt. "Billy worries about you. And none of us can understand. You were estranged."

Nick glanced at him. He did not understand himself. His anger was too deep inside him, too consuming. It seemed to embrace all mankind, but with himself as the centre, and George Moncey as the ultimate objective. She had been his wife, and she had been shot down in front of him. And he had done nothing about it. He had been unable to do anything about it, then. That did not alter the fact.

"You have not been down to Lyme Regis," Castlereagh said. "There is your mistake."

They were descending the stairs, slowly. Each step seemed to rise and fall beneath their feet, and the two men held his arms the more tightly.

"Bob is right," Paul said. "You have been home two months now, and in that time you have done nothing but drink and gamble away vast sums on the most irresponsible wagers. You need a rest. A week, a night, with Anne . . ."

"God damn you for an insolent rogue," Nick said, and shrugged himself free. He lost his balance for a moment, gripped the bannisters. "And you, Castlereagh. Leave me be. Leave my life be. Get out of my sight. Clear off. Eric . . ."

Eric waited with his hat and cloak; the February air was chill. Castlereagh and Paul stood together, gazing at him.

"Nick," Castlereagh said. "If we interfere, it is because we love you so."

Nick hesitated, in the doorway. And sighed. "Forgive me, Bob. But leave me alone. I beg of you." The doors were open, and he was in the fresh air, inhaling deeply. And swaying. Eric caught his elbow, guided him down the steps into the waiting phaeton. Nick sank into the seat.

"Did you win, sir?" Eric asked, settling the rug around him.

Nick gave a brief laugh. "I made Mr. Brummell very happy. Poor fool."

"Yes, sir." Eric climbed up, took the reins, flicked the whip. The horse moved forward. The cold air settling on Nick's face removed some of the dizziness swinging in his head. He had no right to be angry with them. Indeed, they did only seek to save him from himself. And why was he not down in Lyme? The fact was he had written Anne, the day after his arrival in England, and received no reply. So then, she had not forgiven him. Or she had found another lover. Then what of his children? But he did not wish to think about anything, save that so vital body, lying motionless at his feet. And that tall, arrogant figure holding the smoking pistol. There was thought enough to consume a man's mind. There was all he had room for, now.

The phaeton rolled into the yard of the Minnett house; it was two in the morning, but the lights still burned. They waited for the master to come home, as Priscilla Minnett waited in her bed, no doubt still awake, for her son to return to himself. What did it require? An act of will? He doubted he possessed that much will.

Eric assisted him out of the phaeton and up the stairs. Henry the butler stood in the doorway to take his hat and coat.

"Mother?"

"The mistress has retired, sir. But, ah . . . the Garthwaite person is here, sir."

"Garthwaite?" Nick almost shouted the name. "Where?"

"I put him in the library, sir. He came some hours ago, but I thought it best to have him wait. And, sir . . ."

"Later." Nick hurried down the hall, swaying from side to side, pulled open the double doors to the library. "Garthwaite."

The detective had been dozing in a chair. Now he hastily scrambled to his feet. He was a little man with remarkably sharp features. He always reminded Nick of a ferret. Seldom had a man so epitomised his profession.

"Mr. Minnett. I hope I am not disturbing you."

"You are not, Garthwaite. You can never disturb me. You'll take a glass of port?"

"Why, sir, that would be very kind, on a cold night."

"Then put a log on the fire." Nick poured two glasses, then put his own down. His head was just beginning to clear.

Garthwaite took a cut log from the box, thrust it into the dying embers, gave it a stroke, slapped his hands together, and turned to take his glass. "Your health, Mr. Minnett."

"And yours. Now tell me, man."

Garthwaite sipped. "Nothing, sir."

"Eh?"

"I have been to Seend, sir. I have spent some time there. I have spent money, sir, to suborn servants. I have obtained a look at letters, sir. And there is nothing. The Earl and Countess live in total seclusion. They receive no visitors, nor do they ever appear to leave their grounds. Their correspondence, such as it is, appears to be a matter of accounts."

"What of the boy, Alexander?"

"He is there also, sir. He is under the care of his grandmother. But, sir, no one in the village, or in the neighbourhood, has seen or heard of Lord Moncey this past year."

"Aye, well, no doubt he will not risk visiting his home. But there are other places."

"Yes, sir. He was in London, last summer. That seems clear."

Nick frowned at the man. "Last summer?"

"Aye, sir. While you were in Naples. You'll know of the Irish conspiracy."

"Yes, I know of it."

"Then you'll have heard of Lord Fitzgerald's death."

"What?" Nick sat down. "Edward Fitzgerald?"

"Yes, sir. The Duke of Leinster's heir. He had been banned from the country, as you will know, sir. As were his fellow conspirators, Lord Moncey amongst them. Yet did they come and go, clandestinely. They used Hamburg, sir, crossing the North Sea in the guise of merchants. It was on such a voyage, last summer, that Lord Fitzgerald apparently got talking with one of the female passengers . . ." Garthwaite permitted himself a smile. "You know what the Irish are like, sir."

"I know what the Irish are like, Garthwaite," Nick said. "Go on."

"Well, sir, the woman realised to whom she was speaking, and on arrival in London, sir, she went to the authorities. There already was a warrant in existence for Lord Fitzgerald, and this was served, sir, by a squad of soldiers. But Lord Fitzgerald resisted arrest, sir, with the result that he was shot, and mortally wounded. He died a week later, in prison."

"My God," Nick said.

"Indeed, sir. Nor was he alone on that occasion. There were several other men present, conspirators, and one of them was identified as Lord Moncey, for whom of course there was, and is, a warrant also. But he managed to escape. Since then, sir, he has not been seen in London. I have visited all his known haunts, and I have hawked his description through the seaports used by the Hamburg packets. I have even spoken with the captains of the packets themselves, sir, men who are sufficiently familiar with Lord Moncey. And they say he has not been on board their vessels since fleeing the country after Lord Fitzgerald's arrest. It really does seem as if he shall not be returning."

Edward Fitzgerald, dead. How the very name brought back memory. What was Lorna doing now? Marching with the dwindling French army in the Arabian desert? How odd that once he had wanted to do no more than escape them. That had been duty. Now his heart and his mind were there, with them, desperate adventurers, living their lives to the full, instead of waiting . . . for what? To avenge a dead woman?

Garthwaite cleared his throat, finished his drink, shifted his feet.

"To find him," Nick mused, "it seems we shall have to go to Hamburg."

"Sir? That would be highly dangerous."

"No doubt it would. Oh, do not worry, Garthwaite, I shall not drag you along. My thanks for your efforts. Present your account to Mr. Turnbull, if you would. But you are not dismissed. You will keep a continuing watch, on Seend, and on Harwich. He will return to England—I have no doubt about it. And when he does, I wish to be informed on the instant."

"Yes, sir. I'll wish you good night, Mr. Minnett."

"Aye." Nick remained sitting, staring at the roaring fire, feeling the heat reaching for him. Would Lorna know of her brother's death? Edward Fitzgerald, and through him, Ireland, were the only constant ideals in that will-o'-the-wisp character. For Ireland, for her brother, she had said that she would kill. And now he was dead. Another cause for hate. And yet Moncey, hardly less of a will-o'-the-wisp, flitted away to safety, time and again, leaving death and destruction behind him.

So then, Hamburg? As Garthwaite had said, it would be highly dangerous. He could hardly travel incognito, and there was no English fleet up the Elbe. And was not his mother, his sister, his brother-in-law, his friends, Billy Pitt, were they not right when they took him to task for devoting his entire life to the cause of vengeance, when there was so much more to be done?

But could he ever sleep easy again in his mind, did he not pursue his wife's murderer to the very end of the earth, if need be?

He yawned, and leaned back, and listened to the door opening behind him.

"Oh, I shall come to bed, Eric," he said. "In due course. There is no need for you to attend me."

A hand touched his hair. "It will be my pleasure, sir," Anne Yealm whispered.

ii

So then, they had all been right. Had he gone straight to Lyme, had he sought the refuge of these arms, the comfort of this body, immediately on his return to England, he would not have known such despair, and wasted so many precious minutes of his life.

He lay on his back, listened to the sounds of the awakening house. Presumably it was morning; with the heavy drapes drawn across the windows it was impossible to say. And no doubt there was a considerable debate taking place in the kitchen, as to whether or not he should be disturbed this day, and as to whether or not Eric should be replaced by a maidservant for this day.

A pleasant piece of trivia, which restored life to its proper perspective.

He breathed, and the woman moved with his chest, her head resting on his shoulder so that her hair passed his chin and tickled his mouth. Even in the darkness it seemed to glow.

She moved, nestling herself against him, fitting his thigh the

194

more securely into her groin; her left leg was thrown across his, her left hand rested on his chest. She sighed.

He smoothed her hair, ran his fingers down the flesh underneath, all the way, into the deep pit of her back, rippling with muscle from the innumerable times she had bent it to set the sails of 'Golden Rose', over the curve of her buttock, down the backs of her no less powerful thighs. She gave a long, slow shudder, undulating, and was awake as he rolled over, to stretch her on her back, to feel her legs spread as she welcomed him. What a nonsense she made of other women, of other emotions, other passions. Why should a man, possessing this, ever seek a single other pleasure, of any sort.

He felt her fingers on his own back. "You will have to come again," she said. "I was scarce awake."

"And I am spent," he said.

He felt her breath on his ear as she smiled, and then her teeth. "I am content to wait. Here."

He raised himself on his elbows, to look at her. They had not spoken last night. There had been no time for words.

"I could not come before," she said. "Harry had a croup."

"And now?"

"He is better. I have left them both with Maureen, at Windshot."

"You could have written."

Her head shook from side to side, on the pillow. "I wished to come myself, alone. I wished to know if I was still welcome."

"You? Anne?" He kissed her mouth, left his own there, for several seconds. No passion. No passion was necessary, now. "Not welcome?"

"I wished to come with you," she said. "To Naples. I lay awake and wept myself to sleep, endlessly, because I was not with you. Had I come . . ."

"You might have been involved in my danger. I am glad you did not."

"Had I come," she said, "your wife would not have died. As she would not have been in your company."

He kissed her nose. There was no face between them, this morning. "Are you not pleased—that she is dead?"

Little wrinkles gathered between her forehead. "Should I ever be pleased, to learn of death?"

There could be no questioning her honesty. She knew no way to tell a lie.

"Even that of an enemy?"

She smiled. "A rival. I have always counted her a defeated rival."

"Aye."

But she was frowning. "A shadow crossed your face, then."

"She was my wife. And she was shot down before my eyes, Anne."

"And so you must avenge her. I will not dispute that, Nick. But it cannot become your whole life. Surely you can wait for George Moncey's path once again to cross yours? And act upon it, then?"

He kissed her on the mouth, slowly. "Surely I can. I have been a fool. I am always being a fool, in following absurd notions of honour, when I should be in your arms, learning sense. Anne . . ."

There was a rap on the door, and he rolled off her, while she pulled the blanket to her neck. For the door was opening.

"Nick?" Priscilla Minnett peered into the darkness.

"I am here, Mama."

"Henry tells me . . ."

"I am also here, Mama."

"Anne, my *dear*." Priscilla Minnett seized the cord, brought the heavy drapes away from the frost encrusted windows, gazed at the bed. "It is so good to have you here. Now perhaps Nick will be himself again."

"I am myself again." Nick sat up. "Mama. Do we not make a pretty pair?"

"A pretty pair," she smiled. And then her smile became lost in the sadness of her expression. "Oh, how I wish . . ."

"Then wish no longer, Mama. I have decided. Anne and I are going to wed."

"It is hard to imagine," Priscilla Minnett remarked, looking through the windows of the downstairs parlour at the starkly pruned rose bushes, the bare trees which fringed the garden, "that within three months all that will be in bloom, a blaze of colour. That we shall walk abroad without muffs and furs and gloves. Every year I find it more and more difficult to realise that winter is but a transient period."

Lucy Minnett poured tea, passed the first cup to Anne Yealm. Anne sat very straight. Over the past year, she had supposed herself becoming friendly, almost intimate, with these two Minnett women. But now there was a great gulf opening between them again.

"Cream, Anne," Lucy suggested.

Priscilla Minnett stirred. "One sees things differently, in the spring. I often find that decisions, taken in winter, need revision, when the weather becomes warm and bright." She gave a bright smile. "It is the same with human emotions. When dear Percy died, I wished to die also. I wished to do all manner of things. I certainly wished to leave this house, because I knew that everything in it would constantly remind me of him. But now, you know, I am grateful for the memories. They are no longer painful to me."

Anne sipped her tea. She did not see why she should make saying what apparently had to be said any the easier. She was, in fact, keeping her temper under control with difficulty. Priscilla Minnett did not dare face her son on such a matter. She was seeking the easy way.

"It is one of Nick's characteristics," Lucy said, thoughtfully and apparently artlessly. "He is such a . . . a dedicated man." She had, of course, been going to say passionate, but decided it would be tactless. "He throws himself into whatever he is doing with more concentration, more determination, than any human being I have ever known. He is able to shut out all the rest of the world at whim, and dedicate himself utterly to the task in hand, to what he considers important at the moment. This is why he is so very successful, at whatever he attempts, I suppose. But of course, it is impossible to sustain that mood all the while. He must return to the real world, from time to time. And of course, by the same token, when he returns, he suffers the most terrible moods. His spirit soars to the heights, and then drops to the depths. It is entirely natural. Will you take some more tea, Anne?"

"Thank you, Lucy." She was determined to stay calm, no matter what happened.

"And these past few months he has been terribly depressed," Priscilla Minnett said. "It is entirely understandable, of course. You understand it, Anne. To have his wife, murdered before his very eyes . . . my God, I wish to shudder at the thought of it."

But she did not.

"As Mama says," Lucy said. "It is the depths of winter in his soul, at this moment, just as it is the depths of winter here in London. But spring will soon be upon us, and everything will take on a different aspect."

Anne set down her teacup. "And then he will no longer wish to marry me," she said.

The two Minnett women stared at her.

"For that is what you are saying, Mama, Lucy. I confess I do not understand your reasoning, in this case. You are speaking as if this were a sudden decision. Would you not say that six years is a long enough time to come to a decision?"

For a moment longer Priscilla and Lucy continued to stare at her.

Then Lucy gave a smile. "No one could ever argue Nick's love for you, Anne. Our love for you. Our love for Judith and Harry. But as you say, you have loved each other, deeply and dearly, and enduringly, for six years. There has been no previous talk of marriage. So in that sense the decision must be considered a sudden one."

Anne stood up. "Nick could not marry me before, because he was married."

"And now widowed," Priscilla Minnett said. "It is all happening too fast for him. I am sure of that."

"And the wife of Nicholas Minnett must be a suitable person,"

Anne said, quietly, although she could feel the heat spots gathering in her cheeks. "As Lady Caroline was a suitable person."

Priscilla and Lucy exchanged embarrassed glances.

"Caroline was entirely *un*suitable, for Nick," Priscilla said. "We know that. I think even she knew it. But believe me, child, we are thinking equally of you. Nick's wife must bear a great burden. Socially, amongst other things. Her opportunities indeed, for sharing a love with her husband, such as you share with Nick, must necessarily be very limited."

"Unless, perhaps, she already shared such a love, madam," Anne said.

"Anne," Priscilla protested. "We have just acknowledged your love for him, and his for you."

"But you feel sure I will not be able to be his wife," Anne said. "Well, madam, you may well be right. I know only how to love him, and if that is insufficient, well, then, I will have to learn. But madam, he is the father of my children, and he is the only man I have ever loved, or will ever love. I cannot, and I will not, give up that love unless he himself wishes me to. I have lived for six years in the belief that Nick's decisions are my decisions. Last summer we had our first difference, and it may be that this is on your mind now. It was the first time I chose to make a decision in opposition to his, and I knew within a week that I had been wrong. I have told him so. If you would prevent this marriage, you must deal with him. Not with me."

Lucy and Priscilla stared at her, totally taken aback at once by her words, and by the measured way in which she had said them.

As she was perhaps herself surprised. She had known what they wanted, when they suggested an entirely feminine tea, and she had not known how she would respond. Now she felt her knees touch as her legs trembled.

Priscilla Minnett got up. "Anne, dear," she said, and reached for her hands. "You behave as if we are your enemies. And we love you as one of us, equally as we love you for the happiness you have brought to Nick. And will continue to bring to Nick. We wish only to be certain that you both sustain that happiness for all of your lives. And

199

we know, as you must know, that at this moment Nick is deeply unhappy, deeply confused, perhaps, by recent events. All we ask is patience. We do not expect you to refuse him. It is difficult to suppose anyone refusing Nick anything. We would ask only that you ask him to ask you again, in the summer. To be sure. For him to be sure. Is that too much? If you love him, if you are sure of his love and equally sure of your own, can a few months make any difference? And by then he will have quite recovered his spirits, and be the old Nick, and there can then be no doubts in any of our minds."

"There are no doubts, madam, in my mind, now."

Priscilla squeezed the strong brown fingers. "Please, Anne. Do this for me, and in the future you have but to ask."

Anne hesitated, glanced from Priscilla to Lucy, and sighed. "I will ask him to wait, madam. Until his wife has been dead a year."

iv

"The Prime Minister is waiting for you, Mr. Minnett." The secretary bowed, opened the doors to the Prime Minister's room, shutting out the distant whisper of sound which seeped upwards through the Palace of Westminster.

Nick stepped inside, and the doors closed behind him.

"Nick." Pitt seized his hands. "My God, but you look quite disgustingly healthy."

"I am feeling quite disgustingly healthy, Billy." Nick sat down. "I have spent all of last month, and quite a bit of July as well, sailing the 'Rose', lying about Lyme, lying about Windshot. In short, enjoying myself. And feel a new man for it. I do recommend it as an escape from affairs of state."

Pitt sat down, whipping the tails of his coat over his thighs as he did so. "It is merely so enjoyable for you because of the presence of Mistress Yealm. I have no such advantage."

"Then find yourself one, Billy. In any event, it is not always an unmixed blessing. Women I will never understand, if I live to be a hundred and ten. Here I am, a widower, reasonably wealthy . . ."

Pitt permitted himself a gentle cough.

"Reasonably healthy, reasonably attractive, I have always thought. And Anne has been my mistress for six years. So can you consider a better arrangement than that we should now marry? I forgot to mention that she is also the mother of my two children."

"Marriage," Pitt commented. "Now there is a serious step. It is not one I could ever consider."

"You think yourself wedded to the nation. Well, I have no intention of ever becoming wedded to my bank."

"Still, there is some difference in your stations," Pitt suggested, mildly.

"It has not affected our relationship so far." But Nick was frowning. "You think that may be it?"

"May be what?"

"Well, when I proposed the matter, she insisted we wait. For a year after Carrie's death, if you please. That I might be sure of myself."

"Ah. Well, I think she is one of the most sensible young women I have ever met."

"Rubbish. She is herself perhaps suffering from cold feet. In any event, I agreed, have spent the summer with her, and now the time is all but here. You may be my best man, Billy."

Pitt squeezed his hands. "When you marry Mistress Yealm, Nick, it will be my pleasure."

"But you did not request my presence today to listen to my domestic problems. You have news of Bonaparte?"

Pitt raised his eyebrows. "None that is of particular interest. He has retired from before Acre, massacring his prisoners, if you please."

Nick's frown deepened. "Napoleon? I cannot believe it. Indeed, I do not believe it."

"Yet it is true. And there is rumour of plague in the French ranks. You have your old friend Sydney Smith to thank for that, you know, Nick. Without his constant aid, without the support of his frigates and his bluejackets, Acre would have fallen. But now, why, I will wager to you that Egypt is going to be the greatest disaster ever suffered by any French army since Charlemagne got himself encumbered at Roncesvalles. And there will be no Rolandic legend about this one. Should you ever see Bonaparte again, it will be stepping from an English man-of-war as a prisoner."

"Hm," Nick wondered. Although it certainly seemed that his friend had this time bitten off more than he could chew. "But to massacre his prisoners. I'll not believe that, Billy. The man is too conscious of his destiny, of his place in history."

"What nonsense. He is no more than a sans culotte in uniform. Best forgotten. There are more important affairs."

"Ireland? You have raised the matter with His Majesty?"

"Um." Pitt returned behind his desk, sat down. "I have, and regret it."

"He is against Irish emancipation?"

"Against *Catholic* emancipation. Oh, not from any personal prejudice, you may believe me. I doubt the dear old soul knows such a vice. But he is riddled with constitutionalism. He swore an oath, and dreams of it nightly. I will have to work on him. It will take time. But it will be done, or my name is not William Pitt. But even that is not really first amongst our list of problems. Ah. Bob."

The door was opening, to admit Castlereagh, and remaining open, to allow several more men to enter. Nick stood up.

"You'll know Harry Addison, Nick."

"Indeed we do know each other," Addison, a short, sallow man, agreed. "It was I launched Nick on his first French adventure, as I recall."

Nick shook hands. "My third, Harry. But my first official one, to be sure."

"And Bob Canning?"

This was a very young man, who positively exuded energy, even in his handshake.

"One of our future prime ministers," Pitt said with a wink. "You may wager on it, Nick. And of course, your old friend, Lord Ratsey."

Nick hesitated before offering his hand to his rival; they had not spoken for several years.

"You've been in Naples," Ratsey said. He was not very tall,

possessed blunt features and a bristling moustache which accurately depicted his character.

"Indeed I have, my lord," Nick said.

"Expanding your business, eh?"

"I am sure there is enough for us all, my lord." Nick sat down. "Besides, I hope you will not suppose I intend Ratsey's Bank any harm. Am I not your principal shareholder?"

"Why, you . . . you impudent whippersnapper," Ratsey shouted. "I know your game, by God, sir. Buying up my shares. Calling every creditor you have who has pledged Ratsey stock. Why, sir, it is downright dishonest."

"My lord, my lord," Pitt said. "I do beg of you to keep your temper."

"Well, tell this . . . this upstart, to mind his manners."

"My offer stands, my lord," Nick said. "I merely wished you to be sure of that."

"Offer? Offer?"

"Why to purchase the entire share issue of Ratsey's Bank, at a mutually agreed price. As I indicated, oh, back in ninety-three."

"Why, you . . ."

"Gentlemen," Pitt said. "I must insist. We are here to discuss the nation's finances, not your personal rivalry. But I will admit it relieves me a great deal, Nick, to hear you talk of purchasing an entire share issue. It is at least a suggestion that the House of Minnett is solvent. But the nation, alas, is not."

"Oh, come now, Billy," Addison murmured.

"I'm afraid the facts are there," Pitt said. "Last year I asked for twenty-five millions, on the basis of trebling existing taxes. It is all gone. Subsidies to Austrians and Prussians, which are as much wasted as if I had torn up the notes. Yet must we finance continental armies, as we seem to have none of our own. And what am I to do, treble existing taxes again? Why, we shall not be able to afford a glass of port."

"Without which," Ratsey remarked, "the affairs of the nation will grind inexorably to a halt."

Pitt refused to take offence. He merely smiled. "You may depend upon it."

"So what are you proposing?" Nick inquired. "A levy of your leading bankers? Are Morton and Dudley to ride again, with their forks?"

"No," Pitt said. "I agree that would be unfair and unreasonable. We must have an atmosphere in which our trade can grow, and thus we must encourage our bankers to lend their money to their best advantage, and thus, they must have ample funds to lend. No, no, we are in a national war. Our very survival as a nation may well depend upon our victory, and therefore it is right that every man in the nation contributes his share towards our eventual victory. And contributes entirely as he is able. I have in mind a tax, a new tax, on incomes."

There was a moment's silence.

"What did you say?" Ratsey asked at last.

"We have discussed it at length." Addison took up the burden. "Supposing we imposed a ten per cent tax on all incomes. Then, you see, your labourer, with his twenty pounds a year, would pay no more than two pounds, and your Nicholas Minnett, with his . . . what exactly do you pay yourself a year, Nick?"

"Be sure that I would be supporting the cost of the war virtually single handed," Nick said. "The concept is monstrous."

"Nick," Pitt said. "It has been done before."

"A hundred years ago, when William was fighting his interminable wars. We have progressed beyond such tyranny, surely."

Pitt sighed. "Believe me, we have considered every possible other way out of our dilemma. We cannot afford to forget that we are fighting a war against a revolutionary power which does not lack support amongst our own people. Whatever we do must not only be fair, but it must be seen to be fair."

"You'll ask His Majesty for ten per cent of the royal income?"

Pitt pulled his nose. "Well, there will have to be exceptions, of course. And it would make no sense. As His Majesty in any event draws most of his funds from the civil list, it would be no more than a bookkeeping entry to take some of that back again as tax."

Nick gazed at Castlereagh. "You support this, Bob?"

"Well . . ." Castlereagh flushed. "Obviously we must discover some new means of raising money, Nick. Although I cannot for the life of me see how we can force a man to divulge his income."

"We shall appeal to patriotism, in the first instant," Pitt declared.

"And in the second?"

"Well, it will be necessary to introduce certain measures to Parliament whereby if a fellow is consistently recalcitrant . . ."

"You said just now we were *combatting* a revolution," Nick pointed out. "What you are proposing sounds very much like Robespierre and his friends expropriating aristocratic property."

"No one said anything about expropriating," Addison insisted. "But it should be possible to make a man declare his true income, and if he does not, or will not, why then, it should be possible to fine him, so that one way or another he pays his tax."

"Ye Gods," Nick said. "And I did not wish to march with Bonaparte into Turkey, because I had no interest in observing the workings of a tyranny at first hand."

"Now, Nick," Pitt said.

Nick raised his hand. "You must have money. And I assume you have already formulated your plans, and will carry it through the House, with your majority, and are thus doing Ratsey and I no more than a courtesy in informing us beforehand. Thus I cannot stop you, Billy, and you will know that I would never oppose you. But that does not mean I cannot have my say. And my say is this." He ticked off his fingers, one by one. "Firstly, a man's income is the fruits of his labour, or his grandfather's labour. Your father laboured, not only for himself, Billy, but for you. It is not unjust that you should be enabled to enjoy the fruits of his labour, as that is what he intended. Start to place a tax upon income, and you take away incentive, ambition, all the things that take a man to greatness, and the nation with him.

"In the second place, you may use your fines or your threats or your whatever, but the British are not known as a nation of tradesmen for nothing. They will find a way of concealing income. And what will be the net result? You will turn every man in this country into a criminal in the eyes of the law. And once you commit one crime,

Billy, all the others become not only easy, but downright obvious.

"Let me finish, and then I am done. Thirdly, to administer this law, to collect this paltry sum, you will be forced to create an entirely new excise department. They will make sure your eventual profit from this venture is even smaller, at once by their incompetence and by the very nature of government departments. Fourthly, and most important of all, you are placing in the hands of Parliament a weapon which could prove absolutely fatal to the prosperity of this country."

"Oh, come now, Nick," Canning protested. "We ask for but ten per cent."

Nick got up. "*You* ask for ten per cent, Bob. And you may be, as Billy says, our future prime minister. But you will not be prime minister forever. And once that law gets on our statute books, it will be there, forever. Try to imagine a James the Second, a Charles the First, for that matter, with such a law waiting for him to use."

"Those days are done," Addison declared.

"Well, then," Nick said. "Think of Cromwell. Or stay, do not wander so far into history. Think of Charlie Fox. It could happen. It will, when the King dies and the Prince inherits. Think of that, gentlemen. For the rest, my personal income last year was one hundred and seventeen thousand pounds. You are welcome to eleven thousand of that. Good day to you."

He left the room, closed the door behind him, took his hat and stick from the trembling secretary. What an odd world it was, to be sure, where a man, to fight against revolution and upheaval, must create it in his own backyard.

Eric waited with his horse, and with Eric, Garthwaite, still panting.

"Mr. Minnett. Mr. Minnett. I attended you at the bank. And they told me you were here."

Nick frowned at the little man. "And you have something for me, at last?"

"At last, sir. At last. I have come hot foot from Harwich. Lord George Moncey landed from the Hamburg packet but yesterday morning."

17

Nick peered at the man, for a moment unable to believe his ears. "Moncey, in England?"

"I swear it, sir."

"Travelling openly?"

"No, sir. He goes under the name of Broadbridge."

"Then how are you sure?"

"I know Lord George, sir. And this is undoubtedly him. Big. Harsh voice. Arrogant of manner. And accompanied by a lady, sir."

"A lady?" Nick frowned. "What lady?"

"Now that I cannot say, Mr. Minnett. An Irish lady. Soft voice, with brown hair. A rare beauty, sir, although I caught no more than a glimpse."

Nick's frown deepened. Lorna? It could not be. Surely not. Lorna was in Egypt, or Syria, dwindling in the desert with Bonaparte.

"This lady had a husband?"

"I cannot say, sir. There was just the pair. And they hired horses, sir. For Wiltshire. 'Tis not exact, I know. But Seend is in Wiltshire."

It was a year since Edward Fitzgerald's death. More, in fact. If ever the conspirators would renew their plotting, it would be now. But Lorna . . .

"This woman, did you hear her laugh? Or see her smile?"

"Oh, aye, Mr. Minnett." Garthwaite rolled his eyes. "Splendid, it was. A laugh to make a man forget he has cares."

Nick's heart gave a bound. A quite unreasonable bound. He was going to marry Anne Yealm. Her decision, her acceptance, was due in less than a month. So why did his heart start to pound at the thought, the memory, of another woman?

But to see her again. If only for a moment. To know that she was well, that she had escaped the disaster which had overtaken the French army in Egypt. To discover what had happened to Bonaparte and how, in fact, she had made her way back to Europe.

Besides, she was with George Moncey. And he had sworn vengeance on the murderer of his wife.

"Fresh horses," he snapped. "And men. Garthwaite . . ."

"I have five stout fellows, waiting only my summons, Mr. Minnett. For just this occasion."

"Then find them," Nick said. "Get them mounted and armed. Lord Moncey. How long ago did he leave Harwich?"

"Why, sir, this morning, I would assume."

"So we will be twelve hours behind. Saving that our route is more direct. Haste man. We must be in Seend by tomorrow night."

He climbed into his own saddle, and checked, his brows gathering. If Lorna was back in England, then was she also risking the law. And if he took George Moncey, must he not also take Lorna Fitzgerald? Lorna, hauled before the courts as a common felon, sentenced to death for treason? There was an impossible thought.

And one to be solved when he caught up with them. Not to act now, whether out of hatred or out of love, would be never to forgive himself, either.

"Haste, Garthwaite," he shouted. "Have your men at my house within the hour."

ii

They spent the night at Oxford, Nick and Eric sharing a room, Garthwaite and his six men sleeping downstairs. The landlord and his daughters peered at them, and served them in silence. They were too heavily armed, and too preoccupied; eight men about a desperate and violent mission. But surprisingly, Nick slept heavily. And dreamed of that unforgettable smile, those puckered lips, those silky limbs sliding over his.

And awoke in a sweat, and a haste. He roused his men, hurried them through breakfast, had them on their way once more, leaving the high land now to plunge into the lanes and hedgerows which led through the farmland of Wiltshire. It was late autumn, and the crops had been reaped; haystacks crowded the corners of the fields, and where it had stood was turned black earth. The sky was overcast, and from time to time there was drizzle, keeping people off the muddy roads, leaving the group of horsemen proceeding silently, water and mud splashing beneath their hooves.

Seend House was in a valley, and it was nearly nine, and already dark, when Nick drew rein on the rise overlooking the estate. The road divided almost immediately beneath him, one arm running round the estate and leading to the village, lost in the next shallow valley, while the left arm led directly up to huge wrought iron gates, beyond which the drive led through trees, dripping in the evening damp, already shrouded in a clinging mist.

"We'll divide," Nick decided. "Eric, you'll accompany me, with two of your men, Garthwaite. You take the other three and circle the building to the rear. Permit no one to leave until I have spoken with them. No one, Garthwaite."

"I understand, Mr. Minnett." Garthwaite pointed to three of his men in turn, and they rode down the hill, then turned along the road for the village.

"Keep your pistols under cover," Nick said. He touched Belair with his heels, and the stallion moved slowly down the hill; Garthwaite's little troop was already lost in the mist. This was all to the good; so long as they moved quietly the people in the house would not know they had visitors until it was too late.

The gates loomed in front of him. They were closed, and padlocked, and the ditches to either side were filled with water, but Nick never hesitated, turned his horse down the steep bank. The water rose to its haunches, soaked his boots, but did not reach his pistol holsters. Behind him, Eric's horse entered the water with a grunt, then the horses of the other two men. The horses waded along the bed of the ditch, round the stone pillars, and then Nick turned them up the slope again. It took some scrabbling, and he dismounted, digging his boots into the soft earth to tug on the reins. Belair heaved himself out with a tremendous effort and a shake, and Nick remounted.

They walked along the drive, hoofbeats almost silent in the soft earth, even the jangle of their harnesses lost in the sound of the steady drip from the trees to either side. And now they saw the house itself, candles glowing in all the downstairs windows, and most of the upper ones as well. The Earl and Countess, entertaining their banished son? Nick drew rein before the huge portico, waited for Eric and his companions to draw abreast. They dismounted together, taking their pistols from their saddle holsters as they did so. Nick climbed the steps, nodded to Eric, who pulled the great rope and sent the peal of the bell jingling through the evening.

They waited, out of the rain now; one man remained holding the bridles.

The door swung in, and a butler, liveried and wearing a wig, peered at them.

"My name is Nicholas Minnett," Nick said. "I seek Lord George Moncey."

"Lord . . . Lord . . ."

Nick presented his pistol, and the man stepped back. Nick stepped into the hall, water trickling down his boots to wet the parquet.

"Where is he?"

The man continued to gape at him. Eric stepped past him, went to the opened doors to the withdrawing room.

"Lord . . . Lord Moncey is not here," the butler managed. "And you, sir, Mr. Minnett, you are not welcome here."

"I don't doubt that," Nick agreed, and looked past him at the sound of a woman's scream. But the voice was not Lorna's.

210

"Your pardon, ma'am," Eric was saying. "We seek Lord Moncey."

Nick left the butler in the care of Garthwaite's man, joined Eric in the doorway. The withdrawing room stretched for some distance, a series of huge arches, beyond which rugs and occasional tables receded towards the windows on either side. The floor was parquet, but there were several scatter rugs. At the far end the great fireplace was a blaze of light and heat, and in front were four upholstered chairs, but only two were occupied, one by the Countess of Seend, and the other by her husband, although the Earl was now rising to his feet.

"Minnett?" he barked. "What is the meaning of this?"

Nick crossed the room, the pistol still in his hand, although he left it hanging at his side. "I am looking for your son, my lord. My lady, I apologise, but this is an affair of state."

The Countess blinked at him. She was very clearly the mother of both George and Caroline, a tall, still handsome woman, now rather stout, a face with somewhat protruding eyes and florid complexion. By contrast her husband was a thin, haggard looking man, although he also possessed the family height.

"This is an outrage, sir," he said. "An outrage. George? Why should you suppose George to be here?"

"He landed at Harwich two nights ago," Nick said. "Accompanied by a woman I suspect to be Lorna Szen. You may know her better as Lorna Fitzgerald. Edward's sister."

"And you think he would come here?"

"He hired horses, to visit Wiltshire. He would hardly have gone to Windshot. And what do I perceive, four chairs before the fire."

"Sir, you will pay for this intrusion." The Countess spoke in a low, angry voice. "And you, sir, are a bad husband, a bad son, a bad banker, and a bad man. And worst of all, a bad father. Now take your leave."

"I will not leave, my lady, until I have searched your house."

"Until you have done what?" she demanded.

"I will call my servants and have you thrown out," the Earl declared.

Nick raised his right hand, showed the pistol. "Be sure, Your Grace, that blood will be shed. As blood has already been shed. Tell me this. When last did you see your son?"

The Earl frowned at him. "Why . . ." He glanced at his wife. "It would have been last summer."

"Just before that poor Fitzgerald boy was murdered," the Countess said.

"And then he fled the country. Do you know where he went?"

"To Germany," the Earl said. "He is there now."

"He went to Italy, my lord. There to wait for my return from Egypt. I had Caroline with me."

"And you also had her shot down by a band of Italian thugs," the Countess said. "We have heard of that. And you did not even bring her body home, to be buried at Seend. You did not even come to visit us, to share our grief, to see to your son. You are scarce a man at all, Nicholas Minnett. But a fiend. Aye, a fiend in human form."

Nick kept his temper with great patience. "I did not come to see you, my lady, for a very good reason. A band of Italian thugs? Your daughter was murdered by Irish conspirators, headed by your own son."

"You are a liar, sir," the Earl shouted. "A foul tongued liar."

"And it was George who pulled the fatal trigger," Nick insisted. "He killed his own sister. Now, my lady, my lord, do you still wish to hide him?"

The Earl and Countess stared at him for a moment.

"I do not believe you." The Countess's voice was again low. "You . . . you cannot know that," the Earl said.

"I was present, my lord. She died in my arms."

Once again the Earl and the Countess exchanged glances.

"Mr. Minnett." Eric spoke in a low voice.

Nick half turned his head, and Eric pointed. They were standing between the two empty chairs; by the leg of the left hand chair there was a tiny speck of mud.

212

Nick dropped to one knee, touched it with his finger; it was still soft. His pistol came up. "I will have him, my lady. If I have to kill for it. I will have him."

The Countess moved closer to her husband. "I cannot believe he killed Caroline."

"You may believe what you will. Eric, keep them here." Nick ran into the hall, where Garthwaite's man still held the butler, who had now been joined by a maidservant; no doubt the servants had been at their supper, and had commenced to wonder at the absence of their master.

"You," Nick said. "Where is Lord Moncey?"

"Lord . . . Lord Moncey? In the . . ." She licked her lips, glanced at the butler.

"Lord Moncey is not here," the butler said.

Nick seized the girl's shoulder. "Where?"

The girl rolled her eyes. "Mr. . . . Mr. Rollins . . ."

"Be quiet, girl."

"Listen to me, old man," Nick said. "They were here. I know that. Now tell me if they are still here, or if they have left, or I shall blow your head off." He levelled the pistol.

"Mr. Rollins," screamed the girl.

"Be quiet." He was a brave fellow.

"He'll kill you, Mr. Rollins," she wailed. "In the cellar. They are in the cellar. They went downstairs at the sound of the bell."

"Leave them," Nick snapped. He ran along the hall, stopped in the doorway to the drawing room. "Come with us, Eric."

The stairs to the cellars were behind the main staircase. Here the door was closed, but not locked. This he opened, peered into the darkness. Garthwaite's man seized a candleholder from its bracket, brought it forward. Nick took the candle in one hand, his pistol in the other, slowly descended the stairs, Eric and the detective behind him.

Below him there was the wine cellar, row after row of orderly bottles. And not a sound.

"Over there, sir," Eric muttered.

Beyond the bottles there was another door, closed. Nick crossed the floor, tried the handle. The door was bolted on the inside. He gave the torch to Eric. "Hold them here. But be careful. They might make a run for it."

He returned up the stairs, found the hall suddenly crowded with footmen and maidservants.

"Seize him," shouted the Earl, who had joined the throng.

Nick levelled both his pistols. "Take one step more, and someone dies," he snapped. And then raised his voice. "Clayton, leave the horses."

The front door came inwards, and Clayton stood in the doorway, carrying his blunderbuss.

"Gentlemen," Nick said.

The footmen, making a move forward, checked, and turned. Clayton fitted the butt of the scattergun to his shoulder.

"He'll not fire," the Earl shouted. "He may hit his master."

"Cock your piece, Clayton," Nick commanded.

The detective obeyed. The click sounded like a shot itself in the hall. The footmen exchanged glances.

"Get in there," Nick said, gesturing at the pantry. "You too, my lord. Haste, now."

The maids were already backing towards the safety of the doorway. Now the footmen followed them.

"By God, sir," the Earl shouted. "I will have the law on you, sir. Invading a private home."

"As you will, sir. My trial will no doubt take place after yours, for harboring a traitor." He saw the Earl through the door, closed it and turned the key, and was alerted by a sudden explosion of sound from below him.

"Clayton," he shouted, and ran back to the head of the stairs as the sound of Eric's pistol came to his ears.

He stared down the stairs, saw a strange man peering up; ι e wore a riding cape and boots, and carried a pistol. Both men fired together; the Irishman gave a shout and dropped to his knees. Behind him came another and then another. They had uncovered a real hornet's nest here. "Clayton," he commanded.

The detective stood at the top of the steps, his blunderbuss levelled. "Stop there," he commanded. "Throw down your weapons."

The two men exchanged glances, then their wounded comrade raised his arm, lifting another pistol.

Nick fired, and the fellow gave a shriek and fell forward. The other two started up the stairs, and Clayton fired in turn. The roar of the scattergun filled the entire hall, and a cloud of black smoke took away Nick's breath and his vision together. He coughed, and was aware of another series of shots, as well as the thudding of feet.

He swept smoke away with his left hand, and suddenly faced Lorna, wearing men's clothes, her hair loose and her face stained with powder.

"Oh, my God," she said. "Nick. Oh, my God."

He reached for her, and she was thrust aside. Moncey stood behind her, another man at his shoulder, and each carried a sword.

Nick brought up his empty pistols, and Moncey thrust, forcing him to jump back against the wall.

"Mr. Minnett," Eric shouted from the cellar. "Are you all right, Mr. Minnett?"

"Clayton," Nick bawled. "Clayton."

Moncey glared at him, looked around the hallway, clearly uncertain as to how many men were against him, then gave a leap in the air, swinging his sword as he did so, to bring the chandelier crashing to the floor. The candles themselves flared before going out, and the hall was plunged into darkness.

iv

"A light," Nick bawled. "Eric. A light."

Someone crashed against him, and he thought he heard Lorna's

215

voice. He retreated against the wall, swinging his empty pistols to and fro, using them as clubs, hearing the din as the footmen banged on the locked door behind him.

Then the hallway filled with air, as the front door crashed open, and Eric cursed. He had just got a torch lit, and the sudden draught had blown it out.

"Horses," yelled Moncey. "Mount up. Mount up."

"Mr. Minnett," shouted another voice, that of Garthwaite, almost at the same moment as the sound of his hooves reached them, so wet was the ground. "Mr. Minnett."

"Stop them," Nick shouted, running forward and tripping over a body, to land on his hands and knees.

Behind him a light finally did flare, and he reached his feet again, to listen to a flurry of shots from outside, and even the clash of steel, before the hooves started again.

Eric lit another candle, and the hall gloomed, a shambles, with two men lying apparently dead, and two others, one of them Clayton, sitting to grasp at wounds, groaning and cursing. But neither Moncey nor, to his relief, Lorna, were amongst them.

"See what you can do for those poor fellows," he told Eric, and went to the door. Outside there were more signs of battle, with yet another Irishman lying dead at the foot of the stairs, and another of Garthwaite's men wounded. "Where are they?"

"They burst through us, Mr. Minnett," Garthwaite said. "I heard the shots, sir, and as the rear of the house was barred, decided to come round the front. Did I do right, Mr. Minnett?"

"Oh, aye, you did right." He realised they had taken Belair. "Get that man down. I'll use his horse. How many, Garthwaite?"

"Well, sir, two men and a woman."

"Aye. You'll accompany me. And you two." He himself assisted the wounded man to the ground. "Eric is inside, he'll tend to you. Where, Garthwaite?" He swung himself into the saddle.

"They rode for the gate, Mr. Minnett." The detectives were busy repriming their pistols; now they handed two to Nick for him to place in his saddle holsters.

"Haste, man." He spurred his own horse, set it to cantering over the sodden ground. The lights of the house faded, and the rain clouded down. And what did he intend? He had meant to arrest them, to send Moncey for trial, to—do what, with Lorna? He had not really considered. But he had certainly not expected resistance of quite such desperation. Or if he had, he had not suspected there could be quite so many of them.

The gate. He guided his horse back through the water, then reined, waiting for his companions.

"Where, do you think?"

"Harry will tell us," Garthwaite said. "Harry?"

The detective dismounted, crouched on the wet earth, lowered his ear. "That way." His arm extended.

"That is south," Nick said.

"The coast. They will have a ship waiting," Garthwaite said.

"Aye," Nick agreed. Or did they? South of Seend was Windshot, as Lorna certainly knew. What might she hope to discover there? "Ride."

They followed the road. Not only because it led roughly south, but because they could make faster progress on this relatively smooth surface; the rain was growing heavier by the moment. And the road led by Windshot Castle.

They lost track of time. It had been roughly nine o'clock when they had burst into Seend House. It could not have been more than an hour later when they had left. So they rode, into the night, only four now instead of eight, but now each carried the desire for vengeance in his heart.

"Suppose they separate?" Garthwaite shouted, riding alongside him. "It would be most sensible."

"Moncey is the man we want."

"But we do not know we follow the right way."

"Follow me," Nick commanded.

They topped a familiar rise, and saw the castle, looming through the mist below them. It was early morning, but there were lights down there. Nick's heart pounded, as he urged his exhausted horse down the slope and through the gate. "Morley, Morley." He threw himself from the saddle and up the steps. "Open up, Jack."

The doors were already opening. Morley carried a blunderbuss, and was supported by his son. Maureen peered over their shoulders.

"Mr. Minnett? My God, Mr. Minnett."

"Come in, sir, come in," Maureen cried. "You must be soaked through."

"I'd not expected you, tonight, Mr. Minnett. Not after those messengers . . ."

"Messengers?" Nick's heart gave a great bound. "Horses. Fresh horses. Get them out, quickly."

"But, sir, your messengers took our horses."

"Eh?"

"Theirs were blown, sir. And in view of their message . . ."

"You've none left?"

"I have two, sir."

"Then saddle them. Make haste, I beg of you, Jamie." This to Morley's son. He stepped inside, shook water from his hat.

"You must eat, Mr. Minnett. And rest. Your people will take care of the matter, surely."

"My people? Ha. A glass of wine, Morley. And some for these brave fellows. Now, Jack, these messengers. Three of them?"

"Why, yes, sir."

"And one was Lorna Fitzgerald. Did you not recognise her? I meant, Lorna Grant."

"Lorna Grant? Well, bless my soul. I spoke with but one."

"Lord Moncey. Did you not know him?"

"Lord Moncey? Good God. Begging your pardon, sir. He was not the man I spoke with. This fellow had an Irish accent."

"And the others?"

"Remained mounted, and but left their own animals to remount mine."

"Aye," Nick said. He could not blame Morley.

"But what did they tell you, to make you give them fresh mounts?" Garthwaite asked. He had drunk his glass of wine, and recovered some of his spirit.

"Why, sir, they sought Mistress Yealm. A matter of life and

death, they said. There are people out to kidnap her, they said, and you had sent them to see to her safety."

"Kidnap Anne?" Nick stared at him. "Oh, my God. But she is not here?"

"No, sir. They rode on in haste."

"Where?"

"Why, sir, for Lyme. I told them that was where she could be found."

18

"Lyme Regis," Nick gasped. "My God. Are those horses ready?"

He ran down the stairs, vaulted into the saddle.

"I am with you, sir." Garthwaite joined him. "You two follow as best you may."

Nick was already spurring his horse out of the yard. Anne. Of course. There was not only Moncey's opportunity to avenge himself on Nick, finally, but there too was the ship which could take him out of England. As Lorna would have told him.

But they were only an hour ahead. Nick urged his horse faster, following that so well remembered route now, charging over the moors, where he had ridden with Lorna that December evening nearly three years ago. Then it had been cold. Now it was wet, as the rain continued to cloud down, and as the mist gathered; there was only just sufficient breeze to move a boat. But there was a breeze, just sufficient.

Another hill, and the town of Lyme beneath them. In darkness. But already there was a suggestion of grey about the blackness of the night. He had been riding, or fighting, for some forty-eight hours, with only a brief sleep last night. Exhaustion, when it did settle in, would be complete; he could feel it lapping at his consciousness.

Garthwaite still rode at his heels. Nick walked his horse down the slippery cobbles, drew rein before the little cottage, stared at the harbour. The tide was rising, and the ketch was just leaving the ground. And there were people on board; even in the gloom he could see the shimmer of the canvas being shaken out.

"Find a dinghy, quickly," he snapped, and banged on the door of the cottage. And again.

There was no reply, but a window opened next door. "Who's there?"

"Nicholas Minnett, Mr. Lucas. I seek Anne."

"Why, sir, she is on board the 'Rose'. She left but a few moments ago."

"A few moments? But . . . where are the children?"

"Here with us, sir. When we heard the noise, we came out, and she told us the news, and asked us to keep the children for her, until her return."

"Her return? But man . . ."

"To fetch you, sir." Lucas scratched his head, glanced over his shoulder at his wife. "But you are here."

"Of course I'm here. Where do you suppose I was?"

"Why, sir, the gentlemen said you were in France, and in danger, and that the 'Rose' must cross to pick you up."

Nick ran down the road towards the slip, where Garthwaite was waiting with a dinghy. 'Golden Rose' was curtseying to her moorings, her mainsail already set. And he could hear the thumps as they shipped the legs. He hesitated, uncertain whether to shout. But so long as they supposed Anne was helping them they would not harm her. How Moncey must have cursed his luck when his arrival had turned out the neighbors as well; he must have intended to take the children. But not to fight an entire village.

"Sir?"

"Give way." Nick checked his pistols, sat in the stern. Garthwaite heaved on the oars, and the dinghy surged away from the dock. Behind them the church bell started tolling its alarm, and men began to run along the dock, towards the harbour entrance.

Now there came shouts from the ketch, and a sudden cry.

"Anne," Nick snapped. "Ahoy there," he shouted. "Surrender, Moncey, you'll not escape."

The mooring buoy splashed into the water, and the ketch fell away from the wind; the foresail climbed the stay. Either the Irishman with them was a seaman, or Lorna had a very good memory.

Now they were close enough to see the man on the helm. Nick levelled the pistol and fired, but the weapon had been sitting in the damp for too long, and failed. He cursed, and Garthwaite backed his oars as the ketch came round, not twenty feet away now, leaning over as the breeze filled her sails. And two people were running aft.

"Bring her close," he shouted, and reached for the shrouds as the ship loomed above them, the bowsprit soaring past his ear. His fingers locked in the cordage, and he swung himself up even as there came a crunch from beneath him as the oaken hull sliced into the dinghy. Garthwaite gave a yell of mingled fear and anger.

Then Nick was on deck, rising to his feet, drawing the other pistol.

"Don't kill him," Lorna screamed.

The Irishman grinned, and made a sweep with his sword. Nick stepped backwards, brought up the pistol, and was thrown over as Moncey put down the helm to line the ship up for the entrance. Nick found himself on his knees, the pistol sliding from his grasp and across the deck. Now they were close to the pierheads and he listened to the shouts from the men gathered there, while a pistol exploded. He turned, to face the Irishman again, and was struck a paralysing blow on the side of the head.

ii

Consciousness ebbed away for a moment, and when it returned, he was dazed and uncertain of his whereabouts. Noises came to him dimly, shouts in the distance, another series of explosions, the thrumming of the rigging and the hiss of the waves away from the bow.

And voices, close at hand.

"Over the side with him," said the Irishman.

"You'll not do that, Pat."

Lorna was kneeling beside his head.

"He's a dangerous man," Pat said. "Too dangerous for me. We'd be best off without him."

"He's a valuable man, too," Lorna said. "He's our passport. More than the woman. Give me a hand."

Nick attempted to move, and found himself rolled on his face. His arms were seized and pulled behind his back, and he felt a rope being secured around his wrists.

"Waste of time," Pat grumbled, but he gripped Nick's shoulders and began to drag him along the deck. Nick blinked into the lightening gloom, made out her face.

She smiled at him. "Easy now. You'll remember I saved your life."

"You . . ."

"Sssh," she said.

"What have you there?" Moncey demanded from the helm.

"Nick Minnett," she said.

"Chuck him over."

"No," she said. "I want him. You'd best concentrate on steering this thing."

"Where?" he inquired, his voice harsh. "I can't see. Even the shore is gone."

"Get an offing," Pat recommended. "Steer south."

The hatch was pulled back, Nick was thrust into the opening, and released. His feet slipped on the rungs of the ladder and he tumbled down, landing on his knees with a jar, and twisting his body as the ship lurched and threw him to one side, to save his face.

"Mr. Minnett? Nick?" Anne lay on the bunk, her hands also secured.

The hatch slammed behind him, and the cabin was dark.

"Anne? Are you all right?"

"I did not know what was happening," she said. "They said you were in trouble, that I must take the 'Rose' to your rescue."

"Did you not recognise Mistress Szen?"

"Mistress Szen?"

"You knew her as Lorna Grant, the housemaid at Windshot."

Anne made a whistling sound through her teeth. "Her face was familiar. I thought she must have been a guest. A friend of yours. Oh, Nick . . ."

"No one can blame you for that, sweetheart. But we are in her power. Worse, we are in George Moncey's power. We must see what we can do."

"What *can* we do?"

"Untie each other, I hope." He got himself back to his knees, and then to his feet, swaying as the ship lurched. "Where are you?"

She moved her body, and his fingers touched her thigh.

"Your hands?"

"Behind my back."

"Then roll over and face the bulkhead. I should be able to find you."

The bunk creaked as she rolled over, and her fingers touched his. He slid them over her hand, reached her wrist, found the knots. Tightly knotted; tied, unfortunately, by a landlubber.

"Can you do it?" she asked.

"Oh, aye. But it will take time. Did they say where they were bound?"

"They were in such haste to be away. Nick. What of Judith? Harry?"

"Mistress Lucas has them safe."

She sighed. "There was such a to do. If I had only known, I could have had them all arrested."

"Aye, well, don't worry about it. There are only three of them, and if we can get free . . ." His fingers slipped on the knots, and he started again, to find the standing part, to find the end, to find the bight, slowly to trace the rope, his movements restricted by the tightness of his own bonds.

And then the motion changed; 'Golden Rose' came upright and fell away on the other tack. For a moment he thought they had altered course, but the ship came up into the wind and then fell away once again, immediately repeating the manoeuvre yet again. They were hove to.

His head jerked, and he turned, to look up at the hatch, as it slid back, to allow a glimpse of dull grey dawn sky, and his three captors, looking in.

iii

"What did I tell you?" Moncey shouted. He slid down the ladder, seized Nick by the coat front, hurled him across the cabin. "Up to your tricks again, eh? Over the side with him."

"And who'll navigate us?" Lorna demanded. "You're quite lost, George Moncey, and you know it."

She also came down the ladder, helped to drag Nick back to his feet. Anne rolled over once more, gazed at the suddenly filled cabin.

"Lost we are," said Pat the Irishman, also descending the ladder. "We'll never see land again."

"Ah, we'll be all right, Pat," Lorna promised, stroking Nick's face. "He'll tell us where we are. He knows how to do it."

"Can you?" Pat inquired.

"If I get a glimpse of the sun," Nick said. "At noon. But I can tell you where we are, roughly, if you'll give me the exact time you left the harbour entrance, and the course you've been steering."

"There," Lorna cried triumphantly. "What did I tell you?"

"And will he be saying the truth?" Moncey sneered, looking down on him. "He hates us all."

"I hate you, at the least, George Moncey," Nick said. "And I'll see you hang."

"By God," Moncey shouted, starting across the cabin.

"Keep your distance," Lorna cried, pushing Nick against the bunk and leaning in front of him.

Moncey hesitated, big hands opening and shutting in a familiar gesture. Then he turned, suddenly seized Anne by the shoulder to drag her upright, twining his other hand in the bodice of her gown. "Oh, aye," he said. "He'll tell us true, or I'll have this wench of his. She's a charmer, wouldn't you say?"

Anne gazed at him with steady eyes; her mouth was firmly closed.

"Harm her, Moncey, and I'll kill you myself," Nick said.

"Oh, aye," Moncey agreed. "It'll be your ghost, Minnett."

"Will you two stop quarrelling," Lorna insisted. "You say you can tell us where we are, Nick. You'll lay a course for us, as well."

"Where?"

"Ireland," Pat said. "There's no safety in England any more, if the alarm is up so quick."

To Nick's surprise, Moncey and Lorna exchanged glances, to suggest they were not quite so much at loggerheads as they seemed.

"And there's safety in Ireland, now?" Moncey asked. "With Lake running amok and hanging everyone he can lay hands on?"

"There's nowhere else," Pat insisted. "Me sister will help us, for sure."

"But for how long, there's the point," Lorna said. "For how long will she be able? No, no, Pat. 'Tis France we must make for. Why, we must be half way there already."

"France?" Pat demanded.

"France," Moncey muttered. "Who's to say we'll be any the more welcome there? Those gentlemen have poured too much time and money, and men and arms, into this venture. Now it has collapsed, they'll be wanting to wash their hands of us. They'll be as like as not to send us back to the English."

"They'll not do that," Lorna said.

"Then they'll hang us," Pat said.

"The French take off your head," Moncey told him.

Pat rolled his eyes.

"They'll not do that, either," Lorna promised.

"And why not, may I ask?"

She patted Nick on the shoulder.

"Him?" Moncey shouted.

"The man himself," Lorna said. "What, do you not know how the frogs value Nick Minnett?"

"For what?" Moncey sneered. "Oh, I know Bonaparte is fond of the fellow. But he left Bonaparte, lost in Egypt."

Lorna smiled. "Bonaparte values Nick as a friend. There are

those who value him for what he is. Barras, for one. Nick owes Barras money, do you not, Nick?"

"If you say so, Lorna." Nick's brain raced. How did she know of that abortive transaction?

"What money?" Moncey asked.

"Near four years ago, now," Lorna said. "Nick and Mistress Yealm were in Paris, on secret business for Pitt, so they say. And they were taken. And Nick bought his freedom by promising Barras all the funds the House of Minnett had in Egypt. A very large amount, the story goes. Only he got away, I don't know how, without paying up. But they say Barras drinks a toast every night to the Minnett funds. Oh, he'll be glad to see us, if we bring Nick Minnett with us. They'll have his head, George, you can count on that. And the woman's. You can watch."

Moncey stared at her for some seconds, then at Nick. And smiled himself. "I do believe the girl is speaking the truth, Minnett. Judging by your expression."

Nick felt Lorna's hands, apparently at her side as she leaned against him, touch his legs, and squeeze the flesh. Lorna Grant. Lorna Fitzgerald. Lorna Szen. And now, Lorna who? But she had a gift for survival, as she had proved, time and again, not least in her remarkable reappearance from the Egyptian desert. And now playing some game of her own? Oh, indeed, of her own. But why involve him? Because of the moments they had shared together? Or for some further scheme of her own?

He did not know, but he did know that however unreliable she might be, she was the only thing protecting both Anne and himself from instant death.

"She is speaking the truth, George," he said. "Barras would very much like to get his hands on me."

"Ha," Moncey said. "Then he shall, by God. And you shall steer us there, or the woman goes over the side."

iv

"What time did you leave Lyme?" he asked.

"We have no idea," Lorna confessed.

227

"Was it dark, or light?" Nick asked, patiently.

"Well, light," Pat said. "Just."

"So, let's say seven o'clock. It's not accurate, but it's something to go on. Now, where have you steered since?"

"Due south," Moncey said.

"And the time now?"

Moncey consulted the ship's chronometer. "Eleven minutes past nine."

"And the wind force?"

"How should we know the wind force?" Lorna inquired.

Nick sighed. "Look over the side, Lorna. Are there any whitecaps on the waves?"

She pushed her head out of the hatch. "Yes."

"Many?"

"Not all that many."

"And the height of the waves is about three feet, right? I mean, from trough to crest." He could tell that by the motion of the ship.

"Why," she said. "I suppose it is."

"Well, then, that would be about twelve knots. Tide was half up when we left, so let's see, with a twelve knot wind, we'd have been making about six knots for two hours, with about a knot and a half of east running tide. Get out that chart, Lorna, and lay off a line from Lyme Regis due south for twelve miles, then east for three miles."

Lorna obeyed.

"Mark it. You know, it would be much easier were my hands free."

"Well, they won't be freed, so make the best of it," Moncey said.

Nick sighed. "Have you done that, Lorna?"

She held up the chart to show her cross.

"Good girl. Now, take the parallel rule and draw a line from where that position is straight into Le Havre. If you can."

She busied herself. "I can."

"What about Portland Bill? How close does your line pass? There's a race off the headland."

"I would say we'll pass about twelve miles off."

"Well, then, steer that course. Walk the rule to the compass rose. I'd say it should be about one hundred and twenty. That's east by south."

"One hundred and twenty-three," she said. And smiled at Moncey. "Isn't he tremendous?"

"And what about these tides you were speaking about?" Moncey asked.

"It'll be foul in another hour, then fair again six hours later. But they run east and west in mid channel, and should offset each other. Anyway it'll be dark again by the time we approach the French coast, and they show a light on Point de Barfleur, so we can take our position from that."

Moncey peered over Lorna's shoulder. "You trust all of this?"

"I've seen him do it before."

"Oh, I'm not doubting his ability. But how do you know he's really sending us to Havre?"

"It's there, on the map."

"And you'd best get under way," Nick said. "If you drift around here my figures will become wrong."

"Come on, Pat," Moncey said. The two men climbed the hatch, and then looked down at Lorna. "Aren't you coming? You're the one says she knows how it should be done."

"Oh, aye, I'm coming." Lorna gave Nick a hug, and gently pushed him on to the port berth. "You lie there and stay confortable. And behave. I'll be back with something to eat and drink as soon as I can." She kissed him on the mouth, slowly and lingeringly, ran her hands over his shoulders and inside his coat. "Oh, aye, I'll be back." She straightened, glanced at Anne, who continued to watch her, silently. "Oh, I'll feed you as well, Mistress Yealm." She climbed the ladder.

v

The cabin was gloomy with the hatch shut, and damp. No doubt the mist still clung.

"Can you trust her, Nick?" Anne asked.

"I can trust her self interest, sweetheart," he said. "It is all we have *to* trust."

"And her interest in you." Her voice was soft.

"That too, sweetheart, That too. If you will bear with me."

"You do as you think best," she said. "I blame myself for our predicament. Had I been with you, in London . . ."

"Nonsense," he said. "You have nothing with which to blame yourself. Had I not shown Lorna where 'Golden Rose' was moored in the first place, shown her how the ship should be handled . . . the fault is undoubtedly mine."

"Hist," she said.

The hatch was sliding back, and he saw Lorna's boots. She half fell down the ladder, landed on her hands and knees in the centre of the cabin, commenced to vomit.

Moncey climbed down behind her. "Useless bitch," he growled.

"Oh, Christ," she whispered. "Oh, Christ have mercy upon me. I had thought myself cured."

"You'd best lie down," Moncey decided. He held her shoulders, thrust her on to the bunk beside Anne, then hesitated, pulled her back off.

"Oh, leave me be, for God's sake," she begged, vomit dribbling down her chin.

"Oh, aye, Lorna," he agreed. "You're not my sort. Too skinny, by far. But you and Minnett are friends, eh? Puke over him." He thrust her on to the bunk beside Nick, scooped her legs behind her, grinned at Nick. "There's room, eh, Minnett? And room for me on the other one."

"You . . ." Nick strained at his bonds.

"You can listen." Moncey went to the ladder. "You all right for a spell, Pat?"

"Oh, aye, Lord Moncey," came the call.

"Well, then, I'll just take a rest." Moncey pulled the hatch shut.

"Anne," Nick said.

"Aye," Moncey said. "There's the ticket. Talk to her, Minnett. Tell her to be good to me."

Anne said nothing, but even above the whish of the water past the hull Nick could hear her breathe.

"Oh, Christ," Lorna muttered. She raised herself on her elbow, vomited on to Nick's stomach. "Oh, Christ. Moncey. Leave the girl be."

Nick could not see past the woman. He could only hear, a low chuckle from the man, the sound of ripping material, and then again a laugh.

Anne sighed.

"They said you were a beauty," Moncey said. "Oh, aye, they said that. Twice a mother, by God. I've not seen tits like those in a while. And you've a belly made for man, Mistress Yealm."

"I promised," Lorna said, and fell across Nick, gasping for breath as the boat lurched.

He sawed his wrists together, strained at the rope, and could not stop himself listening, to the thud of Moncey's boots hitting the floor, followed by the rattle of his belt as his breeches followed them. Followed by the creak of the bunk and then a sudden gasp of pain.

"Bitch," Moncey shouted. "Bitch." There came the sound of a succession of slaps, and a moan from Anne.

"I'll kill you, Moncey," Nick said. "So help me, I'll kill you, slowly, with my own hands."

Moncey did not reply. He was gasping for breath, as was Anne, and the bunk creaked again and again.

"You've no right, Moncey," Lorna muttered. " 'Tis not decent."

The cabin was silent, for a moment. Then Moncey's feet thudded to the deck. "Now I know why you deserted my sister, Minnett." He grinned down at them. "Oh, aye, I can understand that, now. By God, I've not enjoyed a woman like that in years."

"With my bare hands, Moncey," Nick said. "So help me God, if it takes the rest of my life. I'll kill you with my bare hands."

19

The cabin was quiet, save for the slapping of the waves against the hull, and the groans from Lorna. Nick heaved his body beneath hers in an attempt to throw her off, but she just sighed and clung closer.

"Anne?" he asked.

"I am here." Her voice was calm.

"Anne . . ." He did not know what to say. "I will avenge you."

"You will bring Lord Moncey to justice, Nick. For all of his crimes."

"Anne . . ."

"I am not a girl, Nick. He has not hurt me, physically, beyond a few bruises. Oh, and I think I have been bitten. If you can forgive me for having known another man . . ."

"Forgive you, Anne," he cried. "Why . . ."

"Then it were better to forget what has happened, Nick," she said. "Or it will cloud your judgement, and you may need all of that."

"Anne," he said. "Say now, that you will marry me."

He heard her breath as she smiled. "There is a month yet to come," she said. "I will give you my answer then. If you will ask me again, then."

Lorna groaned, and retched.

"Lorna," he said. "Wake up. Lorna, for God's sake."

She nestled herself against him.

In any event, he reflected, she would be of little value in this condition. But he recalled that she had only been prostrated for a few hours, the last time they had shared this cabin. She might well recover before they gained Le Havre. And in the meanwhile Anne was right. To allow the rage which seeped at the edges of his consciousness to take control would accomplish nothing—would, in fact, make him less able to take advantage of any chances which came his way. Time enough to feel rage when next he faced Moncey, man to man. But then no rage even then. Time more than ever for a cool head, for a cold certainty.

Nor could he do anything for Anne, with each of them bound and separated by the width of the cabin. He could only make up to her what she had suffered when he could again take her in his arms. So he must wait, with that patience which had enabled him to survive six months in a French prison while the world was collapsing about his ears, which had enabled him to recover from the knife thrust in Madame Duguay's salon, which had enabled him to survive Bonaparte's determination to make him Minister of Finance of an eastern dream which had since crumbled into dust.

Which reminded him that he must wait, in the first instance, on Lorna, if only out of curiosity.

The day passed slowly. Pat the Irishman came down, to grin at them. Nick feared Anne might be made the victim of another assault, but he only wanted bread, and cheese, and a bottle of wine. "Mid Channel," he said. "So far as I can reckon. And not a ship in sight, praise be to the Lord. 'Tis the mist."

"We are hungry, too," Nick said.

"Aye, no doubt. But that would be a waste of good food."

He returned on deck, the hatch slammed shut. Nick heaved his body once more. "Lorna . . ."

She sighed, and appeared to sleep. It was late afternoon before she suddenly sat up. "Ugh. The stink." She rolled out of the bunk, gave a sigh, sat at the table, beneath the swaying lantern, peered at Anne. "Well, well, Mistress Yealm," she said. "You made Moncey a happy man, I'll wager."

"Would you straighten my clothes, please, Mistress Szen?" Anne asked, quietly.

"Oh, aye, I'll do that," Lorna said. "Those legs would turn a man's head, they would." She pulled down Anne's skirt. "Christ in heaven, but I am hungry."

"So are we," Nick said. "And thirsty."

She stood in the middle of the cabin, bracing herself against the motion of the ship.

"Do I not look pretty, in men's clothes?" she asked. "You never said."

Nick sighed. "You look splendid, Lorna. You would look splendid in sackcloth."

"And your opinion, madam?"

"I agree with Mr. Minnett."

"Of course," she said. "Are you hungry?"

"Very. And thirsty."

She seized Anne's shoulders, pulled and prodded her into a sitting position on the bunk, legs hanging over the side. Lorna gazed at her rival for some moments, her face brooding, then arranged the disordered skirt, even pulled some auburn hair from Anne's face. She came across the cabin, arranged Nick similarly, pausing to stroke his face and breeches. "Oh, Nick," she said. "To see you alive. We had supposed you dead, destroyed with Brueys and all his crew."

"As I had supposed you dead, Lorna, lost in the Arabian desert."

She made a face, kissed him on the nose, uncorked a bottle of wine, and held a cup to Anne's lips, briefly, then turned her attention once again to Nick. "How did you survive?"

"I was blown into the water."

"With Carrie?"

"With Carrie."

"But she died later. So I heard."

"She was murdered, Lorna. By George Moncey."

"I cannot believe that."

"I was there. As he will murder you, when you and he disagree sufficiently."

234

She gazed at him for some moments, somberly, then turned and busied herself preparing bread and cheese.

"And how did you get back from Egypt? Where is Bonaparte? Where is Johannes?"

She sucked air through her teeth. "Johannes is in Italy, I believe. We separated after our return."

"But how?"

She shrugged. "Oh, you may imagine, there was a great to do when the news of the destruction of the fleet reached Cairo. Bonaparte was half out of his mind with despair." She glanced at Nick. "And with grief, at your supposed death. He really is fond of you, Nick."

"What did he do, eventually?"

Again the shrug. She lifted bread and cheese to Anne's mouth, allowed her to tear off a chunk. "He considered it destiny, that he should march east, having had his boats burned. He spoke of Cortes in Mexico, and a lot of other rubbish besides. So off they went. Into the desert. Mad."

"Leaving you behind?"

She winked at him, held food to his mouth. "I came down with a convenient fever, and Johannes had to stay to nurse me. We were a lot safer in Cairo—they had to leave a garrison, you see—than marching about the desert. Do you know what happened? They got as far as Acre, and laid siege to it. But there were some English warships there, commanded by a man called Smith. Do you know him?"

"Sydney Smith," Nick said. "We were at school together."

"Were you? You do have some odd friends. But this Smith person commanded the defence of Acre himself, and try as he might, Bonaparte could not take the place. And then the army contracted the plague. When that news got back to Cairo, well, I decided it was time we left. There was a senseless end to a promising career, to dwindle away on the edge of some prehistoric town."

"But how did you leave?"

Lorna smiled at him. "We travelled to the coast, with an escort, to look at some ruins, and there I bribed an Arab sea captain to take us to sea."

"*You* bribed him?"

She tossed her head, packed away the food. "Johannes had no money. And I have often wondered . . . it is no matter. The fellow agreed, and turned out to be honest. He set us ashore in Italy, after three nights at sea. As simple as that."

"Providing you have only yourself to think about."

"Oh, indeed. And who else should one be thinking about, may I ask?"

"Lorna, you are probably the most unprincipled woman I have ever met," Nick said. "And something of a harlot, into the bargain."

"I have principles," she said, and to his consternation pushed him flat on the bunk before climbing in beside him. "Ireland, for one. Which is why I am in this mess. And you, for another." She lay beside him, propped on her elbow, her hair trickling on to his face.

"Principles which allow you to betray me, from time to time?"

"Oh, you . . ." She rolled off the bunk. "I would have had no harm come to you. I made that plain." She gathered up the food and the bottle of wine, went to the hatch. "Besides, if you and me are to get on, it must be me alone." She glanced at Anne. "You'd best think about that, before we reach France. Me alone, Nick. I don't share you."

ii

"Nick," Anne whispered. "She would have me over the side, if she could."

"Will you trust me?"

"Of course."

"I must pretend to humour her. But I swear it will be, nothing more than that."

"I trust you, Nick. Have I not always trusted you?"

"Aye. And not always to your profit. How do you feel?"

She smiled. "I haven't feeling in my arms. But that will return, when I am freed. And Nick, it has always been to my profit, at least in so far as I am aware."

Further conversation was ended by the arrival of Moncey. He ate some food, drank some wine, stared at Nick, and then at Anne, and returned on deck. From then on they were visited fairly regularly by one of the men. And Lorna herself came down to prepare some more food towards evening. But the Irishman, Pat, accompanied her, and there was no time for talk. Nor, Nick decided, would it have been much use, had she been alone. She had apparently undergone another of her remarkable changes of mood, no doubt sparked by his lack of sufficient response to her advances. He could only wait for her good humour to return. But before either it or she did, Moncey was back, to his surprise waking him from a doze.

"You're to be congratulated on your navigation, Minnett," he said. "Cap d'Antifer is high and clear to port. We'll be into Havre in an hour."

Nick jerked his head, surprised to discover that he had actually fallen asleep. "What time is it?"

"Just dawn, once again. A fast passage, I would say."

"She's a fast ship," Nick said. But by now he was growing desperate. "Do you really mean to sell me to the French?"

"Can you think of a better idea?"

"I'd purchase my own freedom," Nick said. "And that of Mistress Yealm."

"Oh, indeed? And how much would you value those two lives?"

"You have but to name it, Moncey."

"And a pardon from His Majesty's government?"

"I cannot guarantee that, George. But I would certainly intercede for you. And Billy Pitt knows how to show gratitude."

Moncey stared at him for a moment, then gave a short laugh. "I've no stomach for trusting English politicians. No, no. We'll settle for a home in France and a pension. Safety before profit, in this case. Besides, I want to watch your head roll into the basket."

He climbed the ladder, slammed the hatch behind him.

"Nick." For the first time Anne's voice trembled. "Can he mean it?"

"Oh, he means it, all right. At least as regards me."

"And after you . . ." She would not finish the sentence, but the thought of it drove him farther to desperation. He twisted on the berth, attempted to free his wrists, quite without success, as all feeling had by now left his arms as well. And soon enough he was preoccupied with the rattle of the sails being lowered, and the sound of French voices. 'Golden Rose' had entered Le Havre, and he was now, irrevocably, back in the hands of the sans culottes.

iii

Lorna had disappeared, no doubt too happy once again to find her feet upon dry land. But Nick was beginning to wonder if she was going to prove of any assistance at all, or if it had all been nothing more than a desperate hope. For now Pat and Moncey came down to the cabin, dragged him from his bunk, and placed a black hood over his head; the velvet contained no eye slits, and while he could breathe, he could see nothing. Nor, he realised, could his face be seen.

"What about the woman?" he demanded, his voice muffled.

Moncey gave a brief laugh. "She'll be taken care of, Minnett."

"Should any harm come to her, Moncey . . ."

He was cut short by a shove, which sent him staggering across the cabin. "Be gone with you. 'Tis yourself you should be worrying about. The girl will come to no harm." Pat chuckled. "Leastways, not what I'd call harm."

Nick turned to kick at him, at the same time once again wrenching on his wrists, but all to no avail. Another shove sent him sprawling, and then he was seized by the shoulders and dragged to the steps. And now they had been joined by Moncey's French friends, no doubt summoned by the noise.

"Don't hurt him," Anne begged. "Please don't hurt him."

There was the sound of a slap, and a gasp, and a foot crashed into his ribs.

"Up," Moncey growled. "Or you'll hear the girl scream."

238

Nick struggled to his feet, kept his temper under control with an enormous effort. It would do no good to shout and rave and struggle. He was a gambler, by nature and by habit, and his talent lay in his ability to estimate odds, and his courage to abide by that determination. So, he had been dealt an unplayable hand. He must, therefore, sit and wait. There would be another hand, soon enough, and perhaps that would be better. And eventually, if he took care to keep himself alive and well, there would be a hand strong enough to regain all he had lost. And to enjoy the sweet flavour of revenge.

He allowed himself to be half carried, half dragged, up the steps, and into chill air. It was presumably about the middle of the morning, but there was a faint, cold breeze drifting off the land. He stumbled across the deck, and through the gangway, over another ship, and felt the hard stone of the quay beneath his feet.

At the sight of him a jabber of conversation rose from the watching fishermen and their friends, but comment was silenced by a remark from one of his French captors, to the effect that he was a spy. Yet there was no immediate shout of execration. Like most of those living on the Channel coasts, these fishermen were uncertain where they would stand, if too close an investigation were to be made into their activities once they cast off.

He smelt leather, and horses, and found himself being thrust at the door of a carriage. He scrambled in, pushed from behind, fell on to the seat, and felt someone get in beside him. Then the door slammed, and immediately the equipage began to move. Nick pulled himself upright, waited for the cloying folds of the hood to settle.

"Are you French or English?" he asked.

There was no reply.

Nick tried again, and still the man ignored him. Because it was a man. His nostrils told him that. So he leaned back, made himself as comfortable as he could, and listened, and counted. He had made the journey from Le Havre to Paris before. It would hardly take less than twenty-four hours, he calculated. But the coach was driving fast, far too fast to sustain a hundred mile journey. And driving fast, it was setting up too much noise for him to hear what was happening on either side.

The halt came without warning. The coach slewed round and clattered over a wooden bridge. The driver pulled on his brake, and they scraped to a stop. The door was opened, and Nick's guardian bestirred himself.

"Step down, monsieur."

Nick obeyed, once again listening.

"The tower room," said his captor.

Which told him that he had been taken to a château. His feet stumbled up the stone steps from the courtyard, and into an entry hall, also stone, also, so far as he could tell, uncarpeted. But large and high ceilinged, he estimated, from the echo of their footsteps. Someone seized his arm, guided him to some steps, and he felt a draught of cool air on his face. Then he was climbing, up a circular staircase, his shoulder brushing the wall, two men, he estimated, immediately behind them. Once again he counted, but it was easy to decide the floors, as there was a brief landing at each one, until after the third the landings ceased and he realised they were in the tower. They climbed another fourteen steps before he bumped into a door. A man pushed past him, and he listened to a key scraping in the lock. Then he was pushed forward.

He stumbled, regained his balance, and turned. "You'll take off this hood," he said.

"We have no instructions about that," the guard pointed out. A hand seized his arm, and he was guided forward again, until his knees brushed a bed. He was turned, and made to sit. At least the mattress was reasonably soft.

"You'd best rest a while," said the other guard.

"I have not eaten in twelve hours," Nick said. "Nor drunk."

"We have no instructions about that," said the first guard.

"Nor answered a call of nature," Nick said, desperately.

"Lie down," said the second man.

Nick sighed, and allowed himself to relax. He was, in fact, not especially hungry, or uncomfortable in his belly. But he was extreme-=048ly thirsty. And once again there was no point in becoming either desperate or angry. He could only wait.

He lay down, and even managed to sleep. When he awoke it was late afternoon, and he was now definitely hungry and definitely uncomfortable. But it had been neither of those which had awakened him. A key was turning in the lock. He sat up, inhaled scent, and realised that he was in the presence of Lorna Szen.

iv

Hands touched his head, and the hood was removed; for a moment his eyes were dazzled by the flickering candlelight, for she had placed the holder by the bed. Then he could blink, and look around him—at the surprisingly large tower room, at the narrow slits of windows, glazed to keep out the breeze. And then at the woman, for she had changed into a pink gown embroidered with gold thread, with a gold coloured sash gathered in a huge bow just beneath her breasts. Her hair was loose, and she had recently bathed.

"Well?" she demanded. "Are you not pleased to see me?"

"I'm pleased to see anyone at this moment, Lorna. Even you."

She pouted. "Did I not save your life?"

"I imagine that remains to be seen. Will you untie my hands? I have a desperate urge."

She produced a knife, reached behind him, slit the rope. His arms fell to his sides; he could feel nothing.

"I'd best help you," she decided. "There is a privy drain in the corner." She helped him to his feet, herself undid his breeches, guided him to the alcove.

"I am also hungry, and thirsty," he said, feeling blessed relief seeping through his body.

"And unobservant," she remarked.

He looked over his shoulder; on the table by the door had been placed a tray containing a plate of cold chicken and an opened bottle of wine.

Lorna buckled his breeches, led him back to the bed; feeling was just starting to seep back into his wrists, accompanied by a delicious agony of prickling blood.

"Just sit there," she said. "I will feed you."

She held a cup of wine to his lips, allowed him to drink half of it,

241

then took it away again and finished it herself. Then she held a chicken bone for him to gnaw.

"And I'm curious," he said, with his mouth full.

"You are in a château belonging to a friend of George Moncey," she said. "We have used it before."

"And Mistress Yealm?"

"Oh, she is here, too. Although George would not wish you to know that. She is well enough. She has not even been violated."

The food started to taste better.

"And here we wait until Barras comes for us?"

Lorna shrugged, gave him some more wine. Now he could feel in his fingers again, but he kept that secret to himself.

"Or until you let us out," he suggested.

"Now, why should I do that, Nick Minnett?"

"Because you have claimed to save my life. That would not be the case if Barras lays hands on me."

"I am not sure that you do not deserve to die," she said. "We are enemies. We can never be anything other than enemies. You are Pitt's creature, I stand for Ireland."

"And suppose I told you that Pitt also hopes to stand for Ireland?"

She frowned at him, chicken bone poised. "I do not understand."

"But *he* understands the injustices under which you have laboured, for too long. He would remove them."

She frowned at him, held the bone to his mouth. " 'Tis a question of religion."

"Oh, indeed." He chewed, and swallowed. "But an out-dated one. He would remove all Catholic disabilities. Your family could be restored. Your father could take his seat in the Lords. There will be Irish representatives in the Commons."

"You are dreaming."

"It is what Pitt wants. And he generally has his way."

Her tongue came out, slowly circled her lips. "If I could believe . . ."

"You can, because it is true. But I doubt you would benefit, if you now hand me over to the sans culottes."

Lorna gave him a long stare, got up, and returned to the tray to refill the glass. Her every movement was thoughtful. "I dare not let you out," she said. "George would kill me."

"Where is he now?"

"Oh, he isn't here. He has gone into Paris, to see Barras. But the château is full of his people."

"We will never have a better opportunity, Lorna. But find me a weapon, and show me how to reach Anne. I will take you both from here. 'Golden Rose' is in Le Havre. She will take us to safety. She has done so before."

Lorna turned, gave him another long stare. She raised the glass and sipped from it, then came slowly back across the room. "I fail to see why I should set your doxy free."

"Because she is not my doxy, Lorna. She is going to be my wife."

"Your wife? A fisherwoman?"

"Anne Yealm, Lorna. My wife. And you'd do well to be respectful."

"Bah." She held the glass to his lips, then took it away, set it down, and slipped his coat from his shoulders. "I did not bring you here to discuss another woman, Nick. Do you know, I still dream of that afternoon we spent together, in Naples? I have never had so wonderful an afternoon in my life." His coat was on the floor, and she was unbuttoning his shirt, thrusting her slender fingers inside to caress his nipples. "You and me, Nick. Nobody else. You and me."

His hands closed on her shoulders, slipped up to her neck. "And suppose I throttle you? It would be no more than you deserve."

She leaned against him, gave that marvellous throaty laugh. "Then would I die happy, Nick, as the hands would be yours. Nor would it avail you. The door is locked on the outside, and will only open to my call." Her head tilted back, taking his hands with it, and she smiled at him, and rolled off his lap to lie on the bed.

And he lay with her, his leg thrown across hers as he had held her that very first night in Windshot, how long ago. And once again her mouth was open as she smiled, and her lips were there to be kissed as her tongue was there to welcome his. She wore nothing beneath her gown. She had come here with a purpose. His hands slipped the cloth up her legs as he sought flesh. He was remembering, recapturing the beauty of that Naples afternoon. Deliberately. To lull the woman into passionate acceptance of his will? Or because for him too it was an unforgettable memory, two hours of utter bliss.

As was this, an hour of utter bliss. Her hands freed his breeches, guided him against her; her fingers dug into his buttocks, as he drove again and again, and her head threw back as she laughed with delight.

"Lorna," he whispered. "Lorna. You are a witch. Certainly you have the ability to bewitch me."

"I want nothing more," she said, and stroked his head as he collapsed on her. "You and me, Nick. Nothing more."

But already sanity was returning, awareness, of his guilt, in lying here and being happy, while Anne must still be suffering the torments of the damned. His guilt, in lying here at all, when he should be straining to escape the position in which he found himself. In lying here . . . he listened to feet on the steps outside, rolled off the woman and sat up as the door was thrown open by George Moncey.

20

Nick leapt from the bed, naked as he was, instinctively seeking only to wrap his hands around Moncey's throat, but checked himself as he realised his enemy was accompanied by several men.

Lorna sat up, reaching for her gown with her left hand to hold it on her lap. "Moncey? Why, you look as if you've seen a ghost."

"A ghost," Moncey snapped. "Ha-ha. We *have* a ghost, Lorna."

Nick backed against the wall, hastily looking around for some form of weapon.

Lorna frowned at the intruders. "You've been to Paris? Seen Barras?"

"And like to have lost my own head," Moncey said, coming into the room. "You've had your last tumble out of Nick Minnett, my dear. The Directory wishes none of him. Barras was aghast to consider that he might be in France. As he is, he wants him killed, privily, and his body disposed of. Oh, and that long-legged doxy of his."

For a moment Nick was too surprised to move. Barras, wishing his death before even seeing him, before even attempting to extort money from him?

"I don't believe it," Lorna said. But she got out of bed, and, remarkably, dropped her gown at the same time, to stand naked in the middle of the room between Nick and Moncey, drawing the delighted stares of the other men.

" 'Tis his disappearance, for ever, or our heads," Moncey insisted. "Anyway, it'll be a pleasure. I have our safe conduct from France, and we can weight their bodies in the Seine." He grinned. "Not that we will bury them together. As the pretty thing must die anyway."

He made a step forward, and Lorna threw herself behind him, on to her hands and knees, "Now, Nick," she screamed.

Nick hurled himself forward, and Moncey's arms came up, sword point flickering. But Lorna's shoulder was cannoning into the backs of his knees, and he was already off balance, tumbling over the girl to strike the stone floor heavily. Nick leapt over him, and was into the midst of the other three before they could recover, their attention still taken by the flailing white arms and legs immediately in front of them. He scattered them with a swinging right hand punch, a left hand thrust, and a kick, and then was running down the spiral staircase, panting, brain racing. He could not leave without Anne, and he had no idea where she was. He needed weapons, and preferably pistols; he had never been a swordsman.

Noise came from above him, curses, and the sound of a blow. Poor Lorna. She had, at the end, attempted to save his life. He emerged on to the top floor of the building proper, left the staircase to run along the gallery, found a set of halberds mounted on the wall. He reached up, tore one down. Lacking firearms, this ten foot pike was better than any sword. He heard a sound from the far end of the gallery, turned, pike thrust forward, and saw a manservant peering at him, bemused by this sudden naked apparition.

Nick ran at him and the man gasped and turned, but slipped and fell to one knee, and before he could recover Nick stood above him, the point of the pike at his throat.

"A young woman was brought here," he snapped. "She has long red hair. Tell me where she is confined."

The man rolled his eyes, and from the staircase Nick heard the sound of booted feet crashing downwards.

"Speak, or I'll kill you."

246

"In . . . in the cellar," the man gasped.

"The other staircase?"

The man pointed, at the far end of the gallery. Nick released him, ran to the main staircase, looked back, and saw Moncey and his men arriving.

"He seeks the woman," Moncey bawled. "Get down there. Cut her down."

Nick gasped for breath, ran down the stairs, listening to feet crashing above him. They had divided, two behind him, two to seek Anne. He pounded past the next landing, reached the ground floor and ran into the great hall, at the same moment as Moncey and his companion ran out of the tower. And they were nearer the door to the cellars.

Nick ran forward, pike thrust in front of him.

"Hold him there," Moncey snapped. "I'll see to the woman."

But his movement toward the stairs was interrupted by a sudden thunder of hooves crossing the drawbridge into the courtyard, and an almost immediate rat-a-tat on the front door. Moncey checked, gazed from Nick to his companion to the door in surprise.

"Open up, open up," came the summons. "Or by God I'll hang you all."

Nick lowered his pike in total amazement; that never to be forgotten voice belonged to Napoleon Bonaparte.

ii

As Moncey's companion also knew. "Bonaparte," he muttered. "He is a friend of Minnett's."

Moncey continued to hesitate. "He has no authority here, save by command of the Directory."

"Which may well be his, by now," the man insisted. "You know what happened in Paris last night? You know why he has returned at all?"

The banging resumed on the door. And now the two men behind Nick decided they had had enough. "There is a postern by the river," they snapped.

"Aye," agreed the man beside Moncey. He gave Nick a crooked smile. "No doubt we shall meet again, Minnett." He ran down the steps, half pushing Moncey with him. Nick started forward, but had to turn to face the other two, who were also making for the cellar. They retained their swords, and their blades clashed against his pikehead, but they were interested only in making their escape, and manoeuvred their way past him to the steps, then turned and ran.

He charged behind them, even as the door behind him burst open under the succession of blows. Anne was down there, somewhere. But at the foot of the stone steps the passage divided, that on the left leading to the cellars, that on the right clearly the way to the postern door set in the river bank. He hesitated for a moment, then turned left, threw open the doors to either side, and plunged into the darkness, torch held high.

"Anne?" he shouted.

"Nick," came the answering call.

Panting, he opened another door, again raised the flaring torch, and found her, lying almost at his feet, chained to the wall by her wrists, clothes disarranged, hair untidy, face bruised and dirty, but unmistakably Anne.

"Sweetheart." He knelt beside her.

"I knew you would come, Nick. It was just a matter of waiting."

"What have they done to you?"

"Nothing. Save treat me as a woman. Forgive me that weakness, Nick, and I can forget it."

He kissed her mouth. "You need no forgiveness, dear heart, and I will do the remembering. Now, these chains . . ."

"Let us help you, Mr. Minnett."

He straightened, gazed at Charles Talleyrand-Perigord, ugly face twisted with pleasure, reaching for his hands. Behind him was Joachim Murat, as splendidly uniformed as ever. Then Desaix, who he had last seen when the Mameluke cavalry had broken the square. Then Joachim Castets, of all people. And behind them there were others, while Bonaparte himself was at the back.

"Nick," he said. "Do you always prance around castles in the dark, naked?"

He had forgotten that. "My God," he said. "I must look a wild man. My head spins."

"So does mine," Bonaparte agreed. "Come. I'm afraid those rascals have flown. But we will take them."

"Anne . . ."

Bonaparte peered at the woman on the floor, and raised his hat. "Mistress Yealm. It is too long since we met. My people will cut you out of there, if you will be patient, and brave."

"Your servant, General," she said.

"Get to it, Murat. Talleyrand, you'll accompany me. You *do* have clothes, Nick?"

"In the tower. My God."

"There is more?"

"Lorna Szen is up there. Was up there. I pray she is unhurt." He glanced at Anne, and flushed.

And she smiled. "It seems these past twenty-four hours were best forgotten, on both sides," she said. "You talk with the General. I am sure I will be freed as soon as possible."

"The tower room," Bonaparte told Desaix "Bring down Mr. Minnett's clothes, and anything else you may find. Now come." he seized his friend's arm, led him back up the steps. "Lights," he said. "See to it. And some wine. Nick looks exhausted. And cold."

"Should we not pursue Moncey?" Talleyrand inquired. "He will ride for Paris."

"He will ride for the coast, and make his escape," Bonaparte corrected. "What, go to Barras and tell him he has lost Minnett? His own head would roll in the hour. Now, Nick, they told me you were dead, destroyed in the explosion which ended poor Brueys. Sit down, man. Sit down."

Nick found himself in an armchair, a glass of wine in his hand, candles flaring in the great hall, and one of Bonaparte's soldiers poking wood into the already glowing fire. Very briefly he outlined the events of the battle, and afterwards, in Naples.

"My God," Bonaparte said, when he was done. "To shoot his own sister. I can see why you hate him so. But the way you survive . . ." He turned to Talleyrand. "Did I not tell you that this man was born under a star?"

"So you did," the erstwhile bishop agreed. "And I am coming to believe it."

"And are not you born under a star, Napoleon?" Nick inquired. "To all the world you are a lost man, buried in the deserts of Egypt."

"Ah, bah . . ." Bonaparte looked up as Desaix came down the stairs, carrying Nick's clothes. "Madame Szen?"

"Was lying senseless on the floor, General. I have dressed her bruise and laid her on the bed."

Nick got up. "I must go to her."

"You will get dressed," Bonaparte commanded. "Listen."

From below them they could hear the metallic thuds as Murat struck at Anne's chains.

Talleyrand smiled. "I think your main duty is here, Mr. Minnett."

"Besides," Bonaparte said, leaving his chair to stride up and down, as he usually did when about to make an announcement. "I was going to tell you how *I* came to be here. Oh, things did not go well in Egypt and Syria. I can tell you that, Nick, although I would admit it to no one else. And why? Because you were not there. I do not joke when I claim that you are my fortune. It is proved to me, more and more with every day. Up to the moment you were wounded, why, I could ask for nothing more. From that moment, things started to go astray. Was it not ill fortune that that ghastly madman Smith happened to be anchored off Acre when I approached? Was it not ill fortune that the prisoners I took should have been impregnated with the plague, which they promptly communicated to my men?"

"I have heard you massacred them, Napoleon." Nick pulled on his clothes. "And refused to credit it."

Bonaparte ceased his pacing, turned, frowned at him. "I am a soldier. More, I am a general. More even than that, who can doubt that destiny guides my hand."

Nick's turn to frown. "You mean it is true?"

"I had insufficient food for my own people. And those vermin, as I have told you, were riddled with disease. Believe me, Nick, I did them a kindness. Would you not destroy a dying horse, with tears in your eyes?"

"I would make a certain distinction between a horse and a man."

Bonaparte stabbed the air with his finger. "And you would be wrong. Anything that breathes deserves the same consideration."

"And you murdered . . . what is it, ten thousand men, out of consideration?"

"You seek to quarrel."

"I seek the truth."

Bonaparte sighed. "I had them executed, yes. No doubt you have never had to make such a decision, Nick. I pray that you never do. To a general, it falls continuously. In a battle, which regiment shall you send to its death? Those over there, your favourites, where you yourself served, and who you know can be relied on at the end? Or those, raw recruits, and untrustworthy to boot? Yet boys, of your own nationality, with sisters and mothers and sweethearts to mourn over them? That decision must be taken, every time I face an enemy. A general is trained to make that decision. So should I shrink from a decision which involved either my whole command, or a body of the enemy? For it was as plain as that, Nick. Marching with those men, the entire army would have perished. Without them, my people survived."

"And where are your men now?"

"Ah." Bonaparte threw himself into a chair. "Still in Egypt. Oh, we returned to Aboukir, and do you know, those foolhardy Mamelukes hurled themselves at us again. And were defeated again. No fortune needed there. But by then I knew where my duty lay. Talleyrand?"

The minister took up the tale. "You will have heard, Mr. Minnett, of how the fortunes of France are sinking. All that General Bonaparte conquered in Italy has been lost. We marched into Naples, when they would discard their neutrality, and were as promptly thrown back out again. They laugh at us in Florence. We no longer control the Rhine. And here at home there is too much unrest. We are governed by feeble creatures, who think only of their own pleasure. We need strength. The strength of one man who can stand above the rest. Believe me, sir, the army is entirely of this opinion."

"And so they sent word to Cairo," Bonaparte said.

"And you deserted your men."

"Nick, you do seek to quarrel. Deserted them? I left Kleber in command, with an army quite sufficient to control the Copts. I brought with me only those I need."

Nick pulled on his coat, and felt distinctly warmer. "But how did you get home? Was not Aboukir blockaded?"

"They said so. I had two frigates, and I will tell you this, we saw not an English ship until north of Corsica." He gave a delighted laugh. "Then there was an entire fleet, blockading Toulon, as usual."

"Then where did you go?"

"You English, Nick, are too eager to consider the game won. What, a Frenchman sail, where England rules? There is an impossibility." Again the shout of laughter. "We hoisted the Union Jack, and sailed right through them. Men saluted me, Nick. English tars. Oh, it was splendid. And we made the Gulf of Frejus without trouble, landing at Raphael."

"My God," Nick said. "Someone's head will roll when this news reaches London."

"Deservedly," Bonaparte said. "Oh, aye, there was all history, resting on one commander's shoulders, and he was too negligent to discover it."

"So you returned to France. To a welcome?" Despite himself, he was fascinated by the man's effrontery.

"Ah, well," Talleyrand said. "I had been busy, as you may suppose, Mr. Minnett. As you will know, the Directory consists of five men, and two of these are for the general. The Abbe Sieyes, and Roger Ducos. The other three, who acknowledge Barras as their leader, consider him a traitor, who has abandoned his command and returned to Paris without instruction."

Nick smiled at Bonaparte. "It is a point of view."

"Bah. I go where duty calls. Not where inferior men think to send me. Last night I told them plain, I would have none of them. That there must be a change in the constitution. Sieyes has it all thought out."

"Five are too many," Talleyrand said. "He thinks of three. And nothing so insignificant, so bourgeois, as directors. Consuls. After the Roman model. Three Consuls, with a First Consul as leader, executive, if you like."

"As dictator, you mean," Nick said.

"Oh, no. There will be checks on his power. Oh, it is all very elaborate. Sieyes has thought it out."

"And Barras accepted this?"

"Indeed he did not. But he seeks only to perpetuate his own position, caring nothing that he opposes the will of the nation."

"And is it the will of the nation?"

"Who can deny it? Strength. Firmness. Victory. That is what the nation needs," Bonaparte declared, then bowed to the doorway. "Madame Yealm. A glass of wine to celebrate your freedom."

"I would take that very kindly, General." Anne came into the room, rubbing her wrists. Murat and his men were behind her. "What would I not give for a hot bath and a warm bed. But I perceive you gentlemen are discussing great matters."

"The fate of the nation, nothing less, dear lady," Talleyrand said. "Anyway, Mr. Minnett, to cut a long story short, Ducas and Sieyes took General Bonaparte last night to see their fellow directors, at the Chamber. And it was there that Barras accused the General of treason, commanded him from his presence, said that if he was in Paris tomorrow morning he would have him executed."

Nick stared at Napoleon. "And?"

Bonaparte flushed. "Well . . . I suppose that habits of the soldier, of obedience, are too difficult to disregard, Nick. I admit it freely. I stammered, and lost my presence. I stumbled from the room, and fled to my lodgings."

"Where we waited," Murat said. "I will confess, Mr. Minnett, that I was equally amazed. And distressed. It seemed to me the game was up." He slapped Napoleon on the shoulder. "For this fellow, this lion amongst men, is confoundedly superstitious. He wished us to fly. Us, with all the army commanders on our side, to flee? We argued with him, pleaded with him, to take the bull by the horns, and he would not, muttering about the sanctity of France, until this brave fellow, Castets, came knocking on the door to tell us that you, Mr. Minnett, were in France, and indeed, confined in this château.

"It was my duty, Mr. Minnett," Castets said, blushing. "I could do no less."

"And this made a difference?" Nick inquired.

"All the difference in the world," Talleyrand said. "You should have seen life flood back into Napoleon's body, animate his mind. He was to horse in a moment, and riding here. And just to rescue you, Mr. Minnett. He genuinely conceived himself about to regain his talisman."

"Bah." Bonaparte got up again, as violently as he had sat down. "You may scoff. All of you may scoff. Yet is my path, my destiny, certain, and simple to see. Minnett brings me fortune. He did so at Toulon, he did so on the crossing of the Mediterranean, he did so in allowing me to get my army ashore at Aboukir without Nelson arriving. Had I possessed the sense to keep him at my side, wounded as he was, after the Battle of the Pyramids, India would have been mine by now. And now, of all times, can you doubt it? Here France stands at its crossroads. Here I, even more, stand at the crossroads of my life. You think it is an easy thing, to go against training, against duty, against natural instinct. I am a soldier, not a politician, not a conspirator. I abhor conspiracy in any form. Show me my enemy in front of me, and I will show myself to him. No sneaking around dark corners. But then, France is in desperate straits. And then again, the risk, not only to myself, but to you all, to my family, to dear Josephine. Had I the right to involve all of them in my ruin, should I fail? Or even, you may say, in the responsibilities of my success, should I succeed? It was a consideration of those matters, my friends, that made me hesitate. So, at such a moment, such a never to be forgotten instant in history, what happens? You, Nick, reappear in my life, entirely by accident. You did not know I was in France, and I did not know you were in France. There is no accident. There is Fate. There is Destiny." He thrust his right hand into the flap of his coat, let his left hand droop behind his back, spread his legs, and stared at them. "And there is my decision. We ride. For Paris, and the Council of the Five Hundred."

21

"And you will be at my side, Nick," Bonaparte insisted. "Without you, I doubt that fortune would play its proper part. But it may well be dangerous. Madame Yealm, you will remain here, under guard. Castets, this will be your responsibility."

"The last time you left me secure, under guard, General," she pointed out, "I was in the most dangerous place of all."

"Bah. That was Louis Condorcet. He was a soldier, and a Jacobin. George Moncey is a spy and an aristocrat. He will be too concerned with his own safety to return here. Besides, then I left you in the care of Barras, the man I must destroy. Now you are in the care of Castets. Ask Mr. Minnett if he would not trust his life to Castets."

"My life, certainly, Napoleon," Nick agreed. "My purse, now, there is another matter."

"Why, Mr. Minnett," Castets said. "I do not care to think on how many occasions I have risked my all for you."

"Nor how many times you have considered it in my interest to be betrayed? But guard Mistress Yealm for me, and you may be sure of my debt, forever. Napoleon, I would have a word with Anne."

"Of course." Bonaparte snapped his fingers, and the officers withdrew to the far side of the hall.

"Nick," Anne whispered. "He means to challenge a nation."

"Aye."

"And when he falls, those with him will fall also."

"He will not fall, as long as his resolution does not fail him. I can believe that the army will follow him. He is a general *to* follow. And if there is indeed a party in the Assembly in his favour, and with his brother Lucien president for the day, no, I do not think he will fail. In any event, my sweet, I have no choice but to ride with him. He saved our lives for no other purpose."

"And afterwards?"

"He will let us return to England. Oh, no doubt about that. But you, Anne . . ."

"We said we would not talk of it, Nick. If you must go, then do so, and return, victorious, and in haste. I will have Castets provide me with pistols, and should Moncey return here I will avenge myself. Believe me, I am capable of that." She smiled, and kissed him on the chin. "Besides, I shall have enough to do, caring for poor Madame Szen, will I not?"

He hesitated, and was alerted by the crow of a cock.

"Time, Nick," Bonaparte called. "It is pressing."

"Aye." He took her in his arms, held her close for a moment. The enormity of what had happened to her, the stain that must lie across her mind, could only be removed by him, and by his patient love. "I'll be back by nightfall, sweetheart. I promise. And then we shall be away, for home. And the children and you and me together."

"I shall be safe." She kissed him again, and then released him and went to the stairs. Bonaparte and his officers were already waiting at the opened door, and the horses were stamping in the courtyard. Nick swung into the saddle beside his friend.

"So, once again we ride together, you and I, Nick," Bonaparte said. "Another day to remember. Do you know the date?"

"Ah . . . the eleventh of November," Nick said. "Unless I have utterly lost track of the days."

"Eleventh of November?" Bonaparte shouted. "You are in France, Nick. The day is the nineteenth, and the month is Brumaire. Brumaire, Nick. Remember that. Now, ride."

It was late morning by the time they reached St. Cloud, having crossed the river at Poissy and galloped through St. Germain-en-Laye. Here they accumulated a waiting regiment of grenadiers, and necessarily slowed their exhausted horses. It was time for a glass of wine and a loaf of bread. Few words were spoken; each man knew that by nightfall they would be either the rulers of France, or condemned men. And word of what might be happening had clearly got about; houses were shuttered, and people stared at them from around corners.

And within sight of the palace they encountered Berthier and a small group of horsemen.

"Well." Bonaparte dragged on his rein, and held up his gloved hand for the cavalcade to halt. "They are here, then."

"Shouting at each other," Berthier said. "Both Houses. But united in denouncing military dictatorship."

"What of Sieyes? What of Lucien?"

"The Abbe calls for commonsense, your brother calls for order. And they all look most anxiously at the door."

"The Orangerie?"

"There is work in progress there." Berthier gave a faint smile. "The labourers are not less in a tizzy. The council meets in the gallery of Mars."

"Of Mars," Bonaparte shouted. "Can there be a better omen than that? Murat, you will hold your men here. Berthier, bring a file of grenadiers. Talleyrand . . ."

"I will ride for the city, General," the minister said. "To prepare them for your triumph." He leaned across his horse's head, held out his hand. "God speed you, Mr. Minnett. One day we must sit down and have a long talk."

He turned his horse and rode off, leaving Bonaparte staring after him.

"That man is very much of a scoundrel. You'll stay by my side, Nick."

258

"But only a file of grenadiers," Murat protested. "That is no way to do it. Let me ride my men in there, with drawn sabres."

"It may not be necessary," Bonaparte said. "And if we can do without it, then it is by far the best way. Nick. Berthier." He walked his horse forward, and Nick fell in beside the general. Their hooves clopped on the cobbles, and within moments they were dismounting in the Orangerie, stared at by the workmen on top of their scaffolding, hammers and chisels hanging at their sides. These were the people Bonaparte sought to rule, Nick realised. And certainly they seemed pleased to see him. There was even a subdued shout of 'Vive Bonaparte'.

"Come. Only you, Nick, and stay by the door. Berthier, hold your men, here." He looked over his shoulder, perhaps to reassure himself that Murat really did wait beyond the gates. His face was pale, but his lips were pressed together in a firm line. He had looked no less determined when about to order his guns to fire grape into the Paris mob, four years ago, Nick recalled. That had been successful enough.

Bonaparte threw open the doors, stepped inside. As he had been instructed, Nick remained in the doooway itself. His business was as a mascot, not a participant. But he looked at the scene with a pounding heart. The gallery of Mars was a huge chamber, with ceilings some twenty feet high, with seats and lecterns for the various speakers, with statues of past heroes of France raised on the upper gallery, which was in addition crowded with onlookers. But the most noise came from the floor itself, where the Council of Five Hundred appeared to be in the middle of a debate. This was interrupted by the appearance of Bonaparte, but immediately rose into a crescendo of shouts and yells, the loudest of execration, Nick realised.

"Order, order," shouted the President. Lucien Bonaparte reminded Nick of Napoleon himself, when first they had met in 1793. He possessed the same pinched features, the same fiery glow in his eye.

"Arrest him," someone bawled. "He has no right here."

"Hear me," Bonaparte shouted, his voice cutting across the

hubbub and driving it into silence. "My right is that of man who has fought and bled for France. I stand here in the name of and as the representative for those men upon whom you depend for your very lives: The French soldiers."

The noise subsided to a faint mutter.

"You sit there," Bonaparte shouted, "and debate abstract matters, when all the while you are sitting on the top of a volcano, had you but the wit to see it. Your proceedings are calumniated. You have lost the confidence of the nation. They seek a man of destiny. A Caesar, or a Cromwell. They have turned to me as that man."

He paused, to inhale, and they stared at him, silent now.

"But I come here in no spirit of tyranny. My business is the preservation of liberty, of liberty for all. You well know that with my trusty soldiers at my back I could have seized power long ago, had I so wished. Believe me, my friends, pressure has been brought to bear on me to do just that. That I have resisted such temptation is sufficient evidence of my patriotism. This country has no more loyal servant than myself. But I will tell you this. There is a party abroad in this land of ours who would turn back the clock, restore Jacobinism, give power to the mob and to the gutter journalists, set the guillotine to clanking again. And where do you suppose they will find the heads to feed that monster? From your ranks, my friends. Only I can prevent that catastrophe. Only I can appeal on your behalf to the valour of my comrades, with whom I have fought and conquered for liberty."

He paused again, and this time the council stared at him in shocked silence.

"Consider my words," he said, and retreated into the doorway. Nick stepped back and they were outside, and the soldiers in the courtyard were shouting, 'Vive Bonaparte'.

Behind them there now rose a most tremendous hubbub, as the members of the council shouted their outrage at what had happened, and also exchanged threats and exhortations with each other and with the spectators.

"What do you think?" Bonaparte wiped sweat from his brow.

"A good speech. Which does not mean they will accept it."

260

"They must." He clasped his hands behind his back, walked up and down. "It is for the good of France."

Nick remained by the door, listening. Some of the noise had died, and one or two voices alone could be heard. It was difficult to make out the words. He discovered that he was also sweating. Somehow he had expected an event of this nature to be different, more dramatic. Nations were not seized with words, as a rule.

Indeed they were not. The door opened, and closed again, and a panting man stood on the gallery. "General," he gasped. "Things go badly. They are taking an inviolable oath to preserve the Constitution."

Bonaparte frowned at him. "Bah. Lucien will not permit it."

"He has already taken the oath, General."

"What? What do you say?"

"He was forced to it. They are threatening his life."

Bonaparte gazed at Nick, his mouth open. "We are lost."

"We are, unless you truly act the Cromwell," Nick said. "You yourself said, it is all or nothing, now."

Bonaparte continued to peer at him for a moment, then suddenly slapped his right hand into his left. "You are right." He stood at the balustrade. "You and you and you and you," he shouted, summoning four of the tallest of his grenadiers. "Come with me. You also, Nick. And you, Berthier, summon Murat inside, with his men. The door, Nick."

Nick sucked air into his lungs, then pulled the door wide, was almost thrown back by the gust of noise from within. Bonaparte stepped inside, the four guardsmen at his back. "Stay at the door," he said in a low voice, and took off his hat, to walk up the centre of the chamber, while the noise slowly died.

"I have returned," he said. If he was nervous he gave no trace of it.

"Returned," someone murmured.

"And not alone," said another.

"Look there," shouted a third. "Soldiers. Drawn swords in the sanctuary of the laws."

The council surged from their seats and lecterns, surrounding Bonaparte so that he was almost invisible.

"Outlawry," someone shouted.

"Outlawry," the cry was taken up. "Proclaim him an outlaw."

"Quickly," Nick shouted, and plunged forward, the soldiers at his side. They thrust men to left and right, breaking through them by the very force of their charge, seized Napoleon by the arms. Tearing other clutching hands away, they ran for the door, got outside, panting and gasping, and slammed the door shut behind them.

"General?" Berthier was frowning.

"Lost," Bonaparte groaned. "Lost."

Nick chewed his lip in indecision, wondering if he dared give orders to French soldiers, if they would obey him. But for the moment Bonaparte was too shaken to act for himself.

And from inside there came a fresh chorus of yells and screams and shouts, of alarm and of fear as well as of anger.

"My brother," Bonaparte muttered. "Lucien."

Nick pulled himself together. "Follow me," he shouted. "The general's brother."

The grenadiers moved forward in a body. Nick threw open the door, and the men surged in. Lucien Bonaparte staggered towards them away from his assailants who once again turned to the door in dismay. He had either come down or been dragged down from his rostrum, his hair and clothes in disarray.

"Form a ring," Nick shouted. "Form a ring." He got himself inside, seized Lucien's arm. "Your brother has lost his nerve. It is up to you."

Lucien peered at him as if awakening from a deep sleep. But the grenadiers were again moving for the door, and a moment later they were in the fresh air.

"Now," Nick said. "It must be now."

"That horse," Lucien gasped. Napoleon still leaned on the balustrade, wiping sweat from his forehead.

Berthier helped Lucien into the saddle, and he rose in the stirrups. "Soldiers," he shouted. "The nation is yours to save. There are men in there . . ." He flung out his arm, pointing at the closed door to the chamber. ". . . who were elected to preserve the laws of the country, and who have drawn swords and daggers, endeavoring to have their way by blood rather than by permission. Soldiers, do your duty."

"Follow me," Murat shouted, dismounting and drawing his sword. "Fix bayonets."

He struck the door open with his shoulder, marched inside. There was a howl of outrage from the members, but he stood his ground and raised his sword above his head. "Clear this scum," he bellowed, his voice echoing into the ceiling.

The grenadiers, already filing into the room to form a body to either side, gave a roar, and began to advance behind the bristling rank of bayonets. The members of the council stared at them for one panic stricken moment, and then turned and flooded across the room, clambering up balustrades to gain the galleries, staggering to the windows and throwing them open to leap through. Those who remained shouted, 'Vive Bonaparte'.

"My God," Nick said. "There was a near thing."

"Is it done?" Bonaparte raised his head. "Is it done?"

"Aye," Nick said, and took his arm. "France is yours, Napoleon. You had best set about ruling it."

iii

Charles Perigord-Talleyrand rose to his feet, lifted his glass. "Ladies, and gentlemen. I give you, the First Consul."

The assembly rose with him, glasses high. Nick smiled at Rose Bonaparte—Napoleon had renamed her Josephine, but to Nick she would always be Rose, a memory of his adventures in Paris during the days of the Terror—and then at Anne, wearing a hastily concocted gown, for she and Rose were also old friends. And then at Lorna, her face lopsided because of the bandage which hid the bruise on her forehead, and at the men, the soldiers, Murat and Berthier and Junot and Lannes, who had this day carried their general to the heights, and at the politicians, the Abbe Sieyes and Roger Ducos, their conspiracy at last brought to a successful conclusion.

And lastly at the First Consul himself, for Napoleon was staring at him. He drank, and sat down.

Bonaparte stood up. "I thank you all. I thank you for your loyal support of me, for giving me strength when my own might have faltered. I thank you for being at my side." He raised his own glass. "I return your toast. To you all." He put down the glass, leaned forward. "And now, gentlemen, ladies, to work. Those who fled today, they will continue to oppose me. They must be hunted down." He smiled at their dismay. "I do not plan a return to the Terror. The guillotine is for those who practice active treason, not mere opposition to the will of the country. Yet must they be confined. We will find a use for them, oh, indeed we shall. Cayenne. There they can put themselves to useful work, and harm us no longer." His gaze swept the table, and came to rest on Lorna. "Cayenne," he said.

"No." She started to her feet. "You cannot treat me so. I saved Minnet's life."

"For some purpose of your own, I have no doubt, Madame Szen."

"For love of him." She bit her lip, flushed, and glanced at Anne. "For love of him," she repeated, in a lower tone. "Do not send me away, I beg of you."

"Napoleon," Nick said.

Bonaparte smiled at him. "They say Cayenne is too hot, for a white woman's complexion," he said. "They say she withers like a cut flower, and becomes old before her time."

"Oh, my God," Lorna muttered.

Napoleon continued to smile. "And that were a sad waste of so rare a beauty, Lorna. But France is no place for you, now. You have a husband. Where is he?"

"Johannes is in Naples."

"Then go to him. And stay with him. Should you, or he, be discovered within French boundaries, ever again, it *will* be Cayenne."

"Napoleon," she said. "I am forever in your debt. I—"

"Will leave now, madame," Napoleon said.

She swallowed, looked around the table, then got up. "As I am commanded, General." She looked at Nick. "Until we meet again,

Nick. Mistress Yealm." She gave a mock bow, turned, and left the room.

"Thank you, Napoleon," Nick said. "She did save my life."

"And share your bed," Napoleon said. "You are too much of a gallant, Nick. Gallantry has no place in either politics or business. And she is a dangerous woman. You would do well to remember that."

"I shall," Nick agreed, and stood up. "And now we would also take our leave of you."

Napoleon leaned back in his chair. "Eh?"

" 'Golden Rose' waits in Havre, as my bank and our children wait in England. We have stayed too long as it is."

"Our countries are at war, monsieur," Talleyrand said, quietly. "Do you suppose you can just walk out of our midst, as you choose?"

"The general wishes you to remain ever at his side," Murat pointed out.

Were they playing a game with him, or were they serious? And why should they not be serious? Nick studied Napoleon's face.

"The general," he said, "has ascended to heights which no longer need the assistance of fortune."

Bonaparte rested his chin on his forefinger. "You think so? When ever did a man not need fortune?"

"Would you not say, Napoleon, that a man does better to rely upon his own strength, his own ability, than to depend upon so uncertain a companion?"

Bonaparte gazed at him. "Yet I have a country to rule, to organise, to restore to its former greatness. I will need the help of talented men."

"Of willing, talented men, Napoleon. What, will you shut me away? Be sure you will gain little benefit from that. And as you say, you have a country to restore to greatness. For that you will need peace, not war. Be sure that I also wish peace, for the good of England, for the good of the House of Minnett. Bankers do not thrive on war. You could count on a useful friend, at the side of Pitt, when you make your approach."

"A point, to be sure," Talleyrand said. "Supposing we can trust you, Mr. Minnett."

"Napoleon will know that," Nick said.

"Ha." He glanced at his wife. "What do you think?"

"I think that Nick, and Anne, have served you well enough, Napoleon. And they will remain our friends. Even in England."

Napoleon gazed at her for some seconds, and then gave a brief laugh. "And should I need you again, eh, Nick, I can always send Castets."

iv

"Will you really negotiate with Pitt, for the French?" Anne leaned against him as the coach rumbled down the road to Le Havre.

"Indeed I shall."

"But the French are our enemies."

"The French have been our enemies, since time immemorial. There is no reason why that should not change."

"Bonaparte will never restore the monarchy."

"There will be my biggest problem," Nick agreed. "But only in overcoming British royalism. I personally do not think Bonaparte *should* restore the monarchy."

She sat away from him. "A republic?"

"There have been republics before."

"Great Britain would never acknowledge a republic."

"I fail to see why it should not. We have acknowledged the United States. There is not only a republic, but a revolted part of Britain itself. And we have accepted it. If Bonaparte genuinely wishes peace, I see no reason why it should not be made, and made to last."

"He is a soldier," Anne said.

Nick smiled, and squeezed her against him. "He is a little more than that, I think. And you are a pessimist. Even soldiers like peace, from time to time. France needs time to recover, and he needs time to carry out some of the things he plans for it. I think he wants peace. And I also think that we have talked about him long enough. Oh, Anne, when I think . . ."

266

She placed her finger on his lips. "Do not think, about that. Pretend he was some man I knew, too well, before you came into my life, Nick. Promise me."

"Yet shall I recommence my search for him. And this time he shall not escape me, I swear it."

"That is a private matter. I would talk about us. Supposing you still wish to."

"Still wish to? I wish to marry you, love. At the very earliest possibility."

She pushed herself away, to stare at him. "Are you sure, Nick? Very, very sure?"

"I am sure, Anne."

"There will be opposition."

"I am a grown man, Anne. I am master of my own business. There can be no opposition."

"And your mother? Your sister?"

"Mama? Lucy? Why, they love you almost as much as I do. They will be overjoyed to hear that you have said yes."

She continued to gaze at him for some seconds. Then she sighed, and rested her head on his chest. "And I do say yes, Nick. Yes, yes, yes. It is all I have ever wanted to say to you."

"Sweetheart," he cried, and raised her head to kiss her mouth, and looked up as the coach heaved to a halt. He leaned forward to open the trap. "Why are you stopped?"

"The road is blocked, monsieur," the man explained. "There are horsemen."

"Eh?" Nick released Anne, turned to the door, at the same moment as it was wrenched open.

"Well, now, Minnett," George Moncey said. "Did you suppose you'd escape me so easily?"

Nick gaped at him, for a moment totally surprised.

Moncey smiled into the interior, and raised his hat with his left hand. Nick realised that he held a pistol in the other. "Your servant, Mistress Yealm. And willing to be so. I shall be with you in a very little while."

Anne sat straight, staring at him as if hypnotised.

"Get down, Minnett, get down," Moncey said. "You and I have a business matter to settle."

Nick glanced at Anne, who returned his look in silence. There was indeed nothing to say. But she did not appear to be afraid, although her breathing had quickened. Then he stepped out of the opened door, and down on to the grass beside the road. There were close to a dozen horsemen, all armed with pistols.

"I presume by now that you have had poor Lorna executed," Moncey remarked, taking off his hat and cloak.

"Lorna is safe enough. She has merely been outlawed in France. As are you, Moncey. And for you there will be no second chance."

"I shall be away, and safe, whenever we have settled our matter." Moncey smiled at him. "But we are both gentlemen . . . you *are* a gentleman, are you not, Minnett? We shall fight, fairly. And there is even a prize for the victor, your Mistress Yealm. Believe me, having known her once, I would find life a dismal affair never to feel that strong body beneath mine again."

"You . . ." But now of all times, it would not pay to lose his temper. "You challenge me?"

"Aye. But I also name the time; now, and the place; here, and weapons." He raised his hand, and one of his companions came forward, two rapiers across his arm.

"A weapon with which you know I have no experience," Nick said quietly.

"Alas, my dear Minnett, it is a weapon with which I have no equal. Your misfortune, as I have suggested, is that you are *not* truly a gentleman, but just an upstart clerk. A gentleman, now, a true gentleman, always learns the use of the sword. Do you decline to fight me? Then I think I will have you hanged."

Nick licked his lips. He and Moncey had fought with swords, once before, and he had been the victor. But that had been a surprise, when Moncey had been regarding him as of no account at all. And then they had fought not with rapiers, but with proper swords, which had a cutting edge. Yet now was there nothing for it.

"And will they not hang me, anyway, when I have won?" he asked.

Moncey snorted. "You aim too high, fellow. No, no. Should you win, you will be free to go, because I will be dead on the ground. This is a duel to the death, Minnett. It will be you or I. And these fellows will swear to that."

"Amen," said the man with the swords.

"So be it." Nick took off his coat, folded it carefully before laying it on the ground. His brain was tumbling. To the death. There could be only one way he would win such a fight. And he had never killed a man with his bare hands. But Moncey, now—oh, yes, he thought he could do that. If he could arrange the chance.

"Nick," Anne murmured.

"Keep faith, love," he said. "I will do it, if it can be done."

He straightened, took the offered sword. Moncey already had his, and stood like a guardsman on parade. Then he held out the weapon, and Nick touched it with his own, taking in the evening scene as he did so. The road was empty of traffic, and had no doubt been chosen for that reason. There was no sound save for the slight breeze soughing in the trees, the occasional hoof-clop of a restless horse, and the rustle of the river Seine coursing beside the grass verge on which they stood.

Nick smiled. He had used this river before, as a means to escape. But it was no ally; it was equally dangerous to him and to his foes, and would be again.

"You do have courage, of a sort," Moncey said. "On guard."

The blade snaked towards him, and Nick hastily parried, righting his balance, feet spread, left arm curved behind him. Moncey was advancing, slowly, as yet, also smiling now, confident in his own ability, his own experience. This time his blade moved with lightning speed, sliced past Nick's late parry, cutting shirt and flesh, and whipped back again. Another of those and it would be all over, Nick realised, as the pain began. Just for the moment Moncey was off balance, although he was a superb swordsman, and had his weapon up to parry Nick's riposte. The blades clashed and slithered along each other, and the hafts came together. They were close now, their breaths clouding against each other. Anne exclaimed in alarm as she saw the blood staining Nick's shirt.

Moncey attempted to push him back, but Nick had already placed his foot behind his assailant, and now pushed in turn. Moncey lost his balance and sat down heavily, and in so doing lost his grip on his sword. As it flew from his fingers Nick stepped in and kicked it away.

Moncey stared at him in total disbelief. "You . . ."

"To the death, Moncey," Nick said, and threw his own weapon after the first.

"With our hands? Like guttersnipes?" Moncey looked at his companions. But they were Irishmen, who liked nothing better than a good fight.

"To the death, boyos," one of them shouted. "To the death."

Moncey threw himself forward, still on his knees, locked his arms around Nick's thighs. Nick brought his hands together, used them to club the nape of Moncey's neck, but the big man only grunted and heaved, and it was Nick's turn to strike earth, with breath-destroying force.

Moncey released him, stood up, swung his leg. The toe of his riding boot crashed into Nick's ribs, and knocked out some more breath. Desperately he rolled, as Moncey reared above him again, now intent on using his heel to stab downwards. Nick thrust up his hands, caught the stamping foot, twisted it and threw his man, rose to his knees himself. Moncey cursed and gained his feet at the same instant, swinging his fists. Nick took a short one on the cheek and felt the sudden stab of pain as flesh broke; then he was inside, slamming his fists against Moncey's belly, bringing gasps of distress. This was how he had won their last set to. But Moncey was in better condition now. Even the two driving blows did not bring him to his knees, and once again his arms were locked, this time behind Nick's back, while he strained to get his legs behind and throw his man.

Nick's hands were momentarily trapped. He strained and tugged to get them up, and then Moncey released him, taking him by surprise and leaving him off balance. In that instant Moncey hit him twice more on the face.

Nick tasted blood even as he felt himself rolling down the grassy slope and even as he heard Anne screaming. His entire face, his entire head, was a seething mass of pain, and his vision was blurred. It occurred to him that he had been far too confident of winning, once the contest was reduced to essentials. Because he had won so easily the last time. But Moncey must have gone away and thought about that. Oh, yes, he had thought about that. And done some practicing.

The boots were crashing towards him. Nick rolled away from them, rose to his knees and then his feet. Now his mind was concentrated, with that ruthless determination which made him such a feared antagonist. He stepped forward, and Moncey hit him again with all his force. His lips were drawn back in a snarl, which slowly changed to dismay as the blow merely jerked Nick's head and he kept on coming. Once again the big fist flew, and this time Nick checked it with his own upflung wrist. He was close now. It was time to fight to the death, seriously. He darted his fingers, extended and rigid, at Moncey's eyes, and the big man jerked back his head. Nick swung his right hand, also flat and hard-edged, into the pulsing throat in front of him. Moncey gasped and choked, and fell to his knees. Nick went with him, fingers locked on the throat now, his opponent gasping for breath, drumming fists on his own chest.

Moncey made a supreme effort; he was a strong and determined man. Nick lost his balance and rolled, and they went together. There came a shout from above them, and then for a moment they hung in mid air, before plunging into the hurrying waters of the Seine. Still they clung together, but now Moncey's breath was filled with water as their heads broke surface.

But Nick was himself short of breath, and in danger of drowning. The racing current was sweeping him into the centre of the river, and his strength was failing. He released the throat, kicked and struck out, listened to shouts from the bank. The men were running along in an effort to keep pace with him.

He turned, and swam, and felt his head spinning, and inhaled water, and regained the surface, and gasped and choked, and heard shouts. They had got downstream of him, and one was in the water, held by his fellows, extending his arms as Nick was swept down on him. He reached up, desperately, felt fingers touch his and then lock on them, and was dragged to the shore.

"Well, I'll be damned," said the man who had pulled him out. " 'tis Minnett."

"Then where is Moncey?" asked another, peering into the gloom.

"Nick." Anne came tumbling down the slope to hold him against her, soaking wet as he was. "Oh, Nick. I thought you were gone."

He rose to his knees. "Where is Moncey?"

"Gone," said one of the Irishmen. "There's naught out there."

"No man could live in that," said another.

"Aye, well . . ." They looked down at Nick. "We'd best be away."

Their feet were dull on the grass as they climbed the bank.

"Moncey, " Nick said.

"He's gone, Nick," Anne said. "They were right. No man could live in that river. He's gone, Nick. Forever." She smoothed hair from his face. "And so have the Irish. We'd best to the coach, and I'll clean up your face."

She helped him to his feet. He continued to stare at the water. He could not believe that it had ended—so suddenly and so definitely. He looked down at the woman. "What would you have done, if it had been Moncey they had dragged out?"

"I would have killed myself." She opened her cloak to show him the knife in her hand.

"Anne . . ."

She smiled, and kissed him on the chin, and then drew back her arm and threw the knife into the water. "But I knew you would win, Nick. And now there is naught but you and me. Say there will be naught, but you and me, and the children, Nick."

He gazed once again at the river, growing darker every moment. What news would he have to tell Pitt, of events of France. Of his part in creating a military dictatorship, because that was what it would be. But one governed by a man who was more than just a soldier, he was sure of that. And Pitt wanted peace as much as any man. It could be done.

And then, as she had said only minutes ago, what social problems was he about to set himself? But did it matter? Did anything matter, beside the fact that his feud was over, that Caroline was at once avenged and excluded from his mind, that Anne was here in his arms, now and for ever more.

"You and me, and the children, sweetheart," he said. "Nothing else."